W9-AVF-698

YELLOWCAKE

YELLOWCAKE

A NOVEL

RICHARD MURFF

SAINT BOB PRESS
MEMPHIS, TN

Library of Congress Control Number:Pending
ISBN:
Hardcover   978-0-9796988-1-1
Softcover   978-0-9796988-0-4

This is a work of fiction. Names, characters, places and incidences either are the product of the author's imagination or are used fictitiously, and any resemblance to any actual persons, living or dead, events, or locals is entirely coincidental.

This book was printed in the United States of America.
    1.0

For Maggie & Littlebit

<u>Where Credit is Due:</u>
There are a number of people without whom this book would never have happened: David Seale and Joe Long, my literary ogres of old; and Mark Goodman, an old literary ogre.

Jimbo Lattimore, with his rare combination of creative and business sense, provided excellent editorial advice. We also smoked so many cigarettes over the manuscript that it cured me of the habit (smoking, not writing). Maggie Catmur, not only an inspiration, spotted my legion of typos. As did Jason Higginbotham. My brother Larry and his wife Andrea know what they did, and for it I'm more thankful than I can say. Hugh Mallory thinks I forgot him, but without his two cents our dashing hero would not have been his own man.

Less direct inspiration came from the fellas at the Wolf River Society (F.T.P.O.T.O.T.S), who always enjoy a good story. And Dad, who always saw the method in the madness.

Much obliged.

War, which used to be cruel and magnificent,
has now become cruel and squalid.
*   - Sir Winston Churchill*

One

A Small House, a Beautiful Woman, Dangerous Boating

FRIDAY

THE WOMAN PUFFED THE CHURCHILLIAN CIGAR and settled her heft into the lawnchair, inspiring the plastic webbing to creak mightily. Smoke plumed from her wide mouth and nostrils and she smiled. It was moving closer; the Landcruiser came over the service road that bisected the papaya grove. It bounced and disappeared beyond a hill.

The ancient Landcruiser was knocking violently down the shell road and she squinted into the bright Jamaican haze as it came back into sight, much closer now. The driver was alone. She took another long drag and shifted in the complaining chair.

The Landcruiser turned up the hill toward the aqua green cinderblock house and came to a grinding halt just short of the porch. The driver got out, waving the cloud of road dust from his smooth face. In his hand he had a stuffed alligator, about 16 inches long. Not a plush toy, but from a taxidermist. He squinted in the sun, a comma of shiny black hair fell in front of his eyes, and the faded tee-shirt hugging his athletic frame read *Kiss Me I'm Irish*. He tapped the snout of the alligator against his faded blue workpants. "Miz Cassat, I hope you have something to drink." He said, shading his eyes against the Caribbean sun.

Miz Cassat sneered; she never trusted half-breeds. This one had a proper Black Jamaican mother, Miz Cassat even knew the girl, but his father was Chinese of all things. The fact that the boy looked like an underwear model didn't help. She took the cigar from her lips and showed a mouth full of gold teeth. "Rum all right? It's dark. Dark is pure."

Used to the insult, Robert Chu held up the alligator, "I've got it." He stepped up onto the wooden porch out of the glaring sun. "You fix me now."

She leaned forward and took Chu's hand, pulling her heft out of the chair before Chu knew she was doing it. "First let's see what you've got." She turned around and waddled across the front porch and into the small shack. Chu took a step and stopped, gazing down the erratic line of outhouse sized shacks along the perimeter of the sad little compound. Beyond the house and further up the rocky green hill was a set of steep concrete stairs that twisted upward into gravel clearing.

The inside of the house was roughly finished, but painted a vibrant yellow. A simple white wooden table and chairs were set in one corner, beside a long window shuttered tight with unfinished mahogany planks. Behind the table sat a thirty-year-old stove and a modern refrigerator. On the other side of the room were two pink and green sofas upholstered in sun-faded and dueling tropical motifs. They formed an L along the wall beneath another open window, facing a television that wasn't on.

On one of the sofas lounged a lithe woman in simple floral shift. She was reclining, and appeared long rather than tall. Her skin was a flawless caramel, glowing with perspiration; her long hair pulled up off her neck and over the arm of the sofa. She had a face possessing the strange quality of lazy perfection without one distinguishing characteristic. At first he thought she was black, but then, like Chu, not entirely so. He guessed that there was a white parent and when she made eye contact he was sure of it. She smiled imperceptibly and Chu turned his eyes down the short hallway that led to a back bedroom, a low bookcase lined the wall. It was crammed more with rotting cardboard boxes than books.

Behind him, Miz Cassat set something down on the table with a clatter. She was smiling, her arms folded, standing over a bottle of dark rum and four full jiggers. He crossed to the table and set the alligator down, taking up a glass. Miz Cassat took a glass and they both looked across the room to the lounging girl who got up slowly, smoothing the shift over her round hips. She crossed the room and took up a glass, "Hey Miz Cassat..." she purred in an accent Chu couldn't place, "Listen, about that fourth drink..."

"Dat's for the god Anansi Coupé, don't you touch!"

"I know who it's for, Miz Cassat. I was wonderin' if you'd let me send it to him." She winked at Chu, "Seems like you always get ole Nanci's drink."

"Blasphemy!" Miz Cassat growled, she turned to Chu. "Ugly Sue here don't believe all she should." Miz Cassat grunted-she spat on the floor. Miz Cassat tipped her jigger up and they all knocked back their rum. She wiped her lips with the back of her hand., "Bobby Chu, you believe in Anansi Coupé, don't you? and Olgen de le Flambeau, they real aren't they? Bobby Chu-" Chu's smile faded. It was unbelievably stuffy in the square frame house. "Yes, you believe," she went on. "I talk to Anansi Coupé, yes I do, and he believe in you too, Bobby Chu. He pay you a visit." Chu took a step back from the table. Miz Cassat took up the fourth jigger, "pour Anansi!" and knocked it back.

Ugly Sue drifted back to the sofa with a lazy smile. She lay down and threw her hair over the sofa arm. She began to fan away the heat with last week's *TV Guide*.

Miz Cassat lit some candles and chanted in a pidgin of French and English. Into a clay pot set in the crescent of three fat candles, she poured some dark rum. Then, from a glass-stoppered bottle, she added a dram of clear liquid. She touched her cigar to the pot and a neat blue flame sprang up.

"Did you get it from the girl?" Miz Cassat asked. Chu was still mesmerized by the woman on the sofa. "Bobby Chu! Did you get what I asked you from the girl?"

He turned and looked over Miz Cassat's hulking frame. She wasn't smiling anymore. "Why do we need her?" spat Chu, "Just a spoilt white brat. Dark is pure, remember?"

"Voodoo don't care if you rich or poor, black or white," she sneered, "or half breed. Hah! Voodoo is magic, you must believe..." now she glared at Ugly Sue across the room to the far sofa, "Voodoo only asks that you believe."

Ugly Sue said nothing but smiled over the TV Guide bearing the likeness of Kathy Lee Gifford, also smiling.

"They said you'd be here three days ago."

Chu shook his head. "I had to check in with —"

"Three days, did you get the combination?"

"No. I didn't get it. But she is here now, on the island, at the resort." he picked up the alligator, "I've got this, have you any idea how much this is worth? This is what you're after, what do you want with the girl?"

Miz Cassat snarled and lifted her right hand, clenched like a claw, "Let me decide that! The combination!"

"Her mother is a problem, and she's not the sort you can strong arm, not in her own house. She's got a hold on the girl even if the girl won't admit it."

Miz Cassat lowered her hand and puffed a few more times on the cigar. She poured out two more shots of brown rum. "*Pour Anansi!*-you'd better drink." The two knocked back the glasses and the burn rushed down Chu's insides and he closed his eyes against the glow. "Then you'll have to get the girl herself to do it."

Chu's eyes shot open, "She is not–"

"Anansi Coupé wants!" Miz Cassat roared, "From the temple of the girl! What Anansi wants–he gets! If she hasn't got numbers with her, find out where they are. She know, if not then take her home. Use the girl, flatter her, you're a pretty boy." Chu turned back to the sofa, now Ugly Sue was smiling overtly back at him. "Ugly Sue is stupid in the head." Blurted Miz Cassat. "She don't speak much, and when she do, she don't believe much."

Ugly Sue fanned herself slowly. Chu finally turned and went through the open door. Miz Cassat watched him exit and followed. By the time she had come to rest in the frame of the door, Chu was already about to climb into the Landcruiser. "When can I come back?" he asked.

"You know when Bobby Chu."

"No sooner?"

"You know when."

"I haven't got much time!" He lowered his voice, "It's already started. I see them everywhere!"

"Then you know what you have to do."

Chu ground his teeth and climbed into the Landcruiser. The engine roared; Chu leaned his head out, thought better of it, and shut the door.

Then all Miz Cassat could see from her porch was Chu knocking away down the road. She stepped back inside and closed the door, throwing the deadbolt. Over the table she closed the plank shutters and hissed at Ugly Sue. Miz Cassat flicked the switch, turning on a single overhead light into which the other came grinning.

Miz Cassat moved for the alligator, but Ugly Sue snatched it up, striking it hard once along the lower jaw so that the head came off. She separated the piece carefully and tapped the body against the table as the four .35mm film canisters rolled out onto the table.

Ugly Sue smiled widely now, "Now there's something I can believe in."

THE EIGHTY-FOOT MAGNUM MARNIE 80 yacht thumped against the Caribbean waves. The twin engines pushed the tank of a boat to nearly 50 mph over the open sea. On his 57th birthday, Mikhail Boyorov would have preferred a leisurely tour on one of his sailboats but today time pressed hard. Cuba was fading in the distance behind him and he scanned the horizon. The salt air misted his face and the sun baked his skin. Lean and tallish, he had a round, balding skull covered in short strawberry blond hair that was going white.

Whatever was left of the fair Slavic quartermaster stationed by the KGB in Cuba some thirty-five years ago had long ago burned away. Even before the Soviet Empire had crumbled, Mikhail Boyorov had switched from vodka to rum and adopted the name the Cubans had given him, "Mickey Boy."

Mickey Boy took to island life with the privileges of a Soviet officer. He bought a boat and christened it Kaa, after the wicked, hypnotic snake in Kipling's *The Jungle Books*. The massive hull slapped across the waves and sea mist sprayed his face again. His first mate was a small Cuban named Pedro who'd spent his entire life on a tiny tropical island. However, boats are illegal in Cuba, so the open sea was making him sick. "Mickey Boy!" Pedro said, "Now that we are at sea, you can tell me, what are we picking up in Jamaica?"

Mickey Boy scanned the horizon from behind the polished wood steering wheel. "There Pedro, do you see it?" Mickey Boy said after a long time. "Three o'clock, exactly." He couldn't use the nautical terms because Cubans generally don't understand them. Again, the no-boat thing. Pedro glanced at the Presidential Rolex on Mickey Boy's wrist then gazed out over the sea. "The rock?"

"Ha, the rock." Mickey Boy said and pointed the Magnum Marine to the isolated salient.

"What about Jamaica?"

"We aren't going to Jamaica, Pedro." Mickey Boy laughed.

The mushroom shaped rock seemed to approach the yacht with alarming speed. Closer now, the Magnum Marine began to slow as they engaged a wide arch around the far side of the outcropping.

Mickey Boy cut off the engine in the shadow of the highest cliff. "Put up the flag, Pedro."

"We're going diving?"

"No, I am. Put up the flag."

When Pedro went below deck, Mickey Boy reached under the burled wood panel, removed the ignition switch from the assembly, and slipped it into a waterproof wet-pak that lay atop his wet suit. Pedro returned with the flag, and affixed it to the post on the stern next to the diving platform. Mickey Boy made sure the control panel was securely back in place then stripped and got into the wetsuit, securing the wet-pak around his waist. He met Pedro at the diving platform.

"Why the change of plans, Boss?" Pedro asked as he hoisted the aqualung onto Mickey Boy's back.

"No change of plans, Pedro, we were never going to Jamaica. It's called a lie. Now look, keep an eye out for other boats."

"I don't see-"

Mickey stepped out onto the platform, "Don't take a fucking nap." And plunged beneath the water.

Pedro slipped back up to the cockpit and sat behind the wheel. The problem was that Mickey Boy hadn't told him how long he was going to be under. He had a maximum window of about forty-five minutes, Pedro reckoned, but that didn't mean that he'd be gone that long. After about five minutes, Pedro took a lap around the boat. He scanned the crystal surface of the water and saw nothing of interest. He crossed the length of the boat and ducked below deck. Crammed between the three olive green rocket launchers and a titanium briefcase was Pedro's nylon Nike bag. From it he retrieved a new ignition switch, climbed back on deck, hopped to the control panel and lifted the board. It fit the assembly perfectly. He replaced the panel as it was and stowed his meager insurance back in the hull.

Beneath the surface, Mickey Boy checked his Rolex-he'd been under for fifteen minutes. He was now on the opposite side of the rock from the yacht, but still remained in the shadows of the crevices and small caves of the porous island. He dove deeper and cut on the flashlight integrated into the top of his mask. The water was crystal clear and the silt from the sea floor had settled in the calm weather. He moved into the shadows and reached the drop point in a cave. Drifting easily back into the recess, Mickey Boy extended his arm into the darkness where his body could go no further. He removed the camouflage netting and there it was. It was a canister of high-impact, gunmetal gray plastic, the size of a thermos. He slipped it into the wet-pak and began to back his way carefully out of the narrow opening. He checked his watch again and cut off the light.

The arm touched his back just lightly before it slipped around his neck. He stopped still in the water. Slowly, Mickey Boy let one hand float to the arm closing around his throat as the other drifted to the harpoon gun strapped to his long calf. The arm tightened, slowly and without hesitation. The pressure increased on his back. Slowly, Mickey Boy moved the harpoon over his head and fired the bolt backward. The sound of the bolt splitting the water cut short and the cave was filled with cloudy black ink. Still without struggle, Mickey Boy drifted slowly out of the cave casting the octopus aside. Breaking the surface, Mickey Boy spied a boat on the horizon behind him, making a wide arch around the rock. His hand went instinctively to the harpoon gun. "Blast." His one bolt was still in the octopus drifting lifeless into the waving seagrass below. "Damn ocean livestock."

He dipped back down beneath the surface, staying close in the shadows and thinking again about his retirement. One last deal and go to earth. Then he'd emerge in the South of France as an old Hungarian Count or some such nonsense; something stylish from an Alexander Dumas novel.

Mickey Boy climbed back into the boat and retrieved the canister from the wet-pak. Pedro took up the aqua gear and scampered off to stow in below deck. Cutting the clear plastic coating with a knife, he twisted hard with a grunt and the top moved. Inside were three .35mm film canisters. Squatting down on his haunches, he emptied all three canisters into his palm in turn. Inside each canister was a small velvet sack. One by one he emptied each sack and inspected the diamonds in his palm. Satisfied, it all went into the wet-pak, which stayed at his waist. Now he stood tall in the warming sun. He unzipped the wetsuit and rolled the top half down to his waist, revealing the scar that ran in a half-moon through the hair on his chest. In the cockpit, he snatched up the binoculars and scanned for the boat he'd seen.

It was smaller craft, but he recognized it immediately-he had one. It was a Riva Aquariva, an Italian speedboat with wooden deck popular with rich Americans, in this case a rich man and woman. Mickey Boy replaced the ignition switch. Then the engines growled underfoot as he watched the Riva skip and glide across the surface of the water. The Riva was circling the rock, he was sure of it. In another thirty seconds, they would be passing the *Kaa* in the opposite direction. Mickey Boy pushed the throttle forward and smiled as the boat lurched forward with the pick up of a sports car. From below deck he heard Pedro taking a fall as his feet lurched from under him. Mickey Boy smiled more; he appreciated the little things in life.

Pedro appeared in the cockpit rubbing his head and claiming loudly that he'd been battered. They sped along the Caribbean in the direction and speed in which they came. "Pedro, take the wheel and keep the course. You understand?"

"Of course, hold the wheel steady and be flexible when you push me out of the way."

"That's it." Mickey boy handed over the wheel and pressed the military issue binoculars to his eyes. The Riva was still on its wide arch, then disappeared from sight.

Mickey Boy went further down the beam and sat in one of the leather bench seats before the last section of boat that dropped onto the diving platform. He scanned the sea with his naked eyes, then again with the binoculars. Nothing.

Eventually the Riva came back into view. Mickey Boy stepped back into the cockpit. "You wanna drive, Boss?"

"No Pedro, it's been a long day. You're doing fine. How fast are we going?"

"About 40 now."

"That's fine." He kicked back in the cockpit, his feet up and plopped a worn and shapeless Panama hat over his eyes. This business was getting to him, he thought. They were rich Americans, looking for fish as well as the thrill of skirting forbidden Cuba. Only probably though.

Whether he actually heard something so far off or if it was instinct, Mickey Boy didn't know. He lifted the Panama from his eyes slightly and watched the Riva for a moment before sitting back up. Over the sounds of the speeding boat, he vaguely heard Pedro saying, "Take a nap, Boss, we in the clear now."

"Take it up a notch Pedro." The yacht began to take wide slices in the sea, its heavy wake rolling off from either side behind them.

The Riva was gaining on them for certain. The wooden speedboat suddenly changed its course, cutting across the outside rolls of *Kaa's* massive wake. Then it spun back around expertly and dove back into the rolls until it fishtailed wildly in the center of *Kaa*'s wake. The woman was laughing beautifully, her arm floating at her side so as not to spill the tall highball in her hand.

"Up another notch, Pedro!" Mickey Boy called. "They may just be joyriders, but they need to steer clear." The boat smashed forward through the waves.

The Riva was still in the center of the wake. The driver, a shirtless, sunburnt man in wayfarer sunglasses kept the speedboat steady in the churning wake. The aft fishtailed like a car on ice. The woman howled with delight.

Mickey Boy waved them off. The Riva cut to the right, jumping the rolls and cut back again, keeping parallel with *Kaa*. Now he didn't need glasses to see their faces. Damned rich Americans wanting to play. "Fun time is going to end badly for you." He grumbled and climbed into the cockpit.

"She can't go no faster, Boss." Pedro said before Mickey Boy could open his mouth. The girl, who was dark and beautiful enough to be Cuban herself, was leaning in close to the driver, saying something.

"Sorry Buddy, you aren't getting your ashes dragged at my expense. This is business. Pedro give me the wheel."

"With pleasure, Boss."

The Riva ran alongside *Kaa*, but kept its distance. Mickey Boy turned the wheel and the Magnum Marine roared over the waves at the speedboat. The woman snapped back into her seat and the driver tried his best to put distance between the two boats. The Riva changed course out of the line of *Kaa*. Mickey Boy laughed as he righted his craft and brought it back on course.

Suddenly, the Riva looped around at full throttle. Mickey Boy couldn't believe his eyes. They were going to cross his path in front of him. The woman was now hunched over an open storage bench.

Then she stood, Lily Pulitzer dress bright in the sun against the olive green rocket launcher hoisted to her shoulder.

His squinting eyes shot open-his jaw went slack for the moment. Again he cut *Kaa* onto a collision course, sending waves rolling in front of it. The Riva rocked as the rocket let fly, scorching the kevlar hull of the *Kaa* as it glanced off. Mickey Boy hit the deck and the rocket screamed overhead. The Magnum Marine was careening wildly at top speed. Mickey scrambled to take the spinning wheel. "Pedro, take them out."

The Riva appeared on the starboard side, and the woman was again hoisting another rocket launcher to her shoulder. Pedro leapt from the cockpit, lifted one of the benches to retrieve a Kalashnikov AK-47. She threw the launcher onto the floor and pulled out a long barreled sporting rifle as Pedro put a dozen bullets into the side of the Riva and the ocean. She held steady against the volley and fired once. Pedro fell lifeless onto the deck. Mickey engaged the autopilot and fell to his belly as the windshield exploded with a crack above him. He slithered down the deck and took up Pedro's weapon. Belly down, he hoisted himself up on a leather seat and sent a spray of fire over the side of the yacht. Then he stuck his head over the side to see the woman again taking up the rocket launcher. Another burst of fire and she ducked. Then Mickey Boy stood outright, took aim and fired. The Riva's windscreen burst outward and the sunburned driver, four holes in his back, slumped forward. The Riva spun wildly out of control. The woman fell over backward and Mickey Boy's burst whizzed over her head. He could see the Lily dress crawl to the driver as Mickey fired again.

She took the wheel from the floor and steadied it as the sides of the two vessels brushed. The Riva bounced wildly away, Mickey Boy barely felt the tap. Blindly, he fired downward on the speedboat, splintering the wooden hull. The woman took the seat and blasted full throttle away from *Kaa*, making erratic and chaotic turns. Mickey Boy sent bursts of lead after her.

With *Kaa* on autopilot, the Riva would quickly be out of range of the Kalashnikov. He leapt across the boat and ducked beneath the hull, emerging with his own rocket launcher. He zeroed in and took aim. The woman stood, looking over her shoulder and began what appeared to be another wide flung arch. Mickey Boy fired the rocket. The gas and exhaust of the rocket blurring everything. Through the exhaust he heard the Riva blow up rather than saw it. He cleared his eyes to see bits of wood, smoking and burning, still raining down onto an oily patch of ocean. Quickly, Mickey Boy stowed the launcher and Kalashnikov and took control of *Kaa*.

With a Cuban lagoon looming before him, and the Archipiélago de Los Jardines behind him, Mickey Boy slowed to a cruising speed. He'd consumed half a dozen Red Stripe beers in rapid succession and was looking forward to murdering a quart or two of mojitos at the Club later. Deep in the lagoon, he slowed the Magnum Marine further and checked the area with the infrared. He reached under the control panel and hit a switch. Before him, the thick jungle growth parted with the hum of efficient engines. As the curtain of growth parted on his approach, the shadow of a deep cavern emerged. *Kaa* idled into the huge new hole, and the jungle quickly closed around the gentle wake left behind.

Two

The Mist, the Fog, Cloaks and Daggers

SATURDAY

THE MISTING RAIN HID THE FORM of a man squatting over the skylight as an uneven wind masked the whir of the air-ratchet. The bolts of the skylight came off quickly. Quickly the man pried the aluminum casing from the frame and swiveled the entire pain on its last remaining bolt. There was a coil of black nylon rope at his arm that ran across the gravel roof and was secured to the access ladder. The man peered into the gray office cubicle below, and let the coil drop. Then he lowered himself down into the expanse of the cube farm as the soft rain came down around him.

He was tall, but not strikingly so; his shoulders strangely broad from being on crutches a great deal as a child. His brown hair was starting to get unruly from the course gray coming in underneath, and it curled just at the collar. He had an aquiline nose under green eyes and a cleft in his chin that was offset by a faint scar running along his jawbone. He wore a waxed cotton Barbour jacket and overpants that were covered in mist. Archie Gilmur looked more like a farmer than a thief.

He'd never been to the DeltaComm Components Distribution Center in New Orleans before, but memorized the layout before making the drive from Memphis. The cold mist settled on a picture of a pretty momma hugging a girl in a rabbit costume. Pity, Archie thought, the poor fool who sat under that skylight was probably a nice guy. Archie checked the steel Brietling on his wrist, it read 10:45 pm.

The night vision goggles came over his eyes and the world went hazy and green. Archie moved through the dark, past R & D to the information hub where racks of gunmetal gray servers lined the walls. If his information was right, he knew exactly which server he needed. He counted the boxes as he moved along the wall and stopped. The serial numbers matched. A quick smile of triumph then out of his pocket came a hard drive about the size of a deck of cards, an eyeglass screwdriver and a Blackberry. Archie coupled the hard drive to the server. Then he was at the computer terminal in the center of the hub. The task lamp went on and the goggles off. The pirated access codes glowed up from the PDA. A deep breath, a quick recheck of the numbers, and Archie set the codes in motion.

The transfer began and Archie exhaled. He wouldn't even be missed. Then the lights in the hall came on and his heart stopped. Blood was pounding in his ears as he moved into a recess between the last rack of servers and the wall.

A security guard poked his head in, looked at the blinking lights and drifted away. Archie had left the task lamp on; it was one thing to miss that. If the guard wandered back into marketing, he might find something amiss about a rope dangling from an empty skylight. The dial on his watch read 10:50. The server on the terminal said the file transfer was 30% complete.

There was nothing to do for it but wait until the guard went rushing downstairs to call the police. Then he'd just get out of there with what ever he had. Archie crept out the recess and checked the terminal – transfer 50% complete and still no alarm. The hall lights hadn't gone off either.

At exactly 11:00 pm., the spinning clock icon stopped: TRANSFER COMPLETE. Archie uncoupled the hard drive and put his equipment into his pockets. In the lit hallway Archie heard a voice call out, "Queen of hearts! Damn!" It came from the VP of Marketing's office. Either the guard didn't like Juice Newton or he was playing solitaire.

It is a universal corporate truth that no one voluntarily has his computer screen positioned where it can be seen by passers by. Therefore, it was inconceivable that the guard had his back to the door. Archie retreated back down the hall, found the stairs, and went to the first floor.

The front lobby was black flagstone floors and walnut paneling. The glass double doors would be easy to get through-the Heckler & Koch P7 in the small of his back would pulverize the panel. Tempting but messy, it had no style.

The small TV the night guard brought every night was set on the receptionist's high desk. Archie pushed the set off the counter and it fell to the flagstone floor with a crash. Moving back into the stairwell, he could hear the elevator bringing the guard down as he went up.

Then he was in the cube farm again. He dried the water from the picture of mother and child and heaved his way back up the rope. Hoisting himself through the opening in the skylight, the goggles caught on the lip. Archie pushed himself back to free them and clung helplessly to the rope as the strap came off and they fell to the floor, cracking off the wall of the cube as they went.

This time he dropped to the floor with a thud, shoved the goggles into a free pocket and scrambled back through the skylight.

Flinging himself onto the roof, Archie gathered up the rope in two pulls and swiveled the skylight back into place. The mist and fog were heavier now; it was 11:04. He was about to tighten the bolts on the pane when he saw the guard below, casually looking for the thump he'd heard while trying to reckon just what the hell had happened to his poor television.

The air-ratchet went into the gym bag that went over his shoulder. Archie made his way across the roof, untied the rope from the access ladder, and climbed down. Jumping onto the slick top of the trash dumpster, Archie fell on his side, slid to the edge, and dropped to the concrete. Across the empty back lot was a muddy 1980 International Harvester Scout.

Archie threw his bag in the scout and headed for higher ground. From the industrial park, through the rain at break-neck speed, flashing past the piles of rotting trash and homes left over from the flood. As Archie came into the older quarters of the city where scars of recent disasters were replaced by images of a faded glory. He couldn't read the watch because he was too busy flinging off his wet clothes at the red lights he didn't run. Archie kicked off his blunnies and searched for his black toecaps. Off came the Barbour jacket. He checked his tuxedo shirt and straitened his bow tie. Then, after mounting the corner on a sharp right turn, Archie slipped out of his overpants and was left in a pair of Gordon plaid trews. He pulled up to the Columns Hotel with his shoes on and slipped into a black dinner jacket as he came up the walk.

Molly Pratt was sitting on the front porch smoking with a groomsman. Her coal black hair was up tonight and as beautiful as she was, Archie thought leaving her was a rotten thing to do. He took a fresh pack of Dunhill cigarettes out of his pocket and waved them as he stepped onto the porch. "You've found a smoke on your own."

Molly craned a slender neck around and stared at him, "Forty five minutes for a pack of cigarettes, that's a record even for you Archie."

"Pushing the envelope is the key to self-improvement." He leaned against the column and smiled at her. Molly looked over at the groomsman from Belzoni, Mississippi named John Hanover. "I wouldn't worry about it, Love. Nothing in this city runs on time. I am sorry."

She inhaled deeply, "John here has taken care of me." She patted his hand. John withdrew it.

"Well golly, John, that's mighty neighborly of ya. I need a drink. Molly, can I get you another glass of wine…a catheter of gin?"

Molly glared at him over the cherry tip of her cigarette. Archie unwrapped the Dunhills and this brought a wicked, tense smile to Molly's lips, "I thought you were going to quit?"

"I'm trying to clean up my language too, but that's been a godamm nightmare. Whatta ya gonna do?" He went inside.

Surrounded by the dark mahogany paneling of the bar, Archie lit his own cigarette. There was a pretty redheaded bridesmaid whose name Archie couldn't remember, but she'd been wearing a thong at the rehearsal dinner and that left an impression. She leaned into the bar and turned to Archie. "Oh there you are…Molly has been looking all over for you."

"She's not looking anymore. Smoke?"

"Please." He lit her up and she laughed, "Molly's right, you really don't know the first thing about women, do you?"

"Nope."

"That's gonna be a long drive back to Memphis tomorrow. Did you forget the world revolves around Miss Molly? Now you need a drink hansom. Get a Pretty Baby."

"Beg pardon?"

"Specialty of the house. Molly'll still be pissed but you won't care as much."

Archie couldn't argue with her logic. The harried bartender pointed at him. "Redbreast with a splash of soda."

"Only what you see on the shelf buddy." The bartender nodded to the bridesmaid, "Might want to ask her for that one."

"Workin' on it, thanks. A Jack Daniels then."

The bartender nodded and smiled, he was sick of Pretty Babies.

THE CLOUDLESS SKY WAS FULL DARK when Robert Chu's plane banked left and the pilot announced that they would be starting their descent into Panama City, Panama. Chu looked out the window of the 747 at the city below, he was looking forward to being done with South America.

Gerry Torbel generally felt the same way. He'd come to the Panama Canal Zone nearly fifteen years ago as a civilian working for the US Army's Southern Command, SOUTHCOM.

He sat in a modern building the Corp of Engineers had commandeered from SOUTHCOM when it pulled out of the Zone. Aerial photographs of what looked to be a strip mining operation were scattered across his desk. Gerry loosened his tie and rested his elbows on either side of the photos. A few inches below a hairline that was wild with jet black curls, his eyes scanned the images mostly obstructed by the jungle canopy-they were right, it certainly looked like a strip mining operation. Still he had some questions about what appeared to be sifting vats that sat waiting to be installed. They were different sizes, not just large and small, but graded. Each vat was a little smaller than the last-like nesting dolls.

A screeching of the air conditioner pulled Gerry out of his focus. He looked at his watch, "Hell." He folded the documents, put them in a cardboard wallet, and stowed them in the wall safe. Before closing it, he retrieved a digital camera, slipped it into the side pocket of his blue blazer and dusted off his gray tropical wool pants.

The engineer let himself out the locked building and the guard called "Goo' nite' Mr. Torbel." to prove he hadn't been sleeping.

Gerry waved to the guard and stepped out into the Panamanian night, crossing the parking lot quickly to his Ford Fiesta. He eased the little car into traffic toward the city. With its Lexus's, SUV's and sports cars, Panama City looked as much like Miami as it did anyplace. Panama offered the privacy of numbered accounts and liberal banking laws, styling itself as the next alternative to offshore and Swiss banking. With more than enough drug money pouring in for a good bleaching, the industry wasn't far from realizing its dreams.

Gerry pulled up in front of a Starbucks that was mostly windows in the front and almost instantly a woman appeared in a maid's uniform and hopped into the car.

"You are late." She pouted. She was in her mid thirties, about ten years younger than Gerry, and had a large bosom and thickening waist.

"Sorry. What have you got?"

"Always with business. Take me to dinner."

"Sorry again. Look, those memo's you pulled last month, they've caused a stir up in Washington."

"Is a 'stir' good."

"No, it's like a panic. What I need is anything else that's been added to the file – you remember the one?"

"Am I in trouble? Gerry?"

"No darling – you've done really well. My government is very grateful. We're very close. But we need more information."

"Then I am hero?"

"You could be, yes."

"Then can I come to America?"

"That's being arranged. But we aren't there yet."

"Can I bring Lupé?"

"Absolutely. Nothing but baseball up there."

"That boy, he's getting to like girls now."

"Plenty of those up north too."

She relaxed. "I've done some more snooping – now take me to dinner."

She leaned over and kissed his cheek, passing her hand between his legs. Esmerelda smelled like Pine-Sol.

"I'm gonna to have a wreck! Now stop it. What do you want to eat?"

"You."

"I'm gonna have a wreck!" Then he hissed, "You've got new documents with you – on Independent?"

"What do you want from me? I am just a maid. Besides, Independent doesn't sound Chinese to me. It sounds American."

"British. Or was. It was based in Hong Kong. Before the Brits pulled out, Independent went on the block and was sold to you guys at SinoTel."

For a long moment, Esmerelda seemed to be digesting the information. "Sometimes you can be really boring. But yes, I have something for you Mr. Work-man. First we eat." She looked at him for a long time, her eyes searching, "…and one more thing…I am not one of SinoTel's 'guys'. I work for you, and don't you forget it."

Gerry smiled and squeezed her damp knee, "I won't forget." They got to a joint, not much more than a glorified stall, that served cheeseburgers and fries. Esmeralda was crazy for anything American. The burgers came, they were thin and greasy and sitting on a bed of hot fries. Both Gerry and Esmerelda had finished off their first Budweisers and ordered another round. Esmerelda was talking about America.

"When I go to America, it be legal so they don't send me back."

"Of course. Your work hasn't gone unnoticed."

"I love America, the beer, the food. The movies."

"America isn't exactly like the movies."

"All the men big and strong. My cousin showed me a movie once, made in Texas. All the men had huevos like walnuts and cocks like a forearm."

Gerry choked on a swallow of beer, "So that's why you want to get to America. Listen Esmerelda, don't believe everything you see in the movies, and certainly not the things you see in porn. Real plumbers aren't nearly that friendly."

"Corn?"

"Porn. Those men put their…penises…in machines to stretch them out."

"Really? That's good to know because I saw that movie once with my cousin and then we sexed together, not my cousin, you and me, and I was greatly saddened at first by your penis."

"Your English is coming on fine." The beers came, Gerry looked at the waiter, "Go ahead and bring another round." He said in Spanish.

"No," She continued in English. "Your penis is good, Gerry. Like other men's. I just thought bigger on American men."

"That's a trick of the movies."

"Like Santa Claus."

"Sure." Gerry laughed, "Merry Christmas."

"Oh. Still the burgers are good." She took an enormous bite of the greasy burger and reached for the ketchup.

An hour later, Gerry was peeling the maid's uniform off Esmerelda and hoping he could coax her into the shower to wash off the scent of pine cleaner. Couching his playful request as if it were some perfectly common American sexcapade, Gerry got her into her small, dirty shower. The engineer could never get his head around how a maid had such a dirty bathroom. There was, however, soap and warm lather and squeezing and his thoughts drifted to greener pastures and whiter tile.

In her bed, Gerry lay awake listening to the sounds of the city around. Noise isn't what kept him up, though. The United States noiselessly relinquished sovereignty over the Zone and pulled out on New Years Eve, 1999. Control of the locks reverted back to the Panamanians who promptly awarded the contract for managing both ends of the canal to a Chinese corporation. Since then most Americans moved "up North".

America out and China in. That's what kept Gerry in Panama. He watched the locks, the ships and what they carried. Now though, he also watched the Chinese businessmen who appeared in greater numbers every quarter. They came and took out loans from Panamanian banks now fat on the infusion of South American drug money.

When SOUTHCOM pulled out, the US had given away control of the most important trade route in the New World, a route that ran directly beneath America's underbelly. Now that route was in the hands of the last great Communist power. A power that, despite the onward march of Capitalism, still listed the United States as its number one enemy. Brilliant. A betrayal, that's what it was, nothing less. A betrayal by the politicians against the country they served. But to Gerry, the military and intelligence communities had been betrayed as well.

He climbed out of bed, kissed her on the forehead and put a hand through the hair that was splayed out over the pillow. Then he crept over to a chair where his clothes hung neatly.

"Gerry." She whispered. Lupé was in the den, sleeping on the couch. "It is in my bag…in the lining. It had the mark you told me to look for. It is new. I copied it after hours when the office was empty. The night captain is in love with Nina so things are sloppy."

"You copied it there?"

"Yes. Quickly." Gerry bit his bottom lip as he pulled on his pants. "Don't do that again, the place is wired. All they'd have to do is review the security tape."

"They only do that if something goes wrong. Nothing went wrong." She put her back on the pillow. "Nothing that they know about."

"Be careful." Gerry said, slipping his jacket on and retrieving the document from the lining of her purse. "The original?" He called softly.

"Back where I found it, you idiot."

Slipping the foolscap document from its plain envelope, Gerry looked over the Chinese type and their equivalent of a "Top Secret" stamp.

"There is Independent on the first page." She said. "I know nothing else. My English is bad, Chinese nothing."

"Your English is alright, and you don't see me once a week. You work with them everyday."

Esmerelda smiled, "I don't want to go to China." Then she smiled and closed her eyes, "I don't know. You're the spy, you figure it out."

<u>Three</u>

Troubled Houses

SUNDAY

DAVID MEEKS TIPPED THE BOTTLE of Dewar's into his coffee and lit another cigarette. A short sip made him wince, which came not so much from the heat in a raw mouth, but the realization that for the first time in his life, Commander David Meeks was drinking on the job. Quickly, as the warming in his stomach subsided, the implications of the drinking faded. He thought he was going to cry. Something his buddies from his old Navy SEAL team wouldn't believe and something the CIA didn't need to see. The politics were brutal and any weakness potentially fatal.

Under a large framed print depicting the engagement of the Merimac and the Monitor, he had another drag on the cigarette and a slug of the Irish café au lait. Out the window, Langley, Virginia seemed desolate. Who was he kidding? He was done for and he knew it.

The phone rang once and then again. He remembered what day it was and that his secretary, however loyal, was in church right now. He pulled his eyes away from the text scrolling upward on his computer monitor to check the caller ID. Meeks snarled, if he wanted to talk to his wife he wouldn't be in the office on Sunday morning. The phone rang again and he let it got to voice mail.

The ringing stopped and the red message light on the receiver lit up. Meeks tried to ignore the beacon for about twenty seconds before checking the voicemail. "Hey it's me." His wife's tired and irritated voice said. "I went by the hospital, Doctor Nashru was there. He gave me the results on Amy. Call me if you're interested."

She had to get that last dig in. Meeks thought. Punishment for not sitting in a catatonic vigil with her while the doctors scratched their heads over the unnamed disease ravaging his eight-year-old daughter's bloodstream.

Meeks dialed the phone and took another slug of coffee – it burned his mouth and the whisky fanned out over his gut. The pain kept him focused enough to keep the emotion at bay. The phone rang again and he picked up the receiver. "Hey Sweetie – what's the good news?"

"What's good about it?" she snapped.

"Valerie… I wouldn't know. Why don't you tell me what the doctor said."

"They don't know anything."

"What do you mean they don't know anything? That's impossible. Valerie, they've been testing her for two weeks, they've had another week to study the tests!"

"They took her out of her home and put her in that godamm children's ward! She's eight, she doesn't need to be out of her house for that long!" Her voice was trembling but cruel.

Another drag, another belt of coffee. This really wasn't the time to hate the doctors. "Amy likes the ward. Being around children her age makes her smile."

"She needs to be at home with her mother! They can't love her like I can! No one can!"

Meeks didn't take the bait, "What does the report say, Valerie?"

"It doesn't say anything!"

"DOCTOR NASHU DIDN'T-he didn't give you a sheet of blank paper. Read the report to me."

A very long pause, the breathing on the other end became long and measured. "Maybe you should come home from that that office you hide in and read the damn thing yourself. Amy's ringing her bell. I need to go."

Meeks didn't hear any bell. "Where's Jack?"

"At my sister's."

Again? "I'll pick him up on the way home. Can I pick up dinner?"

"I'll feed Amy, I can't eat. I don't see how you can."

"Alright, I'll pick him up." He hung up the phone and looked at his watch.

There was a double knock on the open office door and a young analyst in a plaid flannel shirt and a sock tie came in with a manila envelope. "Commander Meeks, I think you should see this."

"Look, can it wait till tomorrow? I've got to go."

"They appear to have a bomb."

"Where?"

"Well...here, Sir."

MEMPHIS WAS DARK AS ARCHIE drove away from Molly Pratt's apartment. He'd left her in the den, still hung over and angry. Although Molly couldn't exactly remember why she was mad, she had a pretty good grasp why she was hung over.

Then Archie was making his way through the mansions and sculpted lawns of the quiet subdivision of Chickasaw Gardens. The Scout idled up the driveway of an old Jacobean house and he pulled round back.

Archie set his bags down in the mudroom just off the kitchen where Frank Gilmur stood over the stove, poking at a few pieces of deer sausage with a long fork. Frank looked up, "Hey Archie. You hungry? Venison."

"What's the occasion, Pop?"

"Midge and Derrick are flying in tomorrow."

"Really? Are they coming in from Thailand or Botswana or someplace?"

"Nope, just Virginny. Popping in for a visit, Midge said." Frank leaned in, "She just wants to check in on her little Bra'. Strange thing though, it was that it was all very last minute. You know how your Aunt Midge likes her spontaneity well-planned."

Archie swatted Frank on the shoulder, "Cheer up, Pop, at least Derrick'll be here."

Frank eyeballed the sausage, "Those crazy old Scots love their venison. Listen, we're having a card game tomorrow. Come to the club at seven."

"Hardly fair, a pair of dusty old brains against mine."

"We'll see. Molly doin' alright?"

"Weddings make her antsy. You know how she gets when she's antsy."

"Then marry her."

"You might be deranged, but I'm not."

"Ha! Good one. What about Bunty?"

"Now that's funny, Pop. No fishing off the company peer, remember?"

"Then fire her."

"I need her."

"Won't argue that, son." Frank said, addressing the sausage. "If you do fire her, and have to hire another secretary, you need to remember something…"

"Yes?"

"You can teach anyone to type," Frank said solemnly, "but you can't teach nice tits."

"I'll keep that in mind, Pop."

Frank lapsed into a brooding silence. "Seriously." He set the long fork down on the skillet and faced Archie. "More to life than working, son. Don't let your life slip away while you…" he trailed off. Fat snapped in the skillet.

"How long have you been up?"

"Four months today. And don't tell me to move on. Your sister says that! She was my wife."

"And my mother-"

"My bed is empty. Do you now what that's like after 42 years? Of course you couldn't. They tell me to sleep in the middle of the bed but it's just strange."

"Mine's empty too."

"Now don't you compare stuffin' Molly Pratt with sleeping next to the mother of your five children!" Frank's voice cracked, he turned back to the sausages.

"Wasn't asking you to move on, Pop. You okay?"

Frank picked up the long fork that had been heating along with the sausages. "Gaudammit!" The fork clattered onto the range. "Yeah, I'm okay. Disfigured but okay."

"Wanna play some cards? Gin Rummy? We'll gang up on Uncle Derrick tomorrow night."

"No, I'm fine. We've already discussed it, Derrick and I are going to gang up on you. Listen, I know Midge would love to see you. You got anything tomorrow?"

"Not proud of it...a client of mine thinks his wife is humping her tennis instructor. Wants proof. Oughtta be done by nine, it's an early lesson."

Frank screwed up his face, "I thought you make a point to work for corporations, not people."

"It's a big client, gave me some work right after I moved back."

Frank laughed, "I'd hate to wash that stink off every night. Can you break for lunch?"

"Sure Pop."

"Midge would appreciate that."

Archie climbed the stairs to his room. His mother had overhauled it when he'd gone off to school so the Led Zeppelin and Police posters had been scraped for British antiques. After a long shower, hair still wet, Archie climbed into a low, heavy sleigh bed and exhausted his lungs. His muscles ached. After the congested roar of Dublin, and the screaming clang of New York, Archie was still acclimating himself to the slower pace of Memphis. It had been six months now, and the quiet streets were still conspicuous to him. Just as well, after six years of feasting on venison chops and buckets of whiskey in Dublin and London, and martinis and sushi in New York and Silicon Valley, Archie Gilmur wasn't really sure where he was.

Six months since Archie had come home, four since his father had become a widower. The move back to Memphis to tend to his dying mother and then widowed father hadn't displaced Archie too terribly. He'd only been in New York for a year and a half, which was fine because he'd never really taken to the city. Frank still couldn't sell the house in which Isobel Gilmur had gone on.

Even the Scout he was driving was a relic. Archie was driving what was dubbed the "farm truck" for family properties in Mississippi and Louisiana because he thought the 1969 Jaguar E-Type convertible he'd bought in London was a bit much for Memphis. It sat in the garage below his bedroom window.

Frank Gilmur never drove the old Jag but swore over the second bottle of Vueve Cliquot they split on New Year's Eve that he would "Guard the damn thing with my life. Now when are you gonna give back the farm truck?"

"When I get settled, Pop, of course."

Four

Sly-Boots

MONDAY

BUNTY CARRICK FELT HER BREASTS being admired and didn't like it. She stood up, clutching the file to her black cashmere V-neck. "Can I get anything to drink, sir?" she said to the man slouching in the leather couch by the door marked *Tantallion Group, LLC.* "Sir?"

Conrad Van Clair snapped himself out of the trance he'd fallen into at the sight of Bunty's chest. "Uh, coffee?"

"How do you take it?" Now that she was standing upright, she could feel his eyes moving down her gray Prince of Wales skirt and black leggings. Bunty was annoyed, Mr. Van Clair had ridden up in the elevator with her and followed her into the office. The lights were off when she unlocked the door and she thought that should have been hint enough to wait outside while she opened shop. Van Clair came in after her, introducing himself in the dark and sitting on the sofa while she opened the office. Now she glared at him, "Eye contact, Mr. Van Clair!" She clipped. "Eye contact!"

Conrad Van Clair looked up, taking in the light scattering of copper-colored freckles across Bunty's feminine face. Her blue eyes (that could be green) were punctuated with enormous black pupils that made Van Clair think he could get away with nothing.

Bunty guessed Van Clair was in his mid-fifties, a little paunchy, slightly balding, but not an altogether bad looking man in the obligatory blue pinstripe suit. "Mr. Gilmur had an appointment first thing this morning, should be back any minute. I'll just go and brew some java right up…" she turned toward the small kitchenette on the other side of the room. "…some piping hot coffee, yes sir… you perv."

"What's that?"

Bunty turned, teeth gleaming, "Kenya blend alright?"

Van Clair watched as Bunty started the coffee, her strawberry blonde hair pulled back into a short curl of a ponytail, revealing a nice curve of neck. Van Clair thought that she'd had a hand in the decoration. Before him was black lacquered Oriental coffee table, along the wall facing the door was a kidney shaped pine desk in front of a pine credenza holding a printer/fax, and a wire rack with some files in it. The credenza and desk, with the rest of the front office, were neurotically well organized.

The coffee was hissing into the pot when the door opened and Archie pounded in. "Damn, those new tennis dresses sure are easy to get off."

Bunty appeared from the kitchenette, nodding to Mr. Van Clair. "Hey, I didn't see you there. Archie Gilmur."

Van Clair struggled off the sofa and they pumped hands. "Conrad Van Clair." He looked Archie over; wrinkled gray Oxxford suit at this hour and an Inns of Court regimental bowtie. "Sorry, I thought you'd look different."

"I thought I would too." Archie nodded to the green baize covered door to the left of Bunty's desk. "Let's sit down." Van Clair followed Archie into his office, which was not nearly so clutter free as Bunty's. Archie motioned to the two coffee-colored leather armchairs in front of the huge wooden desk. Papers and files lay scattered atop it. One pile was weighted down with coffee cup and saucer, another with one of those ashtrays built into a plaid beanbag, and a third with what appeared to be a sword hilt without a blade. Behind it, in front of the wide window overlooking downtown Memphis, was a laptop computer on a typing desk. The outside and far walls, behind several glass-fronted bookcases were exposed brick, and the other two walls were painted the color of blended Scotch.

Van Clair looked over the office. "Quite an office."

"Ms. Carrick, who you've already ogled, has an eye for detail. Something to drink?"

"Er... Ms. Carrick is making some coffee." Van Clair said, easing himself into an armchair.

Archie moved around the desk and dropped into a wooden swivel chair. "Who did you say you were with, Mr. Van Clair?" He waved to Bunty as she came in with the coffee service.

"DeltaComm."

The flat smile on Archie's face never faltered as Bunty's eyes bulged and the coffee service went crashing to the floor. Archie was on his feet in a flash, fetching a mop as Bunty collected the pieces back on the tray. Van Clair watched as the two cleaned up the mess without saying a world to each other.

"Let me try that again." Said Bunty.

"Don't bother about it." Said Archie.

"Oh don't worry, I'll bother." She said and disappeared into the front office.

"Sorry about that." Said Archie, as he moved back around the desk.

"Good help is hard to find, eh?"

"Wouldn't say that in front of her unless you want the next pot over your head." Archie folded his hands on the desk and took a breath, "So Mr. Van Clair of DeltaComm Components, what can I do for you?"

Van Clair stared out the window with a smile. "When DeltaComm first moved HQ to Memphis we were in that building across the street." He pointed through the window but Archie didn't follow.

"How the world changes."

"Yes, Mr. Gilmur, in the information technology world, change is all you've got."

"And information."

"Yes. I'm glad you said that, Mr. Gilmur. Information is gold. We like to keep a tight hold on our data."

"Sound policy."

"We're having some security concerns about a move we'll be making, Mr. Gilmur. I can't give you the details. But there are some concerns, do you understand?"

"I think so. Security concerns. A lot of people are having those troubles these days. So what brings you to me?"

"You came recommended, Mr. Gilmur. I'm sure you realize that your specialized…research…is hard to come by."

Archie shrugged sheepishly and took a pack of Dunhill's out of his desk, "Want one?"

"No thank you." Van Clair stared at Archie as he lit the cigarette, "I'm sorry, Mr. Gilmur, it's just been years, hell decades, since I've seen anyone smoke in the office."

"Reckon I'm the boss…my neck on the block as it were." The door opened and Bunty came in with a small cup and saucer, and handed the coffee over to Van Clair, careful to lean away. She sniffed once, and crossed over to the speaker sized air filter near Archie's desk. Their eyes locked for an instant and she switched the filter on. Bunty left and closed the door behind her.

"She didn't bring you any?"

"I'm aware of that. I think she smelled the cigarette. Now, what is it, exactly, you want researched? A security system, I'm assuming?"

"We want you to test the integrity of our systems. Like anything else, information is particularly vulnerable when it is moved."

"Oh a diagnostic?"

"It's not that simple."

"Great." Another deep drag on the cigarette.

"We want you to break into the facility."

Archie leaned forward, "You want me to break into the DeltaComm facility?"

"Correct."

"I don't know what kind of black arts you think I dabble in but-"

"We are actually," Van Clair started with a smile, "very familiar with your work, Mr. Gilmur."

"How about that?"

"You came highly recommended."

Archie crushed the cigarette into the ashtray, "Nice to know I have fans."

ARCHIE STOOD IN THE BASEMENT OFFICE of the advertising agency, watching Kelso Truitt inspect the night vision goggles. "They're broken."

"I'm aware of that." Archie said, "I broke them. How much do I owe you?"

"How'd you break them?"

"Herding sheep."

"Yes, I get lots of nocturnal shepherds in here." Truitt looked up, "Not dressed like that, though."

"I was trying to look like someone with a regular tennis game."

Truitt, despite the February chill, wore jeans and a black tee-shirt that read *Welcome to the Dork Side.* "You're looking very old money."

"Go to hell. Can you fix it?"

Truitt laughed, "You're still trying to clean up the language?"

"Go to hell isn't cussing, it's giving direction."

"It's not preacher talk, how much have you had to pay Bunty this year?"

"Screw Bunty and her cuss jar. And screw isn't a cuss word either. Now can you fix the fuckin' goggles or shall I just shove them up your ass?"

"Archie, some of that is definitely cussing." Truitt laughed and pointed at the goggles, "This? this is easy. I've got a spare lens." he put the goggles aside, "Now let me show you something." Opening a desk drawer, he took out a small plastic device. It looked like a key fob. "Well?"

Archie said nothing and Truitt's smile faded.

"It's not that I'm not impressed…"

"You don't look impressed." said Truitt.

"Would a slight stagger help?"

Truitt considered this, smoothing the tips of a black moustache at the corners of his mouth, "No…at this point, probably not."

Archie wanted to take the device from Truitt and study it, but the computer engineer had odd thoughts about his equipment. "What does it do?"

Truitt jumped excitedly in his chair, "Oh, it's the latest thing!" his excitement rekindled amid the guts of an untold number of disemboweled computers in his bare-bricked basement office. "You can download the entire contents of any PC on the market with this thing."

"Onto what? That hard drive you gave me? Worked like a charm, little slow though."

"No, this is it!"

Archie straightened himself, "That's a hell of a thing."

Truitt set the fob down on a clear corner of his disaster of a desk and Archie picked it up. The plastic was smooth and high-impact, and at a few ounces, was heavier than it looked.

"And you aren't doing anything illegal?" Truitt asked for the fourth time.

"I'm not breaking any *American* laws."

"Not quite a denial." He pointed to the ceiling, "I wouldn't want to lose my gig with the agency."

"That's right, you're an ad man now. What do you do for them again?"

"Maintain the servers for the web hosting. We're a full service agency." Truitt said with a nod.

"Are we?" Archie smiled that way Truitt hated, "So you buy a thousand dollar computer and charge thirty people $500 a month to reboot once every couple of weeks when the works get gummed up. Isn't that illegal?"

"Bit more complicated than that, Archie."

Turning the device over in his hand, Archie moved to sit in one of the tall yellow director's chairs, but there was a disconnected motherboard in its seat. He continued to shuffle around on the concrete floor. Suddenly Truitt's eyes went sad behind his black plastic eyeglasses. "It's not what you wanted, is it? You hate it don't you?"

"Actually, I do need something like this…but what I really need, for this job, is to upload information, not download it."

"Hmm." Truitt leaned back in his chair and sipped Mountain Dew from a mug the size of a cereal bowl with a handle on it. "Sabotage?" A faded picture of Jabba the Hut grinned at Archie from the mug.

"Not really, what I'm looking for is to install a secret back door to the system, not even that, just a doggy door really. So I can get back in."

"Once the system was breached they'd find it."

"How long?"

"Size?"

"Global."

"Chances are the system isn't global, but smaller systems linked globally." Truitt thought again, "Couple of hours if they're lucky, a few days on the outside."

Archie's green eyes bore down on Truitt but he said nothing. He knew Archie well enough to recognize his brain at work: not angry, not impatient, but simply folding in new data until a conclusion was reached. Truitt sipped more Mountain Dew and waited.

Archie and Truitt had met in ninth grade, where they were roommates at McAlistar Academy, a military boarding school in the mountains of east Tennessee. It was at McAlistar that Truitt, admired among the grade school math and chess club sets and nowhere else, was introduced to computers and mechanical engineering. Suddenly, with the conviction of a convert, Truitt knew what he wanted to do with his life.

Archie on the other hand, preferred sleeping outdoors to in, and always seemed happiest surrounded by horses and dogs and a gun across his forearm. Their common bond was that they both loved and despised the rigors of military school at the same time. They quickly became fast friends who never traveled in the same circles-an arrangement that suited both.

Then Archie dug a Berretta pocketknife out of his coat and opened it, running his thumb over the blade. "What I need, is to upload a worm – yes sabotage – something to muddy the waters and then open the doggy door."

"They'll still run a diagnostic."

"But they'll find the worm and stop looking. Won't they? Why? Because they'll have found the problem and be fixing it." Archie smiled, "It's just to buy time, maybe an extra few days."

"You're no friend to the computers."

"I make people like you make better systems." Archie took the motherboard from the director's chair and tossed it onto a blank monitor. "It's tough love."

Truitt watched the teetering motherboard for a moment. The problem with Archie was that he was never careful enough. "If that helps you sleep at night."

Archie looked at his watch, "Can you do it?"

"What do you think?"

"How long?"

"Well Archie, It's not that easy. I'd have to know something about the system, have access to their computer-"

Archie took a hard drive out of the Barbour jacket that had been flung over a chair and set it in front of Truitt. "There's your back door. Got it in New Orleans. Then he pulled out CD-Rom, "and here is the key."

Truitt drained his mug, "Alright, one miracle, coming up. Two days, not cheap."

"Name your price, DeltaComm is footing the bill. Two days huh?"

"Yup." Truitt said and swallowed hard.

"I leave in the morning."

"Well, Archie."

"Well, Truitt, I said name your price." Archie leaned in over Truitt's chair, "But here's the thing. I think you've already got what I need in one of these damn boxes." Archie gestured around the basement room, across the computers that lined the walls. "I think that all you need to do is patch it up to the back door," he tapped the hard drive on the desk, "and we'll be there."

Truitt laughed nervously. "What? Do you think I just sit around here in my spare time and write worms and Trojan horses?"

"You said it, not me." Archie straightened himself.

"When does your plane leave?"

"Atta boy. It'll be worth it." Tapping his watch, Archie said, "Gotta run, write me up an invoice."

"You know I've got a real job now? You, on the other hand, creep around like some sort of spook."

"I prefer sly-boots. Now I've got to get examined by my godmother."

ARCHIE GILMUR WAS NEVER exactly sure how his Uncle Derrick made his money, but Aunt Midge enjoyed smiling at it. Neither was particularly impressed with his having made just shy of three million within three weeks of his thirty-third birthday. As his godfather and namesake, Uncle Derrick was proud of him; as his godmother, Aunt Midge was downright shocked.

The trio sat in a pale red dining room, in chintz covered chairs at a table near the floor to ceiling windows that overlooked the country club links. It was a quiet room. Except, of course, for Aunt Midge telling all that Frank Gilmur really should tear himself away from the golf course and have lunch with his sister and favorite brother-in-law.

"Aren't y'all staying with him?" asked Archie.

"Well, yes, but I'm worried about him. And you, Archie, why were you late?"

"I had to work, Aunt Midge. Testing the integrity of tennis dresses."

"Oh jolly good." grumbled Derrick.

The waiter appeared, padding silently over the padded cream-colored carpet with a tray of drinks. "Archie, Redbreast and soda; Mr. Gordon, your Talisker, and Mrs. Gordon…." The waiter set a tall glass of tea in front of Midge.

"Lester!" Aunt Midge snapped, "I said we were having tea!"

"And there's your tea…don't look at me like that, Mrs. Gordon, I put some vodka in it." Lester smiled winningly, "Go ahead and taste it."

"Lester, I ordered tea."

The laughter that bubbled up from Lester's long, narrow chest only started out low. "Don't worry Mrs. Gordon, nobody'll know."

"Lester, just go away. And take the ice pick with you."

Lester smiled and took Midge's drink as he sauntered back to the bar.

"The club really is going down hill."

Lester reappeared almost instantly with a Cheshire grin and a martini made with a lot of vermouth. He set it in front of Midge. "Will Mr. Gilmur be joining us?"

"Doubtful." Said Derrick.

Midge made a disapproving "tsk, tsk" at her cocktail before taking a sip.

"Archie, what'll you have?"

"Catfish."

"Coulda seen that one comin'" Said Lester. The odd thing about the club was that Archie knew he'd be promoted to "Mr. Gilmur" as soon as his father died and not a second sooner. He and Pop been haunting the place for the last six months. Over the bar in the Red Room, there was a picture of Midge as Queen of Cotton Carnival, laughing over a Martini: she was part of the lexicon that no employee dared to forget even though she was now only in town a few times a year. As for Derrick and his Talisker, well Derrick was the stuff of legend.

Derrick Archibald Gordon, had been in the British SAS at one point, and now owned a few Caterpillar dealerships in Europe he never saw. He had a soft spot for Archie, the sort people do for a puppy that simply won't learn to fetch. He was a tall man, not fat, with a prominent nose and bushy white brows over deep-set eyes. He wore a light Harris Tweed suit and his regimental tie; he'd been in the states for 25 years, and still got his clothes from London. Derrick also appeared to be deaf as a post, but not from anything as heroic as bombs in Northern Ireland. It happened, he explained loudly, from a fishing accident in Tortola, British VI. Then, as a side note he would roar, that it was one of the few really loud fishing accidents in history. That was as far as he'd go, he generally found talking tiresome.

Midge, however, did not. She was speaking now and Archie had to look at her. She was a smallish woman who had been a beauty in her day. The picture over the bar had been pointed out to him since he was old enough to sneak in on Saturday afternoons. But the photo that stuck out in his mind was the one at his father's house, taken when Midge had been touring the Mediterranean as Cotton Carnival Queen, where she was found by Derrick in Gibraltar. She'd first seen him playing polo and that was all it took. He was thirty-five, a confirmed bachelor, and a career soldier. Midge, however, with her drawling accent and Southern manners, was just a little too beautiful. Although Archie couldn't picture it now, Derrick told him that she "just kept me laughing".

"So you kept your godparents waiting at lunch. I guess that means you are at least vaguely employed? Midge had spent over forty years married to a highland Scot–retirement was for the weak, even for thirty five year old millionaires.

"Aunt Midge, don't be daft. I've got a job, I'm a consultant."

"About what, exactly, do you consult?"

"Security issues."

"Security issues." She repeated.

"I get to carry a gun." He winked at her.

"Au Laud, Derrick, did you hear that, he's armed."

Derrick put a wide palm against the dish of his ear, "Eh, what's that?"

"He's just spying. I remember that summer at the lake-"

Lester returned with a shrimp salad, a plate of smoked salmon, and a catfish sandwich. "I gave it a Tabasco bath." Lester said as he set the plate in front of Archie, who was staring at Uncle Derrick's plate.

"I didn't see smoked salmon on the menu."

Lester nodded to Derrick. "I give old soldiers what they want at snack time."

"What am I?"

"You Frank Gilmur's boy." He spied Midge's diminished martini, "Need some more tea?"

"And Lester, make it proper tea this time!"

Lester laughed, "There you go wit that tea again. You sho' is funny, Mrs. Gordon." He strolled off as if the matter were settled.

"Fine fish!" Derrick bellowed over the table. Midge seemed unaffected by the sound waves rolling over her, but it took Archie by surprise.

"The food here is always good." Midge said loudly and pleasantly. Strange how a woman whose sole existence was defined by making life difficult for others could be so indulgent to her husband. "How's Molly?"

"We broke up…I think."

"Well you'd better figure it out, I'm playing bridge with her grandmother in an hour. Very awkward of you to dump the poor thing before my bridge game. You really ought to know where you stand on this sort of thing."

"You've got an hour, Midge. If I leave now I can probably get her on her back before the gossip starts." He looked down at the table, "Hate to miss my sandwich."

Derrick laughed into his salmon plate, "Good one Lad." He wheezed and took a healthy swallow of scotch, coughed, and hit his chest. "Clears the pipes."

"Strange what that man chooses to hear." Midge turned back to Archie, "Don't be vulgar. Now why aren't you two still seeing each other?"

"Maybe the gun scared her."

"It damn well scares me! It's shameful."

"Derrick was always armed!"

"He was in the army. What do you do? Have you got a real job lined up?"

"Shamefully, no."

"When you were little, you wanted to be a farmer. Take over from your father. That's respectable. What's all this business with technology…you hate computers."

"Mom wanted me to go to University in Scotland, if I remember correctly, y'all thought it was good idea. I guess that's what Pop gets for marrying his brother-in-law's little sister."

Aunt Midge smiled, "What can I say, I pick out stunning bridesmaid's dresses." The smile faded, "Isobel was beautiful to the end."

"She was very proud of you, m'lad. All five of you, but you have her wanderlust." He laughed, something he remembered about his little sister.

"You really don't have a job, do you?" Midge touched Derrick's hand, "He's derelict. Without a girl...derelict and lonely."

"Oh, I still get the ashes dragged from time to time."

Derrick laughed loudly into his scotch.

"If you two don't behave yourselves, I'm leaving for more respectable company." She glared at Derrick, "He gets it from your side of the family!"

"Don't be daft, Wife! He's not our child."

"This is too much!"

"Midge don't go." Derrick pleaded. If Archie thought he'd detected a hint of sarcasm, Midge was awash in it.

"There is no need to mock me." She looked at Archie, brimming with compassion, "Derrick Archibald Gilmur, you've got his name, you don't have to be like him." She thought for a moment, looked at her watch and announced, "I think I'd better leave. Archie, call me before we leave." She smiled pensively, "I worry." She stood, they stood.

"Of course, thank you."

Archie kissed Midge on the cheek, precisely where she indicated with a glossy nail.

"Have a good game love." Derrick hollered and extended a large paw, patting her on the rear. He tossed his napkin on the table, "Archie, let's have another drink." Derrick hand signaled Lester and turned back to Archie. "So your pop tells me that you're headed to Jamaica tomorrow?"

"Yes, it's work, not much of a vacation."

Derrick patted Archie's shoulder, "Well alright, let me know if there is anything that I can do."

The bartender came around with a Talisker and Redbreast.

"Sure, did we set Midge off?"

"Don't worry about her, she likes to get set off. If she's still mad later I'll buy her a hat or something." Derrick took a sip and leaned in, "You've never bought a diamond have you?"

"She didn't seem *that* mad."

"Focus boy."

"No, never had a reason to. Molly Pratt thinks I did, but she's John Hanover's problem now."

Derrick laughed; another sip of his whisky. "I buy them, from time to time. Sometimes for myself and sometimes for Midge. Of course, I buy them as a commodity, but the fairer sex doesn't see them that way. Anyway, there is a new diamond and precious metals broker here in town. They are a Canadian outfit, Vanderhorn's. The fella that ran the operation in New Orleans, a Russian immigrant named Viktor Makarin, he's running it. All perfectly legal, I'm sure. The shop is opening soon. My fella in Virginia told me about it before Midge and I left. If I miss his grand opening, could you drop in for me?"

Archie was watching his uncle with a vague apprehension. A long draw of Irish whisky later, he said, "Yeah, Uncle Derrick. Sure, no problem."

"Just next time you've got a free minute downtown. I've learned not to take Midge into retail jewelry stores."

Archie laughed, "I don't blame you."

Derrick waved him off. "I can get the stone, and have it mounted for about half the price, you understand. Not trying to be cheap you see, but there isn't any reason to throw your money away."

"I'm of the same mind. What exactly are you looking for?"

"Cocktail ring. I'll need a small square cut, blue white and very near flawless. Reckon they'll need some clusters around it, not chips, proper diamonds, say three carat total weight...one carat for the center."

"That's some ring. Are you in the dog house?"

"Oh Lord no. Never give a woman diamonds to get out of the dog house, Archie. If they think it's profitable to forgive your sins, they'll make sure you have a lot to forgive. No, she's just still funny to me."

"Fair enough. Hope one day I get there. Why me? I don't know anything about diamonds."

"Nonsense, you're a quick study. And I don't want to get nabbed doing my homework." Derrick paused, "Well, he's new in town, check him out if you can."

"Check him out?"

"You got a good gut, Archie, let me know what you think. Have fun in Jamaica. Are we still on for cards?"

THE ANTEROOM WAS EMPTY, Archie found Bunty in his office. She was matching the items laid out on the tall plantation desk to the type printed list in her hand. Bunty's eyes moved over the items again and she checked off another bullet on the list. A zippered case lay on the table with a small torque wrench and three small dentist picks, along with:

- Gym bag, medium w/ shoulder strap
- 1 pr - paper over shoes (lift from hospital)
- 2 - 2X4's 18" long
- 1 sml box - heavy duty carpenter's nails
- 1 sml box - rubber bands (lrge)
- Flask 12 oz – Redbreast

Missing from the table were:

- Portable hard drive (+ hrdwre)
- Night vision specs
- DeltaComm ID lamys
- Digital Camera (+ disk)

Archie came in and took off his coat, "Truitt can fix the night specs and he's having the ID's laminated. I can pick 'em up this afternoon."

"Good." Said Bunty without looking at him. She made another check on the list. Bunty glanced hard over at him, "Did Elaine come down to give you the nickel tour again?"

"I think she was at a meeting. She must do a lot of web work because I've never been there when she didn't have to come downstairs."

The depth, the absolute blackness, of Archie's blind spot for women put Bunty into a state of shock. "Funny how that happens." she said and looked at the list again "I've mocked up the Glemworth

Insurance ID cards, I've just got to print them out. I'm reformatting the hard drive right now."

"No need." Archie showed her Truitt's devilish key fob. Bunty bit her lip and wrinkled the side of her nose. "You don't like it?"

"Don't you think it's weird?"

"That this bottle opener can store more information than a computer the size of a cow? I guess that's weird, but let's call it innovative."

"No, Archie. The fact that this DeltaComm fella shows twelve hours after you break into their distribution hub and steal a decade worth of financials."

"Steal? No I just copied it..."

Bunty stared at him.

Archie crossed over to his desk and fumbled with a cigarette. "Van Clair isn't sending me to New Orleans. They want me cracking into their OEM in Jamaica."

"The one on a papaya plantation?"

"That's it."

Jamaica, obviously, was not in Archie's blind spot. "Why?"

"He *said* the plantation was there when they bought the place." Archie shook his head, "Strange place to have an equipment manufacturer."

"Strange. Bordering on unlikely."

"Bunty, it's just a job."

"Do you think it's a trap?"

He sat at the desk, "Bunty, why would they do that? If they knew I'd been poking around in New Orleans the other night they'd have the police on me like Elvis on bacon. Why all the cloak and dagger foolishness?"

"So you think it's a coincidence?"

"Didn't say that."

"It's just too weird. You don't think it's a trap?"

"I don't know what it is Bunty. No worries, you won't get stinky if the shit hits the fan."

"Maybe I'm not worried about my skin."

Archie smiled. "Besides, I want to go to Jamaica."

Bunty laughed, "Now that even creeps me out. I booked your flight, got you into that hotel on the Black River. It sounds like a resort to me."

"It's a dump."

"The prices don't look dumpy."

"Property values are nuts down there."

"Sure. Listen you're hauling a lot of equipment down there, maybe I need to go to, you know, to watch our kit."

Considering the change in plans, Archie rubbed his chin. "How are you going to watch our kit if you're laying on the beach half in the bag?"

"Archie, if it's DeltaComm's facility, why'd the cuddly pervert give you a set of blueprints called Independent Manufacturing, LLC?"

"DeltaComm owns 28% of Independent. It was an old British firm, used to be Colonial Telegraph and Wire. When the climate changed, and the Brits lost the Empire, they changed the name. Now a Chinese telecom, SinoTel, owns most of Independent."

"You can be really boring at times."

Archie shrugged his shoulders, "You asked."

"SinoTel, I thought the Chinese were communists."

"They claim to be. They're smart enough not to believe their own bullshit." He laughed, "You'd be amazed how rare that is, you really would."

Five

Black River Papaya Make You Dance Long Time

TUESDAY

UNCHARACTERISTICALLY, Archie had resisted Bunty's demand to be taken to Jamaica to "case the beaches". Now he was flying first class on DeltaComm's dime and enjoying a complementary cocktail at 8:30 in the morning. Archie supposed leaving her behind was a rotten thing to do. And while something nagged at him, it wasn't Bunty. She'd get him back, she always did.

The hypnotic drone of the engines lulled Archie and he tried to focus. Something in the manner in which Van Clair had drifted in and out of nervousness unsettled Archie. He couldn't quite put his finger on it so he deliberately thought of something else.

Last night played over in his head. Uncle Derrick and his father had ganged up on him again and given him a royal flogging. No telling what those two old bastards were doing with the four hundred dollars they'd liberated from him. Losing twice wasn't nearly as bad as trying to figure out *how* he'd lost. Those two had scammed him somehow – he knew it and was sure they knew he knew.

The pilot announced that the plane would be preparing its descent into Kingston soon. The flight attendant came by for his glass so Archie washed down the remains of his whiskey, folded up his tray, and went to the restroom. He fished the passport case out of the inside pocket of his sport coat, and tossed his blue US passport on the sink. From the back pocket of his washed out poplin khakis came a worn red UK passport. Archie put it in the case, and shoved the US passport into his back pocket. Then he actually used the facility and went back to his seat. He sat, legs crossed and strumming his fingers on his white bucks that were badly in need of a cleaning.

The stewardess came by again and suggested a seatbelt.

After an annoying wait in the stuffy airplane, Archie stepped out into the breezy Jamaican air and crossed the tarmac into the heat of the airport terminal. A line was forming at the customs gate; tourists mostly, draped in ridiculous tropical silks. Then Archie stepped up to the uniformed woman shadowed by a bored looking soldier. "Passport Please." Came the lady's voice.

Archie handed over the red passport.

"Very good, Mr. Gilmur. Have you any vegetable matter with you?"

"No, I'm on the Atkin's diet."

As Archie pulled his rented Land Rover Discovery out into the chaotic streets, he called Bunty to check in. "You confirmed the reservation at Hotel de la Rio Negro? …Good, I don't want to spend the night in the Disco. This island is a dangerous place I hear…. How are things in Memphis?…The tennis pro, huh?….I guess the lesson went well enough…Did Van Clair get back to his masters?….Yeah they've got me for four hundred dollars…I don't know, Bunty….What do *you* think an eighty year old Scot and a sixty five year old widower do with that kind of money?… Yes, I studied the maps on the plane. I'm driving straight on to the resort. Now I've got to get into character; some damn bored-to-death-corporate-drone who's managed to get sent to Jamaica without the wife on the company's dime. Hold on, let me try a few boring faces… What's with the compliments all of the sudden Love? You miss me already?"

Bunty's cackle came over the phone with such profound volume and clarity that Archie knew for certain he wasn't on one of DeltaComm's phones.

The cramped streets of Kingston are loud and noisy and Archie realized how quickly he'd grown used to the quiet. He laid on his horn violently because Archie was a firm believer in the "when in Rome" style of travel.

Then he was crossing the island toward the Black River. The Caribbean-it's colors and the manner in which they stand boldly against each other without blending-is impossibly beautiful. Even the slums and hovels appear to white eyes as if they have been rendered in Technicolor film when the rest of the world is on videotape. Archie followed the southern coastline of the island west. He was maneuvering the Discovery through a hairpin turn down a sloping rain forest when he began the see signs for the Hotél de La Rio Negro and the brightly colored building that made up the resort came into view.

He'd lied. It wasn't really a dump. Exclusive club – resort that featured some of the finest beaches on the island was a hair more accurate. Of course, Archie wasn't about to tell Bunty that, it was only last week she'd demanded a raise for the six months hard labor she'd put in at Tantallion Group.

The resort was beautiful, if not a little too well maintained. Soon the chain link and razor wire that kept the impoverished cut-throats way from the rich tourists would be forgotten. He waved to the well-lit guardhouse, and stopped to show his red UK passport. He scanned the guard's hut: a lot of surveillance equipment but very little firepower.

Archie hated himself for thinking that way, but that's life.

The resort was painted bright Caribbean colors and topped with a red tiled roof. Under the grand portico, Archie was swarmed by bag-hops. He handed his keys and a generous tip to the oldest valet and his took his own bags in through the wide glass doors. "So glad you arrived safely." Said the tall concierge with short-cropped hair. Archie couldn't help but smile back. "A parcel arrived for you earlier, Mr. Gilmur."

"Can you have it sent up?"

"It's already in your room, sir." She said, "May I bother you for some papers."

Archie handed over his passport.

She stared at it for a long time and said without handing it back. "You do not sound British, sir."

"I grew up in Zimbabwe." He smiled and tried to look tired. Generally, few people know what a white fella from Zimbabwe sounds like.

In the room, Archie checked the closets and the locks, and threw the safety latch. In the parcel were two plastic cases, inside the foam inset of one was a Heckler & Koch P7. In the second case were the contents Archie and Bunty had packed from the plantation desk. He slipped the pistol into his waistband at the small of his back pulled on his jacket. The camera came out of the suitcase, and that was it-the rest of the gear was left in the bag under the bed.

Archie knew the hotel – it had been sixteen years since he and Vivie had managed to sneak down under her parent's radar. The Oaks thought their oldest daughter was on a trip with her sorority sisters. They'd been down three out of four high school summers, but that last trip was the only one where they'd didn't have to sneak behind a sand dune to have a go. Archie was fairly sure he could still find the bar. What he didn't want to find was Vivie. Surely she wouldn't be in Jamaica in February - *Surely her children are in school by now.*

Now he had work to do. The valet brought the Discovery around and Archie hit the road. Circling the papaya plantation to the north. Then he was off the road and onto a clearing. It ran off into two ruts that served as a road. Bunty thought it a blasphemy not to have a convertible in Jamaica; Archie would have to call her tonight to tell her he was right. Then even the Disco could go no further and he headed on foot.

The digital camera with the telescopic lens went on the tripod and Archie had a seat to survey the compound below. Mostly it appeared to be exactly what Van Clair claimed. A papaya plantation that was somehow deemed essential for business by a Chinese telecommunications giant and an America components manufacturer. There was one large complex on the north-west corner of the farm. A large pre-fab building in front of which Archie could just make out a faded Independent Manufacturing sign. Nearby, a small mobile home park was arranged like a barracks. Across the huge property, closer to the ocean, where the groves gave way to a cluster of steep hills, there were some small shanty houses. At the top of the highest hill, there was a clearing where a bonfire had been recently dowsed.

Archie was packing up the camera when something caught his eye. Zooming in, there was another building, but further back, obscured mostly by a thick tree line that appeared to cut off the grove. This was another pre-fab building, but larger. And this compound was itself surrounded by a fence. An old school bus sat out front, it was painted yellow and green.

He slipped another disk into the camera and began taking shots of the far compound.

IN MEMPHIS, DICKEY O'SHEA PULLED the gray microfibre pants up over his bare behind. Mrs. Oaks smiled from the bed, tired and vaguely confused. "Wonderful, Precious, just wonderful." Mrs. Oaks always seemed unable to stay awake after lunch and a hump and this made Dickey nervous because when the old girl did slip off, it was a task of Arthurian will to wake her and extract his money.

"You were fine too, Mrs. Oaks." He said with a twinkle in his smile. Purring in that strange accent Mrs. Oaks could never quite place.

"Um." She sighed, her normally pale cheeks flushed.

Now Dickey was tucking a French blue shirt into his pants and thinking that loud and cheery wasn't enough to keep Vivian Oaks in the world of the waking. "Did you say Mr. Oaks was back in town tomorrow? Or is it the next day? I'll just bet you'll show that globetrotting husband of yours how much fun it is right here in Memphis."

She rolled her eyes and lifted her head from the pillow. "I could wear a raincoat to the bed before he'd notice."

"Oh, now, Mrs. Oaks. I find that hard to believe."

"My, my, what bedside manners you have. Would you be a dear and hand me my purse?"

Dickey took the purse from the gilded Louis XIV writing table across the room and softly tossed it to her. It landed almost silently in the mounds of fluffed Frette duvet covers. Mrs. Oaks was sitting up and clearing her throat. "Speaking of Mr. Oaks," she was saying, "he is starting to wonder why I'm paying so much and the house looks exactly the same as it did when I hired you."

"He's got a good eye to see all that from Hong Kong."

"He was in town last month, that week you left me for business."

"Business no, Pet. Interior design is an art, and an artist needs time."

Mrs. Oaks laughed, "You are an artist aren't you, Precious. But seriously, the formal dining room could use a face-lift, don't you think? I see something French. Not fussy French, you understand…New Orleans!"

"You want me to flood your house?"

"…Very grand. Well, we'd best show something for our efforts because Mr. Oaks is asking questions. And I've got a party to throw, remember? We'll give it a Mardi Gras theme. That all fits."

"What kind of questions is Mr. Oaks asking?"

"Tara's even flying in for the party. God I hope she's not an embarrassment."

"Mr. Oaks? Asking questions?"

"Oh, don't worry about that, he still thinks your bread is buttered on the wrong side."

Dickey's well-tanned face twitched. This business of everyone thinking he was gay was starting to annoy him. Why? He didn't think he acted gay, didn't look gay; clearing his throat in a manly way-he pulled the flame orange tie into a knot around his neck. On the other hand, the margin on interior design wasn't nearly good as some of his other services. The misconception certainly put him beyond suspicion. Still again, simply cramming Mrs. Oaks' dining room with French antiques might prove less tiresome.

"I suppose I could make the dining room into Sazerac Hotel. But still I wonder…if your husband is off in the Far East blazing new trails for *your* dear big daddy's company, and it is those cuddly yellow bastards and their loaned out pandas we're throwing this party for…then maybe an Oriental flare just might be the ticket."

"I don't want them to feel too comfortable, Dickey. The last time Walt had those folks from SinoTel here-"

"The who?"

"The Chinese. The last time they were in town, some young buck kept trying to bed Tara."

"She's an attractive girl." He said with a wink. "The apple doesn't fall far from the tree."

"Yes. But getting laid by some commie whiz kid isn't going to help her current condition. You know she's failed out of school? We sent her down to the beach house to get away from her crowd."

"Not sure that crowd of professional vacationers in Jamaica are going to be any better. Glowing skin, sure… but…safer?"

"No no, not Oriental." Not one to have her lackluster parenting questioned, Mrs. Oaks pressed on. "That Far East look went out with Beehive hair. What I want them to do-and I mean this-is to go away and take their overfed raccoons and peckers with them!"

"Try not to be so vague with your feelings Mrs. Oaks. Besides, the Pandas aren't actually coming to your house, they'll be at the zoo." Dickey pulled on his coat. "Now look, this is a family business. Your father is the chairman of the board, your brother is the CEO, and your husband is the head of the Asian Division. Now you are going to have to step up to the plate."

"Dickey darling, why do *you* even care?"

"That's it, we'll make the place into the Lost City, everyone's impressed; the Chinese, the city, the papers, your dear brother, and the Memphis Zoo. Hell, even the godamm Pandas will be impressed. Your big daddy will be impressed. We'll just put Tara into a Kimono she can't easily get out of-"

"Houdini will be impressed."

"THEN, and then, when old Walt and the gang goes back to China and everyone makes pots of money and your stock goes through the roof...we'll loose the red lacquer and cover everything in gilt. Go Bourbon Street – the classiest whorehouse in the Quarter!"

"Dickey darling, you just want to be paid twice for the same house."

"Hell for that matter, persuade dear big bro' to transfer Walt to a more...stylish...division...say Western Europe?"

Mrs. Oaks let out a laugh. "Now you've got me worked up. Dickey come her and help me relax."

Dickey crossed the room and gave her a flourished kiss on the forehead as he stuffed the check into his pocket. "You know I'd love to, but I have another appointment."

"It's that Cookie Macmillan isn't it?"

"I can't say."

"She's not your favorite."

"Of course you are."

"Good, she's a vulgar bitch."

"That may be, but her living room does need some work."

"What about her bedroom? I've heard that needs some work too."

Dickey laughed, "I don't know what kind of interior design...guy...you think you've got here, but I don't do this for just anyone."

Mrs. Oaks looked as if she'd been presented with a bouquet of flowers from behind his back. "I am your favorite, aren't I?"

"Of course you are." Dickey was trying to keep the compassion in his eyes and read the crystal clock at the same time. Mrs. Oaks turned to see what had divided his attention. Their eyes met, "That clock has got to go."

"My mother gave that to me. It was a wedding present."

"And see where that's gotten you?"

Mrs. Oaks didn't quite know what to make of that. With more flourish than before, Dickey kissed her forehead. Then he was smoothly drifting back over the carpet towards the white and blue double doors across from the bed. She seemed satisfied, or tired, enough to let him out.

"Oh Dickey!" She called before the door had completely closed. He had been in the progress of digging the check out of his pocket, but crammed it back in and poked his smiling skull back into the enormous boudoir chamber, "Yes, Pet?"

"Remember what we talked about this morning?"

"I remember everything you say," Dickey braced himself for the monumental effort of maintaining a carefree smile. "Why don't you freshen my memory." He suggested, white teeth gleaming.

"The caviar."

There was a sinking feeling in his stomach, "Yes?"

"After that show Cookie put on for Carnival last year, she's the one to beat. Those Chinamen will be showing up with the godamm Panda's in ten days, Dickey. The press will be here…if I can't top Cookie's show, I'll have to move to China with Walt. You said this reception would be a topper…you promised Dickey!"

"Indeed I did, Mrs. Oaks. I remember it well." Dickey kept smiling but tried to appear dramatically concerned as well. "Again, though, caviar really isn't a traditional Chinese dish."

"Don't ask me to find a caterer who'll roast a puppy! Besides, no one really *wants* to be Chinese."

"I can't imagine why you don't travel with your husband more often."

"I need that caviar! And I'll have it in time for the party."

"Well now, this isn't as simple a just going down to the market—"

"I know dear, that's why I asked you."

"I'm an interior designer, Mrs. Oaks, I don't normally deal in black market caviar."

"Hush now," she said lazily from the bed, "I'm sure it's not as complicated as all that. Now Dickey, a promise is a promise."

"Of course it is." He cooed.

"Certainly for your favorite."

Dickey was still smiling, but he was sure the delightful gleam had gone out. He looked at his Pierre Cardin watch; if he was expected to fulfill his promises, he'd never get anything done. "Well, this will ruin the rest of my day."

Mrs. Oaks smiled with lethargic and spent satisfaction. "Hush now." She threw in a wrinkled pout for good measure. "You promised."

"You shall have your caviar." Dickey replied with a slight bow and backed quickly out of the room.

He skipped down the grand staircase and into the marble foyer. With a quick glance back upstairs, he dug the check out of his snug pocket and unfolded it. "Feeling generous, Pet."

The maid, a pretty girl of about twenty-five with insanely crimped hair, came around the corner with an armload of neatly folded linens. "You transform the bedroom yet?" She asked with a smirk.

"As always." He said, stuffing the check back into his pants.

"Wish the old lady paid me that well."

He swatted her playfully on the behind. "Oh no you don't, Fantastic, the old bat makes me work for it." He turned and almost skipped out the wide black oak double doors that opened onto the arching circular driveway, where his white Porsche Boxster sat in front of the house, top down, black leather interior glistening in the sun.

Dickey left the well sculpted and walled subdivision behind, bolting past the guardhouse and roaring down the heavily wooded street as the chilly air blew through his gelled hair. Then he came out of the quiet trees to an open intersection where the zoning changed, and pulled into the first gas station he saw and bought a diet coke. Dickey hopped back into the car and headed back the direction he came.

He was waved through at the guardhouse, and returned quietly up the circular driveway. The maid let him in, "Working overtime?" she smirked.

"Good Lord no. The old bat has list of antiques she wants me to buy and if I get it wrong I'll never hear the end of it." Dickey sang and softly took the staircase three steps at a time.

Mrs. Oaks was snoring softly when Dickey padded into her room, past her bed and into her huge but crowded dressing room. The jewelry box was open. Dickey carefully selected three items, slipped them into a blue velvet sack. He made his way to the front door without seeing the maid.

He drove downtown. The place for which he was looking was a single green door in an old building. Directly behind was a steep flight of stairs that went directly to another door. Dickey ascended the steps and opened the door without knocking.

Vanderhorn's still smelled of fresh paint, and the cases of diamonds glinted brilliantly in the strategically placed lights. Vik Makarin stood over the cases and buzzed Dickey through the glassed in alcove in the front of the store. The old Russian was smiling in a way that made the conditioned hairs on the Dickey's neck stand on end. "You might have told me you were moving shop from New Orleans. Throws a monkey wrench in my operation. All a little too close for comfort."

"I haven't moved, Dickey, I've expanded. The shop on Canal Street is still open. But New Orleans is…well diamonds aren't a priority there right now. I'd have thought you'd be happy not to drive to New Orleans once a month."

"I like the feckin' trip."

"They say you Irish Travelers can't stop moving."

Dickey's charming eyes went hard and furious, "Careful you old kike, I left them behind when I was seventeen."

"Ha." Vik laughed. "And I left Russia. I was in the army once too, Dickey, just like you. It doesn't bleach your blood, I'm still just an old Russian Jew and you're still a damn Irish gypsy."

"I'm not Irish, I'm American."

Vik shrugged his shoulders, "How patriotic."

"So why Memphis?" Dickey said quickly. "What the feck brings ya here?"

"Same reason you are here. Lots of money…old money."

Dickey was glad to get down to business. He fished a pale blue velvet bag out of the tote he was carrying. Vik looked concerned. "Is there a problem, Viktor?"

"You carry a purse?"

"It's a tote, it's European."

"Very well." Vik shrugged. He'd grown up in Europe and wasn't sure he agreed.

Dickey opened the bag and set two cocktail rings and a diamond pendant on the glass case.

Vik said nothing, took the pieces and shuffled off into the back. Dickey followed him into a small room crammed with equipment. Vik looked over the pieces and sat down at a small table, working one of the rings into a small clamp. Carefully he attended the ring until he lifted the large square cut diamond from it's setting and the cluster of smaller diamonds around it. Dickey glanced back at the front room. Vik was examining the lifted stone with a glass, "The measurements you faxed me in New Orleans are perfect, Dickey. You should have been a jeweler." He removed the smaller diamonds and began replacing them with stones that appeared to be identical. Then Vik released the clamp and help up the ring for Dickey to admire. "You've moved up in the world for a fucking Gypsy."

"What's it worth now?"

"Two and a half carats pure Moissanite, flawless. Street value of absolutely nil. Not a damn thing. Ha, maybe you haven't moved up."

"Feck off Vik and change the other stones out."

Vik secured the second ring in the clamp, "No not worthless, just a fraud. Nine out of ten jewelers would be fooled without a glass. Like those fading Southern Belles you play with."

"Are you hard of hearing? Viktor, didn't I tell ya to feck off! Besides, grandma's diamonds are the real thing."

"Two and a half carats though, personally I think unless she has fingers like cigars, two and a half carats of anything is too much for a ring."

"If the ring fits. The real stones are what I promised, yes?"

"Yes."

"Then I don't want to hear anything about commodity pricing. We agreed on payment."

"Dickey, Dickey, of course, have I ever tried to cheat you before? That you can prove?"

"Don't go there, I can find another jeweler to work on less margin."

"Be fair, I have to make a living too, Dickey. I've got overhead, two U.S. shops now, and another in Toronto. Besides, in our business, quality of work matters. You might find it cheaper, Mr. O'Shea, but not better. And discretion, don't forget discretion, it's worth the premium." Vik smiled, "Speaking of discretion…how is your other line of work going? Interior design…with a niche for the bedroom, yes?."

"Shut up you feckin' foreigner. The old cow had champagne for lunch, she'll sleep till four or so. I've got to get her pieces back to her before she wakes up."

BY FIVE O'CLOCK, ARCHIE HAD CHANGED into a pair of hiking shorts and hit the ocean for a swim. Bunty had also thought it blasphemous not to take a bathing suit, he ignored her on that one as well. Admitting there was a beach the island would have only aggravated Bunty. Now he saw no need to call and say he was wrong.

Archie emerged from the crystal waters, the heat of the sun warming his wet skin on contact. Rows of sunburnt women, smelling like coconuts, lay oiled and glistening in the sun across the hot sand. In the grand courtyard, overlooking the powder white beaches, Archie took his seat and had a Mojito. The Caribbean brine had dried, leaving the scent of the ocean on his tightening skin. That's when she caught his eye.

The girl was moving casually up the sugary beach. She seemed familiar to him in a distant sort of way. The fact that she was here, on this beach, was entirely normal; coincidence, surely, but not a fantastic one. Her loose blonde tendrils were pushed back from her face with a blue headband that matched her blue linen cover-up. It was unbuttoned, revealing a stark white bikini beneath. Archie watched her stop to talk to someone, another girl, with cool enthusiasm. The other hoisted her perfectly tanned body off her towel and the two continued together up the beach, onto the sandstone stairs that put them in the grand courtyard. *Question: How much aggravation in my life is random and how much do I bring on myself?* She passed, glancing over at him as he nursed his drink. The other turned his way, but only to see what had caught her friend's attention. Then she leaned into the blonde and said something. *Now they're talking about me. This gig is making me paranoid.* The two passed onto a familiar gang of professional vacationers at the bar.

Archie was trying to find some other girl to occupy his thoughts when he heard a voice and immediately put it to the blonde he could hear approaching, "Archie, Archie Gilmur? Is that you?"

He turned and smiled, "I'm wearing his shorts."

She was smiling broadly and the cover-up drifted off her body as she came at him, "I'm Tara, Vivie's little sister."

"Good God, it is you. I thought you looked familiar. Hell of a thing finding you all the way down here."

She hugged him, smelling of coconuts, brine and sunburnt skin. "Oh, not so strange," she said, "Just had to get out into the sun."

"I'd forgotten y'all had a place down here." He lied.

"Dad's still got his chunk of this place. Don't know why, he hasn't been stateside for more than a month in years. Mom doesn't really use it. Uncle Mike has him stuck off in China now. Did you hear?"

"Actually I had-"

"From Vivie?"

"Yes."

"Y'all talk?"

"No, I haven't seen her since Mom's funeral."

"She's got three children."

"So I hear."

"Mmm, sore subject?"

"What is?"

"Vivie."

"That was high school, Tara. I've had a few girlfriends since."

"Not like Vivie."

"I'll give you that. So what have you been up to? Last time I saw you I think you were thirteen." Archie stood back from her, "You've had your hand in the hormone jar, little girl."

"She'd have married you, you know, if you hadn't run off to Oxford."

"It was Saint Andrew's"

"That's still England."

"Scotland."

"Same island."

"So, what've you got going on here in Jamaica?"

"Oh nothing, it's just Jamaica Dahlin'." Tara pulled away further from Archie, like a mime about to perform. "Besides, there's a jewelry store in Kingston I *absolutely* love. I think its black market. Isn't that wicked?" She let that sink in. "So how'd you get here from Scotland?"

"Went south and took a right in Tangiers."

"Alone?"

"No, the plane was full of Moroccans."

"Smartass. I mean are you alone here?"

"Yes, for work."

"Well you'll play with the gang then, they're loads of full." She took his hand and positioned herself so Archie could see the gang at the bar. "There's Margo, who you watched come from the beach with me, there's Quail, he wants into Margo's pants-" Tara glanced over to the bar, "Don't we all. There's Beau, he's a fag but he's European, so it's okay, he's a scream."

"Does he want in Margo's pants?"

Tara waved her finger at Archie, "Clever, actually *I* could make him break rank. So what's your story?"

"Like I said, down here on business."

"I mean a story with a girl."

"I think I'm going to take up tennis. Folks seem to have a spanking time with tennis lessons."

"Really, Vivie told me you learned to swordfight in college."

Archie shrugged, "A renaissance man."

"Let's go meet the gang."

The gang, it appeared, spent a great deal of time grooming themselves. There was the dark haired and olive skinned Margo, who turned out to be from the Oklahoma, the daughter of one of the largest ranchers in the state. Quail was from Connecticut and was the guy Ralph Lauren had made millions imitating. He laughed longer and louder than anyone at Margo's wisecracks, this seemed to annoy her more that anything. Fortunately she felt it her obligation as one of the beautiful people to keep Quail twisting helplessly on the line.

"Oh my, look what Tara caught herself!" Beau squealed, patting his little pot-belly. The well-tanned blonde Spaniard was so effeminate that at first Archie thought he was joking. Quail only gave Archie a cutting glance to size up any possible competition for Margo.

Tara beamed, "Hands off Beau, he's mine."

"She's already possessive. Is this one for your sacrifice tonight?"

Tara ignored the comment as Archie looked at Margo and smiled, "Archie Gilmur-I know Tara from way back." She offered her hand and he took it firmly.

"Nice to meet you."

"Archie here used to date my sister Vivie." Tara chimed in and pulled Archie closer, "This is Quail..." They shook hands but Quail went cool. Archie smiled, Quail retreated further and began to sulk. "...and Beau."

"The pleasures all mine." Beau cooed and offered an extremely firm handshake. "are you going tonight?"

"Going where?"

"Oh my my, Tara hasn't told you yet."

Archie looked at Tara, "What haven't you told me, Love?"

Then she was smiling wildly, she glared at Archie and licked her teeth.

"Well," Beau chimed in, "your old friend here is into the voodoo. That's why she comes down here when her parents think she's 'decompressing'. Anyway, we're all going tonight." Tara sang, "You up for it?"

"On the plantation?" Archie laughed, "Who isn't going?"

Beau clapped his hands together, "Oh my, we've got Alistair Crowley himself."

"You've been?" Tara's eye narrowed as she turned the toothpick umbrella in her murky orange punch.

Quail kept silent, studying this creature who'd upset the field he'd incorrectly assumed was sloped in his favor.

"No," Archie kept laughing, "but it ought to be a hella'va good show."

After the night went full dark, Archie had changed into a worn out pair of twill khakis and a hunting shirt and took the Discovery bouncing painfully up the rocky hill. The smell of earth made Archie look down, Tara was holding a bag of mushrooms under his nose. "We're 'shroomin', want one?" Tara was in the passenger seat, wearing a simple floral shift."

"Have you washed those?"

"More natural this way. We're all doing it."

"Better not." Having a keen eye for things of great import, Archie knew Tara wasn't wearing a bra but was wearing a thong, he wanted to stay sharp. Quail was in the back, with Margo on his lap.

Margo was ignoring Quail for Beau, who was decked out in a great deal of silk and complaining that too much cocaine might make him straight. The Discovery ground to a halt next to a dusty Landcruiser.

"That's the priestess's house." Tara said in a breathy hush. "They call her 'Miz Cassat'... she may not have a first name." Tara pointed to the coral colored concrete four square. "There."

Archie tried to appear intrigued. "What about her driver's license?"

"Well we can't all fit in there or we'd all go Bi-" Beau yelped from the back.

"It's at the top of the hill." Said Archie.

"I thought you said you'd never been?" snapped Tara.

"Uhh.." In the back, Margo started singing a few bars of *Tainted Love*. "Where else would you hold this sort of thing."

They all piled out of the car and marched up the hill. The drums were pounding atop the clearing and the smell of a wood fire, still faint, spoilt the Caribbean air. At the steps, Tara took the lead, squeezed Archie's hand and charged up the narrow steps.

"We've got her worked up now!" squealed Beau. Tara hit the top of the stairs forgetting her entourage before the wild scene. Her grip on Archie's hand grew tighter.

At the higher elevation, the smell of the wood fire was over-powering. Flames licked up the side of the round cast iron pot. Around it lithe, sweating Jamaicans danced, wailing indecipherable noises that sounded African.

Tara's face was wild with delight, her small white teeth reflecting in the firelight as she bit her lower lip in anticipation. Then there was Miz Cassat herself, an enormous woman in a wild kaftan with a great cigar clenched in her teeth. She too was wailing, with her arms flung out and upward to the heavens. Her jabber wasn't faux African gibberish, but lousy French.

Archie started laughing to himself, this postcard voodoo was almost as good as the postcard gay Spaniard getting his groove on a few feet over. He'd never met Miz Cassat before, never heard of her before today, but that was her alright. This was her party-harder to reckon was just how she was getting rich off the gig. Donations had to be the ticket. Rich Americans and Brits tired of the logic of a modern age were the target. Far too hip to be something so old fashioned as Christian or Jew, they'd managed to bleach out all the mystery in their lives. Miz Cassat gave them mystery combined with adventure, and a bit of black magic showmanship thrown in where the saints and Elijah had failed to keep up.

Tara pumped Archie's hand and her slim hips moved slowly to the fast beat, somehow in rhythm. Poor thing, she'd probably signed over as much as she could get of her colossal trust fund over to the witch. Neither of the Oaks' children had much in the brains department, but Vivie had horse sense and a kind heart. The jury was still out on Miss Tara.

Someone is watching me. Archie scanned the scene and looked at Tara, she was still enraptured with the mêlée. His itch grew, a pair of eyes were following him. Beau was lost in his own world, fingers snapping high above his head. At the caldron, Miz Cassat didn't seem to know they'd arrived. Beyond the priestess and the cauldron, more attendees looked on, all taken in by the service. Archie glanced back over his shoulder, Margo was watching Tara's hips swaying to the music. Quail was transfixed on Margo.

Archie shook his head, trying to clear out the paranoia. Then Beau drifted closer to the circle and Archie's eyes snapped to the left, catching a young man who appeared to be both Chinese and Black at the same time. He was the one. Archie turned his head, their eyes met and Archie gave him a nod. The other didn't flinch and there they stood. Archie's hand was being pulled. Tara was moving toward the circle. The other watched Archie and Tara as they moved to the circle.

Miz Cassat sent a blue plume of cigar-smoke upward into the wake of her clapping hands. Her head went level and she yowled deeply. The drums stopped. "You white sister!" she called, her hands still clasped above her head, "Look all! Sista Tara come back."

Tara said nothing but let Archie's hand drop.

"Has Sista Tara brought what Anansi Coupé demands?"

"What's that?" she asked blankly. Tara failed to keep the drama raging.

"What does Anansi demand?" Miz Cassat growled, and turned to the crowd. "Brotha Bobby Chu, do you know? Do you know what Anansi asks?"

He snapped his attention from Archie to Miz Cassat. "Sista Tara knows."

"Anansi wants my devotion." Tara said. Even Archie could tell it was a guess.

Chu began to creep toward Archie and Tara. "The girl knows. Tara, remember what I told you Miz Cassat needed?"

Tara stepped closer into the circle, the firelight giving her skin a glow. Miz Cassat started again, "Brotha Bobby Chu, do you not hear what Anansi says?"

"I do. The white girl don't hear too good."

Back to Tara, "Do you have what Anansi wants?"

"I thought Bobby here just wanted in my pants." She said in a spasm of honesty. Then it seemed that whatever it was the mob was demanding from Tara became suddenly clear, "Yes, that's it," she smiled now, "I did bring them."

"Them?" Chu said.

Archie squatted on his haunches, setting his legs to spring forward in an instant. As he did, a pretty caramel-skinned woman in camp shorts and white undershirt hunched herself in the same position opposite him.

"The numbers…" Tara added, "access…"

"Yes…access." Chu and Cassat urged her on.

Tara rubbed her temples, "Yes, I wrote them down…father's secrets…"

"Yes…the combination…" Chu was close to coming unhinged. He pushed the oily comma of hair from his forehead and closed in on Tara. Archie stood slowly and Chu stopped short. Out of the corner of his eye, Archie saw the woman stand and drift his direction.

Tara shook her head, "I don't have them with me, they're at the hotel. I wrote them down," Now she was beaming, she stood up straight, "all of them, birthdays, anniversaries. I wrote them down, wrote them all down!"

Chu froze, the horror on his face clear. Miz Cassat roared into the night, her eyes bulged from her skull like a frightened rabbit. "Chu you fool! Speak clearly! Anansi wants what he wants!" She snatched an earthen jug from at her feet, plucked the wet stump of a cigar from her mouth and took a long drink. She hurled the jug at the cast pot where it smashed and took to a clear blue flame up the side. Wiping the spittle from her mouth with the back of her hand, she wailed "How you think to know the voodoo if you cannot see what the power want?"

Beside Archie, Tara was starting to shake and cry.

Miz Cassat turned her attention to them, "The numbers, not to his life, but his mind!"

"The safe…yes the safe…safe." Tara mumbled, trying to unravel some knot in her mind. Then she turned to Archie.

"Safe." She muttered again. Her eyes were terrified and confused. "Archie, can you take me out of here."

"You haven't introduced me to your friends."

"Archie, please, can we go?"

"Yes."

Chu had retreated into the shadows and the girl in the camp shorts squatted back on her haunches.

"The combination to his secrets; the safekeep of his horrors" Miz Cassat cooed loudly. "You come tomorrow, you bring the dates…and I will tell you what Anansi Coupé wants. At midnight."

Tara took Archie's hand and turned to the narrow winding steps that descended to the level ground where the Discovery was parked. Now Archie was at her side, taking the slope. "You won't tell Vivie will you." She pleaded.

"It'll be our secret, Love."

They jumped into the truck amid the grunting curses of Quail being pushed off Margo. The back seat had been laid down to make a bed "Godammit, don't you people knock?" Quail snarled.

Archie started the car, "Quail, this is a rental, you're gonna have to have more style than that."

Margo pulled down her skirt and rolled over on her belly, her ankles crossing above her rear end, "Don't worry about it Quail, you're getting further. That's something." She smiled at Tara, "Sweetie, what's gotten into you?"

"Mojo baby." Tara snapped her fingers. The panic that had gripped her on the top of the hill seemed to have evaporated from her face without a trace. Her eyes, though, still glistened with fear.

"What about Beau?" Margo asked, "Did he find himself a voodoo queen?"

"Ah you know Beau, he's like a cat…that pussy always lands on his feet." Tara put her hand on Archie's knee, "Aren't you glad you came down? Nothing ever happens in Memphis."

During the short drive back to the resort, Quail made it clear that he wasn't forgiving anyone until he got his ashes dragged.

On the pretense of being tired, Archie had left Tara and the gang at one of the resort bars and returned to his room. He checked the P7 that had been in the small of his back all night and slid into a web shoulder holster. From his closet came a worn Willis & Geiger poplin sport coat – it was the sort made for travelers with a half a dozen hidden pockets – he pulled it over the holster. Into the pockets went a laminated ID, Truitt's key fob, and a pick case. Into the bag went the 2x4's with the nails hammered into the end and bent at a 90 degree angle. The nails were wrapped in rubber bands. On top of that he put the night vision goggles.

There was a knock on the door and Archie crept across the room and looked through the fisheye. "Blast." He murmured under his breath.

Beyond the door, Tara stood unsteadily, smiling in her own fumes.

He swung the door open, "Tara, did you lose your way to the bar? Just follow the rhythm of leaping Spaniards."

"You sure wear funny PJ's Archie. I thought you said you were going to bed."

Archie pointed to the camera, "Gotta take some pics, Love, I'm down here on assignment. The Jamaican mountains, natives getting' jiggy in the moonlight, that sort of thing."

Tara swerved across the room and plopped down on the bed. "No point in going outside for that." She smiled, "As for that mountain, there are less challenging things to climb on around here. Me, for example. Can't have too much scandal. People will forget about you." She reached around Archie's back and cupped a cheek.

"What about the combination?" Archie asked.

"A little excitement, some tasty drinks and a willing girl. What more of a combination do you need?

"No Love, the combination that caused the fracas tonight. The one you don't seem to have on you."

"Oh, my father's safe."

"Now we're getting somewhere."

"Dangerous things in there I guess." Tara purred.

Archie leaned back on the low dresser, facing Tara. She was slouching further back on the bed, supporting herself with her elbows. "What has your father, way off in China, got in his safe in

Memphis that they want so bad down on a papaya plantation in Jamaica?"

She popped forward eagerly, "The cache of secret fears he instilled in me…it's keeping me down, suppressing me…away from the power… your parents did the same to you…"

"Oh I see, this is self-help voodoo. Thank God, I thought you were down her wasting your time."

"…the key to his secrets, his fears, will unlock mine…" she went forward, closer, eyes ablaze again, "…set me free."

"That's a hell of a thing. So what's really in the safe they're so whipped up about?"

She snarled at Archie, then pouted, "I told you, the voodoo is real, it's good mojo."

"…and your father's legal safe, will fix you?"

The fire in her eyes cooled, "Archie, I'm tired of all this. Let's take a nap." She began to work the top button of his shirt.

Archie thought for a second before crossing the room to the telephone and picking up the receiver, "Yes, Gilmur here, I need a bottle of Vueve Cliquot…and a pizza. Everything on it, drag it through the garden. Yes, that'll be fine." He hung up.

"Champagne and pizza?"

"You'll love it." He snatched up an ice bucket on his way to the door. "Let me go down the hall and get some ice for us."

"Hurry back." She said as the door shut behind him.

He went down the hall quickly, tossing the ice bucket into the janitor's closet without stopping.

Archie crossed the papaya plantation that sat like a mysterious cloud among the Byzantine accounting practices of DeltaComm Telecommunications Corp. He passed the hill with the window rolled down, warm air blowing over his skin. The gumbo ya-ya at the top of the hill had died down a bit. Archie dowsed the headlights and made his way with the running lamps.

The dirt road wound a narrow path, first cutting right along the tree line and then turning into a small gap in the trees so black that Archie almost missed it.

In the next field more papaya stretched out and Archie stopped and put on the night vision goggles. In the green haze, Archie picked up the long low pre-fab building compound beyond the papaya grove. The area around the front entrance was well lighted, but the rest of the second compound was shrouded in night.

Stopping at the edge of the last grove, Archie surveyed the distance between the dark grove and the pale yellow corrugated building. He rolled up to the grass next to the fence. There were no other cars, so Archie checked his kit, slung the gym bag over his shoulder and climbed out of the Discovery. Taking the two 2x4's from the bag he moved through the shadows towards the fence. Hooking the two bent nails into the fence high above his head, Archie placed the soles of his boots onto the chain link. Now the fence could be wired like a casino and he'd be safe as long as the rubber bands on the nails didn't tear. Of course if they did, he was fucked.

Getting himself over the top was the tough part. That entailed walking himself straight perpendicular to the ground using the hooks as hands to pull himself over the top. Then he leapt far enough out to clear the bag slung over his shoulder and hoped he remembered how to take a fall. He crossed the rest of the lot under the glare of flood lights.

The front door was a simple, single steel door. From the kit came a slender torque wrench and a pick. Then he saw it, the control panel for the alarm system. It was a white plastic box near the door with a row of lights along the top and nothing else. Archie flipped down the guard panel to reveal the keypad when he noticed that the armed light was dead and the green pass light was on. No car in the lot. He returned to the lock, inserted and turned the torque wrench slightly, holding it in place. Then he racked the pins with the pick. A bit more pressure and the wrench and the racked pin held inside the chamber. He began to lift the pins that remained.

The door opened silently. Sliding into the darkness, Archie shut the door behind him and listened hard. Nothing-but a nothing he didn't trust. Everything was now back in the gym bag and he pulled it tight against him and adjusted the night goggles. If the alarm was off, someone had to be here. Creeping down the hall, peering into one office after another, the place seemed to be exactly what DeltaComm claimed it was, the original equipment manufacturer of a telecom.

In a green grainy field of vision, Archie followed the simple building plan past the cheap reception and front offices paneled in flimsy wood grain. Then past the wide and open testing labs and back into the electric heart of the building. Bundles of cables and wires came through the white soundproof ceiling tiles in the hundreds, breaking off along the walls to the unpainted plywood panels along the perimeter of the room. Along the panels, the bundles opened into thousands of individual wires, each coupled to a connection tacked to the plywood boards. Toward the center of the room were some freestanding racks housing flat gunmetal gray routers and telecom switches. In the dead center of the room were four black metal army issue desks that had been pushed together to form a block.

Taking the key fob from his kit, Archie crawled under the desk behind the thick tower of the humming computer and attached it to the outlet Truitt had sketched out for him. Then he was back at the keyboard with the PDA in front of him. Glowing in the dark were access codes Archie had lifted from the DeltaComm job the other night. Then he set the codes in motion. In the silence of the place, the whirling of the computer at his feet seemed deafening.

Bunty was right. The coincidence of it all was unsettling. Van Clair waiting for him twelve hours after the break-in at New Orleans. *Question: What would DeltaComm have to gain by sending him on this wild goose chase if they knew he'd broken into the HQ?* Archie couldn't get his hands around what they could be up to if they did know. It would be simpler to just have him arrested. Entrapment. He considered the prospect. Possible, but that would put DeltaComm in as bad a bind as Archie if they were caught.

Archie stood and crept back into the darkness of the complex, the luminous dial of his watch read 2:30 a.m. The upload of Truitt's doggie door/worm decoy combo could take up to ten minutes. To his right, there was a door, like the others, but slightly ajar.

He took the doorway and found himself in another nondescript hallway. Through the grainy green of the night vision specs, Archie could see one of the double steel doors at the end of the hall was ajar. It was being held open by a yellow legal pad. Slowly, Archie eased the sliver of space between the steel door open and until he could peer inside. It appeared to be a gymnasium. He eased the door wider still, and unholstered the P7.

The markings and lines of a basketball court were on the floor, and along the far side of the room, collapsible bleachers stood along the wall. At the far end of the space, just barely visible was what looked like paper targets. Then something was missing. At first

Archie couldn't think what it was and as he scanned the walls for some mysterious component that he thought should be there he noticed the wall closest to him, opposite the bleachers, was a rock climbing wall. It was a poorly designed one. The footholds weren't randomly placed at all, but fell into discernable patterns of square groupings and parallel grids. Then, to the far right of the wall was an enormous clear cylinder. The height of the structure struck Archie, three stories he reckoned. He took another head check out the door and crouched a bit, moving quickly along the wall toward the cylinder. Then he ran into it. The wall of the thing gave a little and bounced back, sending Archie onto his back. He dropped the P7 into his coat pocket and reached a hand out, passing over the seamless and invisible wall. *Plexiglas? Yes. Antenna? Maybe.*

Archie checked his watch and returned to the communications hub. The transfer was complete, so he stowed the fob in his kit. From his haul in New Orleans he knew the names of the officers stationed in Jamaica. There were two. One was Leonard Cox, in the sales office in Kingston. Raised in San Francisco, Cox's mother was a Chinese national and he appeared to be part of the original SinoTel deal. The other one was a DeltaComm man; poor old Walt Oaks. When Archie and Vivie had dated Mr. Oaks had his fingers in so many pies that she was never even been certain what he did or who he worked for. His directorship wasn't odd, but the fact that DeltaComm seemed to think he lived in Jamaica was. His two daughters and the rest of Memphis was certain that he lived in China.

The gun barrel pressed into the side of his head wasn't what Archie found nearly so unsettling as the fact that he'd heard no one approach.

<u>Six</u>

Ugly Sue

IN THE COURSE OF A SINGLE DECADE of her life she bore no resemblance to the thing she had been before. Ten years ago, at twenty years old, she was already jaded by events that she had not chosen. Daisy Adries was no longer capable of simply letting things happen. In a frame by her bed was a single phrase, from Goethe, set like a photo of a loved one. It was in German, although it wasn't her best language: *Du Mußt Amoß oder Hammer sein.* Translation: You must be the anvil or the hammer.

Her parents had been French Algerians, her father a French Colonial soldier and her mother a local. Their life together started well enough, but in 1960 the gig was up for the French in Algeria. Captain Adries married his mistress and got her out of the mess exploding in her homeland. The new Mde. Adries, being Algerian, didn't have to liquidate her family's possessions when the rest of the French were selling their colonial lives for a song. They actually made a little money.

Then the couple found themselves on an army base outside of Paris. In 1965 M. Adries retired from the army, and they moved to the Caribbean Island of Martinique.

To Daisy, born in the lush sunshine of the Antilles, it seemed her parents were always in love. *Peré* had cast off the structure of army life with vigor and *Meré* had not been in France long enough to conform to European sensibilities. They seemed wild and fantastic to

Daisy, but distant. Eventually, they sent her back to Paris for a proper education.

It was in her second year at the University in Paris when the tall blonde Austrian walked her home from the nightclub. He gallantly walked her up to her grubby student apartment, she kissed him on the doorstep. She let herself in, waved to the gorgeous man, and closed the door–or at least tried to.

The nurse thought it was strange that the man hadn't touched her face in the assault, but never said Daisy had been lucky. Her ribs had been cracked, her body brutalized, right wrist and left ankle broken, but he hadn't touched her face. The nurse had been there, she wore a thick lump on the bridge of her nose for it. She wasn't glamorous or fantastic to Daisy, but she wasn't distant either. They talked well into the night, every night.

Looking back, Daisy thought it had been the nurse who'd told the DGSE about her, but she would never be sure because she never again laid eyes on the older woman after her release from the hospital.

When they first contacted her, she scoffed at the idea. She wouldn't be another helpless cog in the machine-she would never be helpless again. But they were persistent, and Daisy began to feel as if she were being courted. Not the breathy, claustrophobic wrestling match that passed for courting in her short childhood. This was different, they pursued her like a gentleman. Persistent but distant, creative yet formal, and then let her decide. If she wasn't going to jump in with both feet, they didn't want her any more than she wanted them. It worked.

Six months after their first contact, nine after her release from the rape unit of the women's hospital in Paris, she agreed to their proposal. They seemed delighted but not surprised, and they never smiled. These weren't smiling people, they knew too much.

She asked why they had chosen her. They wouldn't say, but told her if that was a problem; she certainly was still free to leave. There would come a time, however, when she wasn't so free to go. She stayed.

First there was training and they sent her far away. It came easily because her childhood had been short and she saw the world as a logical set of predictable consequences. The technical schooling fell easily into place. The jungles of Polynesia reminded her of the

Caribbean. The brutal hikes designed to whip her into shape were merely invigorating to a body raised on a steep mountainside. Her frame, lean but incredibly strong from propelling herself up canyon walls, was nimble enough to curl around rocks and trees and growth.

Gunplay wasn't natural to her, but the mathematical simplicity of projectile trajectories was almost boring in its simplicity. Fighting-hand to hand and with a knife-came easily to Daisy because of the rage in her. The discipline they were drilling into her gave that anger a mortally efficient method of delivery. She focused until it was simply fuel and then it was spent and they put her under a male trainer and pushed her onward still. Her trainer was an American ex-patriot who had dissolved himself completely into the French Foreign Legion. He was a tall man with Scandinavian name and he looked it. He watched her, blue eyes set in a face that never seemed to brown, even after years in the Pacific sun, but had become a permanent violent pink. She told him that she would be a machine. He cringed. "A machine...no...not possible...not you."

"You don't think I can do it?" She barked, exhausted after a four-hour race to a distant bridge in the jungle armed only with a knife.

"It isn't a lack of faith, oh no." He laid back at the foot of the rope bridge. He'd run the course hundreds of times, but still had only narrowly beat her to the target. "A machine is detached, yes, you can do that. I mean, you've done a hella'va job of divorcing yourself from your soul. But a machine...a machine is man-made and no man could make you... too beautiful... absolutely flawless."

Her eyes tightened as she reached for his canteen, "Are you going to try to seduce me now?"

"Oh no," he said, kicking her hand away, "you'd never have that. But you are beautiful."

She continued to look at him cruelly.

"I'm sorry." He said, the smile fading from his face, "Something's wrong." He tossed her the canteen.

"It's alright." She took a small sip.

To lighten the moment he said, "I'll have to call you something ugly and common to get you out of my head."

"What's that?"

He was out of breath, "Sue." He said. "Ugly Sue."

"So you aren't going to try anything?"

"I'll let you make the first move."

She never did. The name stuck and then it became an official code name in the Direction Générale de la Sécurité Extérieure - a.k.a. DGSE – a.k.a. the French Secret Service.

The training camp in Polynesia gave focus to the rage, controlled it like a regulator on an IV tube-instead of a flood there was a steady drip of hate.

It was in a $1,200 dollar a night hotel in Toronto that she became the creature now called Ugly Sue. It wasn't her first assignment, and it was simple enough-but it managed to break one person from the other.

She stepped away from the noisy Toronto street, through the grand revolving door and spotted him. The German arms dealer, looking almost identical to his dossier photograph, was on the other side of the opulent lobby. He was sitting at the marble table, nursing a large draft beer. Tall and a little thick, his white blonde hair was long and teased, and his red triangular eyeglasses Daisy found bizarre. He had secrets to sell. A brown Louis Vitton leather briefcase sat between his feet. She pretended not to see him and scanned the room. Picking out four subjects in particular.

Number 1: A man, young. Far end of the bar…trying very hard not to signal the German.
Number 2: A woman passed between she and the German. Her newspaper hits the unused chair at his table. Daisy can't see but knows something has dropped into the chair in which she is supposed to sit.
Number 3: At a marble table opposite the room from the German… traveling businessman looking for a little company on his vacation away from the wife and kids. Dismiss as not a threat.
Number 4: She passed him on the way in-sitting by the door reading a Thomas Mann novel. Lean but strong. Could be trouble.

The German was beautiful and looked remarkably like the man who'd put her in the hospital in Paris. She wondered only for a moment if that was a coincidence. There were no coincidences.

At the time it was almost disappointing how easy he was to seduce. She strolled up to him, took a seat in a chair he hadn't expected her to take. The tiny black speck on the seat where her rear would have been, she guessed, was a tracker. So what. She pretended to not totally know what she was doing. She had to admit he was quite charming.

Still, she couldn't enjoy the feeling of him thumping away inside her, but this time she had targeted the man, not the other way round. He cupped her breasts and she squeezed her thighs tightly over his hips until he looked as if he was about to lose control and she stopped, hopping off him and he rolled after her. She bit his ear playfully and he was on top of her. Her ankles locked behind the small of his back. His arms were locked, holding his chest above her as he started again. Her arms looped under his and pulled up, biting at his chest. His thick arms folded and he covered her like a blanket, breathing hotly into her ear. That's when she reached between the headboard and the mattress, took hold of the thick plastic cylinder buried there. She moaned lightly before she drove the syringe into the base of his skull. It was a fast acting and nearly untraceable poison so accuracy wasn't as important as simply a good deep thrust into someplace vital.

His muscles tensed up and his jaw locked and his eyes bulged in revolt to the poison–making a happy ending quite impossible. A happy ending for him was something that she would simply not have.

She pushed his still rigid body off hers and went to the bathroom to take a shower. Then, fully dressed, she cracked the en suite safe, took all the contents and stuffed them into the German's briefcase, which had been hidden under the bed. She conducted a thorough search of the room, which included finding a false bottom he'd installed in the bottom drawer of the dresser.

The search, and the contents in the safe were her excuse for killing the man, which wasn't her assignment. They'd told her to find out what was in the briefcase. She told them they got the bonus plan. After the arms ring had been broken, the DGSE gave her a bonus and increased security clearance…then she knew the truth behind the death of Charles De Gaulle.

Ugly Sue never did *that* again. But the change had happened, and whether or not it was done in a similar hotel room, emerging from the bathroom where she was "getting comfortable", her silenced .25 Beretta blazing, or in a crowded subway with another poisoned needle, she had become something different. She had become the hammer–leaving a shattered anvil behind.

THE VULNERABILITY OF LIFE IN THE RAPE UNIT was distant to her now. Still, Ugly Sue had just seen her partner shot in the line of duty, smelled his sunburned skin as she pulled him out of the captain's seat to get herself out of their botched mission and to some safety. She never knew why she turned around when she did, as opposed to concentrating on the escape. Something told Ugly Sue that the Russian's rocket had a tracker on it.

Even the hammer was mortal, and to know that was the only way to stay alive. She saw the rocket aimed at her boat from the hulking Magnum Marine and had made the violent decision to abandon ship.

She was under the azure crystal waters when she saw the bottom of the boat lift out of the water and the insulated explosion from above. The concussion from the blast shoved her deeper through the water. She had a breathing device taped to the inside of her leg, not much larger than an obnoxious fountain pen, and she didn't blink as she ripped it free. The breather sustained her while she swam in the opposite direction of the Magnum Marine. She stayed hidden for about ten minutes, spitting out the breather as it exhausted itself. Her arms and legs still pumping for distance as the canister drifted slowly downward into the waving sea-grass below. There was the horrible feeling of her lungs collapsing on themselves. Ugly Sue pointed her frame upward and kicked hard, breaking the surface.

She scanned the horizon for the Magnum Marine. Nothing. The Russian she'd been sent to kill had stopped looking for her.

She wriggled out of the Lily sundress and tore off the buttons, cracking open one to start the homing beacon housed inside. The other she slipped in the front of her swimsuit bottoms and continued on toward the rock they'd circled earlier.

Hours paddled by slowly and still she swam. Every time her muscles cramped and water filled her mouth, her mortality flashed before her. At long last, Ugly Sue reached the rock where she'd first targeted the Russian. She checked the homing device and waited. It was a bad place to be baking in the sun like a goddess. If Mickey boy came back, she was dead. That wasn't the real problem. Ugly Sue had two bosses. It wasn't entirely different from an affair-the lover knew all about the cuckold, but not the other way around.

Three hours passed, then a large and ugly fishing boat seemed to appear out of the fine sea air. Her heart stopped. She couldn't tell, the boat was coming at her, junky stained and spewing black vapor into the cloudless blue. There was music, but Ugly Sue couldn't be sure what it was. One of the crew spotted her and signaled to the others. Nothing to do for it now but to stand and let them come. Faintly she began to make out the music coming from the boat. It was blasting Santana's "Black Magic Woman" from the deck. She smiled. The cuckold was still in the dark.

She dived into the water towards the fishing boat.

NOW SHE PRESSED THE COLD END OF THE SILENCER into the neck of the man traveling under the name Archibald Derrick Gilmur. He stopped typing and held his hands up, moving them slowly to either side of his head. Ugly Sue smiled in satisfaction, this one knew the drill. "Why are you here?" she asked calmly.

He laughed lightly, "I'd have thought the first question is 'who are you?'"

"I know who you are, Mr. Gilmur, and who you're with. What I want to know is what you're doing with Tara Oaks in all this voodoo gumbo and, what's even more pressing—" Ugly Sue put the barrel of the silencer harder into the pink flesh of his neck, "—why have you broken into to this place."

"The alarm was disarmed, I thought y'all were having an open house."

"Watch it."

Her voice was completely even, not amused, not irritated. That was a bad sign. "I'm going to stand up now." Archie said.

"Oh, no you aren't."

"Yes I am. You might want to take a step back so I can't get a jump on you."

"You're going to stay put."

Her bland American accent wavered the tiniest bit. "You, see," Archie slowly raised out of his chair, the silencer still pressed against his neck, "I'm curious, Love, as to just who you think I am."

"Don't turn around."

Archie swallowed hard, "Again, if it makes you feel better, safer, please take a step back. Because you're not going to shoot me, not now at least." He laced his fingers over the top of his head in the most relaxed, non-threatening manner he could and slowly turned around.

She took hold of his hair. "Stop!"

He had only caught a glimpse of her muddy boots and camp shorts. "You've been watching me all night. I really don't think I am who you think I am."

"Archibald Derrick Gilmur…born in St. Olaf's Hospital in Edinburgh, Scotland in 1971. Yet remarkably, you have no residence, you just disappear. You appear to be the son of a Frank Gilmur, of Clarksdale, Mississippi. But you arrive in London periodically throughout your childhood. You appear to have attended McAllister Boarding School in Tennessee, and Saint Andrews College, Scotland…"

"Very well."

She reached in to the back of his pants. "Where is it?"

"Left it in the hotel"

"A little far fetched, don't you think?"

"So my father is from Clarksdale and my mother was Scottish…how do you know all this, and more to the point…Why?"

"Your first permanent address after college is in Dublin, Ireland."

"Very well."

"Stop saying that."

Now Archie turned around, Ugly Sue's hand twisted his hair but still he turned, "Stop!"

He looked at her full on and she shoved the silencer in his face. Archie brushed it away and it came back. Again he pushed it away, gently. There was something in his eyes that terrified her, something one didn't see in the eyes of spycraft…amusement.

"I seem to have made someone mad. Did my mother violate some Celtic purity laws?"

"Why are you here?" She pushed the gun in his face.

"I already know you aren't going to shoot me, ma'am. You wouldn't have learned all that about me just to kill me. I can take one look at you and tell you're more efficient than that."

She spied the strap of the holster under his jacket, "Are you trying to flatter me?" She reached inside and felt the empty holster.

"You have a gun in my face, how bad can it hurt?"

"Well accidents can happen in this line of work, Mr. Gilmur, you know that."

A rock sunk in his stomach, "You have beautiful eyes."

"Watch it…I might swoon and get careless!" she spat.

He'd hit a nerve, he back peddled, "Ma'am, I'm a security systems consultant. That's all, DeltaComm pays me to break into places and see what I can steal, then they go complain to their vendors and security teams-and I'm guessing that's you-about how easy it is to crack their systems." He looked her over and smiled, "I was expecting a black polyester uniform, but this *is* paradise."

Ugly Sue didn't respond.

Archie's smile faded. "I don't know who the hell you think I am but that's it."

"Tara Oaks."

"Ms. Oaks, nice to meet you. I wouldn't guessed that name was so common."

"Why were you with Tara Oaks?"

"I used to date her sister in high school…we broke up because she went to the University of Tennessee, and that, truly, is unforgivable."

Ugly Sue didn't quite know what to make of that. Then Archie leaned back against the metal desk his back went rigid and rubbed his eyes hard. "Ah shit." He said.

"What?"

Archie said nothing, but wouldn't look up.

"What is it?"

"I just told you."

"What, all you said was 'Aw shit'."

"Well I don't usually get guns stuck in my face."

"And?"

Archie looked at her, "I just shit myself."

"Ahhhh!" Ugly Sue dropped her armed hand, just slightly and reached out with her other. Then the reddened face in front of her came crashing into her skull, great black blobs exploded before her eyes.

He had her wrist, twisting it horribly outward. Then his feet, were between hers and she was lifted slightly off the ground as her wrist came crashing down on the metal desk. The gun fired a muffled shot that split one of a dozen gunmetal gray terminals. It sparked violently and a flash ran to the far end of the rack, the power outlet flashed and began to smoke. He smashed her hand into the desk, this time rapping along the knuckles.

The gun clattered to the floor and Archie kicked it away in the darkness. Then there was a blow to his solar plexus, knocking all the air out of him in a single violent shot. He lurched forward, pushing the girl off him and onto the floor. He remembered vaguely the P7, but guessed that this one knew how to take it away. Archie ran, leaping over Ugly Sue as she scrambled off the floor. She wasn't immediately on his heel, she was searching for the gun. He pushed further, his empty lungs burning and gasping for air. From the look of those long legs, Archie guessed that she would outdistance him quickly–especially if she had the advantage of at least some oxygen in her chest.

Then he heard her feet coming after him. A shot rang out and something shattered around his ankles. Archie reached for the P7, jumped to the side and twisted his torso to fire twice down the hall, shooting high so he'd miss her. From down the darkened corridor, a body hit the floor and stopped. He turned and barreled through the lobby and out the front door, locking the handle as he went. Archie stumbled through the dark parking lot, falling once. The power had gone out with the fire, at least he hoped it had.

Archie fell into the fence and nothing happened. He scrambled up and over the top and fell to the asphalt below.

Then he got to the Discovery and climbed in, starting the engine and grinding it into gear almost simultaneously. The front door hadn't opened behind him, and by the time he'd crossed the tree line and passed the main papaya groves the adrenaline that had locked down his system relaxed slightly. He yanked up the hand-brake, opened the door and threw up. He circumvented the dark guardhouse and hit the road to the *Rio Negro*. The thought of the unopened front door plagued him. Had he killed the girl? He stopped again, this time getting out of the car and vomiting wildly on the side of the road.

Slowly, Archie drove back to the resort. He waved to the guard at the *Rio Negro*, parked, and drug himself back to the room. Outside his door, there was a bottle of Vueve Cliquot champagne in a silver plate cooler, the ice three-quarters melted, and pizza on a mahogany butler's tray. Archie opened the door and took up the tray, setting it inside on the dresser. In the bathroom, he washed his mouth and brushed his teeth.

The room smelled of cigarettes and stale liquor. Underneath it was the wonderful scent of sunburnt girl. That made up for the full ashtray. The still shape of Tara Oaks lay in the bed, the sheets turned down, wearing nothing but one of his white shirts. He opened the bottle of champagne with a soft pop and took a pull. On the corner of the bed he sat and put down two pieces of cold pizza and half the bottle. Then he moved Tara over and put his head down on the pillow.

Seven

The Morning After

WEDNESDAY

ARCHIE HEARD HER GROAN and ignored it. Then she turned over, her breath was incapacitating. "Oh fuck." She moaned and rolled away. The room was light now and he could see Tara's clothes slung over the back of his chair. Then her voice softened, "Well this is something, Archie. Wonder what Mom would think?"

Archie rolled out of bed, "Love, you gotta brush those teeth."

He turned to see her sitting up in bed, still in one of his white shirts, "That's not very nice."

"Neither is your breath." Archie stumbled off to the bathroom. He was still in mid flow when Tara came in and took up his toothbrush and squeezed out some paste. "Jesus, Tara! Don't ya'll have a condo with your own bathroom somewhere in this building?"

"Ours has an ocean view, but you knew that, didn't you?"

Archie shook and stowed everything back in his underwear, "1117, if I remember." He flushed and pushed her out of the way to wash his hands.

"Are you trying to get rid of me? Ya know, you never struck me as the love 'em and leave 'em sort." Tara said with a mouth full of foam.

"You where 13 back then, how would you have thought one way or another?"

"Girls develop faster than boys."

"That's what every half-grown girl has always told me."

"Had a huge crush on you. Did you know that?"

"Of course I knew that. I was your big sister's boyfriend. I could have looked like Rasputin and it would have still been puppy love."

She laughed and handed over the toothbrush. "I've waited a long time for last night."

Archie stared at the toothbrush for a long time.

"What? I don't have cooties." He heard her say.

"Little girl you keep some strange company. Listen, just as a medical precaution, call room service and order a couple of bloody marys."

She splashed water in his face and went into the other room. After he'd brushed his teeth, Archie took off his boxers and stepped into the steaming shower. Hot water ran over his body and he realized how bad his head hurt. There was a bruise on his shoulder where he'd rammed the front door.

Gently the shower curtain opened and Tara stepped in. "Hi." She said girlishly. She seemed almost embarrassed.

"Did you lose your room key?"

"You're no fun. Oh God! That is a nasty bruise." She stepped closer to inspect it. The hot water hit her hair and the cigarette smoke from last night came up in swirls of steam. In an instant the smell had risen away all that was left was the scent of sunburnt skin, well rubbed with coconut oil wafting between them. Her breasts pressed against him and a leg moved between his and he felt himself coming back to life. Tara inspected the black blob for a long time. Archie just let the water roll over and between them. Finally she said, "We've got to get you put back together honey." She took a small bottle of shampoo and squeezed it into his hair. Her long fingers massaged his head and the tension that had racked him since last night began to fade.

"You're relaxing. I can see it in your face. It's the first time since I've seen you down here."

He opened one eye. A thick white dollop of soap fell from his head onto her breasts that seemed larger pressed against him. She guided his head under the running water and washed the soap down between them. She stepped away to get a bar of soap, and he sprang to attention. "Hello." She said and reached down. Archie stepped away and out of the shower.

"Hello...goodbye...uh...Archie, you alright?" came the voice from behind the shower curtain.

"I'm fine." Archie dried himself off furiously.

She poked her head out of the shower. "Water too hot?"

"Water's fine, Love. Perfect in fact."

"What's the problem?"

"Mental anguish."

"We can shampoo again, that seemed to help. Lather, rinse, repeat?"

"No, I don't want the anguish I'm gonna get from another rinse cycle."

"You're still in love with Vivie!"

"Who?"

The lapse was only for a second but Tara's head disappeared behind the curtain. "Yes! I won!" He saw her fists come over the curtain in a Victory stance.

"I didn't forget about your sister-"

"You can't even say her name!"

There was a knock on the door. Archie wheeled in the cart and got dressed; white shirt, khakis, and poplin sport coat. Tara came out of the shower and pulled on his shirt again. She was beaming and there was none of the spoiled temptress about her. "You know," Archie said, "if I could keep you away from other humans, you might be fun to have around."

"Why'd you get out of the shower Archie?"

He handed her a bloody mary. "I told you."

"But after last night."

"When I got back to the room last night, you'd passed out in my shirt."

Tara was profoundly disappointed. "Oh. We'll have to do something about that. Why all dressed up?"

"Because I've got a job to do."

"You always were a big ole boyscout."

"That's me; thoughtful, good manners, honest..." Archie was peeling through the blue vinyl business card wallet, pouring over pages of clear plastic sleeves. Then he extracted a somber business card with the Glenworth Insurance Company logo into the plastic sheath at the end of a lanyard, "...and always prepared." He slipped the card in his pocket to hang around his neck. "I'll call you when I get back."

In the daylight and up close, the straight groves of the papaya plantation were depressing against the wild beauty of the mountainsides. The occasional tractor or light truck would come grinding down the service road and Archie would pullover and tip his DeltaComm baseball hat as it passed. Then the green and yellow school bus came trundling along, from the manufacturing facility and headed for the break in the tree line.

While the bus moved beyond the tree line, Archie fumbled in the Discovery, putting a set of forms into a clipboard. Then he was off again, bouncing up the road to the far compound. In the light of day, the buildings appeared much larger than he'd guessed the night before. Now he rolled past the fence and into the lot that was full of service vehicles. The empty bus was on the far end of the parking lot.

Both DeltaComm and Glenworth ID tags hung from his neck as he climbed out of the car and pulled the bill of his hat down against the sun. In the front office, Archie was greeted with a volley of unwelcome stares-the Chinese men, either in blue suits or drill fatigues said nothing. Even the receptionist was Chinese. She stepped away from the group, "May I help you?" Her English was near perfect.

"Archie Gilmur-I'm with Glenworth Insurance. The folks at DeltaComm said we had a little bit of a mishap down here."

"We have not filed a claim." Said one of the suits curtly.

"*You* didn't have too, Mr. ...ah..."

"Quan."

"Mr. Quan." Archie scribbled this on the form. "Like I said, DeltaComm alerted me last night. Hell, I guess it was this morning. Hopped a jet in Puerto Rico and drove over to see how we could help."

Without saying a word, Mr. Quan stepped forward and inspected the two ID tags. He stared at Archie for a moment and silently stepped aside. Archie gave the gang an "aw shucks" grin and ambled down the hallway.

The information hub was a wreck. The wiring that had run along the walls was gone in a mass of melted veins indistinguishable from the wall around it. Most of the servers were little more than scorched metal boxes stacked in listing racks. The computers in the center of the room were gone, leaving clean square footprints on the otherwise sooty desktops. Archie took some notes on the clipboard to look official. He'd scrawled: *How to explain to Van Clair??* Then he scratched that out.

Moving back down the hallway, Archie made his way to the double steel doors. They were locked and beside them now sat a metal folding chair with a Chinese newspaper badly folded on the seat. He looked at the lock, then the chair, *do insurance adjusters pick locks?* He continued down the passage until he was looking up a recessed staircase. The bare bulbs in the stairwell were out. Archie found the darkness comforting. At the top was a single door – locked with a standard mechanism. He hunched down and went to work, picking the lock quickly. Beyond the door was a narrow room without furniture overlooking the gymnasium below.

In the glare of the overhead lights Archie could see the enormous Plexiglas cylinder on the far wall. A small lean man was climbing the rock wall with a large pack on his back. To the right, the bleachers had been pulled out from the wall. An athletic woman in her mid-twenties was running sprints up and down the bleachers with a backpack and weights around her ankles. She wasn't Chinese, too tall. Archie had a good look at her face. She was Arab. He looked over to the climbing wall. The short man was moving along the top of the wall. He was Arab as well. He moved nimbly, gracefully along the wall towards the cylinder. The climbing wall – its straight lines and right angles suddenly became clear. Archie wrote *clear antenna – top secret* on his pad, tore off the piece of paper and stuffed it in his pocket. "Fantastic." He heard himself say.

Through the glass windows of the room, something was said loudly and quickly. Archie looked up to see the small man dropping off the wall via the safety line. He hit the ground and disappeared beyond the climbing wall. On the bleachers, the tall woman was staring at Archie, her arms planted firmly on her hips. Archie smiled and waved at her in an "oops" sort of way. He left the way he came.

Mr. Quan was still in the front office but the rest of the suits were gone. "Have you made your inspection, Mr. Gilmur?"

"I have. It's official, you boys had a fire."

Mr. Quan didn't laugh. "If you will excuse us, we have a great deal to do to get the facility back on line."

"I can see that. You'll have my report in the next few days."

"Good day." Mr. Quan said formally.

The morning air was bright and hazy with moisture. There were no cars at the small house. Archie made it back to the Discovery and headed for Miz Cassat's Voodoo love nest. Leaping onto the porch, Archie knocked loudly on the front door and called out, "Miz Cassat, I'm with Glenworth Insurance, for DeltaComm, could you open up?"

Nothing. Archie looked down and noticed the heavy industrial lock. *What in the Hell does the old bitch need a lock like this on a cardboard door?* After a couple of nervous head checks, Archie managed to pick the lock and tumbled inside.

The interior was early Caribbean poor. The air was thick with an odor that was not unlike having an entire can of Copenhagen crammed up the nose. It was from the large saucepan on the stove. Tobacco was mashed and boiled and in a thick clump in the pan. On the counter nearby, four small bottles were filled with brown, translucent liquid.

Archie stepped down the hallway until he saw three large spiders set about on the floor. Two seemed to be facing off in mortal combat as the third hung back, waiting for the stronger of the pair to wear itself out. It must have been the brains of the trio.

Archie stepped over the spiders and looked into the back bedroom. It was a plain space with off-white walls broken by one window and some louvered folding doors. A single bed was pushed against the wall under the window. Archie checked out the closet and found nothing but some enormous underwear in a cardboard chest of drawers and two kaftans hanging nearby. He dropped to his belly and pressed his ear to the floor. Under the bed, there was an outline on the floor. Back onto his feet, Archie pulled the bed away from the wall. There was a metal rectangle covering the cut-out in the concrete floor.

Archie wedged the sheet metal away from the floor with his pocketknife and pulled it free. Below was a shallow hole with a small portable fire safe the size of a small suitcase. It was left unlocked. There, inside, was a small stuffed alligator without a head, inside of which were several velvet bags. Archie knew what they where before he emptied the loose diamonds into his palm.

Outside cars passed nearby. Archie stuffed the velvet bags into a hidden coat pocket and began to put everything the way he found it.

Then he saw the small black book in the safe. Mostly of the names were initials: BC, MB, GGL – there was Ugly Sue scrawled sloppily across a single page. Archie pocketed the book.

In the hallway, the spiders still stood in gridlock. Archie stepped over them again and headed to the truck. There was a problem, its name was Bobby Chu and it was peering into the driver's window of the Discovery. A few yards away, standing beside an open top Jeep, was a small, fierce looking Chinese man in a blue suit and bold red tie with an enormous full Windsor knot. He wasn't speaking to the SinoTel security guard in khaki drill fatigues who leaned against the jeep, hand on the grip of his side arm. The man in the blue suit just stared at Chu, arms folded over his chest with a look of disgust on his face. Something non-congenial was barked in Chinese and Chu snapped his attention away from the Discovery. "What are you doing here?" Chu spat at Archie.

"I'm the man from Glenworth – we handle the insurance for DeltaComm." Archie started. "And what's the meaning of last night's performance?! Really sloppy." The blue suit rolled his eyes violently and looked to heaven. "Are you Go Lin Lee?" The suit looked suspiciously at Archie. That was when Archie first saw the disfigured side of his head. The man was missing an ear. "Mr. Lee, you're going to perform some drug tests on the workers. I don't know how you people in the Middle Kingdom run your operations, but that Bobby Chu hangs around a queer bunch. I think there were drugs involved… violent, fun sorts of drugs. And if there weren't, well, then you've got a real problem!"

Neither Mr. Lee nor his blue suit moved.

"And another thing," Archie dug into his pocket for his keys, "Just what the hell is going on in here!" He waved grandly back to the small house with his keys. "Are you running some sort of narcotics gig with our manufacturing plant?"

Chu laughed and turned to Mr. Lee, "I think the man from DeltaComm knows exactly what is going on here and in the compound beyond the trees because the man from DeltaComm- Archie Gilmur- was caught on surveillance tape just before the fire broke out."

"Is this true?" asked Mr. Lee.

"Of course it's true. I've got a key."

Mr. Lee grunted something in Chinese and another SinoTel security guard appeared from the other side of the Discovery.

"Good God they're a lot of you! This is really sloppy, really sloppy. I got into the facility with a wrench and a dentist's pick."

Mr. Lee said nothing. Archie dropped his voice, gave them a winning smile, "Look, they sent me down from DeltaComm. I know you're working on some sort of antenna here. Gonna replace all the cell towers. Great, but my job is insurance. And I work for DeltaComm. I know whatever you've got is hush hush. I don't want to leak any information, get anybody into trouble, but I've got a report to file here and-"

The blow to the kidneys was a violent one. Archie dropped to his knees as the other guard delivered a blow to the torso. Chu took a fist full of hair and punched Archie in the nose.

"Take him inside." Mr. Lee barked.

The security guards pulled Archie back onto the porch and began to wrestle him into the house when Chu screamed, "Wait!" there was tinge of childish panic to his voice.

Mr. Lee rolled his eyes again. "What now, Mr. Chu?"

"Spiders in there."

"And?"

The security guards tried to keep Archie still while they waited on the order.

"I'm not going in there again, not till they clear out the spiders."

"That witch has made you useless, Mr. Chu." Mr. Lee explained as Chu crossed himself and kissed a talisman that hung around his neck.

Archie strained against the guards and got another kick in for good measure. He buckled, dragging both guards with him for a moment before they straightened themselves out. It was enough. Archie clawed into his coat pocket and fired off a round through his jacket, into one of the guard's boots. The guard howled and collapsed.

Straightening himself up, Archie stepped away from the second guard, "Nobody is killin' me indoors or out. I've got to get to Memphis tomorrow. If I don't the whole world will be down here."

The boot to the side of Archie's skull, delivered via a powerful roundhouse kick, sent Archie flying off the porch and onto the rocky clearing. He hit the ground hard but never lost hold of the pistol.

"As you can see, Mr. Gilmur, we take our security very seriously down here. Go tell that to your masters."

Standing, his knee boomed with pain, "Okay. Maybe I'll gloss over this last bit. You people seem to be very sensitive about it."

"I will be in touch with Memphis." Mr. Lee growled.

"I'll be at the office tomorrow night, so-"

"Goodbye Mr. Gilmur."

There was nothing to do for it but get into the Discovery and get off the plantation. He started the car, leaned out the window and shot the knee of the guard who'd round housed him, and made for the main road.

"I DIDN'T REALIZE HOW UGLY IT WAS until you took your pants off."

"Just what I wanted to hear." Archie said. The torn khakis were coming off slowly, they were at low thigh, "Tara, get me a glass of water." The torn and frayed fabric at the knee was matted with blood to what skin was left. Tara brought the glass and Archie tipped it over his knees and peeled the pants away before propping his leg up on the low bamboo dresser. It was torn, the red blood and black skin was dirty. "Well fuckity do!" His foot went to the carpet and the knee throbbed. Tara giggled. She was sitting in one of the bamboo armchairs near the writing table. "What's so damned funny?"

"You're charming even when you're wounded."

"You're an impressionable girl. What's the laptop say?"

On the writing table sat a computer and a digital camera wired together-sending it's information through the ether to be received and sorted out in Memphis. "Sixty eight percent complete." He heard her say. Archie sneered at the machine, technical marvel thought it was. "In college, when I was home from Saint Andrews, Vivie would smuggle me down here because the phone systems were so bad your parents could never hope to catch us. Now look at the place, might as well be Atlanta."

"You think too much, Archie."

"Think I'm gonna take a shower-alone-and get my ass back to Kingston."

Tara popped forward in her chair, "I'll go with you."

"Oh no you won't, Love. I'm going to the airport and flying home."

"When's your flight?"

"Tomorrow afternoon, but I'm not waiting that long."

"Kingston is dangerous."

"I'll take my chances."

Tara sat back, her eyes narrowed, "Hum. You can't drive these prehistoric roads with a torn knee. Not in a hurry you can't. I'll drive you, we'll catch an early dinner and I'll make sure you're awake for the first flight in the morning."

Archie dismissed her with a causal gesture. "You don't eat early dinners, you soak. Don't lie to me. Now I'm going to lick my wounds in private."

Tara was smiling wildly now. "…no, too easy."

She left Archie to his wounds. The blue and purple cloud over his ribs was tender and puffy to the touch-so he quit poking himself there. The knee needed attention. Archie pulled back the loose skin and cleaned the wound in torrents of hot water. His face was angry and red and the blood and pain rose violently under his skin. Turning away from the spray, Archie dosed the open wound with hydrogen peroxide. The joint foamed over like a thin lager. Archie let fly a litany of Anglo-Saxon.

Then he was in clean boxers and an undershirt, laying on the bed recovering from the shower. Tara came through the unlocked door wearing a wild and mostly yellow shift of a local print and carrying a small suitcase.

"Christ almighty." Archie said.

"Now you owe me a bottle of champagne." Tara said with a smile.

She was, Archie reckoned, as beautiful as she thought she was. Those loose blonde curls fell around that sun burnt face and Archie didn't think she was wearing any makeup. He needed to put some pants on, quickly.

"Let me think," she said, "We'll go to the Polo Room."

"What?" Archie rolled off the bed.

"In Kingston, the Polo Room, for champagne."

"We had champagne last night."

"*You* had champagne last night. I woke up and three quarters of the bottle is gone. It's not good to drink alone."

"I wasn't drinking alone, you were there."

"I was asleep."

"Not my fault you couldn't stay awake till I came back with the ice."

"The machine must be closer to my room." She pulled the belt free of the torn khakis and handed it over as Archie pulled on a pair of white ducks. "You know the British left the island years ago."

Archie ignored the comment, they were his last pair of pants. "What's Vivie up to these days?" He pulled on the shirt Tara had spent the night in.

"Oh you know…" her voice was louder than expected, "the rumpled soccer mom thing. Pity you two didn't get married, I'd have had you to play with every Christmas and fourth of July…"

She was still talking. Archie didn't know why he'd agreed to let her drive him to Kingston. Maybe she had a point about the bad knee, but there was no way he was carting Little Miss Vixen back to Memphis with him. Archie applied the blazer.

"…lose the coat, you'll be the sexiest man in Kingston."

Archie kissed her, firmly, but not for very long. He had to. "Maybe I want to be the second sexiest man in Kingston. Lets go."

The keys to the Discovery were left with the front clerk. He stowed his kit in Tara's rented Mazda Miata, and she pulled out of the Rio Negro with enthusiasm. "Well now Archie, I've got a question… I've seen you boozing at a five star restaurant, dancing with the locals, making only a half hearted attempt at seducing your first love's fairly willing little sister, only to twice disappear into the wilderness-and come back broken each time."

"*Fairly* willing?"

"Just what the hell do you do, Archie?"

"Odd gig, actually. Listen Tara, before we get into the champagne, or otherwise altered, can you tell me about this safe of your father's that's caused all the ya-ya?"

Tara experienced the odd sensation of not wanting to talk about herself. "Well." The Miata sped up as they came to a turn. Archie pressed himself into the seat and said nothing. "The safe, it's just an office safe." She shook her head and flew past a man and his goats as they went scrambling off the road to safety.

"What is poor old Walt Oaks up to these days?"

"Still working for DeltaComm. They've got Vivie's husband, he's there too now. Granddaddy and Uncle Robert made daddy the head of Asia Division. He's in Hong Kong most of the time. I hadn't heard a thing from him until he tells mom that he's struck up a deal with the Chinese government to bring these pandas to Memphis. Said it's great press for the company on both sides of the Pac-rim. Asia is a huge market."

"Clever."

"If you're into huge raccoons that look like saddle oxfords."

"So what's in the safe? Secret formula for panda chow?" Archie was tracing the alphabet on the tiny floorboard with his toe to keep his knee from becoming stiff.

"I don't think they care." Tara said after a long time. They roared along the narrow road and she seemed to have drifted into the same haze that Archie had seen last night. Again, like last night, she snapped out of it almost instantly. "Enough about me, tell me about your 'odd gig'."

"Really isn't anything to tell." Archie traced a passable Q on the floor mat.

"What about Ireland?"

"Small island of vaguely alcoholic poets in the North Sea."

"Funny. Why were you there?"

"Because it's a small island of vaguely alcoholic poets in the North Sea."

"Rumor had it you were dating a beauty. Her father had a title."

"Not true."

"At least he had buckets of money."

"So does yours."

"It's mom's money. So what happened to your pretty Irish heiress?"

"We broke up."

"Sweetie, you're going to have to give me more than that. It's a long way to Kingston."

Archie pointed to a bend in the road. "Mind the goat, Love."

WHEN YAVI OMARI HEARD THE WOMAN called Alice bark "get out" he immediately dropped off the top ridge of the climbing wall. The nylon of the safety line slid through his fingers, his feet hit the floor softly, as he was trained to do. Yavi unfettered himself from the safety line and was making his way around the Plexiglas cylinder, when it occurred to him that Alice was looking towards the observation room, and not talking to him at all. Behind the climbing wall, Yavi slung off his backpack and moved down a short damp smelling hallway to a small locker room.

He set the pack down and kicked the metal bench before him. If he hadn't looked guilty, scrambling down the wall and running off, he certainly looked scared. He wasn't scared of Alice, he told himself again, that was certain. Even the thought was ridiculous. What caused Yavi to kick the bench a second time was something different.

She was going to come back here and lecture him about safety and training. He wasn't scared of her. She was just a headache, that's all. But now he'd had enough. His wife didn't speak to him in that way. True, she didn't speak to anyone in that way, but that was why she was a good woman. Now he had to spend his days with this pushy slut and he'd had enough. Now Yavi relished the thought of her impending attack. He'd put up with her since January – when the plans had changed.

He heard her come down the bleachers. Yavi Omari hated a change in plans-they usually ended badly.

Yavi was an engineer by trade and a mathematician at heart: in his world the equations never changed. Nevertheless, back in Paris, at New Year the call came and he had to obey. He'd been praying when the phone started ringing. "Oui." Since coming to Paris, he'd been trained to react the way expected.

The French are fairly open to foreigners as long as they are kind enough to act, speak and look exactly like the French. His own daughters had had their headscarves confiscated at school for being "ostentatious" religious symbols. Eventually, Yavi, his wife and daughters agreed to the humiliating compromise of having his daughters show a forelock of hair so as to transform the "provocative headscarf" into simply a headscarf.

It was times like these that made Yavi put up with a phone call during his prayer. The code was delivered in French and then confirmed in French. Then the speaker switched to Farsi-"We've moved up. Go to Crik Crok. Same order as last time."

"I will not see my girls before I go?"

"You will see them in Paradise, they will follow your example." The line went dead.

Yavi hung up the phone. The Crik Crok was a cheap cafe around the corner in the industrial suburb of Aubervillers where he lived in a safe house. The Crik Crok didn't mean the Crik Crok, though. It meant Renard's on Rue de Borgne. Yavi took a moment to collect his thoughts and come to grips with the fact that his short life would soon be fulfilled as a martyr.

In the bedroom of the small flat he kissed the photo of his two daughters and wife he was forbidden to have at the safe house. Family photos would connect him with the outside world. Yavi kept them anyway, and shoved them into the lining of the Nike gym bag he'd already packed. Switching out the lights, he placed the keys to the place in a small box beneath the sink. Turning the self-lock, he stepped out into the hallway.

As the door swung shut behind him, Yavi's eyes bulged in his head as his memory jarred and he turned himself around. He swung the Nike bag into the door, stopping it before the lock caught. Back in the kitchen, Yavi filled the coffee maker and started it. Then he was back in the hall, the door locking behind him.

When he got to Redard's, or even before, a call would go out to the cell and someone-Yavi didn't know who, would come by, sweep the place for prints and throw the deadbolts. Yavi smiled, they might even enjoy a pot of strong Turkish coffee.

Yavi went down three flights of stairs onto the street and took a block before descending down into the Metro station. Fare paid, he squeezed into the subway and found a place in the crowded car. In a pair of Levi's knock-off's, and sweater and a large shabby overcoat, Yavi faded quickly into the milling Metro passengers. Where he was heading, however, he'd stick out like a mangled thumb.

So this polluted, dirty city was the most beautiful city in Western Christendom? No wonder the West was so violently confused. Whirlwinds of fast French whirled around his head without revealing itself to Yavi. He recalculated his route to Renard's in his head and leaned back against the glass.

The French that came over the loudspeaker was slower, more deliberate. His stop was approaching and he stood as the car slowed and stopped. Then he was moving with the crowd up to street level before breaking away south to the Rue de Borgne. From time to time he flexed his wrist, causing the bag in his hand to jump. It's heft, the fact that everything he had packed was still there, comforted him. It gave him a sense of control as events were sweeping him off to his destiny across a distant ocean.

Set along the avenue among the expensive retail stores, Yavi spied Renard's. Personally he thought it a waste to front an operation at such an expensive location, but kept it to himself. Then, standing before the shop, he caught himself staring awestruck through the plate glass storefront. The place looked more like a chic disco than a high-end jewelry store. White neon splashed across the walls spelling words like Amore, Sexy, and XXXOOOXXX. Small focused bulbs hung from the high ceilings, and glinted off the diamonds in the inside. It seemed to Yavi that they were feeding the very monster they were trying to kill.

Stepping through the front door into a glassed in alcove, Yavi pressed the buzzer. An extremely pretty young man, they said his name was Chu, looked up, glanced at his watch and sneered. He came around one of the glass cases, his patent leather pants glinting in the light beneath his close fitting black turtleneck. He aimed a remote at the alcove and the buzzer sounded. Yavi pushed open the door but was stopped halfway through by Robert Chu. Behind them the quick thump of techno music hissed through the air.

Yavi said, without glancing at his watch, "I'm about nine minutes late."

Chu reckoned the number confirmation without blinking, "I only noticed about four minutes ago." Thirteen. The West's unlucky number. Chu didn't move out of Yavi's way, but looked him over quickly, "Deliveries in the rear please." He shut the door and went back to a bored and waifishly thin woman staring at an insane piece of Western decadence inside.

For a moment, Yavi looked at his shabby-self in the reflection of the plate glass. Perhaps the contact was only being cautious. Stepping back onto the street, Yavi found the first alley and followed it around to the back of the block. The back door of Renard's wasn't nearly as grand as the front. A gray steel door set into a gray concrete wall with Renard's stenciled with spray paint on the door. Yavi rang the buzzer and the door opened as if Chu had been waiting there.

"Get in." Chu said and closed the door shut behind them. "I thought the cell had provided you with suitable clothes."

"For what?" Yavi said looking at the stark concrete walls on the back passageway.

"Travel. You look like a hobo."

"A what?"

"A criminal. You'll be stopped at the first check. Didn't they give you a suit?"

"Yes."

"In the bag?"

"No. I forgot it. I left in a hurry."

"Not good enough. We've got too much riding on this to leave it to a scatterbrain."

"No, they chose me, I will go." He stood defensively. "I look average, I will blend in."

"You look like a terrorist." Chu stomped away and turned up a stairwell. Yavi followed. Upstairs was only marginally more fashionable than the back passageway and Yavi wondered if he were still in the same building at all. They came into a small office and Chu went to the safe and opened it. "You are traveling first class. It costs more, but the authorities don't eye you quite as long. But you, my God, you'll stick out like a lump of shit in crystal." He took out the envelope and tossed it on the desk. "You will be traveling to Spain by rail, then to Kingston, Jamaica. In Kingston, you will go take a cab to the Le Meridian Pegasus. You will not check in but go to the Polo Room and wait for my opposite to take you to the compound."

"And the code?"

"Twenty one. A passport and papers are provided."

"They say there is a witch on the island."

Chu looked at Yavi hard, "Catholic nonsense." He spat, "Once you leave here stay in character. Which means don't leave until we fix you." Chu walked around him twice. And pointed to a door off the office. "Go to the bathroom." He ordered. With Yavi protesting but compliant, Chu shaved his head. "Strip."

"What?"

Chu began to take off his clothes.

"What is wrong with-"

"Strip!" Chu barked. By this time his turtleneck was laying on the back of the toilet and he was pulling off his steel tipped cowboy boots. Yavi moved back into the office and began to take off his clothes. Moments later, Chu was pulling on the sweatshirt and Yavi was trying to wriggle into the patent leather pants.

"I look ridiculous." Yavi whined.

"No, I look ridiculous." Chu growled, "You look chic." His beeper went off and Chu read the screen. "They've broken the safe house, did you make the coffee?"

"Yes."

"They'll think you're coming back. But they won't wait forever."

Yavi looked to heaven, "This is for the greater good." He said in Farsi.

"This better be worth it." Chu said in English.

Chu went back to the desk and handed a newspaper to Yavi. "And try not to look like you're learning a part. Your ride is downstairs."

But he *had* learned a part, training on this lush, humid island. The smell of the locker room was moist and dank. She was coming around the rock wall-Yavi stood and balled his fists. Alice came into the room, "Try not to look so guilty-I wasn't telling you to get out."

"I wasn't listening to you." Yavi spat.

"That man, the westerner, in the observation room, did you see him?"

"No."

"Then why did you run away?"

Yavi looked at the floor and scratched his head, "You need to learn to control-"

"Oh shut up Yavi!"

"Don't use my name!"

"You're pathetic. Did you see the man or not? Who was he?"

"I said I didn't see him. How could I-"

"Just stay here." Alice commanded. Yavi stood his ground and kicked the bench again after she'd left.

ALOGRYTHM, THOUGHT GERRY TORBEL, ALOGRYTHM. He threw his hands up in the air as the crew foreman-a man with most of an elementary school education-questioned Torbel's figures for the fourth time. "This was created by a very sophisticated algorithm." Gerry repeated.

The word was lost on the foreman. Gerry ground his teeth, snapped shut his notebook and handed the grimy sheath of papers back to the foreman. "Just do it! Like it says!" he used the corner of the notebook to point down the hill. "There." Workers were erecting the supports for the suspension bridge that would span the serpentine river that cut deep through the Panamanian the mountains.

Gerry turned with a grunt and headed to his trailer. The foreman was calling after him in a style of Spanish not taught by the US State Department. Gerry waved him off and kept on towards the trailer. Inside, he sat down at the desk and looked at the earth that still clung to his Rockport shoes. He was in his uniform of tropical gray pants, and short sleeve white shirt that Esmerelda teased him about incessantly. The sun-faded blue blazer hung loosely on the back of the chair. A small desk fan pushed the stale air around the cramped trailer and Gerry opened his notebook to review his figures.

He'd built dozens of bridges. They were scattered around the undeveloped corners of the world and he was sure that, even on the off-chance that he had made a mistake, an undeveloped crew foreman would not be the one to catch it. Still the seed of doubt had been planted, and Gerry Torbel, being Gerry Torbel, needed to review his figures before he did anything else.

The chattering of Chinese outside his thin window distracted him. Panama seemed an odd country for the Chinese to overrun. Gerry thought something more Pac-Rim would be more their speed, nevertheless here they were. And they were everywhere. The information he sent to his handlers in Virginia would sort out the Chinese situation and make sense of it all. But there was a window. A predictable formula of events that was bound to unfold. Once enough of them had arrived, men and women, to form a self-sustaining society, it would be closed off to outsiders. Whatever Gerry was supposed to be collecting, he reckoned he only had about three years to do it.

The chatter passed. They were laborers discussing the drunken stupor they were both still suffering. Gerry packed up his notebook and told one of the gopher boys that he was going up the mountain for an overhead survey. While Gerry thought that this sounded impressive, the talk was that the American engineer was just going up the mountain to take a siesta were the workers wouldn't find him.

The road wound through the forest covering the side of the mountain. It was civilized enough for the Fiesta, but just barely. The radio was off and Gerry reveled in the near silence as he bumped along with the tall ceiling of the forest above him. Then a clearing opened up and before him, far below, was the building site. That was as far as the Ford Fiesta could go.

Shutting off the engine, Gerry climbed out and let the silence wash over him. Wonderful silence-that would clear the head.

There had been variables to consider when Gerry first weighed his government's proposal for some specialized "patriotic work". He'd run through the offer like any other problem to be solved. There had been one variable that Gerry had never been able to factor accurately. Now he was staring right at it.

Simply put, Gerry Torbel was worried that Gerry Torbel wasn't cut out for this sort of work. He rubbed his face and sat down on the hood of the Fiesta, staring blankly at the foundation of the bridge he was building. He stared, but nothing registered.

Something stirred beyond the clearing and Gerry shot to his feet, turning frantically several times before his fear gave way to a frustrated laughter. "Hello." He called. Nothing. He picked up a palm sized stone and hurled it into the bush. Suddenly there was a rush of movement and a shriek. Gerry ducked behind the hood of the Fiesta as the brightly colored bird took flight from the bush and off into the air.

Gerry forced himself to giggle to prove to the woodland spirits that he could laugh at himself and therefore wasn't coming entirely off the latch. Breathe Deep. Gerry got back onto the hood of his car and tried to clear his head. Again the silence crept back into the clearing and left only the feeling of blood pounding in his ears.

Rocks shifted behind him. Gerry's back stiffened. Then the crunch became a slide and stopped. Gerry breathed deep and told himself not to succumb to the fear-not to turn around Then the silence came back and was too still.

He could stand it no more and popped off the hood and spun around. The soldier was staring at him and it took Gerry a moment to realize that the man in the camouflage fatigues was not Panamanian but Chinese. They froze, then a lighting quick flutter of the soldier's eyes.

All went black. Rough material was pulled loosely over Gerry's head from behind, then the material was stuffed into his mouth. It tasted like gasoline. His arms were pulled behind his back and his wrists cuffed together. Then the sack came off his head and a sock was stuffed into his mouth and held in place with duct tape and the sack came down again.

Now the muffled Chinese was not the idle chatter of drunks but the hard barks of military men. He could hear them but couldn't make out what was being said. Pushed down into a squat, Gerry was frog marched across the clearing. Then, in the bush, he was lifted by his armpits and half-dragged through the undergrowth.

He was stopped roughly and lifted into the back of a flatbed truck. Thrashing out, Gerry kicked something over and the smell of gasoline again hit him with a rush as the butt of a revolver came crashing into his brow. A heavy boot kicked him in the solar plexus twice, emptying his lungs with a crash. The gas fumes mixed with air burned his lungs and he pushed the vomit back down his throat. The boot came down again and he though he was going to die.

Hands came under his armpits and ankles and he was hoisted into a box. His arms, cuffed behind his back, were pinned underneath him. He kicked again into the heavy plastic case. Gerry sensed that one of the soldiers had leapt from the truck and gasoline vapors again wafted across his nose. The remaining soldier was then setting a lid atop the box and whatever light filtered through the coarse black material around his head went black.

The darkness was complete-the silence all encompassing. Both arms had cramped and gone numb. In the shriek of thoughts that came without any distraction Gerry began to wonder about the thin wisps of air he was breathing. He was crammed into a box that, if airtight, would soon be his coffin. The fear crumbled before a cataclysmic panic.

Somewhere, he was aware that the truck was moving.

BEAU WALKED UP THE STREET under the dim street lights, away from the discothèque, meandering slowly to a less revered establishment. After the Hotél de la Rio Negro, all of Kingston seemed to be a pool of filth and poverty. The building he turned into had probably been a brilliant sea foam green but now looked like infected mucus. Inside the jukebox played old Motown hits. That was fine-he'd had enough calypso music to hold him for a year.

Without stopping at the bar, Beau went to the back of the place and mounted a narrow staircase on the far side of the nasty toilets.

The top of the stairs opened up into a narrow hallway lined with narrow doors where the working boys and girls rented out the rooms. Beau passed the rooms and his disgust began to turn. The fact that perfect strangers were humping away like dogs just beyond the thin walls did something for the Spaniard.

The room at the front end of the hall took up the entire façade of the building. Between the baby grand piano and the bar, the room was insanely cluttered with chairs and small round tables. At the end of the bar sat Robert Chu, his beautiful almond eyes moving across the room under that oiled comma of hair. He wore a tight undershirt and a not quite so tight pair of black microfibre pants. Chu smiled but never looked directly at Beau, who went directly to the bar and ordered a screwdriver.

After two sips of his cocktail, his disgust with the place was completely overpowered by anticipation. He slid off the barstool and took the drink with him back down the hallway. Then he collided with a small girl in the hall. "Hey!" the girl called. She was no older than fourteen and almost pulled a knife until she saw his face. "Hey Beau, watch where you goin'-slow down, we all have happy endings here Baby."

"Having a good night, honey?"

She smiled, "Actually, I am."

Beau took what was left of the screwdriver and continued to the end of the hall. He knocked on the last door and tried the knob. The door was unlocked. An Oriental dressing screen blocked the interior of the room from the hallway. Beau moved around the flimsy piece of discretion and into the narrow room. It was the size of a dormitory but still managed a double bed and a chest of drawers. Looking at his watch Beau finished off the screwdriver and began to unbutton his shirt. The mirror and the razor blade came out of the top drawer and he poured out a small mound of cocaine.

On the other side of the screen the door opened and closed again. "Lock it please." Beau whined. The bolt was thrown but Beau never took his focus off the mirror. "Hey sweetie, this shit's been cut with baby laxative, so it may get wild."

Chu came around the screen with a charming grin.

"I think I know what's going on in that pretty head of yours."

"Oh I doubt it."

"Well I just love surprises." Beau cooed and leaned over the mirror with the dollar bill he'd just rolled. With two long snorts the lines were gone and Beau was wiping his nose and rubbing the tips of his fingers over his raw gums. "Now for your dose."

Closer now, Beau saw the glass syringe in Chu's hand. It was the size of a cigar.

Beau looked up, "Oh no honey, I learned my lesson on heroine. NOT...FOR...ME. You can have every bit of that devil."

"Where's your sense of adventure?" Chu asked and jabbed the needle into Beau's paunch and slapping a hand over his mouth. Holding their bodies close, Chu depressed the plunger evenly. The mirror fell to the floor, dusting Chu's black pants.

Then he was standing over Beau, capping the syringe and sliding it into his cowboy boots. "Be careful, that bugar sugar will kill you sweetie. You're now having a major cardiac arrest, and when they find you, in say... how long did you rent the room for us? All night? You are a romantic. No matter, when they find you, you'll have had a simple heart attack. And with the cocaine in your system then there'll be no need for an investigation. You always said I was a clever boy."

Beau tried to scream but only heard a gurgling hiss come out of his foaming mouth.

Chu came out of the room and into the hallway. Casually he took the narrow staircase to the bar below and went out the back door. Then he was on the sidewalk and it wasn't crowded but alive: breathing and coughing with all the souls that animate red light districts the world over. He stopped and smoothed his hair in the plate glass reflection of a pawn shop window. No one cared, but a few roving eyes passed over his trained physique.

His destination was in the same quarter as the brothel from which he came; it was a small and dingy building, three stories high. Walking up the creaking steps to the third floor, Chu opened the door to a dirty and small flat. It was one room and in a far corner, by the sole window, was a military issue cot. A pine armoire held a wardrobe entirely too trendy for the seedy dump. On the other wall was a sink, and enough counter space for a double burner. Beneath the counter was the refrigerator. There was a folding table and chair near the sink and on the table was a glass box in which sat a large black spider.

Near the door where he entered was a closet door that was closed and locked with a Krieg industrial lock. As an added precaution, the closet door itself was steel with a paper-like veneer of pine. In the closet was the telex equipment the Chinese army had assigned him.

The truly curious visible detail about the place was the walls. Scrawled on the dingy white walls were voodoo hexes and gris-gris bags hanging from nails every few inches.

Chu locked the door behind him and checked the window. It was still nailed shut along the bottom and sides. As an added measure he'd painted over the nails with a thick latex paint. Chu studied the ceiling nervously before retrieving the paint can from under the cot. Then he dragged the chair under a crack in the ceiling that had been painted over with several thick coats of paint. Chu inspected the crack, winced, and smeared on another coat.

With the crack re-painted, he put the paint under the bed, took up the glass box and set it near the head of his bed. Then Chu stripped and climbed into bed, one hand on the glass case, murmuring "Anasi, Anasi Coupé." He never really slept.

Eight

It Rolls Down Hill

THURSDAY

MIN FA HAD BEEN A PROFESSOR of Political Studies in Beijing for 20 years. He'd been a spy for ten. Min could never be sure, but he suspected his wife first raised the flag on him. Things had been strained and distant and then artificially close. The day she'd gathered up their son and said they were going to visit her mother up north for a few days the alarm bells clanged in his head. He had helped them pack, walked them to the bus station and saw them off. Min never set foot in his house again.

He took a bus in the opposite direction. The bus reached the coast and he hired a car to the nearest port. There he stowed away in a ship, emerging from its dark hull in Hong Kong.

From Quayside, Min made his way to the financial district and found his stock-broker at the DFCrenshaw, Inc. office. Min owned no securities but the nice man at DFC was also the CIA's man in Hong Kong. Min Fa was in Langley, Virginia 72 hours later.

That was five years ago.

For this reason Min was indignant that David Meeks-who spoke no Chinese-asked him if he was certain of the translation.

"Quite certain, Commander Meeks."

Meeks looked at the aerial photographs of the graduated mixing vats that Gerry Torbel had sent him. "They're buying yellowcake." Meeks said to himself.

"Yellowcake?" Min looked at the original Chinese.

Meeks rubbed his head, "Uranium. Fissionable material. The specs you've translated from Panama have a Chinese construction company buying unrefined Uranium 238, which you can't make a weapon out of. You'd have to mix it in your lemonade to make it deadly." Meeks looked at Min, "As far as I know you can't make a building out of it either."

"But it isn't the Uranium you can make a weapon out of?"

"Well, not until it's refined. Uranium 234." Meeks tapped the aerial photos laying on the desk. "and this is how they'll do it. Those mixing vats are the wrong size. That isn't a strip mining operation."

"Don't we have a man in Panama to take care of this?"

"Of course we do. Min, you just translate. I just gather and pass on." He pointed upward, "Then there are those who coordinate."

"Well shouldn't they know about – "

"Yes. And as soon as you leave I'm going to pass the report on."

Min smiled, "They'll take care of it?"

Meeks sneered, "Hardly. When I first joined the company, we pulled all our people from the military. Now we get them from corporations... godammed CEO's turned spies."

Min only smiled because he wasn't sure just what Commander Meeks was going on about.

Then Min Fa was gone and Meeks was left alone with his cigarette and small fan blowing the smoke out the window. He was staring at a picture of Amy and thinking he didn't really care if the Chinese jabbed a nuclear spear up through America's Texan underbelly or not.

Then he made the call to Rowan.

"Is Mickey Boy still in play?"

"Yes." Rowan said. He was annoyed and this gave Meeks a cruel smile, "Our girl in Jamaica pissed in her whiskey."

"How bad did she miss?"

"Badly...not really sure what happened." Rowan lied. "Haven't got a report, she's gone underground."

"This shit needs to be handled by the professionals."

"Well, Commander, she came highly recommended."

"By who?" Meeks winced as soon as he said it.

"By you. She was on your list." Rowan laughed, "It looked like a professional list."

"Alright."

"Neatly typed...clean..."

"Alright. You used our girl and she fucked up. Pissed in her whisky as you say. I got it, where is she now?"

"Gone to earth. I've got another in Jamaica – he's a little flighty but reliable. They're in the same orbit."

"Not your little Spanish fag?"

"That's the one."

"Found him dead last night in Kingston. Cardiac arrest, the local screws think it was a drug overdose."

For a long time Rowan said nothing, then, "Reckon she'll come up for air soon enough. Is that why you called?"

"We're increasing the priority on Mickey Boy – we need him taken out, now."

"I'll get it done if I have to do it myself. I'll have a man in Havana by first light. He's been sitting on that pile of old Soviet material for thirty years now, why the sudden step-up?"

"We've gotten a report from our man in Panama – it looks like we've found Mickey Boy's biggest customer, a construction company in Panama – owned by a Chinese business man, a Mr. Lee of SinoTel fame – appears to be building the capacity to refine Uranium yellowcake."

"In South America?"

"Yeah, they don't appear to have the capacity to fire it at us though."

Rowan breathed out hard. "At that range they don't need a missile. All they need is a Volkswagen."

THERE WAS PRESSURE ON HIS FEET and the lid opened, filtering light through the heavy gauze of the sack. Then Gerry was falling forward and his head hit something hard. His eyes opened wide, bulging with tension out of the front of his head. The sock taped in his mouth had long absorbed any moisture from his tongue. Heavily shod feet shuffled nearby and suddenly the sack was pulled off his head without warning and his skull thumped again on the concrete floor.

The light was white and harsh and a long while passed before Gerry could make out the images that lay before him. An assessment of his new surroundings eventually emerged: concrete floor, unpainted; white walls, the harsh lighting was harsh and unshaded.

Then he saw the give-away, the drain in the middle of the floor, Gerry Torbel was in an interrogation room.

One of the soldiers bent over him and tore the tape, pulling the sock out of Gerry's mouth. If he could have screamed, it would have been for water.

Most likely he was two or three floors below ground. With the affection that Gerry knew the crew foreman held for him, it might be a day or two before his absence on the site was officially questioned. At the office, they would assume he was on a job site. Then again, how long had it been? No windows, no clocks, the lights always on…there was no telling how long he'd been gone. At one point, locked in his coffin, his ears began to pop. He vaguely remembered thinking he'd been put on a plane. He racked his brain for the first person that might miss him.

Esmerelda.

"Oh, God!" Gerry moaned harshly.

This was met with peels of laughter from the soldiers who came over and lifted Gerry by the armpits. His limbs cramped, bloodless and numb, they exploded in pain. Across the room he was dragged to a simple wooden stool. Before him was a long wooden table, on the other side of it, four chairs, all empty, faced Gerry. Then, in silence, all left the room but a stocky Manchurian in a rumpled white shirt and wrinkled blue suit pants. He had only one ear. The Manchurian began in accented but passable English: "Mr. Torbel, an honor to have you with us. We have a few matters to attend, and your cooperation would help to get you back to your bridge as quickly as possible."

Gerry nodded that he understood. Mr. Lee poured out a small glass of water from a carafe on the table handed it over, "Drink it slowly." Gerry did not. He swallowed hard and choked a bit. "We do not want you getting sick." Gerry handed the glass back and Mr. Lee refilled the glass. This time Gerry tried to sip the metallic water. "I trust you enjoyed your journey?"

"Where am I?"

"Not in Panama."

"…" Gerry looked up, dumbfounded.

"Yes, we know that you revere silence, Mr. Torbel. That is why you were up in the clearing. You go there often, but not to sleep, as your crew thinks. So you made our journey in total sensory depravation. It must have been a refreshing dream. But, unfortunately, all dreams must end."

"Fucking nightmare." Gerry choked.

Mr. Lee smiled in a manner Gerry didn't like. "I am sorry, do you need some stimulus? We will leave you with soft, soft music. Then I shall return and we will talk." With a short bow he left the room.

Somewhere in the glare of the harsh white lights, speaker cracked on. The clanging came at a deafening 130 Decibels -first the metal against metal followed by gunshots and smashing glass. Beneath it all was the screech of a telephone line logging into the internet.

About twenty minutes later, the LSD that had laced the water carafe began to take affect, and then the harsh, constant lights went out and the strobes began blinking wildly.

Six hours and a hundred years later, the cacophony of manufactured noises and pulsing light cut out at once. Two soldiers entered the room. One jabbed him with an electric cattle prod and Gerry moaned sadly. Then they lifted him out of his vomit, urine and feces, and dragged him from the corner back to the stool.

The images before him ebbed and waned out of focus in a slow, fluid wash. Then he could make out Mr. Lee sitting at the table, hands folded politely in front of him. "You have torn the flesh from your face, Mr. Torbel. Not advisable."

Gerry's fingertips were caked in blood.

"We have a question for you, Mr. Torbel-" The screeching was still tearing at his brain, the sight of his fingers burning his eyes, and Gerry had to struggle to follow what was being said. "-we know that you were spying on us. Annoying but quite routine, as is our meeting today. What we need from you is a list of your…" Mr. Lee made a quick check of his notes, "I believe that you call them 'assets', in Panama."

"Please…quiet…rest."

"The question, Mr. Torbel."

"I'm an engineer…not a spy…I'm trying to help these people down here."

"Again, you are no longer in Panama. Please listen closer."

"Where then?"

"No matter."

Gerry caught the cattle prod in the kidneys and he jumped and crumbled to the floor. His stomach lurched and retched bile over himself.

"Tsk Tsk Tsk." The soldiers placed Gerry back on the stool. "You Americans are so dirty. Call a maid!"

Moments later the door opened and a battered Esmerelda appeared freakish with a broken nose, fat lip, and wearing a tiny French maid's uniform. She saw Gerry, tried to run to him but the guards took hold of her. Her arms reached out and the engineer saw that both her thumbs had been broken.

"We had to go into the jungle to find you, Mr. Torbel." The Manchurian was saying, "This one we picked up in the very room we saw her making copies for you."

"Oh God!"

"Gerry…save me…take me to America!"

"We have broken her body, Mr. Torbel. She even gave us all she knows, we just need you to confirm."

They threw her on the table and one soldier held Esmerelda down while the other took down his pants.

"Gerry-I tell them nothing! I swear it."

"Your man in Jamaica, the homosexual, has already been liquidated."

"I told them nothing!" She spit on the soldier as he positioned himself between her bruised legs. He hit her in the side with the cattle prod for good measure and she screamed out.

"Stop it!" Gerry shouted.

They did. "Yes?" Asked Mr. Lee.

Gerry chocked back the vomit. "What do you want to know?"

THE BLACK NYLON BAG TOOK the crest with a thump and slid without grace down to the conveyor belt. The baggage claim of the Memphis International Airport was loud, overhead noise and announcements, but not crowded. Archie was trying hard not to look like he'd just witnessed a voodoo blasphemy, possibly committed a justifiable homicide, and lost his shirt trying not to stuff an ex-girlfriend's uppity little sister. He was pretty sure he was doing a passable job of it.

What vexed him were the diamonds. The lot of them stuffed into a sock in the black suitcase trundling along with the other baggage on the belt. Archie went silently through the sparse crowd, not rushing but moving with purpose.

He was in a blue pinstripe Brooks Brothers suit, a fresh shirt and a sober, loosely knotted bowtie-something inconspicuous and harmless. A hand reached out for the bag; a woman, possibly in her fifties. Archie craned around her. "I believe this is mine." He said quickly, "Yes, there's my name…pity everyone has the same luggage these days." He was talking too much. Turning to the sliding glass doors he took a breath and held it to a five count.

Archie stepped out into the winter sun at just after three in the afternoon and felt dirty. Scrolling through the numbers on the mobile phone, *it* caught his eye. So much for the disappearing act. He squinted and stared up the long line of cars coming up the ramp and smiled. "You silly bitch," he muttered, "you actually went and did it!"

The 1969 Jaguar E-type is beyond the perfect car, it's sublime. It is the reason all other cars strive to be more than they are. Every English speaking male – no every English speaking person – should drive one before they die. The E-type makes a pretty girl hot, and a hot girl pure destructive perfection. Although it won't make a man make smarter, it will make him better looking and more charming-which trumps brains every time.

Bunty was sitting behind the wheel, well aware how good she looked. His remark never made it to her and she wouldn't have cared if it had. She was wearing thick tortoise-framed sunglasses and a plaid scarf over her head. A single strawberry blonde comma twisted out over her forehead.

Archie hit the auto-dial and the other end started ringing. Bunty answered her mobile with a smile, "Nice tie. I don't like you in blue pinstripes."

"How'd you get the Jag? Did you sleep with Pop or just get him drunk?"

"Embarrassing really, he told me to put my shirt back on so I had to hit him with the bourbon."

"You silly bitch-you're sick." Archie said, taking up his bags and moving towards the car. "Listen, I gotta go, my ride's here."

"Who's that?"

"Stunning girl, spanking car."

"You lucky, lucky man."

By the time the mobile went back into his coat pocket, Bunty had popped the trunk. Archie threw in the bags, came around the left side of the car and slid into the tan leather passenger seat. "So how ya like the right-hand drive?"

Bunty said nothing. A quick head-check, "I'll show you." She cackled and roared into the traveling lane. The E-type came down the ramp and in seconds was coming up behind an SUV. Bunty glided them around the truck and up to the parking attendant who waved them through. Then she bolted, pushing the E-type out of the airport lot and onto the expressway like a bullet in third gear. She cut a glance at Archie who was suspiciously quiet. "Hey Archie, that suit doesn't exactly scream 'Welcome to Jamaica, Mon, have a nice day."

"This is a suit I can disappear in."

"Oh Lord, did something go wrong... other than burning the place to the ground?"

"You could say that." Archie said staring out at traffic. They said nothing as she shifted around a large tractor trailer. Finally, Archie rubbed the bloodshot eyes under his sunglasses and said, "I may be in trouble."

"You should've brought me." It was weak and she knew it.

"You don't want a dog in this fight." He said, looking off into the skyline of downtown standing off in the distance. "There was a shooting."

"Oh my God! Who?"

"She knew who I was, spat back huge chunks of my life: where I was born, went to school, where I lived when I got out of college. Less clear on other things. I saw her at some voodoo ya-ya on the papaya plantation."

"A what?"

"Some voodoo priestess and her cult live down on the plantation. How's that for local color?"

"Real voodoo?"

"Hardly. She's a tourist trap at best and a pure con game at worst. There is a voodoo god called Anansi Coupé. He's a big ass spider and this wailing side of beef has got the natives scared shitless."

"I hate spiders. Who was shot?"

For a long moment Archie let the chilly air fill his coat sleeve as they sped along. "I was downloading what I was paid to get, right, when this gun goes to the back of my head. The place was dead quiet and I didn't hear her come up. Not a fuckin' sound. A little too good for a rent-a-cop out on the islands."

"Possible that she was down there for the same reason you were? For another company?"

"Doesn't explain why she knew all about me. I suppose she could've gotten my name and passport from the hotel, but why? I hadn't done anything strange at that point."

"Who were you at the voodoo ya-ya with?"

Archie shifted in the low seat as the E-type took the ramp off the expressway that took them downtown. "Just some folks I met at the hotel."

"Ah...locals." She trailed off and the silence lasted too long.

Archie grunted.

"I told you that business with DeltaComm was fishy. I said 'Archie huney, you need to watch out. That's nothin' but trouble'." She slapped the steering wheel.

Now Archie looked over. "You didn't say that. You've never called me 'Archie huney'."

"I said something like that. Maybe they're trying to set you up."

"How would DeltaComm explain having me under a service contract? And you didn't say anything like that Bunty."

"Look Asswholio-I know what I said. And if I didn't say it I'm sure I thought it."

"That's not exactly the same, is it?"

"Maybe she was working for a competitor. God knows you've had enough of *those* jobs."

Archie grunted again. Bunty took the E-type up the off ramp that put them downtown. Still Archie said nothing. She maneuvered through the afternoon traffic and let Archie go wherever it was he went in deep thought. They turned onto Monroe Avenue and Bunty roared into the parking garage.

"You're leaving it exposed in this place?"

"Where else would I park it? That castle your dad lives in is a hike from here."

She had a point.

"I have a question." Bunty explained again.

Archie said nothing as they walked down to the street. "It's too much of a coincidence." He started, stepping into traffic.

Bunty went after him but with more caution, "What is?"

"That gal being down there the same time. I suppose it's possible that DeltaComm knew about an attempted break-in and wanted to test the system. Bit of a stretch. Wonder if it could be another buyer, that would drive up the stock price."

"I have a question."

"It is questionable. But that's it. Somebody, a major stockholder, would have known about my contract, gives my info to a competitive bidder – interest is piqued – the price goes up. He'll screw DeltaComm, but he gets out smelling a little richer." Archie clapped his hands, "That's it, that greedy bastard. The question is who's the rat?"

On other side of the street Archie opened the door to the office building that dated from the thirties. A wave of forced heat hit them in the lobby.

"That's it. And somebody knows about my visit to New Orleans…" Archie kept on, "that's how that woman knew who I was." He hit the button for the elevator.

"I have a question." Bunty repeated.

"And that is?"

The doors closed around them. "Who was shot?"

Nausea rolled over Archie's gut and up to his face. Bunty waited for him to speak.

The doors opened and they went into Tantallion Group and sat in the two leather armchairs side by side. "She had a gun in my face. I faked a seizure."

"Clever, what kind of seizure."

"Actually it was diarrhea." He said finally.

"Oh shit."

"Explosive. It put her off, and I knocked her gun to the floor, and took off."

"You faked a poop!"

"You come up with something better with a gun in your face. Who's comfortable around loose bowels? It's awkward. Besides, who'd shoot an unarmed incontinate?"

"What if she'd been a doctor?"

"She'd have to put the gun down to get the block of cheese or whatever it is she'd need to stove up an explosive ass."

"Language. You'll have to feed the cuss jar."

"Ass isn't a cuss word. It's geography."

Bunty conceded that he had a point. "So you got away..."

"She came after me. I kicked the gun off into the darkness but she found it and came after me and took a shot. I fired back. It was pitch black. I heard her hit the floor. I just kept running."

"Maybe she was taking cover. It was dark."

"That's what I keep telling myself. I need to get online and find a Jamaican newspaper."

"Any problem at the airport?"

"No. Entered and left Jamaica as a Brit and entered and left the US as an American." Archie climbed out of the chair and crossed over to the barrister case with the liquor in it. Bunty followed and stopped him before he got there. She took his hand, "Archie, it was self-defense."

"Keep telling myself that too." He said. She was leading him back to the chairs without his realizing it. She sat, he sat. For a long time they were silent. He shook his head violently and asked, "So what's happened on the home front?"

"The Tennis Pro over at the Racquet Club stopped by. He seemed pissed. I thought I'd let you sort it out. Said you'd be back the day after next."

"Christ." He bent forward and took a cigarette out of the box on his desk. "Want one?"

"No thank you." He lit it and inhaled deeply and Bunty didn't stop him. "The big question is what type of redundancy the computer system in Jamaica has."

"Pardon?"

"Redundancy. It's where you have two or more identical systems constantly writing over to the other system, so in case of a fire you don't lose all your information. If the system is efficient, it won't matter that I torched their IT hub, because my doggie-door will have written itself over onto the other box."

"Probably not what they had in mind when they got two systems."

"Probably not." Archie snapped his fingers. "Oh yeah, I've got maybe a quarter million dollars worth of smuggled diamonds in one of my socks."

THE HELICOPTER BANKED LEFT over the Arichipelago de Jareues and Mickey Boy pointed to hulking shape below in the distance. "Cuba." He said.

Miz Cassat craned over to see the island below them from cramped seat of the Mi-28 helicopter-still in use by the Soviets until the late eighties. Another one of the toys Mickey Boy had managed not to return to his Soviet masters. Now the thing was painted a flat black, but beyond that Mickey Boy had made no other modifications. Miz Cassat said nothing, only grunted. "You know," Mickey Boy started again, "For all your magic, Miz Cassat, you aren't too keen on heights. I thought witches could fly." Still she said nothing. "I'll have to blindfold you now."

At this she growled, "How long have you known me, Mickey Boy?"

"How long have you known me, Miz Cassat?"

"It's about to be dark. I couldn't pick the place out if I had to."

Mickey Boy laughed, "You might pick out the right side of the island, that would put you 50% there. Ha! Miz Cassat, I take precautions, as do you." Then he turned to the back of the chopper, "Miguel, if you would be so kind."

Miguel folded the kerchief neatly and leaned forward. "Miz Cassat," he said from just behind her head, "Please." Miguel came from the same village as the late Pedro-and shared his superstitions. He thought it best to be as polite as possible to a witch.

Still Miz Cassat leaned forward and out of Miguel's reach, "You'll dump me over the sea."

"Don't need a blindfold to do that. Besides, I don't want to kill you until the deal has gone through, paid in full." He laughed alone. "It was a joke, Miz Cassat."

She didn't laugh, but figured if he was planning to keep her alive he wouldn't be blinding her. She leaned back and heard Miguel say in Spanish, "Excuse me, Miz Cassat." And the world went black.

The whirling but rhythmic *whup thump* of the rotor blades overhead began the form a pattern like a slow heartbeat in her mind. Now she began to wonder how many other pieces to *the deal* were out there, scattered like the tiny islands below her.

Time in the darkness warps a little. The helicopter dropped onto the concrete pad. The *whup thup whup thup* of the rotor blades suddenly became a thunder as the air moved hit the concrete walls of the pit into which they descended and moved violently back over them, creating winds within winds coming from all sides. The noise was deafening. "Where are we?" she shouted but knew the rotors drowned her out. Then the engines were cut but still air whopped furiously off the walls and back over them. Someone, probably Miguel, opened her door and helped her down to the pad. She sensed machines were moving around her as the rotors finally slowed to a halt.

"Miz Cassat," came Miguel's polite voice, "may I remove your blinds?"

"Now." She spat.

What she saw amazed her. The helipad was sunk 50 feet below the surface into a deep circular concrete pit. It was dim in the pit, but the night was clear and the stars were out. Miz Cassat rubbed her eyes, she was hung over and thought Mickey Boy had probably drugged her as well.

Where the hell was he? She found him a few yards away in the gloom, standing tall in his olive green flight suit. He was speaking to another man in fatigues, he looked like a Russian mechanic. Her eyes crept upward to the clear night above. The stars shone down like perfect pinpoints without a single cloud among them. No, something wasn't right, the stars weren't as they should be. In fact, the Cuban cosmos seemed to exist in well-laid grid. Not a perfect Caribbean night at all, just the ceiling of the bunker.

Her mouth went dry and Miz Cassat licked her teeth. She glared at Mickey Boy and he hit the button for the lift behind the walls the gears began to grind. Finally she began to walk, but slowly, from the helicopter to where Mickey Boy stood rocking on his heels. The door opened. She was going to make the bastard wait.

Mickey Boy stepped into the lighted car and hit a button on the wall, waving to Miz Cassat as the doors slid shut. The cables again began to whir and grind beneath the walls.

When Miz Cassat finally waddled up to the lift, she mashed the single button and listened, the car was still being lowered deep into the earth. Now her anger was turning to fury. She was going to have to get a hold of herself. Eventually the car began to come back up. "Olgen give me focus." She muttered. The gray doors slid open and she stepped in.

There was only one button on the panel of the drab-gray elevator. She hit it and down the car dropped. The grinding of the cables and the wheels above stretched out for seconds then minutes. "How far down am I going?" She muttered before thinking that the car was certainly wired for sound and she'd better keep her cards closer to the chest.

Finally the lift stopped and the doors opened. Miz Cassat found herself in a cavern of a room. The construction of the place had the straight lines and utilitarian air of a military facility. The furnishings were a different story. The room, from one end to the other, was filled with sleek European luxury items. They were grouped into a number of different themed seating areas: one area grouped chrome and black leather sofa and chairs and a glass table, another vignette was red and black lacquer tables that looked like an Italian trying to update Japanese furniture, still another was decidedly German in its futuristic appeal. But nowhere in the 50 square yards of mismatched furniture was Mickey Boy. In fact, there was no one there at all. Then the lift doors closed behind.

Footfalls began to echo off the concrete and stone walls. These were not approaching army boots – these were four-inch heels coming her way. The hallway from which she emerged was dim so Miz Cassat didn't get a good look at her until she was moving past the absurd German chair that looked like it had been stolen off one of the newer *STAR TREK* sets. She was a beautiful Cuban girl dressed in a pale pink Versace suit and *that* was no small miracle on an island like Cuba.

"Miz Cassat." She said politely with a nod. She was one of the most beautiful women Miz Cassat had ever seen: the product of several generations of European, African and Amerindian genetics. A few steps more and Miz Cassat could smell the Chanel perfume. "Come this way." Still polite, but not a request. She nodded again and turned on a stiletto heel.

Into the darkness of the far hallway they went along the walls were no more overpriced settees but gray green steel boxed stenciled in white Cyrillic letters. At places they were stacked eight high. The Cuban girl showed her into an office that shocked her.

The place was stripped of the ostentatious luxury items and looked rather like old photos of the British Raj in India. Mickey Boy was behind a large teak desk, flipping through a thick file. "Miz

Cassat, sorry I lost you. You really need to keep up. Concepión here seems to have tracked you down. Have a seat, excuse the mess, I'm having a fire sale. Got to move that inventory."

"Speaking of inventory," Miz Cassat spat, "Chu is telling me that SinoTel wants their first delivery."

"Yes, I suppose that they do. I received the payment, everything was in order. Strange thing though…got shot at after the pick-up."

She said nothing, could still smell the Chanel.

"You've got a leak, Miz Cassat." Mickey Boy's eyes went to a laser focus.

"I do not. Probably the Cubans."

"There's only one Aqua Riva on this island and I own it. The boat came from Jamaica. Had military hardware. Picked up any new hires lately?"

"No."

"Who are you hanging around with? I don't want to jump to any conclusions, but I've got to assume the Chinese run a tighter ship than a second-rate Carib witch. I hear you've got some Westerners in your flock.

Miz Cassat sneered, "The locals are faithful, but their wallets don't do me no good."

Now Mickey Boy laughed, "I can sympathize." He absently flipped through a few more pages of the manila folder. "Please sit."

"I'm fine."

"Your man Chu – he was in Paris over the New Year."

"I don't know. He travel a lot."

"He was in my store in Paris – we helped him move some Iranian ex-pat out of France." The slight upturn of his lips was unmoving and the rage in Miz Cassat was to the boiling point.

"Mickey Boy! Won't do you no good to cut me out. Robert Chu, he believes."

"In what?"

"The Mojo…he'll poison the Chinese on you."

"You're joking."

"No. He need me, so the Chinese need me. And you be careful the way you talk or I'll put one on you."

Mickey Boy laughed again, "Oh, I haven't got time for that sort of nonsense. So your man at SinoTel thinks you've got a voodoo hex on him. That's fantastic!"

Miz Cassat leaned forward with a snarl, "Oh now, don't you threaten me! He more than 'jest think' about the voodoo! You hear me, I got something better than voodoo-I do and they know it. I got me a U.S. Senator, and an American who sits on the board of six Fortune 500 companies. Word is, he'll run for congress next term. That makes one Senator and one congressman. Got them both in my pocket. The Chinese'll quit your dirty bombs, but a spy is forever."

The smile was still spread across his sunburnt face. "I'm impressed."

Her hulking frame leaned back. She stood proud, arms akimbo. "Oh now! That's right. You'd better be impressed. Now listen here, we jest gonna have business as usual right?"

"Now how have you managed to deliver that pair of fatted calves?" Mickey Boy looked over her shoulder and motioned to someone. The mechanic from the helipad came in with a steel army-issue briefcase at his side. It was wide and reinforced at the corners. "Ivan Petierovich, here." He pointed at his desk. "Miz Cassat here was just about to tell us how a small-fry Jamaican thug passing herself off as a church will deliver…what was it? Yes, one Senator and a future Congressman, to America's number one global enemy, as spies no less."

"Is dat the yellowcake?" she spat.

"That, can wait. You must tell me your scheme."

"Don't you worry about me and the Chinese-I put this deal together and I can take it apart."

Mickey Boy smiled, "Of course you can." He nodded to Ivan who opened the lid. "Ex-soviet yellowcake, Uranium. Not suitable for a warhead. But as you can see, will fit quite nicely in a suitcase."

Miz Cassat looked at the container in the lead-lined case and tried to look like she'd seen the stuff before. "Very good."

Ivan closed the case and took it up and a faint waft of Chanel announced Concepión's entrance. Now she was in a snug flight suit and, as evident from the low front zipper, little else. "Concepión will fly you back to Jamaica, Miz Cassat. Send Robert Chu my regards."

Ivan handed over the case and Cassat was on Concepión's departing footsteps.

"Ah, Ivan Petierovich!" Mickey Boy said when the footfalls faded away, "Let's see what that old dyke thinks about Concepión's Mojo."

Ivan Petierovich looked at Mickey Boy for a long time. "The diamonds she paid you with are not real?"

"Moisionite, Ivan, not worth the bullet it would take to shoot the old cow." Mickey Boy cocked his head, "You didn't give her real Uranium did you?"

"Of course not. You say whip up a kilo of fake Uranium, I'll whip up a kilo of fake Uranium. But the first one who takes a good look at the stuff won't be fooled."

"Oh don't worry about that, I just want to fool our all seeing priestess."

"She paid you with fake diamonds, why not kill her yourself? You aren't getting lazy are you?"

"Old and fat, Ivan Petierovich, old and fat. What I wanted to see was if she knew she'd scammed me. She didn't. As for rubbing her out, well I'll just let the Chinese do that." Mickey Boy drifted off, "still, I wonder about that senator of her's."

AN AFTER HOURS BREAK-IN WOULD HAVE BEEN EASIER, but Vanderhorn's was inpenetratable. At least it was with the equipment Ugly Sue had hauled up from Kingston. She'd have to go in tomorrow, and drop a bug under Makarin's nose. That would be risky. She didn't want to think about it.

Now she stood in the doorway to her own room in the Eureka Hotel and scanned it, locked the door and performed a second sweep. She took the suitcase from the amoiré and powered up the laptop inside. Then she noticed it, the USA TODAY lying on the bed.

Her heart jumped. Taking a pen-sized black light from her case, she turned to the Money section of the paper and passed it over the masthead. *Graceland. Tomorrow. 1ˢᵗ Tour. –R.*

She tore off the masthead and burned it in the bathroom. Then she was on the phone with the concierge, "This is Norah Clark, listen, I just can't stay in Memphis without seeing where Elvis slept. How early do the tours start?"

Nine

Grosser Blood

FRIDAY

ROWAN HAD FIRST CONTACTED HER in Cannes, the only place she actually thought of as home. A summer shower had broken open with instant passion and sent swimmers and sunbathers frantically to their cars and the shelter of waterside cafés. Ugly Sue, still dripping with ocean brine when the clouds broke, threw her cover-up over a modest one-piece swimsuit and towel over her shoulder. She made her way up to the street where her Vespa waited.

The warm rain ran down her face and soon the streets and beaches were deserted. She saw, idling next to her Vespa, a crimson Jaguar. She approached, and the Jaguar didn't move. Her pace slowed and heart quickened.

So this was it. Her own people had finally come to pick her up. After all she'd done-her discovery and ultimate protests-she was now on the outs with her government. They'd let her lay fallow, dangling, for almost a year. Now they'd come for her.

But something was wrong-what was it? Fine hairs on the back of her neck were standing at attention despite the wet. This wasn't a master coming to stamp out an errant servant. The French government would never send its patriots out in Jaguars.

The back door opened and he got out. He was tall, older than she was expecting, but in good shape. Confident and graceful, he emerged from the car as he opened an umbrella. His thick eyebrows struck her as aristocratic and he certainly dressed like one: a flax colored linen suit and an ascot tucked into his open collar. Under the umbrella his French was formal: "You cannot ride the Vespa in the rain, Mademoiselle, it is dangerous."

"Thank you, I can manage."

"I have work for you, Ugly Sue. I wouldn't want to cut short your holiday, but it has been a year."

"What's that?"

He turned and walked back to the car and a driver was holding the door open for them. Then he was sliding next to her and closing the door, shutting out the rain. "They call me Rowan." He said and the driver started the car.

"You said you had some work, Rowan?" She said.

Rowan studied her for a moment, she recognized the name. "I need a man taken out of a very dicey equation.

"You aren't French."

He laughed, "Really…" he said in English, "How about that?"

"They say you're English but you don't sound English to me."

"Is that what they say?"

"I work for France."

"Ugly Sue, you haven't worked for anyone in a year. Not since Iran."

She looked down at her feet like a scolded child. His voice softened. She thought she detected a brogue but that wasn't it. "Governments are bigger than their citizens-Nations have character, but they don't have souls. France isn't the only country selling God knows what to every third world lunatic with a cause. The sin you committed against your country was connecting the dots. We are supposed to remain in our boxes, you and me. To think more takes grosser blood."

"France has no knowledge of-"

"But you do…and you've been blackballed from the only thing you know how to do."

"So what's your offer? Of course, I'll report anything you say to my superiors."

Rowan smiled. "Of course you will, Ugly Sue." It suddenly dawned on her that Rowan, whoever *he* was, knew her real name. "There is an arms dealer in Cuba, an ex-KGB quartermaster. Name is Mikhael Boyorov. I believe you know the Caribbean well."

THE LATE ELVIS AARON PRESLEY'S TASTES IN DÉCOR were not entirely subtle. She spotted the man she knew only as Rowan on the bus taking them up the drive of the outwardly elegant home of the King of Rock & Roll. He still looked like an aristocrat to her: a checked shirt and worn khakis underneath and Barbour thornproof and a crumpled fedora. Rowan never looked at her on the tour bus, but had the unsettling habit of chuckling to himself every time she secreted a glance his way.

In the mansion, they stayed close in the tour group but never made contact. They walked through the jungle room and stood in the blue and yellow TV room with three sets built into the wall.

It wasn't until they reached the gravesite that Rowan approached. Again, his French was formal: "What brings you to Memphis? I understand that Mickey Boy is still quite alive, and I am short one Aqua Riva, among other things."

Ugly Sue glanced quickly at the small crowd that was now moving on from the gravesite to the King's collection of Cadillacs. "There is more to this than a simple arms thug."

"Really? Why, Ugly Sue, that's a hell of a thing." Now his lips were almost touching her ears-his hands firm but gentle on her shoulders. "You weren't paid to be a detective. I have a heavy down payment in you, as well as a dead operative, and my target is still sailing about playing pirates of the Caribbean."

"Rowan, trust me."

"I don't. And won't until you prove yourself. What, exactly, do you think is going on here?"

"Mickey Boy makes his arms money clean somehow. There is a precious metals and diamonds brokerage in the US & Canada called-"

"Vanderhorn's..." Rowan finished, "New Orleans, San Francisco and now, of all places, Memphis. What, exactly is your point? At the present, your target is still operating because, for some reason still unclear to me, he is still alive!" he hissed. "You were supposed to cut off Vanderhorn's head, not give it cancer."

"With all due respect, there is more to this than Mickey Boy."

Letting go of her shoulders, Rowan laughed in the cold morning fog. "Always the soldier. Yes, there is more. And my desk still needs you, but only if you finish the job you've been paid to do. If you can't finish the job you're useless to me. A liability, really."

Ugly Sue said nothing.

"Speaking of being paid, my dear, I also understand that not only is Mickey Boy still alive-he rather a bit richer for his troubles-"

"No he's not. His down payment isn't real."

"Clarify."

"I replaced the diamonds that voodoo mama was sending him with moisenite replacements."

Rowan smiled, "Clever girl. So where are the diamonds."

"That's my business-"

"Your business is my business, Ugly Sue." He guided her closer to the pink Cadillac, "Beau Barrendo…I believe that he was a friend of yours?"

She swallowed hard, "Yes?"

"Dead…cardiac arrest in a brothel. The local police seem to think it was a drug overdose."

"Who?"

Rowan shrugged, "Can't say for sure. Spiders all over the place I understand. Damned strange."

"All I want is a name. I'll do the rest, for free."

"You'll finish your job before you start your hobbies." Rowan continued, "Our man in Panama delivered to us an…alarming document, to say the least. Forty-eight hours later he disappeared from a job site as did his asset who recovered the document. Then operatives began to be liquidated."

"There will be an investigation?"

Rowan stepped away, "Eventually, I suppose I'll conduct an informal one. No agencies involved."

"Beau was a friend."

"He was also deniable…just like you. A homosexual with no family dies in a tramp brothel. It isn't an international crisis. Yet here you are, in Memphis with your knickers full of smuggled diamonds, not in Cuba at all…and the question is why?"

It had started raining harder, there was sleet mixed in, and the group moved for cover. "After the attempt, he'll go low- Mickey boy that is. I want to be able to get to him."

"So why did you come here?" Rowan hissed.

Ugly Sue stopped and took a step back defensively. "There was another operative. He was at the facility in Jamaica."

"What where you doing there?"

"That voodoo priestess Mickey Boy is hooked up with-she's the front. Acts as a sort of broker for his arms deals." Rowan glared at her and for the first time since becoming the thing that was Ugly Sue, she wanted to run. Run far. She gritted her teeth and pressed on. "How do you think I knew where the target was going to be out in the middle of the sea just then? I'm getting close to Miz Cassat…I was at her campy voodoo service."

"Why were you at the SinoTel facility? I'm not paying you to snoop around. Need I remind you how dangerous connecting the dots can be?"

"Why is it such-"

"Those are my reasons! Answer the question!"

The pressure was building inside her head, "There is another operative, he was with Tara Oaks, the daughter of Walt Oaks he's-"

"I know who Walter Oaks is!"

"He was with her – looked out of place – I went to the facility to see if I could connect him to the target. She was speaking so quickly that Rowan was having trouble following her French.

"Yes." He said in English.

"The operative was there. Since the target had gone underground, I followed the op to see if he'd lead me to the target. He came here. A fellow named Gilmur."

Rowan squeezed his eyes shut. "Why is the target, Mickey Boy, still moving?"

"Rowan, this is part of a bigger puzzle!"

"You were sent to hit a target, not put together a puzzle. Isn't this why your government put you to the curb in the first place? I want a report. Everything you've got so far, on this mystery operative too. And get back to work. If Mickey Boy is still hiding in Cuba…go to Havana. You'll catch a flight from Kingston!"

"What was in that report from the Chinese?"

Rowan leaned in close. "A deadline, Ugly Sue. One of you will be dead in ten days."

ARCHIE HAD SEEN Hasidic diamond merchants in London, Antwerp, and New York going to and fro. He knew that they might be carrying several hundred thousand dollars worth of diamonds on them: in a coat pocket or in a greasy paper bag. The theory behind that insanely lax security system was that it was less conspicuous than titanium briefcases shackled to the wrist. You could get you arm cut off doing that...nobody ever got robbed for their tuna salad sandwich. It was a sound enough theory for Archie. With Miz Cassat's diamonds in his pants pocket next to his other jewels, Archie ascended the narrow staircase Uncle Derrick had told him about.

At the top of the flight, he opened the door and stepped into a Plexiglas walled alcove. A buzzer sounded and Archie stepped into the showroom.

"Welcome to Vanderhorn's!" exclaimed the old Russian with a face like a saddlebag. Viktor Makarin drummed his fingers on the spotless glass case. "What can I do for you, Mr. ah..."

"Archie Gilmur!" Dickey O'Shea called as he stepped out of the back hallway, "How the hell are you?"

Archie found himself laughing for some reason he couldn't quite place. "Hey Dickey, how are ya? You in the diamond biz now?"

"Not quite. Heard dat you were in Ireland." Dickey asked, coming around the front of the case and settling into a chair.

"I'm back. I thought a boy-chick like you would be on the receiving end of the gifts"

Dickey showed a charming glint of teeth, "Must be losing my touch. So...getting married or just in trouble?"

"There's a difference?"

Vik's foreign accent purred, "Vhat's vrong with Amoré? You two a couple of fags?"

Archie turned to Vik, "Now how the hell do you expect to sell me a $15,000 hunk of pressurized coal if you call me a fag?"

Vik pointed to Dickey, "Bad influence. What can I get for you? Something for a bonnie Irish lass?"

"If there was a bonnie Irish lass in the picture, I'd still be in Dublin."

Dickey slouched back in an arm chair, "Mr. Makarin, I think the bonnie lass is who drove Mr. Gilmur out of Ireland. Like the pied piper."

Archie found the conversation tiresome. "Speaking of snakes." Archie said as he kicked the heel of a blunnie boot into Dickey's crotch.

By the time Dickey had slumped onto his knees, testicles in hand, Vik was in a fit of schoolgirl giggles, "Mr. Gilmur, you shouldn't rob a man of his livelihood."

"So Ivan-" Archie started.

"Viktor Borisavich-"

"Of course. So, is this place a pawn shop?"

Vik became very serious and didn't seem to realize that Dickey had leaned over so dramatically that his chair was about to tip over. "As you are no doubt aware Mr. Gilmur-diamonds and precious metals are commodities and those who trade in them have made and lost great fortunes. No, this is not...vhat you say...a pawn shop."

Finally the chair tipped and Dickey hit the floor, still holding his jewels. "Godammit Archie!"

Vik peered to the floor. "Please don't harass the other clients, Mr. O'Shea. Now, is there something I can do for you Mr. Gilmur?"

"There is." Archie fished a small velvet sack out of his coat pocket. Gently, he emptied the diamond into his palm.

Vik's eyes lit up. "Very nice – you want it mounted?"

"Well yes, but there is more to it than that. You see, this was originally part of a pair and I'd like you to find me a matching one."

Vik put a glass in his eye, "Hmmm... blue-white, internally flawless, or very near, table cut. Very nice, Mr. Gilmur"

"Family piece – originally in a set of earrings. They were split up during an inheritance dispute."

"Yes..." Vik said, still enthralled by the diamond. "...family is a wonderful thing. Would you mind if I had a closer look at the piece...it is quite exquisite."

Now Dickey had hoisted himself off the floor, "For fuck's sake!"

Archie shrugged his shoulders helplessly. "I can only be me." Then to Vik, "Please, could we go in the back? Not that I don't appreciate the peanut gallery."

"Very well. Mr. O'Shea, will you excuse us?" They walked into the short back hallway and Archie bent over to tie his shoe, hopped forward, and found himself alone in Vik's office. He was able to scan the room twice before Vik cleared his throat behind him. "Ah hem, the lab is the other way."

The lab was a small room fitted with the machinery of the jeweler's trade: Sets of tiny and well-organized tools, cleaners and magnifiers. Vik was already putting the stone under the lens of a huge gray electric magnifier when Archie strolled in. "Mr. Makarin, how long ya been here?"

"Not long. I came from New Orleans, a disaster. Please excuse the mess." He was studying the diamond intently. Suddenly Archie needed to sit down. He gripped the door jamb, "Really, New Orleans…where was your place?"

Vik's head never came up from the eye-piece, "In the French Quarter."

"A bit risky for a diamond broker."

At this Vik laughed, still without moving his head. "You could say I'm an expert on security measures." Then his head came up from the eye-piece, "May I hold onto the stone while I search for the match? To ensure we get as close as possible. Of course, in addition to my security measure here, I am quite insured."

"Certainly."

"A family piece, eh? Do you know what happened to the other?"

"Couldn't say. An aunt of mine got it, but she's got a gambling problem. I think the old bat fenced it."

Archie was picturing Bunty, a block away in the office guarding the other stones. What he didn't see was that Bunty, at that actual moment, was prancing around in front of a mirror with her sweater pulled up and a diamond in her belly button.

"Interesting." Vik mumbled to himself.

They emerged ten minutes later, Dickey was again in the righted chair, studying a small gold pendent. He looked up but said nothing. Vik was clapping Archie on the shoulder, "Mr. Gilmur, I shall call you when I've located what you seek."

"Thank you." Archie said as they shook hands, "Look forward to it." He stopped, "Dickey, always a pleasure. Let's do lunch sometime."

"Yeah fuck you too."

The buzzer sounded and Vik watched the door long after Archie had disappeared down the stairwell.

Turning onto the sidewalk, Archie retrieved his mental snapshot of Vik's office: the box that he had at first taken to be an intercom was coupled between the line and the phone, which really isn't where an intercom ought to be installed. Archie didn't know a great deal about phones, but he had been pretending to be an executive from DeltaComm Communications Firm. *Odd what you picked up without really trying.* Stranger still about Vik's intercom was that there wasn't anyone to call, no secretary and no place to put one.

Fishing his cell phone out of his coat pocket, Archie began to scroll through the numbers. A well-tanned woman with long dark hair passed him quickly. She was speaking rapidly on a cell phone, her hair covering her face. Quickly she passed without making eye contact. The tiniest whiff of perfume hit his nostrils and the hair stood straight on the back of Archie's neck.

He stopped and spun around as a small voice came over his line. A pair of well-shaped legs disappeared up the stairwell to Vanderhorn's. The perfume had passed and was replaced by the faint exhaust and smells of city garbage. Still the memory of the scent lingered. He took a step towards Vanderhorn's when the voice on the line boomed with an annoyed brogue. "Bloody Hell, Archie, I know it's you!"

"Uncle Derrick-"

"I said hello five times boy, I thought I was the deaf one!"

"And you'll always be the deaf one to me, Uncle Derrick. I mean that."

"What's the drama, m'lad? Did you get my message?"

"No. Look, I'm just leaving that diamond broker. Don't buy anything from Vanderhorn's, it's probably all hot."

There was a sound of rustling papers over the line and Uncle Derrick started again. "Really, how intriguing. What makes you say that?"

"Dickey O'Shea was in there."

"Who the devil is that?"

"A real shithook I went to McAlistar with. He's from an Irish Traveler clan, can't reckon how he found a boarding school in East Tennessee. Think his momma, she left the clan, worked at the school. Anyway, I understand he went into the army and came out an interior designer.

"So he's a pikey, that's queer but not illegal."

"He's a thief. Always has been, he almost got sacked from McAllister for it."

Again another pause. Derrick seemed to be taking notes. "...and how does that make Mr. Makarin a crooked?"

Archie sensed that Uncle Derrick already knew the answer. "It doesn't, necessarily, doesn't help either. Why would a legitimate broker have a Clayborne scrambler on his phone?"

"Security reasons."

"This isn't a corporate precaution, it isn't even a retail item. It's for government use only."

"How would you know that?"

"I've spent the last week living and breathing all things DeltaComm and SinoTel. I went through the government inventory on the plane."

Derrick laughed. "You're working too hard, m'lad. I like it. Thanks for the legwork." Another pause, he was writing again. "...oh, and I think I'll go through my regular man on those diamonds."

Back inside Vanderhorn's it was tense. Vik Makarin was annoyed with Dickey, who was still slumped in the chair by the display case. "I'm trying to run a business here!"

"Yeah you're an up and up guy."

The buzzer sounded and both turned toward the beautiful but otherwise unremarkable woman in the glassed alcove. Vik buzzed her in and both couldn't help but take in those long legs bringing her across the room. Dickey popped out of the chair, his disfigured crotch miraculously cured. "My name is Norah Clark." she said, her hand thrust confidently at Dickey.

"Dickey O'Shea." He said with a smile.

"I understand that you are an independent precious stones and metals broker. I don't need some milksop running to corporate all the time."

Vik cleared his throat, "Ma'am, I am the proprietor of Vanderhorn's. " He bowed his head formally, "Viktor Makarin, at your service."

She looked hard at Dickey, "-and who are you?"

"He is a loyal customer. Nothing more."

Dickey smiled widely, "Who appreciates objects of great beauty."

"I've got a gun." Ugly Sue mentioned with a charming smile.

"God that's hot."

She stared at Dickey until the moment became awkward and Dickey's face went blank. Ugly Sue placed a sleek briefcase on the display case and turned to Vik. "Mr. Makarin, if you can loose the peanut gallery-I've got something you're just going to die for."

Ten

Boiling Brer Rabbit

FRIDAY NIGHT

TARA OAKS INSPECTED THE SCAR RUNNING from the corner of her mouth and straight back to her ears. She inspected the other cheek in the bathroom mirror for reference, and turned to the new scar. In truth it was really an angry scratch-which was a pity because it was fading and Tara was starting to like it. Her sunburnt skin made the fresh jag seem well worn. Then she tried on a hat with an enormous sunflower on the front, tried on a few pouts for the mirror, and tossed the ridiculous thing onto the floor.

From downstairs she could hear her mother and that decorator bickering about overhauling the house in Louis XVI, and was that really appropriate for a diplomatic delegation from China? Vivian Oaks' shrill voice cracked through the marble foyer, "Oh for Chrissakes Dickey! Those awful people aren't flying halfway around the world to watch me imitate the Laundromat in their backyard!"

Dickey was laughing. "No wonder Mr. Oaks left you here. Now they may not be coming to see the Imperial City but they aren't coming to see Storyville either." Dickey leaned in to share a final tidbit, "I assume they go to New Orleans for that."

Vivian dismissed him, "Hell, it'll keep them on their toes, Dickey, it's good for them. Besides, it wasn't my idea to throw the party on the Mardi Gras."

Tara suspected that Dickey was stuffing her mom-and Tara was just going to have to get to the bottom of that one. Might be good for a little more slack on the trust fund. She came out of the bathroom and ascended the top of the marble staircase in a pair of black lizard skin pants and a gold lamé top.

"Well hello nurse!" said Dickey to her pert, unsupported breasts. He was standing in the entrance hall with her mother.

"Hi." She cooed. "I'm Tara, Mommy's naughty daughter."

"Tara Oaks," Vivian whined, "Dickey O'Shea – Dickey here is a master of colors."

"That's not his only talent, I hear." Now she was drifting downstairs.

"You're going out in that?" Vivian asked. It's forty five degrees outside!"

"Oh, I'll just find some strong man to keep me warm." Tara touched Dickey's arm.

"A coat might put up less of a fight." Vivian pointed out.

"Dickey, you're not going to work all night are you?"

"I've got a party to host!" said Vivian, watching the stupid grin on Dickey's face grow wider. "Oh he's pulling an all nighter that's for sure. I'm not paying him to sleep."

"I'll bet." Tara winked at him and made her way back to the kitchen.

"That child." Said Vivian, "I wish she were more like her sister."

"No, you don't," said Dickey, "Vivie takes after Walt-dependable and boring. Tara takes after you."

Vivian smiled at this, "Yeah, we may be here for a long time tonight."

Outside Tara slipped into the Lexus roadster that gleamed under the porch light like red enamel. She slid into the leather seat and guided the car around the house and didn't floor it until she was careening down the wide circular driveway. Guiding the roadster with force through the walled subdivision, past the enormous houses that filled the huge lots, the heater roared against the frigid night as her nipples pointed the way forward. Checking herself once more in the rear-view mirror while the gate opened up, she roared onto a public street and made her presence known to the masses.

IN HER ROOM AT THE EUREKA HOTEL, Ugly Sue studied the global positioning sevice before her. She knew where she was, but the receiver she'd planted under the bumper of Miss Oaks' car was now moving. Dropping all four legs of the chair to the floor, Ugly Sue studied the data pouring forth from the GPD...the girl was moving fast.

Then she was on her feet, slipping into a black cocktail dress hanging on the amoiré door. Ugly Sue pulled on the dress and smoothed the wide satin ribbon across her flat stomach. It tied in a bow over her rear. That sort of flummery generally wasn't what Ugly Sue went in for, but it did hide the pistol in the small of her back. She took up a small black purse and was still studying the GPD as she stepped out into the hall.

The roadster was moving west toward the hotel.

IN THE PARLENCE OF A MORE ELOQUENT TIME, the act of copping a look down a ladies neckline for an eyeful of cleavage was referred to as "gazing down Pennsylvania Avenue." Pennsylvania Avenue...precisely the boulevard down which Frank Gilmur now peered. Bunty was bent over the kitchen counter, reading a newspaper article about the crawfish farm the family owned in Louisiana. Derrick, whose 'wee Midge' was standing nearby, had been more discreet. Frank recovered his manners and looked away. Archie was staring at him, reached into his Redbreast and shot a sliver of ice at his father's forehead. Archie missed, but not by much.

"Sorry."

Bunty looked up, "What are you boys doing?"

"Nothing!" they said in unison.

Midge, who had witnessed the whole thing, just shook her head and announced she was going to bed early.

Bunty swayed her hip into Archie and smiled at Frank and Derrick, "So what are you two silver foxes going to do tonight? Whip some poor bastard in cards again?"

"My dear, at our age the options are limited." Said Derrick.

"Somehow I doubt that."

Derrick shook his head. "To be in Archie's clothes tonight. Where are you two going?" The old Scot's flirtations were such a part of him that Bunty figured he wasn't aware of it. Still, though, after all these years, it seemed to annoy Midge. Bunty would have never played along but that Midge seemed to be a woman who liked being annoyed.

"I'm taking Archie out tonight…to see a show, the boy needs to relax."

"He needs to find himself a girl!" Midge divined grandly.

"Midge," Frank pointed out, "he's standing right there."

"Little brother, I know that. Archie you need a girl. A nice one."

"Aunt Midge, I think you're right."

Then she turned to Bunty, "Bunty, you're a girl."

Bunty double checked, just to be sure, "Mrs. Gordon, I think you're right."

"I noticed that too." Said Frank.

"I saw you notice." Midge sneered.

"Oh it's alright," said Derrick, "I figured it out too."

Midge rolled her eyes, "Naturally."

"Can we stop?" asked Archie, "please." Then to Bunty, who was blushing madly, "You – let's get the hell out of here."

"To the Jag!" she declared.

"No, ya silly bitch, we're returning the E-type to it's lair. We take the Scout."

"I think we've located why you haven't got a girl."

"Bunty, help my godson out. You're a girl."

"Bloody hell, not this again!"

Frank leaned forward, "Stay strong son."

"Bunty! To the Scout."

"Alright Asswholio." Then she stood defiantly, arms akimbo, and proudly said, "I'm a girl."

Outside the boy helped the girl into the Jaguar. Archie wasn't clear how that had happened. The engine turned over and idled for a full minute before backing out of the driveway.

Tara had put up the top of the roadster and was lighting another cigarette when she saw the E-Type come out of the driveway. She let the car move up half a block before starting the car and slowly moving after him. There was no hurry – she knew the subdivision well and there was only one way out.

Still further back, down the street and across an intersection Ugly Sue's Ford Taurus rental was blocked by a huge Georgian house. The GPS lit up and Ugly Sue watched for a moment to let the roadster out of sight before starting after it.

For a caravan of three, it was a short drive. Archie looked into the rearview mirror. "Someone's following us." He said flatly.

"You're just paranoid."

The E-Type pulled into a parking lot across the street from Newby's and Tara pinched her lip when she saw the girl get out of the passenger seat. She roared on, putting her cell phone to her ear to hide her face, unaware of the Taurus lagging behind.

THE SILK SHEETS HAD SLID AWAY FROM THEIR BODIES and in the dim moonlight coming through the second story window, Dickey watched his tanned hands grip the white of Vivian's round hips as she pulled him into her. Vivian flexed her thick waist into him, her painted nails scratched his thighs while she pressing her enormous bosom toward him. *The older ones really were better at this*, Dickey thought.

Vivian was saying something dirty to him. Dickey hoped that it wasn't anything requiring more that a grunt because he was tapping all his brainpower to morph Vivian's face into Tara's. Then her nails where coming through his tousled hair and brought his face into the enormous divide of her bosom. There, Tara could not compete. Somewhere beyond Vivian's guttural groans and rasping breaths Dickey heard a tiny electric version of *Danny Boy*. The first bar, repeated once then again. Someone was calling his pants, slung over the end of the bed. If Vivian was aware of it, she didn't react.

Vivian rolled him on his back, fresh air bathed his face before she mounted him and the close musty air pressed between them.

Dickey had no idea how much time had passed. Vivian had actually gotten rid of the clock she'd gotten as a wedding gift. She was out and nothing would wake her now-spread eagle on her back. Dickey was confined to a teetering edge of the mattress, grateful for the dim light.

Rolling off the bed, he pulled on his pants and checked the call log. One message, one new number: *Naughty Tara* it read. The little vixen had gotten a hold of his phone. He listened to the message, "Hey Dickey, when you're finished with my mom come down to Newby's – Endangered Species is playing – it's cold."

He dressed quickly.

ARCHIE PAID THE COVER FOR HE AND BUNTY and the enormous rectangular bouncer waved them in. "I think we were followed." Archie said over the dim of the crowd, mostly postcollegiate sorts who hadn't conceded to family life. The band hadn't started yet and Cheap Trick was blaring over the stereo.

Bunty waved him off, "Archie, leave it – nobody followed us. Enjoy the show, you're working too hard." They moved through the bar and into a messy brick enclave that connected the place to an old movie-theater. Bands played there, it made them feel big. Bunty waved at a girl who was enraptured with a young man in an expensive suit. "Oh look, there's Penelope – she's loose – I ought to introduce y'all, that might distract you."

"What about Molly Pratt?"

"Y'all are finished, forget about her."

"How do you know that?"

"Bunty knows all."

"Convenient." Archie looked back to the door for the second time.

"The all-knowing Bunty needs a beer."

By instinct, they had arrived at the bar. "I need a girl beer and a Redbreast over ice."

The bartender stared at him, "I got plenty of girl beer, what's that other thing?"

"Forget it, just give me a Jack Daniels."

Bunty scanned the room again, "Hey Archie, I've got a question...what does your Uncle Derrick do?"

"He's in construction."

Bunty was about to say something and stopped, her eyes went icy and cold. Archie turned.

"Archie Gilmur! How about that?" screamed Tara. She wrapped her arms around his neck and kissed him full on the mouth.

"Hey Tara – I thought that you were in Jamaica."

"Can't spend all my time in the sun."

"Bunty Carrick, this is Tara Oaks. Her big sister was a friend of mine in high school."

Tara leaned in to Bunty. "I hadn't seen Archie here in years since he and Vivie were such a hot item. Then I see him in Jamaica-"

"How about that." Said Bunty.

"Who are you here with, Tara?"

"...So imagine my surprise when I woke up in bed with the man Vivie almost married."

"Beg pardon?" asked Archie.

142

"I'm gonna go see what Penelope's up to." Before Archie could stop her, Bunty was weaving her way to Penelope, still chatting up the fella in a suit suspiciously well-pressed suit for ten o'clock on a Friday night.

"What was that all about, little girl?"

Tara sucked the straw of the pink cocktail in her small hands. "Did I say too much? I played down the shower. So what's with the girl? Listen, you never told me, what happened in Ireland?"

"My God, what happened to your face?"

"Oh the scar, isn't it cool?"

"Only if you're a man called Horse."

She touched Archie's face, "It matches yours."

"Well just think of the hideously deformed children we'll have." He was looking for Bunty but couldn't find her. Then someone else passed into his field of vision. "Good God!" He left Tara where she stood.

Endangered Species cut into their first song and there was a rush through the darkness to the stage. Over Penelope's shoulder, Bunty watched Archie cross the room and knew instantly that he wasn't coming toward her. Tara looked after Archie and then saw her as well.

When Ugly Sue finally spotted Tara, she hadn't expected to see her with Archie Gilmur and now he was closing the gap between them.

"Damn I'm glad I didn't kill you!" Archie blurted out. He touched her arm.

His touch shocked Ugly Sue. She didn't draw her arm away. *Guilt*, she thought, *He actually feels guilty for shooting at me.*

"Don't worry," she said, now focusing enough to slowly removed her elbow from his hand, "it happens all the time."

"Really? That's a hell'ova thing. Lemme buy you a drink, Danger Girl."

"I don't think so, you're the dangerous one."

"You aren't dead."

"You're a lousy blind shot." She added. "What are you shooting?"

"H&K P7."

"Nice." She smiled, "You seem to have recovered from your bout of dysentery."

"Beg pardon?" He was pointing her to the bar, his hand in the small of her back.

"The issue you had just before you hammered my wrist and tried to kill me."

For the first time, Archie noticed the bruise on her wrist. "Yes well, sorry about that. I lied. Now why did you shove that gun in my face? What are you drinking? I'm trying to get a Redbreast, but I don't think they've got any." He flagged the bartender, "Jack and soda." He turned to Ugly Sue again, "What do you want on your ice?"

"I'll have a Benedict."

Archie turned to the bartender, "Can you do that?"

"Benedict? Sure."

"Thanks." Back to Ugly Sue, "Of course he can make a Benedict, but he's never heard of Redbreast. Well, sorry about the wrist, you really ought not sneak up on folks like that-it takes people off guard."

"Sort of the point." She couldn't believe she had said it.

The bartender set the drinks before them, Archie paid. "So why shove a gun in my face, what were you playing at? And how the hell did you get the thumbnail sketch of my life and, more to the point, why?"

"Who do you work for?"

"Deltacomm, on contract, I told you that the last time you asked me. Maybe you found the gun distracting…I did. By the way what's your name?"

"Norah."

"Norah huh, well you're clearly lying." Archie took a sip of his drink. "Well at least there isn't a beautiful dead body riddled with my bullets on some damn papaya plantation."

They stared at each other for a long time, finally Ugly Sue peered over her shoulder at the dancing throng. "It looks like your girlfriend found a new beau."

Archie searched the room for Bunty but Ugly Sue nodded in the direction to Tara. In front of the band she was writhing in a sloppy grind with Dickey O'Shea.

"What the hell's he doing here?" they both muttered, looked at each other and took a step apart. Tara turned caught sight of Archie and grinding her rear into Dickey's hips. She smiled at him defiantly.

"So what's the deal with you and the Oaks girl?" Ugly Sue asked. "You've been to Hong Kong?"

"I travel a lot on business. Just like you."

"What do you do? Aside from breaking into manufacturing labs in the middle of the night?"

"Security consultant."

"That's no good, I'm using that line." Archie laughed. "Wow! that Tara's a limber little thing."

She was on her haunches, her knees set wide from her body, her head inches away from Dickey's gyrating hips.

"Where'd a Southern boy from Scotland like you pick up that taste for Redbreast Irish Whisky?"

"Where do you think?" He looked back to the dance floor-Tara and Dickey were making out amid the smoking lights. "So what brings you to Memphis...Norah...to make sure your Miz Cassat gets into Walt Oaks' safe? By the by, I don't believe the voodoo ya-ya for a second.

"Oh, I was just checking out the local color."

Archie stared at her face. Her eyes seemed to pass through haze he couldn't read. "The con is a fairly simple one. What I can't figure out is how you fit into it."

"Maybe I don't."

The all-knowing Bunty broke away from Penelope and her well-pressed man and came to them. "Hey Bunty," Archie said, "This is the gal I tried to kill in Jamaica."

"Nice to meet you, Bunty Carrick."

Ugly Sue took her hand, "Nice to meet you Bunty, Norah Clark."

"Norah here is clearly lying about her name." Archie added cheerfully.

"Norah honey," Bunty drawled, "You're lucky to be alive, Archie doesn't miss much." She turned to Archie, "And you, after sleeping with Tara, you're lucky you haven't got the clap."

"I didn't stuff anybody. Can we just listen to band?" On the dance floor, Dickey was giving Tara's ear a good plunging with his tongue.

Ugly Sue looked at Bunty, "Let's go to the bathroom."

"That doesn't sound like a good idea at all." Archie said. "Let's all have another drink."

"No offense, Norah," said Bunty, "But you pull guns on people."

Archie moved behind Ugly Sue and put his hand over the bow at the small of her back. "She's armed. Miss Norah, it's illegal to bring firearms into a bar. And there's a cop right there."

"Mr. Gilmur, let's go into the other room where it's a little quieter. Bunty, lovely to meet you, would you excuse us?"

"What happened to the bathroom?" asked Archie, "You know once I get the idea into my head it's all I can think about."

"Mr. Gilmur, your spastic bowels won't get you out of this one. Now can we talk alone?"

"Bunty can hear anything I can hear."

"Then tell her later if you have to."

"Archie, it's okay."

"Want to step outside?"

"I'd rather not." She said. They moved out the old theater and back into the other bar. It was in the back, near the fire exit, where they found a tiny booth lit by a tiny banker's lamp and table with a backgammon board built into it. The pieces of the game were evidently the marriage of about half a dozen different sets.

They squeezed into the tiny booth and sat with their foreheads inches apart. "You wear Chanel No. 5."

Ugly Sue smiled, "You're wearing Bay Rhum. I thought that went out with colonial wars."

"I'm a traditionalist."

Ugly Sue took a deep breath and looked around, "Mr. Gilmur, I don't think that you know what you're involved with here."

"Care to enlighten me?"

"I'm going to ask you again. What were you doing in Jamaica?"

"I'm just like you-a security consultant. We're just alike. My name isn't Norah though." He snapped his fingers, "Oh that's right, neither is yours. That's two things we've got in common."

"Mr. Gilmur, this is serious. Rowan may be able to call me off your case, but the Russian is a different story."

"Mighty neighborly of Rowan."

"This isn't funny!" Ugly Sue growled. "The Russian doesn't give a shit about Rowan or his money."

"Miss Jones, everybody gives a shit about money." Then for some reason Archie couldn't place he finished, "I can handle the Russian."

"That boy-toy Tara Oaks is with-what's his part in all this?"

"He's small fry-just a petty thief-forget about Dickey. My turn, why do you want in Walt Oaks' safe?"

"Look, Archie Gilmur, man with no home, we are the same. Both work for Rowan and in the same capacity. He doesn't want his deniables connecting the dots. You know how he is. Rowan will have us both killed."

Despite the flogging Frank and Uncle Derrick given him over the card table, Archie had a remarkably good poker face. He never lost eye contact with Ugly Sue and was sure she did not detect the sinking churn in his gut. "I've been briefed. Now just what the hell do *you* think is going on?"

Suddenly the image of Brer Rabbit, poised to throw that first fateful punch at that tar baby, flashed into his mind.

Inside the old theater the band was giving it their all. Bunty had been approached by two fellas almost simultaneously and was now enjoying the show as they tried to peacock for her attention. They looked oddly alike-save that one was taller and fatter-and seemed to share a common personality. Bunty taunted and teased them and decided then and there that she'd go dance with the first one to have an original thought. Then the band announced that it was taking a break. Now she'd have to settle for drinking the winner under the table.

"Aw swell," she muttered. From the dance floor came Tara dragging Dickey in tow.

"Hey there!" Tara sang, "Listen, sorry about earlier. Didn't mean to run your boyfriend off."

"You didn't, we just work together."

Now the two lotharios were reassessing the situation with Tara and Dickey in the mix. Sure there would be more competition, but with Tara, who carried herself like a devoted slut, the final prize was well-defined.

"You work with Archie?" asked Dickey. Tara didn't like the way this was developing. "I went to school with him. Y'all in the diamond business now?"

"Hardly."

The shorter of the two lotharios leaned back on the bar, "Now look," he said to everyone, "I can out-charm the tall one here, but the boy-chick is just plain better looking than me."

Bunty laughed and touched the end of his nose, "We have a winner."

"Pardon?"

"That was clever. Buy me a drink. A cosmo."

"Let me get that." Said Dickey.

"You'd better get two!" spat Tara.

"Funny boy's getting mine."

Funny boy smiled at Bunty and ordered a cosmo.

"So is Archie seeing anybody?" Tara asked.

"I don't get into his personal business, Tara-" Bunty tried to sound exasperated.

"I'm kind of a physco-chick sometimes."

"Really?"

"Her mom's a real rabbit boiler too," chimed Dickey. "The apple doesn't fall far from the tree. Now what exactly do you and Archie do... exactly?"

"We're lion tamers."

"I see I'm not going to charm this out of you."

"Funny boy's got you by one."

Funny boy handed Bunty her drink but was now having second thoughts. He could see his tall, fat former nemesis across the room, chatting up some reasonably pretty thing without any competition at all. "I gotta piss." He said and walked off to the bathroom.

Bunty shook her head and looked at Tara, "Little girl, you can sure thin out a crowd."

"No really," Dickey nagged, "What is it that y'all do."

Tara stomped her foot. "Where is Archie by the way?" She didn't wait for an answer but moved away quickly out of the old theater.

ARCHIE, BEING A QUICK STUDY, quickly realized that Viktor Makarin was not the Russian Ugly Sue had been talking about.

"After the Cuban missile crisis, the US assumed that there were no nuclear devices in Cuba. But the Russians kept smuggling the stuff in with food staples – from France and Spain of all places. For thirty years, the Soviets dumped their excess nuclear material in the jungles of Cuba."

Archie leaned in, "But without any missiles, how did they hope to deliver the warheads?"

"Conventional air power. Dirty bombs. The grand plan had been to build sites further away, say in Nicaragua. Remember? Communism was supposed to sweep across South America. But that never happened. The fact is they wanted to point their spear at the soft underbelly of Capitalist America."

"But the Empire crumbled-we out spent them."

"And the Kremlin recalled their soldiers from the far reaches of the Empire. The smart ones stayed put. So what if they lost their lousy jobs and pensions. They weren't being paid anyway, hadn't been for months. They lived like kings strong arming the locals anyway, the rubles didn't really matter."

Archie digested this information and wished desperately he hadn't let Bunty talk him into going out. "So why now? So why does Rowan suddenly want Mickey Boy dead?"

"A document surfaced from a CIA operative in Panama. The Chinese were planning to pick up where the Russians left off. Only they aren't taking over South America with guns and dogma-they're doing it with money."

"...And they're paying for Mickey Boy's outdated yellowcake with untraceable diamonds."

"Yes." She said after a moment. She smirked.

The name on the note came to Archie after struggling on the skirts of his memory for most of her explanation. "Tell me Ugly Sue, where did the diamonds come from?"

The code name took her by surprise. She looked around and stammered, "I can't say for certain."

"But we can guess Africa. The Chinese are…uh.. making themselves known there." Since living in Dublin, Archie had been a loyal reader of *The Economist* so he was good at faking expertise on any number of world affairs.

Ugly Sue looked at him hard. "That's the assumption."

"And this Miz Cassat you're hooked up with, she's acting as some sort of broker between Mickey Boy and the Chinese. Why do they need her at all?"

"Muddies the water. Quite frankly, she's in over her head. Either Mickey Boy or the Chinese are going to liquidate her soon enough."

"She was your way to get to Mickey Boy?"

"You try and find some ex-KGB quartermaster holed up in a mountain fortress in Cuba."

"Good point. I'm glad we're on the same page. While I'm flattered, curious, and more than a little disturbed by the attention you've paid me-" Archie leaned in, "-there has been a mistake."

"Archie."

"Look, you've got the wrong guy. I really was just checking a security system."

"Archie," she touched his hand before he could say anything, "I believe you but the fact is-and listen, don't try to interpret-I'm not the only one who's got the wrong idea about you. You've managed to get on the radar of some bad people. People who won't sit for a little chat to clear things up. How did you get my code?"

"Ugly Sue. How the hell did you get a code like that?"

"Focus Archie."

"I put it together. Your name was in Miz Cassat's house."

"Where are you with Rowan?"

"Let's not connect anymore dots, Ugly Sue."

Tara, her breasts cold behind a thin veil of lamé, bounded out of the darkness. "Well hello Archie Gilmur-hey your girlfriend in the other room is being hit on. Listen, Archie babe, you're starting to creep me out with all this lurking in the shadows business."

"You're not the only one. Tara do you know...Norah was it?"

"No, Tara Oaks. So where do you fit in with Mr. Gilmur here? Or does he fit into you?"

"I think y'all have met."

Ugly Sue kicked him under the table. Tara studied Ugly Sue but her face, half obscured by shadow, didn't register. "I don't think so. But nice to meet you. Now Archie, you're living here right? My father is having some diplomats in town-something to do with some damned pandas at the zoo-but we're throwing a hell of a party for them. Dickey is revamping the whole house. You ought to come by...it's black tie, your father already got an invite."

Later, when contemplating the smoking crater beneath his office window, Archie would wonder why he said it, but it just came out. He took Ugly Sue's hand, "We'd love to come." He could almost feel the pitch oozing between his fingers as he landed a second punch at the tar baby's solar plexus.

"Vivie'll be there." Tara cut a wicked look at Ugly Sue, "Archie's first love was my big sister. So imagine my surprise when I run into him in Jamaica-" Tara's pale face went almost luminous white when she caught the whole of Ugly Sue's face and a dreamlike memory came rushing back to her. "Uh hawth…" she cleared her throat roughly. "…The more the merrier. Archie you remember where I live? Come through the front door. No reason to climb through Vivie's window anymore." Tara retreated from the table and out of the pale green pool of light over the table.

Archie and Ugly Sue looked at each other. "I need to check on Bunty." He said.

"We aren't done."

"I need to check on Bunty. Call me."

"What's your number?"

"I'm positive this Rowan fella can get it for you." Archie got up quickly and moved toward the old theater. "Whoever the fuck that is."

She jumped up after him, "Archie wait, let's step outside, it's late. I need to go."

"Bunty's in the other room. Gotta dance with the one I came with."

Ugly Sue leaned in a kissed him gently on the cheek. "Good night then."

He watched her go and headed for the bar. "Jack Daniels." He patted his coat for his wallet. "Hell, never mind. She stole my wallet."

"Want me to call the police." The bartender asked.

"No, it wouldn't do any good. She's not after the money."

"Was it that perfect thing you were in the corner with?"

"That's the one."

The bartender laughed and passed him the drink. "Here, have one on the house. And watch those pretty ones-they'll get you every time."

Then Bunty was at his arm, "Archie, kiss me."

"How?"

"Drunken teenagers."

"Okay. Why?"

"Funny Boy has had enough to become Captain Courageous."

While Archie wanted everyone to stop speaking in code, he owed Bunty action. They kissed, deep and probing with wandering hands.

The bartender was embarrassed for them.

Eleven

A Really Good Dress

SATURDAY

THE SMOKE IN THE DAWN AIR didn't smell right. Robert Chu's khaki Landcruiser knocked along the road to Miz Cassat's house. This was it - the scheme would be executed: the Arabs would have their jihad, the Chinese would seize the vacuum in Central America, and Miz Cassat would have her money-more than she could ever spend. Chu had done everything that she's asked of him, even betrayed his masters in Beijing. She would have to remove the curse now. And when she did he would leave the islands and voodoo forever. He didn't know whether he would retreat to the land of ten thousand Buddhas or Western secularism, but Robert Chu was damned sure he was leaving the world of Anansi Coupé and Olgen Flambeau and all the other crackpot voodoo gods.

Anansi Coupé the spider god, hung over his head since he'd first brokered the deal with Miz Cassat. She had nothing he wanted, but was the contact point for the one they called Mickey Boy and a pile of outdated yellowcake he was sitting on. But Chu had grown up on the islands and the night he woke up to find his naked body crawling with spiders and the candles burned down on the alter he knew what had happened. Then he was wailing for Miz Cassat, or Anansi Coupé at least.

In the dim light of the dawn, Chu saw the smoke coiling up from the top of the windowsills. The smell hit him. This was not a wood fire and Chu ground the truck to a stop and leapt out.

In the sky a helicopter circled, from a distance it looked like an American Apache, but he couldn't be certain. He got back into the car and headed for the far compound.

ARCHIE WAS MOMENTARILY STRUCK SENSELESS by the view down Pennsylvania Avenue – both of them. Bunty and Ugly Sue were bent forward over his desk, rendering Archie oblivious to why they had gathered round his desk entirely too early on a Saturday morning. Without noticing it, Archie lifted a cheek and checked the wallet in his back pocket for the third time in the last half-hour. Silly really, because if the girl really wanted to keep his wallet, she wouldn't have called him at dawn thirty and asked to meet him downtown to return the damn thing. "I don't know how it wound up in my purse." She had cooed over the phone. Then he was on the phone to Bunty and having to listen to her assessment that Archie had, in fact, broken into a foreign global corporation's computer system, yet had to call his secretary to get the alarm code for his own office. If her analysis ever reached a conclusion, Archie was in the shower before she got there.

Bunty looked up first. From her boss's relaxed eyes and peaceful smile she knew he was buried neck deep in someone's cleavage. "Archie," she said. They were nowhere near eye contact.

Ugly Sue looked up and smiled, she nudged Bunty. Bunty cut Ugly Sue a look: an unamused, predatorial glance that was unmistakable.

Archie was visualizing how much he could see if Ugly Sue lost one more button.

"Archie." Bunty said again.

"I'm sorry, Love. What?"

"We know the front door will be open-and the kitchen-" Bunty growled. "...but how do you know this side door is going to be open?"

"Goes to the patio."

"Great...it's February."

"It's also black tie. Cigars and whiskey."

Ugly Sue never looked up from the Oaks' floor plans laid out across Archie's desk. "Man stuff." She said, "Ridiculous man stuff."

"That's about the thick of it." Archie said, leaning back in the desk chair. "I'll probably make my exit out of Vivie's bedroom window. I know how to get down that tree."

Bunty rolled her eyes, "Why've you gotta jump out a window Arch?"

The smirk had quit Ugly Sue's face, "These plans, Archie, you did them from memory?"

"Yeah, we dated for four years, I'm pretty sure I remember the layout of the house."

"Your memory is not what I'm questioning. I'm sure it's dead on, and if we where pulling this stunt in 1989 that'd be fine. But those girls have moved out and I'm guessing the bored Mrs. Oaks has rearranged the house a few times."

"People don't do that Norah."

"Men don't." said Bunty. "Mrs. Oaks has been left alone in that house 10 months a year for nearly five years now. What do you think she's been up to?"

"Well, see, I'm sure she's screwing the pool boy, but not the interior designer-they aren't usually built that way. Besides, the basics won't have changed." Archie stood and forced his attention on the very flat surface of the floor plans, "Downstairs: reception and dining rooms, there in the back, the home theater. You know, to mask the fact that none of them have anything to say to each other. Upstairs: the master bedroom suite will be the same. Vivie and Tara's bedrooms might be guest rooms or work rooms, it doesn't matter, they'll still be in the same place. So will Mr. Oaks' office."

"Why do you say that?"

"First, Mr. Oaks was the only male in that house with three spoiled pushy women…you don't know what he was like about that office. Monasteries don't get that much reverence. Second, moving that wall safe out of there is a bit out of the pale of an interior designer's spruce up."

"I'll buy it." Said Bunty. "Just tell me the kitchen has been remodeled."

"Bunty!" Archie slapped the heels of his palms into his eye sockets, "Are you still mad about that?! Look, if you want out just tell me. I never hired you for this kind of work, Lord knows I don't pay you enough for it-"

Ugly Sue was now standing straight up, arms akimbo on her hips. Bunty looked her over and said. "No, Archie. No...we both know you're useless without me."

"Well, I wouldn't say use-"

"But why am I posing as a caterer? Here is the social event of the season and I'm crashing the damn thing through the back door. That's no good. I just picked up this black velvet number from Oscar De La Renta – it's dead sexy..." she turned to Ugly Sue, "Simple A line cut, scoop neck..."

"Oh, sounds nice. Their stuff really does fit well. You can't go wrong."

Archie made a pleading gesture to his creator. "Will you two please stop it? Bunty, I'll make it up to you. I'll take you out, you pick the spot...platters of caviar and buckets of the Veuve."

Bunty sneered at the offer, "That's no good. Just you, me and the dress. I need a crowd. The dress needs an audience."

"She's right." Ugly Sue said, "You do need a crowd for a dress like that."

Now Archie called his creator by name. "Look, all that's changed in the house is the wallpaper. I'm quite sure the kitchen has been refitted twice since the late eighties. And let me assure you of something else as well, nothing will be worn out because Mrs. Oaks can't – no, won't - cook and went to great lengths to ensure that her daughters couldn't either. But you aren't actually cooking, Bunty. We're breaking into a safe. As for your dress, I really am sorry but I told the nympho I was taking Ugly Sue here."

Bunty looked at Archie's date, "I thought her name was Norah."

"Jesus Archie!" Ugly Sue screamed.

"Who cares what the fuck she's called! The one I'm pointing at..." Archie waved a finger at Ugly Sue.

A strange calm settled over Bunty and then spread over the room. She was looking at the ceiling and appeared to counting. "Eight seventy five."

"Beg pardon?"

"Remember the cuss jar, that's a double fine." To Ugly sue, "He owes me a double every time he ends a sentence with a preposition."

Ugly Sue stared at Bunty in awe. "How'd you get him to agree to *that*?"

"I never agreed to anything of the sort." Archie rummaged through the desk drawer and handed Bunty fifty cents. "That's two fines for the cuss jar. Your prepositions can fuck themselves."

"It's okay Archie, I'll be the maid."

He shook his outnumbered head, "How did we get here?"

Ugly Sue pressed her lips together. "We really need to focus. Archie, you seem to do okay on industrial locks, but have you ever cracked a safe?"

"It was really more like a big locker."

"Okay, that's fine, we'll better leave that to me. I'll need some gear but that's fine, I've got the case with me here in town. It's about the size of a bread box."

Archie looked at Bunty, "You take the case through the kitchen, act like you're going to the bathroom with it and hightail it to the office upstairs. The desk is huge…really sinful, the front is closed so you'll be able to hide it under the desk for the time." Then to Ugly Sue, "Is that it?"

"If I can't crack it by eavesdropping, I'll need to get the drill up there. It's about yea big." She set her hands about a meter apart.

"Not sure that's gonna fit in a casserole pan." Said Bunty.

Archie cleared his throat. "We can get it up from the outside…"

"Vivie's tree?" Bunty said with a smirk.

"Brilliant! That's it. I'd forgotten."

"Uh huh."

Ugly Sue relaxed a bit. She crossed the room and looked over the decanters in the bookshelf. "The drill is just a backup, of course. Surely I can crack some fool's home safe."

"Surely."

Archie and Ugly Sue would come in through the front door with Archie in black tie and she in any dress but Bunty's black velvet number. They would be fashionably late. The case would be waiting for Ugly Sue as soon as Tara emerged from the throng to separate them. Then Archie would press Tara for information. He would try Vivie as well because she wasn't so self-absorbed as her little sister and had a chance of knowing something about Mr. Oaks' situation with the Chinese.

"I'll get up into Vivie's old room, probably a guest room now – if so I'll just hoist the drill up from there…we'll need a cord."

"Where will you put it once you get it in the house?" Ugly Sue asked.

"If it's a guest room, under the bed."

She shook here head. "No, that won't do. We are attempting to crack a safe and steal the contents while the house is full of people – dangerous people. Archie, Bunty, you two may be great at spying on inventory lists of mildly crooked companies, but this is different. Stowing our backup under a bed that may or may not actually be there isn't good enough. All this…this is what I do, but I can't have you two getting hurt."

Archie and Bunty looked at each other until Bunty burst out laughing, "That's dear. You tried to shoot Archie last week. I'm as fickle as the next gal but that's a bit much."

"You did, didn't you?"

"Well we're on the same side now kids. And we have to find out what, exactly is in those rooms. Archie, it looks like you're gonna ask Miss Tara out for drinks."

"I'd really rather not."

"I'm not sure that's a good idea." Bunty chimed in.

THE HELICOPTER CAME DOWN SOFTLY in a hurricane of dust, as Chu made his way past the chain link fence. Inside, Concepión had barely touched down when Mickey Boy's hand went to the door. He stopped, "What did you say he was scared of?"

"Spiders. The old witch told me that before I dropped her off somewhere between here and there." She was referring to the stretch of Caribbean Ocean between Jamaica and Cuba.

"Any particular kind of spider?"

"He was cursed by Anansi Coupé, a voodoo spider god. I don't know if he is a god of all spiders or just certain species. Sorry boss, I didn't think to ask."

Mickey Boy stared at the group of men at the fringe of the clearing, shielding their eyes from the whirling air. "Don't worry about it, Dear. Being genetically Buddhist, my guess is Mr. Chu doesn't know either. I am just curious by nature, I suppose. One more thing," Mickey boy patted the metal suitcase from between their seats, "Do curses of this sort have death-puts?"

"Pardon, boss?"

"Now that the old bat is dead, is the curse gone?"

Concepión laughed, "Oh no, she had to make that abundantly clear to Mr. Chu. It was the only way she could ensure he wouldn't kill her and go to you directly, Boss. It was her life insurance."

Mickey Boy shrugged his shoulders, "Pity." Then he was out of the chopper, walking low and fast towards the group of men on the fringe of the clearing. Beyond them still, the trees that hid the complex from the rest of the plantation, blew and swayed madly in the eddies of dirt and air.

From Miz Cassat's sneers about underwear models, Mickey Boy guessed that the young one coming to him now, hand outstretched, was Robert Chu. "Mr. Boyarov?" Chu shouted.

"That is correct, and you are Mr. Chu-Yes?"

"Yes."

"It is convenient to meet with you face to face. Our middleman was more a hindrance than help. But, perhaps you and your partner were friends indeed. Or perhaps there was unfinished business." Mickey Boy winked. Chu said nothing and the small man in the blue suit and red tie did not move, nor did the three guards in khaki fatigues. "You are Go Lin Lee." Mickey Boy said.

Mr. Lee nodded only slightly and Mickey Boy, who knew an insult when he saw one, tipped his head not at all. He stared down his long Slavic nose at the Manchurian.

"Have you got it? The yellowcake?" Chu asked before things got too tense.

"It's in the Mi-28."

Concepión had the chopper hovering just feet above the ground. Mr. Lee looked around Mickey Boy. If there was a fury or frustration building in the small being, it didn't show on his face. Mickey Boy had to admit Mr. Lee was cool.

Which was more than he could say for Chu, who clapped his hands like a nervous salesman, "Yes, you'll want to see the payment."

"Yes. I will." Mickey Boy said to Mr. Lee. "I've got to demand payment in hand because I'm not certain I like doing business with you. That broker you people picked out was really sloppy. Very second rate."

"Who else would you sell your mountain of half-processed uranium to?"

"Anyone outside of NATO, Mr. Lee, anyone outside of NATO. Of course I mean no offense – I'm a businessman. I want to unload my inventory and go to earth. That's all. I want to retire. And here is SinoTel, wanting to buy my whole inventory. I guess you gentlemen want to set the state of Texas glowing. Great. But it's a sloppy operation down here. I don't want things to blow up before endgame and have half the world looking for me." Mickey Boy stopped and pointed a long finger just inches from Mr. Lee's short nose, "Retirement. Mr. Lee. I don't want to think about work after I retire. It's not convenient."

For Mickey Boy, that's when the tell came. From the still, almost dead face of Mr. Lee, came the words that betrayed a furious and bruised ego that was impotent to act on its rage. "Mr. Chu, show Mr. Boyarov that his product will be put to good use. I'll present the terms." With that he barked something authoritarian in Chinese and the security guard went scrambling after him into the jeep.

Mickey Boy followed Chu up a paved footpath to the rear of the prefab building. "How important are you, Chu?"

"Pardon?"

"Is my English that bad? I said, how important are you?"

"I have my place."

"We all do, Mr. Chu. The question I have is where, exactly, is your place? How I mean is this-are you disposable?"

"No."

"Dangerous thing to say. Am I walking into a trap? Are they willing to kill you with me?"

"I see." Chu mumbled after a moment. "No, they need me alive. In fact they're sending me on a diplomatic mission tonight."

"Fair enough."

Chu produced a ring of keys and got them through the back door. They went down a narrow hallway and the air was thick with the scent of paint and burnt dust. "We're undergoing some construction."

"May I inspect?" Mickey Boy reached for the handle of a closed door but Chu put himself between them.

"No, you can't. It would be of no interest to you." They continued down the hall.

"I'm glad I have this moment alone, Mr. Chu, there is something we need to discuss."

"I keep no secrets from the company."

"Of course you don't. Loyalty, there's a dying cult. But there is the matter of the, I suppose we'll call it the brokerage fee. What your Miz Cassat took for her services. Services that she never rendered."

"That's really between the two of you."

"Yes I understand you've got unfinished business with her. So do I. Think about the future, Mr. Chu. You see I had my girl Concepión ransack her little shack and the diamonds-owed to me in good faith, were no longer there."

"Not my problem, Mr. Boyarov."

They stopped before a pair of steel double doors. "Well, you see, I think it is. Because Miz Cassat was very unlikely going to rob herself and even if she would have, she would have hardly done it after she was dead. Someone cleared her out. And you, Mr. Chu, were her partner in this…what's the word…endeavor. And, it has not escaped my attention that you hardly seem worried that your share has been looted. Which might, were I a cynical man, lead me to believe that you have not actually been looted."

Chu said nothing but opened the twin steel doors. Beyond them lay the gymnasium. One set of the bleachers were open with set on the opposite wall folded flat. On the far wall a small man scaled what looked like a badly laid out rock climbing wall. "Yavi!" Chu called and walked into the gym.

Mickey Boy followed but did not run to catch up, "Mr. Chu, unless you're about to demonstrate a game of Atomic Basketball…we have not concluded our business."

The one called Yavi cocked his head and backed down the wall, descending some thirty feet backwards with remarkable speed. He had a gym back slung over his back and when his feet touched the floor he slung this off a came trotting over to Chu.

To the left, the tall woman who had been running up and down the open bleachers had stopped and was watching them. Mickey Boy thought she was very tall for an Arab, but her face was unmistakable. Her chest heaved for breath and she placed her hands on her hips in a very Western way as she watched them.

Yavi came to Chu and he slapped the small man on the back. Yavi seemed to glow at this.

"So this is our delivery boy?" Mickey Boy called, slowly striding up to the pair.

Yavi screwed up his face and asked Chu in French, "I'm a delivery…what did he say?"

"He asked if you are the one to deliver God's vengeance." Chu responded.

Mickey Boy, who spoke French passably, chuckled to himself and pointed to the woman on the bleachers, "Is this the partner? You people are getting smarter."

Chu looked at the woman coming down the bleachers, "That's Alice. I don't know what her real name is. We told them they needed a couple. They were against it at first, but saw the light. A pair of Arab men just raises too many eyebrows."

Mickey Boy smiled at her and said loudly, "It's amazing what concessions you'll make when dressing politics up as religion."

This Yavi understood clearly. "No! Not politics! The Will of Allah. The Fist of Allah! I will smite the most decadent holy day in all of Christendom!"

"Wow!" Mickey Boy laughed, "That's fantastic!"

"Silence!" spat Alice. "Say no more Yavi!"

Yavi's brown eyes bulged in his head, "Do not speak to me that way, you are unclean! Like the rest of them!"

"Silence! We are on a path to Allah and I will not let you destroy it with your boyish boasting!"

"Unclean! Unworthy!" Yavi seethed.

Mickey rubbed his face, "Listen Alice, I know what Yavi thinks he's getting paid, but do you get seventy two virgins as well? Is that even something you want? A quick awkward lay for eternity?"

She glared Mickey Boy down, "Back to work!" And she ran back to the bleachers. Yavi spat "Whore!" when she was well out of earshot and ran back to the far climbing wall.

"Crack team you've got here." Mickey Boy turned and started back towards the open double doors. In the hallway, Chu caught up with him. "Where's Mr. Lee's office, and more to the point, where are my diamonds?"

"This way."

"Listen, I don't know what you were trying to illustrate back there, but those two don't exactly fill me with confidence. Just let me get to another hemisphere before you play whatever trick you've got in mind."

Chu didn't want to talk about Miz Cassat's missing diamonds. "Alice went to University in the West. She comes from a wealthy and, by their standards, liberal Arab family. She is busy being a perfectly normal student, just was with the wrong boy and gets a burning case of syphilis. Her family disowned her, thinks she's been defiled, she thinks she's unclean. Here's the rub. This is the only way to make it right. She can't ever have a good fundamentalist Muslim home because of the VD."

"That is inconvenient."

They came to an elevator and stepped in. Mickey Boy felt it prudent to remind Chu-"I haven't got the yellowcake on me. And Concepión isn't loyal enough to stick around for my sake."

The doors opened and they stepped into an office that looked eerily like the throne room of the Forbidden City. Mr. Lee was leaning against a wide lacquered writing table patting a metallic suitcase. He opened it and let Mickey Boy approach. Fishing a jeweler's glass out of his pocket, Mickey Boy inspected one of the diamonds at random. "They are African?"

"Yes. Serria Leone."

"Fine. Beautiful. If I find out half these are Moisonitte, I'm going to be very put out."

"Pick another."

Mickey Boy did. Then a third. Mr. Lee showed no signed of impatience. Finally Mickey Boy put the jeweler's glass back in his pocket. "They are beautiful. Lock it up, let's go outside, for my end."

One of the guards shut the case and took the handle. Mickey Boy moved again, clamping a pair of handcuffs around the SinoTel guard's wrist, linking him in one fluid motion to the case with the diamonds. "We'd hate to mix up our cases on the trip back to the chopper."

Silence from Mr. Lee. Nothing to betray either anger or admiration for Mr. Boyarov.

"Listen, Mr. Lee, one more thing." Mickey boy continued, "The original broker on this deal was lost at sea. Tragic really-helicopter fishing accident. But when my girl Concepión ransacked her quaint little shack in search of the diamonds she never delivered, they were gone. You can't expect me to pay a broker who failed to deliver?"

"Miz Cassat took her diamonds out of our payment to you, Mr. Chu."

"But where are they?"

"We certainly do not know the finer details of your arrangement with Miz Cassat, but they are hardly our business. This is a lawless island, if she was robbed I can't seem surprised."

"I heard of a CIA operative in Panama who was liquidated three days ago. But not before he managed to get his asset, a cleaning woman no less, to get a copy of a report into the hands of Washington. Have you heard that story?"

Mr. Lee sighed, long and hard. "Rumors, Mr. Boyarov."

"I heard that the Americans are looking out for an Arab attack on US soil-Easter possibly, in the capital maybe." Mickey Boy stepped closer, "Let's see if this sounds familiar...you send a Muslim holy roller to an Easter parade. Set off a dirty bomb, infect women and even more so, children. 'Smite the most decadent holy day of all Christendom', Does that sound right? Then the US and Britain, the world's boy scouts, begin again to pound the Middle East. And then South America and its proximity to America's underbelly recedes just a bit further back on the American paranoia radar. Washington spends all its time smashing the Arabs and trying to get the French to love them for it.

"All the while, you, SinoTel, China, the Middle Kingdom, continue to buy up South America and refine my vintage Uranium in it's jungles until Uncle Sam wipes the sweat from his eyes only to find an enormous nuclear spear pointed at it's groin by the most populous nation on the planet. Does that sound right?

Mr. Lee said nothing for a long time. "I believe that we can make whole the agreement with our agent. Miz Cassat was regrettable. Here is your payment, Mr. Boyarov. I believe you have a product to deliver in return."

Mickey Boy checked his cell phone signal and punched a number on the speed dial. "Concepión...we're coming up. Don't touch down until you see me. Set up the scrambler, I've got to make a call."

THE CALL FROM MICKEY BOY had left little to nothing to the imagination. There had been no pleasantries, just simply that the old witch was dead and she was cooking up some deal with the Chinese to get into Walt Oaks' safe. There was something in there that the Chinese were going to pay well for.

That was fine and not a problem, Vik had assured his Mickey Boy. In fact, he had a half-wit pikey thief who'd already done all the legwork for him.

Not good enough, said Mickey Boy, the old witch had cracked under Concepión and he knew that the girl, the one they called Ugly Sue (had he heard that right? The girl's name was Ugly Sue?) was on her way to Memphis.

Vik assured Mickey Boy that he could handle her.

Mickey Boy assured Vik that he had better. But there was something else, for some reason Mickey Boy wasn't privy to, Robert Chu had left on a plane to New Orleans around eleven.

Vik hung up the phone and found his thoughts wandering to the beauty who'd come into the shop last week. Vik tried to picture her face, but it seemed vague to him. He could clearly recall her caramel cleavage as she leaned over her desk. She had wanted to sell him uncut diamonds- had a hundred thousand dollars worth in her purse. He was certain she was crooked, but liked the look of her.

Then something went wrong with his image. From where he stood in the doorway of his office, Vik was aware things weren't as they ought to be. He studied his office for a long time and slowly moved into the room. Swinging the never used door closed he examined it before moving to his desk.

Under the front lip of the desk Vik moved his fingers softly until they moved over a small plastic object. He knew immediately what it was and tore the microphone and transmitter free. A wave of fury washed over the Russian. It was followed by calmer thought, and Vik set the bug on his desk.

ON THE OTHER SIDE of the crumbling downtown brickwork, the interior of McConnell Black Advertising was a Latin Carnival of furniture that looked better than it felt. Truitt opened the door for Archie and the two descended into the dark recesses of the interactive department without talking to the skinny, hairy college dropouts huddled over their keyboards, writing code in torrents of caffeine, oblivious to the day of the week.

A Monty Python movie played silently on his Truitt's Macintosh. "Glad to hear you aristocratic sorts work on Saturdays too."

"I thought I'd slink down here with my precious and ask you a question."

Truitt cocked his head to a Lord of the Rings poster and smiled, "What can I do for you?"

"I need some help."

"You don't look like the old Mr. Sunshine." Truitt took up his dinghy of Mountain Dew and stroked the corners of his mustache, "What sort of miracle are you looking for today?"

Archie scratched his head and pretended to look for a place to sit despite being far too agitated to even stand still. "Well I don't know how to put this...I've got the earphone, the receiver, for Bunty, I need to put a microphone in a watch or a cufflink or something like that. You see, it's black tie..."

"Oh for God's sake! Don't tell me this is the party for those damn pandas!"

"Yeah, that's the one."

"We're working on some DVD's about China. Mrs. Oaks wants to play them on these flat-screen plasmas television she's hanging on the wall like art. Can't imagine the money she's dropping on this party. They must be loaded. Do you know the family?"

"I dated the older daughter over my summer's home from McAllister."

"Of course you did. Vivie Oaks, that was her name, wasn't it? God you used to go on about her." He looked at Archie for a long time, "Why don't you sit, you know you're gonna sooner or later." Truitt sipped his Mountain Dew. "So what's the deal, why you gotta have secrets with Bunty, why not just whisper them like sane people."

"Can you do it?"

"I don't see why not. Your watch'll never be the same though."

Archie dug into his pocket and slapped a Rolex Presidential on Truitt's desk. "You don't want me to wreck that thing do you?"

"Pick it up."

Truitt snatched up the watch and rolled his eyes, "Let me guess, the suitcase you bought this out of wasn't an authorized Rolex dealer."

"Something like that."

"Are you in over your head, Archie?"

"Yes."

"No jokes, no smartass comment?"

"No. Just in over my head, Truitt."

"So why do it...whatever it is? You're a mercenary."

"They know my name, where I went to school. This business with the Oaks-they knew my name before I knew they existed."

"Can you run? Lord knows if anyone can disappear it'd be you. Jesus, you've got two passports, isn't that Scottish Uncle of yours hooked up with the army somehow."

"SAS. Retired."

Truitt leaned forward, "There you go, Archie. That's it. Disappear into some foreign army. You loved that shit at McAllister-the military structure and tradition. The British Army's got tradition in spades. That's honorable work-not this stealing inventories and R&D reports you call a job you've got now. Go...disappear. Your Pop will be fine. Hell he grow'd you."

"I can't run. Not now."

"This isn't the time for machismo-"

"Shut up Truitt, it isn't that. God you ought to know me better than that by now."

"Then what is it?"

"Bunty."

"What about her? She'll get another job, Archie."

"Of course she'll get another job! Jesus, Truitt she's smarter than I'll ever be, of course she'll get another job. What part of what I've said don't you get? These people, and I'm not certain who they are, know everything about me. That means they know about Tantallion Group, that means they can get to her. And if I run they will, to smoke me out. And her. I'm a corporate thief, you know that as well as I do. I'm not sure how I got into this mess, but I probably deserve it. She doesn't. Once she decides what the hell she wants to do with her life she'll be one of the great ones. No, she can't burn all that running away from a gang of overblown criminals."

Truitt watched Archie's head drop slowly then dig the heels of his hands into his eye sockets. He sipped his soda and waited for Archie to come back from wherever he went. "Archie, let me ask you a question."

Archie dug into a coat pocket and handed over a small plastic bag. "Already picked it up, just need you to put it together."

Truitt looked at the bag, "Well he can be taught."

Twelve

A Day Of Rest

SUNDAY

IT WASN'T THAT MRS. OAKS NEEDED TO LOSE a few pounds to pull off the pants she was wearing, she needed to lose a few years. Dickey was studying her rear because at the moment, it was all he could see. No, he decided, it wasn't a matter excess mass, it was simple gravity and years of sitting down to smoke and drink.

"This is a great space." Dickey heard himself saying, "But if we've got a diplomatic mission coming half-way around the world, it'll need a touch up."

"Dickey darlin' we ain't doin' a thing to this room. Walt would flip. Besides, after the price you just gave me for that Czarina Caviar, I think I'm running out of money."

"But I found the caviar, didn't I, my sweet. I told you it wouldn't come cheap."

"Yes, well, maybe just one tin of the stuff and the rest we can pick up at the grocery. You know, the stuff they sell on the aisle with the frozen fishcakes."

"I'm sure I don't know anything about frozen fishcakes. Mrs. Oaks, I called in a huge favor to get this caviar. Not only is it not approved to sell over here, it comes from a fishery owned by that Russian oil tycoon. The fucker they threw in jail over taxes. It's great scandal food."

Mrs. Oaks winced, "Operating a fishery and an oil company? Is that safe?"

"Of course it isn't safe, that's why it's black market." It had occurred to Dickey several times that an international diplomatic party, even one in honor of a pair of oblivious pandas, was not the place for Mrs. Oaks playful flaunting of the international law. She was, however, on the verge of writing Dickey an enormous check so he kept it to himself.

He focused himself back on the office before him. On the wall behind Walt's desk was a dramatically framed family tree. "Let's move that desk." Dickey declared, "over there, under the window."

"No!" barked Mrs. Oaks. "Mr. Oaks would never have that. No, we'll leave this place the way it is. We'll get Simone up here for a proper dusting but I'm not touching anything."

"Well who wears the pants in the family?" Dickey wished he'd used a different phrase.

"Look, you can't move the desk because Mr. Oaks has some thing about sitting in front of the safe. Ridiculous really, all that security is over-kill. High Drama. I mean if someone had the wherewithal to crack through the safe behind that family tree, then they wouldn't be put off by someone like Walt at his desk, frowning at them."

"Behind the family tree eh? What the hell has he got in there anyway?"

"Hell if I know." Spat Mrs. Oaks.

"Company information?"

"Why would he lock that away from me? All the real interest in the company is in my name, not his." She shook her head. "Who knows."

Dickey smiled, "Let's have a look." He swatted her square behind.

"After that caviar, I can't afford another roll in the sheets either."

"You'll make Cookie McMillian die with envy."

Mrs. Oaks smiled at this.

"Say, you and Mr. Oaks ever do it in here?"

"God no. He'd be pissed if he knew I was in here right now."

Dickey cleared off the desk with one push, "Alright ole girl, up you go."

The logistics of Mrs. Oaks passing out on top of desk were simply too difficult. She wandered back to her bedroom in a pantsless haze, with Dickey's soft, manicured hands leading her.

Four minutes later she was out and Dickey was back in the office, running his fingers between the wall and the family tree. He was less focused on his job and more on the fact that Mrs. Oaks had slipped off without paying for services rendered. He'd just have to mark up her caviar another notch.

One side of the family tree was hinged like a door. He found a simple latch and swung the frame off the wall with ease. Recessed into the wall was a Klieg 5200 wall safe. Dickey didn't know it, but it was the same model used by the government.

Archie, who was actually the first to defile Mr. Oaks' desk, knew this already.

IT WAS THE MEMORY OF VIVIE'S seventeen-year-old backside perched on that polished desk that made Archie smile as he pulled up the wide circular driveway. Of course now he had Tara with him and she was full of champagne and his current plan involved even more booze.

He pulled up behind the white Boxter and parked. Archie stepped out of the Scout into the chilly damp day. Measured by any standard other than the American South it wasn't a cold February. That didn't stop Tara from wearing a hat to lunch that would have made Doctor Zivago's Lara proud. Originally Archie had been hoping to take the girl out for some hot wings but it was Sunday and the hat seemed far too grand for hot wings. So he took her to the club where you could get buckets of champagne and really majestic hats had room to breath. The club, however, doesn't serve hot wings.

Opening the passenger side of the Scout, Tara practically fell on Archie as she climbed out of the truck. "Oh my!"

"Damn girl, those crab cakes are weighing you down."

"Go to hell, Archie!"

"I've got something for us." He said and pulled a small suitcase from behind the passenger seat.

"There's a shady box of tricks. What the hell have you got?"

"The green fairy."

The pair went through the front door and Tara motioned for quiet. Upstairs Mrs. Oaks could be heard talking loudly to a voice Archie swore was Dickey O'Shea. Tara removed her ridiculous hat and tiptoed with exaggerated stealth toward a mostly glassed in garden room. With a touch of a button some music came on-it was old and soft and in French for some reason.

"Now tell me about this green fairy of yours."

From the case, Archie drew two glasses shaped like small parfaits, a wildly ornate slotted spoon, and cube of green sugar and a bottle of Absinthe. "We'll need some ice."

"Is that the real stuff. You know, made with wormwood?"

"What do you think?"

"What does it do?"

"Well, Oscar Wilde said it came in stages, the first was like any other drink, the second was when you see cruel and monstrous things, and then all the beauty of the world in the third stage."

"That sounds like a wild trip." Tara went to the bar and came back with a bucket of crushed ice. "What do you say about it?"

Archie smiled, and dropped a handful of ice into a glass and set the slotted spoon over the mouth, "In language you can understand? It's like having a cocktail and smoking a fatty at the same time."

"Nice."

Slowly, Archie poured the green liquor over the sugar cube and through the spoon. Over the ice it came and within the green floated like a cloud a milky white luce of ice and sugar.

"It's beautiful." Tara said, mesmerized. Archie handed her the glass and she sipped with greed. "Tastes almost like licorice."

Archie began to make another cocktail and by the time he'd created a second milky luce, the first was gone. He handed over the second glass. Tara didn't seem to notice. "When do I see cruel and monstrous things?"

"We'll try to skip that part."

Directly overhead it sounded as if someone had cleared the entire contents of a desk onto the floor. "What's going on in your father's office?"

Tara looked at the ceiling. "Oh who knows, Mom's having the whole house redone. I guess she's on dad's office right now. Huh, brave girl."

"What's your dad up to these days? You said DeltaComm had him off in China?"

Tara was smiling at the absinthe cocktail, "Hummmm...I see a green smiley face."

That did it, now the green fairy was smiling at Archie. He made a cocktail for himself and took a sip. The stuff really did taste damned awful, but it had character. He took another long pull. It wasn't so bad, really. The only problem was that the green fairy himself lacked focus. "Listen, Smiley…" Archie started, "Your parent's place in Jamaica-"

"Where we were just at?"

"That's it. Was your dad down there with you?"

"He works in China, silly." Tara took another long sip and slouched back on the small sofa. She scrunched around like she was in bed and took Archie in a long look. "Don't know that I'd gotten into the whole voodoo routine if daddy'd been there."

"I thought he had some business in Jamaica?"

"Well, he does. He owns part of that resort, you know the one with the big roomy showers you don't like to have sex in." She put a hand on his knee.

"Oh, I see. DeltaComm owns the resort."

She squeezed his knee. "So what'd you think about my hat?"

"Have another drink, Love." It seemed that neither Tara nor the horny green fairy where going to be much help. "I need to run to the bathroom."

"Need some help?"

"You know…that's not even sexy."

Archie tried to causally move out of the garden room before Tara felt obliged to give him directions and hopped up the wide central staircase, taking three steps at a time. There where people upstairs. Creeping down the hallway, Archie closed in on the office. Through the sliver of space where the door was ajar, Archie saw something that would have turned Lot's wife into a pillar of salt.

God's Holy Trousers! Screamed the voice in his head. And he crept back down the hall and made his way to Vivie's room. Vivie's room was a happy, safe place. Of course, so had Mr. Oaks' office until the all too real sight of Dickey humping Mrs. Oaks had been ungraciously burned into his mind's eye.

At one cavalier point in Archie's life, the window in the corner of Vivie's room had been his favorite entry and exit from that house of Walt Oaks. The tree outside was still there, just like before, but the iron bed, floral wallpaper and Duran Duran posters were gone. In their place was a Stairmaster, some powder blue dumbbells, and a long floor mat, all facing a huge television. Beyond that the room was strangely bare.

Archie found the ladies Oaks defiling and redecorating of his favorite adolescent memories a trifle annoying.

There was movement in the hallway. With an ear to the door, Archie reckoned that Dickey and Mrs. Oaks crept back into the master bedroom. He waited and was down the hall again and slipping into the most hallowed place in Walt Oaks' matriarchal world. He knew the room well. The safe, the Klieg, was behind the questionable family tree. Walt claimed to be a descendant of Oliver Cromwell, which explained quite a bit. While the tips of the tallest branch had been amended to include the names of Vivie's three children, the root system made no official connection to the Lord Protector.

There was a time when he and Vivie would sneak into the office-to Vivie that was being bad. Then Archie would take the gambit further, opening up the frame and looking at the safe. "Close it!" Vivie would hiss. Archie would ignore her and go too far. He'd crouch and spin the dial deliberately, pretending to try and crack the safe.

"Archie, that's a military grade safe, you can't get into that thing. Now stop."

Archie would smile, "What the hell do you think they teach us in those military schools?"

"Archie, don't, that's not funny!"

"Shhh! I've only got two more tumblers to go, we'll be in!"

"Archie stop, maybe there's an alarm! I'll bet there's an alarm!"

"Maybe there's not. One more to go."

"We'll get caught."

"Vivie, aren't you just the tiniest bit curious as to why your dad's hair never moves? The answer is in here I reckon." Archie, who would not learn to even pick a lock until he was in college, would turn around as Vivie eyed the locked door and pulled her blouse over her head. Later, but not until years later, Archie would wonder if it was the whiff of danger that got Vivie going or if she truly believed he could crack the safe and was merely trying to divert his attention.

Archie had never gotten into the safe and wasn't going to today. Across the room, however, there was a closet door that had always looked even more promising than the safe. It was flush with the walnut paneling, and apart from the lock and a small brass pull, you'd hardly know there was a door there at all.

Crossing over to the closet door, Archie fished the tiny torque wrench and pick from his coat pocket. Downstairs, the music suddenly got louder as he dropped to his haunches and began to work the lock. The panel swung open and somewhere below Tara ran into the coffee table. "Please don't wake up mom!" he thought, but it wasn't his voice in his head, but Vivie's husky drawl.

Behind the door was a walk-in closet but there where no clothes inside. The walls were fitted with shelves that were loaded with random electronic equipment and appliances. On the back wall was mounted a small television monitor set atop a bank of buttons. Archie moved deeper into the shadow of the narrow closet and switched on the monitor. Instantly he was looking at the fairly nude Mrs. Oaks lying face down on her bed. "God, not you again." Beside the bed Dickey was getting dressed. Archie stepped to the door and closed it. The music from downstairs was cut off completely.

In the incandescent glow of the monitor, Archie inspected the bank of buttons beneath the screen. None were labeled so he touched the one on the left. Then he was looking at the empty workout room and its new, lonely equipment; then the guest room where Tara's wild clothes and Louis Vitton accessories lay scattered about like a Visigoth hangover; then he was looking at the back garden; then the front door and his own car set behind Dickey's Porsche. Eventually, Archie found Tara herself dancing to the jazz music he could no longer hear. Then she stopped dancing long enough to focus on rolling a joint. "Jesus girl." Archie muttered in the colossal silence of the small closet. Then the pretty Hispanic maid appeared to give Tara a hand. Archie's frustrated mind went wild with the possibilities.

One more button and Archie figured he needed to check it out and then he could get right back to the garden room. Then he was staring at the on-screen image of Dickey O'Shea, dressed thankfully, coming into the office just beyond the closet door. Dickey stopped and peered back down the hallway in the direction of the master bedroom. Then he moved into the office.

Softly, Archie moved to the door, waving his hands over his head until his right hit the ball at the end of a dangling chain. The closet emerged in a dim wash of red light, which Archie thought was more than a little queer. He squinted through the light to the lock on the door. There was no thumb latch so the lock couldn't be thrown from the inside without a key. On the monitor, Dickey could be seen pulling open the family tree and examining the safe behind it. Turning back from the monitor to the unlocked closet door, that's when Archie realized what lined the shelves of the closet.

Tiny cameras, three of them; a handheld photocopier; and a travel alarm, the sort one hangs on the doorknob of a hotel to shriek if the door opens; and a titanium pen-light like executives addicted to PowerPoint presentations use. Archie flashed a red spot on the ceiling but couldn't see it given the red light washing the closet. He looked back to the monitor to see Dickey still studying the safe and returned to the shelves. There was a Walther PPK – the smallish police gun from the James Bond novels. "Jesus, Mr. Oaks." The pistol was unloaded, which was comforting. It went into his coat pocket.

Again, Archie looked back to the monitor. The office appeared empty. The safe was still in full view, the family tree still open in front of it. No, Dickey was in some corner not covered by the camera.

The closet was flooded with light and Archie spun around. Dickey was standing in the doorway, shocked. From some strange reflex Archie pointed the penlight at him. Dickey moved, fast, hitting Archie square on the bridge of the nose, sending him back into the monitor. He took Archie by the coat lapels and pulled him away from the equipment, swinging a polished Chelsea boot at Archie's crotch. Archie buckled a knee and took the kick in the shin.

Now Archie was groping the small of his back for the P7 and taking another blow to the nose. With the penlight in his tightly curled fist, Archie connected hard with the side of Dickey's head and then again with the nose. Dickey leapt forward and drove them both into the bookshelves. Archie hit back and the two locked up, stumbling past the leather armchairs into the middle of the room. With a sweep of the leg, Dickey knocked Archie's feet from under him and they went tumbling onto the oriental rug. Dickey reared his arm back to drive the final point up Archie's battered nose and stopped. He never saw the gun, but knew what was now pressing into the soft flesh under his chin.

"I win, Dickey. Now get off me."

"Win, how do you figure that?"

"I've got the gun, you stupid gypsy."

"But ya can't use it. Ain't your house and I'm here on contract with the owner. Not to mention unarmed. Not even you could squirm out of that bucket of shit."

"Let's call it a draw. Now get off me."

Dickey dropped his fist and hopped up. Archie got up and dusted off his pants.

Leaning against the huge desk, Dickey chuckled. "H&K P7, nice piece Archie. But all things being equal, I won."

Archie pistol-whipped Dickey once. "All things aren't equal."

Dickey lunged from the desk. Archie turned and crooked his arm around Dickey's neck, then, with a foot to the back of the knee, forced Dickey to the floor. Dickey's softened head connected with the small table between the armchairs and tipped it. The table wobbled and righted itself. The vase atop the table wobbled. Tipped over and rolled to the edge. "Ming vase!" Archie thought he heard Dickey mutter. Knee still in Dickey's backside, Archie lunged forward and caught the vase as it made for the floor.

"Please don't wake up Mrs. Oaks!" Dickey hissed.

"If she didn't hear us fall, she won't hear that damn vase." Archie tossed it into the seat of one of the armchairs.

Dickey gasped for air. "Very expensive. She'd hear the money break."

Archie knew it was true. He released Dickey and stood up. After a frantic draught of air, Dickey made it to his feet and quickly placed the vase back on the table and set about arranging the armchairs just so. Archie took a large silent step back and holstered the P7. Dickey swung violently around, throwing a punch that ended somewhere between them. Archie flashed the penlight at Dickey's face. Suddenly Dickey's hands went to his right eye and he fell back into an armchair with a scream.

"Dickey, what the hell is wrong with you? Don't wake up Mrs. Oaks!"

"My eye!" He yelped, "I'm blind."

"How?" Archie flashed the penlight in the palm of his hand. The instant sensation was akin to cauterizing a wound he didn't have. "Good God!" He growled, blowing into his palm, "That's a real damn' laser." The spot in the middle of his hand was already looking like a blister to be. "Sorry about that Dickey. I really am."

"I'm blind!"

"No drama, Dickey, you've still one in working order." Then a little less convinced, "I'm sure it's temporary."

"I'm feckin blind!"

"Listen Dickey, what the hell are you doing in here, snooping around Mr. Oaks' safe?"

"I could ask you the same feckin' thing!"

"Yeah, but I've got the silent blinding laser."

Dickey moved his left hand over his left eye. "I'm the interior designer, Archie, what the hell do you think I'm doing?"

"Redecorating his safe?"

"No. This damn Panda Party. China has rented a pair of damn bears to our zoo and Walt had made bucket of political capital out of it."

"I know about the party, Dickey. Why so interested in the safe?"

"I'm not. I'm sprucing up the place. Came in here to see what I had to work with." Without moving his hands, Dickey nodded to the family tree. "Apparently that god-awful thing is here to stay."

"But you aren't an interior designer."

"That's what Mrs. Oaks is paying me for. Go ask Tara."

Suddenly the French jazz went off and what sounded like German techno-music came on. Dickey was lying but the story was plausible and there was no way Archie was going to get the truth out of him. "Listen, let's go back to our corners. Tara is waiting for me downstairs, you've got the lady of the house to deal with...call it a draw."

Still holding his eyes, Dickey sat up, "Why don't we switch corners?"

The grainy image from the monitor, that of Tara and the maid rolling a joint, danced through Archie's head. "Well Dickey, since you can't see so well, why don't you opt for experience?"

DOWNSTAIRS THE MAID, SIMONE, AND TARA, while still fully clothed, looked as adorable as ever. "Care for a hit?"

"No thanks." The bottle of absinthe was three quarters empty the dregs in the two highball glasses on the coffee table was bright green.

"Good God, Tara. You drank all this and now you're getting stoned?"

"C'mon, get that ridiculous hat of your's. We need to get out of here."

"Does that mean I need to get back to work?" Simone groaned.

Archie smiled, "Mrs. Oaks is asleep. Mr. O'Shea is not." She perked up at the news. "I hear he's developing a wonderful sense of touch."

Tara snatched up her hat and thought it wonderful that Archie whisked her out of the house with the force of a linebacker. Simone leaned back into the garden room sofa, still what would be called *stoned as a lab rat* when Dickey came stumbling down the stairs. He was clutching one eye and threw her the keys to his Porsche. "You've got to drive to the ER, Fantastic! The old bat's asleep and won't wake up."

"Will I get fired?"

"Only if the man with the grand vision for this feckin' party goes blind."

With one eye burnt out and the other foggy with tears, Dickey couldn't be sure that the SUV's and station wagons Simone was weaving in and out of were as close as they seemed. But his screams of terror had reached such a pitch that she started laughing at him so he just bit his lip until the car stopped and he stumbled into the emergency room.

Simone was still a bit smoked up, but mostly just blissfully sleepy when Dickey appeared back in the waiting area of the ER. She waved and gave him a glassy eyed smile. "I like the eye patch. You look like a pirate."

It was a gray plastic patch and Dickey demanded Simone drive him to the Eclectic Eye Boutique and picked out a suitable black leather patch. Dickey looked at himself in the mirror. He thought he looked like a fool. The sales girl thought it looked great…considering. But she was trying to sell him something. Again Simone said it was manly and felt his crotch.

"Hey Fantastic, can you take me on one more errand?"

"Can I drive your Porsche?"

"You'll have to-" Dickey said, like a child who's realized that broccoli is the only path to dessert. Dickey made a quick call and they went screaming downtown.

At the top of the steps the buzzer sounded and Vik waved him in and trodded off back to the office. Dickey followed, digging the crumpled calling card out of his pocket. It was a heavy stock ecru card with Vivian Oaks' wildly scripted name emblazoned in a violent purple.

Vik eased himself into his enormous leather desk chair and stared at Dickey standing in the doorway. It started to make Dickey nervous, then pissed, because he thought that now they were partners he really ought to be offered a chair. "Your eye…"

"Long story."

"You look like a pirate."

"Yeah feck you to."

"You have something for me?" Vik asked.

Dickey looked down at the card and studied his own handwriting, "Klieg 5200…" said Dickey and hoped the information would mean something to Vik.

Vik leaned back from the desk and cleared his throat, "Put it on my desk." Dickey did as he was told. "Let me ask you something, Dickey…" Vik trailed off but held aloft a tiny black object between his thumb and forefinger for inspection.

Dickey strained his remaining eye to see what it was. Vik studied Dickey's face. "What's that?" asked Dickey, "It looks like a microphone? Are we recording this?"

Whoever planted the bug in his office, it wasn't the pikey brain cloud standing before him.

"No Dickey, no one's recording us. Don't be paranoid." Vik put the dead bug mike into his desk drawer. "That woman who was in here the other day, Norah Clark, do you know her?"

"I wish I did."

"Find out who she is. Someone who looks like that surely must be well known in a pig-path like Memphis." He leaned forward and inspected Mrs. Oaks' calling card. "Klieg… 5 series, tricky but doable. How many people are going to be at this damn party tomorrow night?"

"Two hundred." Dickey wanted to explain the eye-patch and the fight that led to it to Vik, it seemed important. Archie hanging around with Tara was making Dickey nervous, but why he couldn't exactly place. Vik might think he was being paranoid, and Dickey wasn't in the mood for that kind of abuse; or Vik would see a problem that he hadn't, and doubtless blame Dickey for it. He wasn't in the mood for that kind of abuse either. "Yes," Dickey said again, "Around two hundred. It's a big house."

"Good God. Alright, will they be upstairs?"

Dickey smiled, "The old cow runs a tight ship, she'll keep them all where they can bask in her glory."

"Fine. What's Mr. Oaks like-is the desk very grand?"

"Like a solid block of walnut."

"Fine. I have a kit-I'll need it to crack the Klieg...you'll stow it before the party under the desk." Vik glared into Dickey's one open but dim eye, "Dickey!"

"What?"

"Can you do it?"

"Sure. Put your suitcase under the desk. Got it."

Vik wasn't wholly comforted. "If there is a problem, I'll need a drill. Dickey, you know the house, what would be the best way to sneak it in?"

"Huh? Oh, sneak in a massive drill, sure. That'll be a pain in the ass the night of, the place will be packed." Dickey shifted in his seat and cleared his throat in a manly sort of way, "We'll have to do it beforehand. Yes, that's it. But even that won't be easy. But I know the place to hide it. The dude has a secret closet he's proud of. It'll be dangerous." Dickey kicked his heels onto Vik's desk and sucked his teeth. Vik's eyebrows scrunched so tightly they almost touched-he said nothing. Dickey snorted confidently and laced his hands behind his head, "Say Vik, what's in that safe you suddenly want in? You think the old cow's got more than diamonds?"

"No." said Vik, "Unlike you, I think beyond the next smash and grab job."

Another snort. "Care to let me in on the vision?"

"Not really. You see Dickey, you aren't very smart."

"Hey!"

"An associate of mine would like delivery of the contents of that particular safe. That is all you need to know."

"Another Rooskie?"

"Shut up, Dickey." Then Dickey was saying something and Vik rubbed his eyes. "I beg your pardon?"

"You aren't a spy are you? Cause I'm a patriot."

"A patriot? Aren't you some class of Irish Gypsy? Not American in any legal sense of the word – can you vote? Certainly not Irish. No Dickey, you're just an idiot. No one here is a spy, this is just commerce, Dickey, the wheels of capitalism."

"Okay." Slightly deflated, Dickey put his feet to the floor. "Is anyone else after this safe?"

Vik smiled, "I can assure you no. Just be sure you get my kit under the desk before the party starts."

Dickey smirked, "Oh the desk. It'll never be the same."

THEY HAD TAUGHT YAVI OMARI TO THINK in the language of his host country and now he was in America. *Vile* was the only word that kept coming to mind. He sat in a rickety hotel chair, staring down the Rue de Bourbon. They called it Bourbon Street here. Even the very language here was crude and revolting. Just vile. They had dropped him on the most vile strip of that sewage drain of America called the French Quarter. Around the whole city were piles of rubbish, toxic and rotting, as if Allah himself had finally tried to wash the place into the gulf. For the glory of Allah Yavi found himself far away from the beauty of his dry, brightly lit desert home; on the run from the French and Interpol, looking down on the most vile street of the most vile quarter of the most vile city of a country that was the most powerful adherent to that vile Western culture.

The soggy stink of the city had clung sickly to his skin since they had arrived last night. The drive from Atlanta had been long and the further they got from that relatively dry city, the hotter the air had become. Hot and soggy. Yavi now found himself showering constantly, but here even the water was dirty and grimy.

He'd taken a shower before bed, woke in the middle of the night to take another, and then another still this morning. It was just after ten in the morning and Yavi had showered three times in roughly twelve hours and felt as dirty as when he arrived.

Yavi looked out the window and focused on the targets outside: two couples walked down the street hand in hand. All four were men but only one wore a dress-but for the mustache Yavi would have thought it was a woman. Not far behind, a drunken student in an undershirt stained red and festooned with bright beads fell to his knees and vomited into the street. His friends howled with laughter.

This elicited a humored glance from the homosexual quartet, but not much else. Then the student, exhausted by the violent expulsion, laid his head on the filthy sidewalk a foot or so away from a pile of horse dung left by a mounted patrolman.

At this point, two of his friends came over to help him up, still laughing. Another browsed the selection of trinkets in a shop front window. Some girls came by, five of them. They all seemed to know each other. They wore snug, low slung jeans and tee-shirts that were so tight that even from Yavi's distance he could make out the outline of their underwear.

Yavi wanted to be disgusted, told himself that he was. It was vile beyond description. Still he couldn't bring himself to look away. He would disown his daughters dressing that way, wouldn't he? Kill them even? Secretly Yavi doubted if his devotion ran so deep. Still he couldn't stop himself from watching. These girls- exposed, cheap and unashamed. The beauty of their forms was undeniable – but why sod it by exposing it to everyone? They should hide it away, hide it from all to see.

Stepping away from the window, Yavi thought about the sunrise out in the deep desert sand. The way the dunes in the east glow like purple halos in the dim fading night. Its unfathomable beauty and glory that was a gift from Allah to his people. The desert sunrise was made even more beautiful by its proximity to the base, man-made cities of gray steel and pipe that blotched the cloudless sky, chugging oil from the earth. All for the greater glory of the vile west.

A quick slap to the face, then another. Yavi focused again on the suitcase at the foot of his sagging bed. He needed to meet a man at the Port Authority.

In came Alice and threw a wet towel on her twin bed. She seemed taller in western dress. Like the ones on the street, her physical beauty was useless to deny. She was dressed like the others, generally; flared jeans, tennis shoes, but she wore a loose linen smock, unpressed and wrinkled from her bag. Alice had her hair pulled back simply from her face.

Yavi smiled and muttered, "You look very nice."

Alice breathed deep, she was looking beyond Yavi out to the street. "So this is it." She said in English without a hint of accent.

"Yes." Said Yavi, "For Allah."

"How long have you been away from your family Yavi?"

"Two years."

"Your wife, is she pretty?"

"She is a good woman. Pure. I am proud of her. Very proud."

"Do you love her?"

"Yes. She is a good woman."

Alice smiled, "You never answered my question, Yavi. Is she pretty?"

Yavi found himself chewing the question around in his head as he looked over Alice's cheekbones and nose, so open with the hair pulled away from that face. "Yes." He finally said.

"Yavi-it's about to be over for us."

"Over? Eternity is forever."

"Have you ever had a day of fun in your life?"

"When I was a boy-"

"When you were a boy? How about since you started shaving?"

"When my girls-"

"Your girls? Yavi do you believe that happiness is only for children?"

"No."

"Let's have some fun, before it's too late. We'll still be martyrs. We will still have our rewards."

Yavi swallowed hard. "You…you are unclean."

Alice didn't flinch. "Yes, I am untouchable. All the things you have, are so proud of, I can't have. Upstanding home, fine children. But you are about to give it all up. Why? In two days we will be the same, you and I." She was close now, he could see the swell of her breasts against the clean linen.

"Yes." Yavi stammered, not exactly sure about what he was saying yes too. "But if I am with you I will be unclean too."

"Possibly. But we'll both be clean in two days. What does it matter?"

Even the shape of her ear was beautiful. He couldn't remember his wife's ears. He was sure he'd seen them before though. She was his wife. Then Alice put her hand on his leg. "What does it matter, Yavi Omari?"

"For Allah. It is wrong."

"It will all be right when your job is done."

Yavi looked into her face, "My job. What about your job?"

"I will be made clean too." She kissed his cheek.

The curve of her waist was smooth under his palm. He pulled the linen off the skin and it was made more beautiful by the absence of clothes, tight jeans or shapeless burkhas. It was a beautiful form.

Later, as they walked the dirty street, Yavi lost his focus. Now Alice had caused a tremendous incongruity in Yavi's violent but simple worldview. Yavi found this terribly inconvenient. What had happened in that vile hotel room had been like nothing he'd ever experienced. Now he was a faithless husband and quite possibly carried whatever pox defiled Alice. Still his heart leapt in his throat and he tried not to think about it. They walked down the street, scanning the rooftops of the old Quarter buildings. The French Quarter hinted, just slightly, of a Moorish influence beneath the Spanish architecture. That gave the place some hidden and decaying charm. Yavi wanted to hold hands as they walked, for cover, of course. But Alice said they were supposed to be a couple, not actually in love. There was a difference. That, Yavi knew, was true.

"There." Said Alice and they stopped. "That's the place."

Before them was an enormous Plexiglas cylinder was being offloaded and righted off the flat bed of an eighteen wheel trailer. A small but adoring throng of students stood in silent-almost reverent-awe to the monument being erected. They knew what it was.

Yavi looked at it for a long time. The Plexiglas seemed too flimsy and out of place to be an addition to the ancient building behind it. Finally Yavi asked, "What's that?"

"That, Yavi, is an alter to everything you find vile about the West."

"Yes, but what is it?"

Alice strode across the street to a rough wooden stall, brightly painted and wedged into the narrow space between two crumbling building. It reminded him of that huge bizarre witch who lived on the hill in Jamaica. At the wooden bar, the hairy vendor was selling frozen drinks out of three drums that churned behind him. Alice paid the man and he filled a large clear plastic cup with a bright red frozen concoction. She came back to him and shoved it under Yavi's nose. "Drink."

"What is it?"

"Drink it."

"I cannot."

Alice smirked, "Yavi, you have a venereal disease from laying with an unclean woman – not your wife - during your 'jihad' into the vile west."

Alice had a point, in two days they would be clean. Yavi took a sip. It was sickly sweet and then burned in his stomach. If they failed he would be unclean forever.

Alice nodded to the Plexiglas cylinder now erected in front of a building. "That," she said, "Is an enormous one of these." She took a sip herself. "I want you here, at the three story hurricane. I'll take the other." Alice checked her cheap tourist map, "Let's go look."

The New Orleans Port Authority building is a mostly glass structure-Bauhaus in design-set in concrete along the lacing ironwork of overhead bridges and dock works. The taxi turned off Henderson street onto Port of New Orleans Place and Yavi found himself counting the skinny stick trees jutting out of the concrete before the endless glass of the building. Just more Westerners obsessed with exposing themselves.

Then things got decidedly more festive as they approached the Julia Street Cruise terminal, where the rich and idle boarded luxurious ocean liners that took them nowhere, just to float around in the ocean and do nothing, only to arrive at the same terminal from which they left. These people were bizarre. Yavi was aware that Alice was paying the driver and the taxi had come to a stop. She nudged Yavi and told him to grab the suitcase. It was a new black nylon case on wheels with a long handle. Yavi preferred to carry it.

They both went into the cruise terminal, directly to the restrooms. They emerged with the same quick but casual movement, this time moving away from the lines of taxis and limousines before the cruise ships. The light was beginning to fade as Yavi and Alice made their way from the cruise terminal to the industrial and ugly sea of concrete of the Robin Street Wharf. Quayside was a dimly lit freighter under a Panamanian flag. Between them and the ship were long rows of cargo containers-red, blue, purple and white-stacked four and five high in long walls beneath the tall harbor lamps and even taller cranes that moved them like children's stacking blocks.

The sun was dipping away, making a beautiful sunset for the gay crowd embarking on a cruise-but cast deep shadows along the alleys created by the walls of containers. *A lot of activity for a holy day of rest.*

The information he'd gotten was good and soon Yavi and Alice were far away from the noise and traffic of the cruise terminal. Yavi stopped and turned at a break in the stacked wall. "How can you be sure that this is the place?" Alice hissed.

"I am certain. I will make no mistakes."

Alice smiled, "Someone's got himself a sudden boost of confidence."

Yavi said nothing and fished a cell phone out of his shirt pocket. They flattened themselves against the wall, in the shadows, and waited for the call to connect. "Bobby, you can't miss this Mardi Gras." Yavi sang into the phone. It was hollow, Yavi was a remarkably bad actor.

Alice couldn't hear what was coming over the line, she didn't really care because it was a code she wasn't privy to. Within three seconds Yavi was off the phone and took up the suitcase again. He started down the alley. Alice said nothing and followed.

Two more breaks in the wall and Yavi turned again, then right, doubling back on themselves. He stopped at a rust red GATX trailer marked 12679. Within two minutes, a lone figure could be seen coming towards them. The figure stopped, stuck a cigarette in his mouth and tried to light it. After three attempts, he threw the lighter away and lit it with a match.

"That's him." Yavi said.

The figure turned at a break in the wall. They followed.

Yavi and Alice followed the slow moving figure through what was left of the maze of shipping cargo. Then they were in a construction site. The dusty concrete and steel jumble that was soon be the Erato Street Cruise terminal. No ships were docked there yet. They followed the figure into the shell of the cruise terminal, followed him until he stopped at a single crate, leaned against it and crushed a cigarette out underfoot.

The man wore a western suit, stylish cut but of cheap fabric. His dark hair was cut close to the skull and dark circles puffed beneath his eyes. Alice stopped walking and held back and Yavi continued to approach the contact. On closer inspection, Yavi saw the man was Chinese, and seemed to know Yavi and Alice on sight.

The man opened the top of the crate and removed a steel case. From inside came the device. It was a long plastic cylinder with a timer glued to one end. The case that held the timer and the battery came two wires. "Yellowcake." He said and set the cylinder into a larger case, lined on four sides with plastic bags, connecting the wires by hand. He spoke a little louder than a mumble, "The explosive is low grade, will cause more wind than fire. Do you understand? It will kill you if you are standing near it, a few around you, but the cloud is what is going to do the trick. Do you understand?"

"Yes."

"Set one off on a roof, say three stories high. Another in the street." He looked at the one suitcase. "Here is the other." The man pulled another case out of the crate and extracted a second cylinder. "Where is the other suitcase?"

"Tourist backpacks are in the hotel. We'll transfer them there. Down here, we need a suitcase."

The contact didn't like it, but shrugged his shoulders. "Let me show you how to set the detonator. And be careful, I don't want this thing going off until I'm back in Panama."

Thirteen

A Really Good Caterer

MONDAY

For a number of reasons, Bunty was not in the habit of renting clothes. When raiding Archie's closet to find the tuxedo shirt he demanded she wear, Bunty happened on the very one that Archie had worn to the junior prom with Vivie Oaks. It was like rooting around in a time capsule, going through the childhood closet of a grown man. The shirt was a relic of the last time that he and Bunty would be even remotely the same build.

Bunty was in black tuxedo pants from Anne Klein which fit exactly right. The effect was that, despite following Archie's wardrobe instructions exactly, Bunty did not look like the catering help.

She pulled up and around the back of the Oaks' house, where a small army of workers swarmed the house, and parked as far away as possible. The gleaming white van that was the trademark of Mira Semmes Catering had been pulled oddly close to the back door. From the van and into the kitchen the harassed employees of Ms. Semmes, caterer, swarmed.

Bunty moved around the side of the house unnoticed with the Nike bag. Archie's recce of the place had been sloppy or the tree service had been out in the last thirty six hours and removed the operative branch for getting in and out of young Vivie's room. Bunty studied the scar on the trunk: *Yes, no doubt about it.* She thought, *This is*

Archie's fault. Still…I've got to remind asswholio not to go leaping out of the window for old time's sake.

She kept moving around the house and came around a well-sculpted topiary and onto the wide semi-circular driveway. Catching her reflection passing in one of the windows, Bunty took great pleasure in going through the front doors, pushing them both open and coming into the entrance hall amid a great flush of sunlight. "God Almighty." She muttered when she saw the staircase. Archie's placing of it had been accurate enough in the plans he'd drawn but she never imagined that anyone but French royalty would need such a conveyance. She stole up the grand staircase with the bag over her shoulder and stowed it in Vivie's closet.

Down the hall, Walt's office was exactly as Archie had described it. No surprises of scale. Archie had gone to great length to paint a vivid picture of the room, not because she needed to know every inch of the place but, she suspected, because Archie was suffering from office-envy.

The walnut panel across the room swung open and there stood Dickey and his eye-patch.

"Ahoy matey." Bunty said.

"Who are you?"

"I work for Mira Semmes, caterer."

"Well I'm the designer for this party, so feck off. We aren't serving food up here."

"Hey, I don't do parties in houses like this everyday, give a girl a break."

"We'll see what Ms. Semmes has to say-"

"Why don't we see what Mrs. Oaks has to say."

"What?"

"Redecorating Mr. Oaks' closet are you? Does the old lady know you have the key?"

"Mrs. Oaks and I-"

"There really is no way you'll make me believe that Mrs. Oaks gave you the key to her husband's office, so waddaya up to?."

"Who are you? Have I seen you before?"

The syrupy sweetness returned to Bunty's voice, "I'm sure you've designed lots of parties, Mr. O'Shea," Bunty moved into the room and Dickey took a tentative step back, "and I've worked quite a few."

"Maybe."

"We've probably seen each other out. You look pretty hip." Dickey relaxed a bit in the shoulders. "Ever go downtown? Luvs me some martinis. What's you're favorite party food?"

"What?"

"That'll be my tray."

"Very nice of you."

"Not all the way nice, though." Bunty said and Dickey chuckled and touched her arm. "So, waddaya got in the closet?"

Alarm bells were attempting to go off somewhere in Dickey's head but his hormones were doing a passable job of smothering them. "Silver polish. That's where they keep the silver polish." Dickey stepped forward and moved them far enough into the office to swing the panel shut.

"You'd think they put it closer to the silver closet."

"The rich have their own logic. We've got work to do." Dickey finished, almost pushing Bunty back through the office and out into the hallway. Dickey shut the office door.

Bunty smiled, "I like the eye-patch, it's manly."

"So am I."

The effort of forcing her eyes not to roll to the back of her head was physically painful. Dickey turned to the master bedroom and Bunty headed downstairs. In the great room, Truitt's wide behind stuck out of the gleaming white cabinet near the television. "Kelso Truitt? What are you doing here?"

His head popped out of the cabinet, "Oh, McConnell Black has the Zoo account and so we're helping them throw this party for the pandas. We made some videos of the pandas, they're gonna play on those flat screens during the party." He pointed to the enormous silver-tone televisions, two of them, which hung on opposite walls on the great room. "They must have spent a small fortune on this stuff." Truitt smiled at her in a sad sort of way but said nothing.

Bunty looked down at her clothes. "Oh this, I'm just earning some extra money, you know, picking up a little weekend work. Archie doesn't part with money easily."

Truitt smiled, "I thinks it's sad that they throw this party for pandas… those poor animals get shipped across the world and sit in cages while all the muckity mucks toast the poor things and slap each other on the back."

"Does seem rude."

"Are you gonna see Archie before the party?"

"I plan to, yes."

Truitt struggled to his feet and leant over the black nylon laptop case. "Listen, you can save me a trip." He handed over a small leatherette case originally made to carry a cell phone. "Take this to him."

"What is it?"

"Well, I'll let him tell you, I guess. Actually it's for you, though."

Bunty opened it and looked at the small earpiece and the Rolex inside. "I see. That's clever."

"Uhmph…" Truitt scratched his head, "This has all got him worried Bunty."

"Nah," she laughed and closed the case, "Archie has some completely unfounded confidence that seems to carry him through this sort of foolishness."

"He's worried about you."

"I can take care of myself."

"It'll all be okay. Somehow."

She hugged Truitt and surprised both of them. "Thanks."

Truitt slowly and awkwardly lowered himself to the floor. "Now I've got to crawl back into my hole to make sure this colossal waste of energy and money goes off without a hitch."

THE TUXEDO WAS LAID OUT WITH CARE on one of the two double beds. On the other, beneath the cheap hotel watercolor was spread out an enormous map of the city of Memphis. Robert Chu stared at his lean frame in the mirror; clad in black briefs and a silver tone cell phone at his ear. The phone was ringing but like the four previous attempts, there was no answer. Hanging up, he checked the number he'd dialed, as if his phone shuffled numbers from time to time. No, he was calling Tara's number and she wasn't answering the call.

Chu snapped the razor-thin phone shut and tossed it on the Versace dinner jacket. On the desk in the corner, his laptop hummed-Chu leapt across the room and logged onto the search engine to look up the landline to Walt Oaks' house. He already had the address, which was memorized on the map. He dialed up the landline from the hotel phone. "Hello?" Came a woman's stern voice.

"May I speak to Tara?"

"Tara Oaks?"

"Of course."

"She's not here. At least I don't think that she is. I haven't got time to go searching for her. Try her cell phone."

"Who is this?"

"Mira Semmes, caterer. Can I take a message?"

"No, Mrs. Semmes, that's alright." Chu slammed the phone down, fuming.

His eyes now fell on the candles, unlit, arranged around the rough clay pot atop the cherry veneer of the dresser. In the basin of the pot was a spider; or rather a ball of his own fine black hair wound up in a ball with black pipe cleaners to look like a fat, unkempt arachnid. Chu was pretty sure that's the way Miz Cassat had told how to stave off the wrath of a vexed Anansi Coupé. There was something, he thought, about devotion to Anansi Coupé wooing a vexation to favor…whatever that meant. Of course, they had both been pretty drunk at the time.

Solemnly, Chu lit the candles around the clay pot, from those flames he lit some incense in long gray sticks through the ghastly hair spider. "Anansi spare me." He muttered.

Then a thought occurred. Chu moved across the room and typed "Archie Gilmur". Within two minutes, Robert Chu had a lot more information on Archie than Archie would have liked. There was a cross referenced number for Tantallion Group; a legal address that appeared to be the home of a Frank Gilmur with the address recorded and marked and memorized on the big map. Both Archie and Frank and a few other Gilmurs all seemed to have interest in an outfit called 6-K Farms, which owned a truck-a 1980 International Harvester Scout with Tennessee License plates.

Again he studied the map on the screen and then the one of the bed. He studied and took a stiff shot of rum. The windows didn't open, and Chu checked the ceiling for the second time for cracks. There was a place where the seam of the wallpaper was blistered, but he'd super glued it back down. It wasn't great but it would have to do.

Then he got dressed.

ARCHIE THOUGHT UGLY SUE looked like a bridesmaid, only not so giddy. She was wearing black pants and her hair was worn up with great care; she wore a man's shirt she could get out of without disturbing her do. The man who owned the shirt was Archie and he was sure he'd seen the last of two shirts in as many hours. Did Tara still have his shirt from Jamaica? He'd have to ask her.

Ugly Sue's dress, unseen by Archie, hung in a black plastic bag from the door to the office. Archie was a little further along in his plaid trews and evening shirt, the rest of his tuxedo was hung over the back of his desk chair. He was standing before the plantation desk and, again, checking the items before him against a printed list.

"Bunty's got your kit and the drill. She should be done stashing them by now." Archie checked the list again. "Truitt is supposed to deliver the comms for Bunty — I've got to call him. And there's my P7 and holster…"

"Are you sure you ought to be armed?"

"I'm sure I'm not walking into that empty handed. Now: rubber gloves, two pair; crazy glue, one tube; cigarettes, one pack; playing cards, one deck."

Ugly Sue leaned on the plantation desk, "Why the cards?"

"You won't catch me at a party this size without a deck of playing cards."

"Great, are you going to itemize the condom in your wallet?"

Archie looked down, "You know the girls really dig the pants, maybe I should get one…or two. How many can you fit in that wee purse of your's?"

"Focus on the job."

Archie crossed back to his desk and lit a cigarette. "Norah?"

"No thank you."

"Good, it's a filthy habit. I'm just nervous."

"You'll do fine."

"It isn't me I'm worried about. It's Bunty. I need to get her out of there as soon as I can."

Following him across the room, Ugly Sue looked at the quiet cold downtown street outside. "Look Archie, I know you think you two are in way over your heads, and well, you are."

"Thanks Love.

"Just listen. The only way you are going to get Bunty and yourself through this is to just push on through to the other side."

"When in Hell keep going? I'm sure you mean well, but from where I'm sitting that sounds very self-serving."

Ugly Sue shrugged her shoulders. "I guess I need to change."

Archie pointed to the door, "Go into Bunty's office, it's cleaner. There's the bathroom."

Then the phone was ringing. Archie hit the speakerphone, "Archie Gilmur."

"Archie, it's Bunty."

"You alright?"

"Fine. Before I forget, Truitt was there rigging up some DVD foolishness, he gave me a watch and earpiece."

"Great, hold onto them."

"The drill is in Vivie's room, in the closet. Just like we said."

"And the kit under Walt's desk?"

"Yeah, about that…I went to stash the thing and there was a nearly identical kit already there."

"What?"

Ugly Sue had been taking the dress off the hook and spun around, "What did she say?"

"That's not all I found in Ole Walt's office. Dickey O'Shea and his eye-patch were coming out of a secret closet in the paneling…"

"Yeah I knew about the closet, what was Dickey O'Shea doing there?"

"Not real clear-"

"Bunty, where are you now?"

"In the back yard."

"I think you need to get out of there."

"I'm not finished."

By now Ugly Sue had crossed the room, she was lightly rapping her knuckles on Archie's desk. "Did you say Dickey O'Shea?"

"Don't tell me you know him."

Ugly Sue leaned in, "Does he work for a fella named Vik Makarin?"

"Not that I know of. I did see him at Vanderhorn's. Is Makarin a Russian fella?"

"He was there when I dropped in too."

"Why in the hell where you there?"

Ugly Sue's eyes were the most intensely focused things Archie had ever seen, but her mouth, that full mouth of hers, retained a half grin that was almost casual. "Well Archie, I was unloading some diamonds I'd picked up in Jamaica."

"Oh shit!" Archie and Bunty said at once.

"Vik Makarin works for Mickey Boy." Ugly Sue said as a point of fact.

"Oh yes, Mickey Boy, the one who is surely going to kill me?"

"Yeah that's the one."

"Oh dear-" Came Bunty's voice over the phone. "Archie, I'll leave if you promise not to come."

"No, you'll just get the hell out of there."

"Please Archie, let's leave this to the pros."

"The pros have lousy aim."

"Archie," came the small voice over the speaker, "I'm doing my puppy dog pout."

Ugly Sue said, "Bunty, that'll only agitate him."

"Bunty," Archie said, "Go home."

"Are you still coming?"

"Yeah, I have to."

"I'll see you here."

The line went dead.

THE LIBRARY IN FRANK GILMUR'S HOUSE was a large room made much smaller by the cramped bookshelves and the taupe curtains drawn closed against the cold night. Opposite the closed off bay window, two leather wingchairs faced a small glowing fireplace. When Isobel Gilmur had run the house, the chairs would have faced inward, towards the center of the room with it's comfortable couch and long writing table; a much more social direction. Now the chairs faced the fireplace and the pretty setabouts that once decorated the side tables had been thrown in drawers or stood cowering under the threat of large male feet.

The snifter of Talisker was warming in Derrick's palm as he read the e-mail he'd printed earlier. Now the letter was so obscured by his own hand written notes that both the original content and his notes were rendered into an indecipherable jumble of characters. He was wearing an immaculate Gordon plaid dinner jacket and the high collar of his evening shirt was perfectly starched.

"You clean up nice." Said Frank as he came into the room. "I feel underdressed." He was wearing a pair of washed out khakis and flannel shirt. He poured himself a bourbon and drew a splash of branch water.

"Go put on a dinner jacket…come with us."

"They're called tuxedos here."

"You're still not wearing one."

"Thanks. Y'all are nice to look after me, but y'all go have your date." Frank settled down into the seat of the second wing chair. "Besides, I've forgotten how to wait on Midge with any style."

Derrick laughed, "It's easy with practice. Lots of practice." He sipped his scotch. "How are you doing?"

"I'm coming on fine, I suppose. I feel like a drag though, with everyone coming to check on me. I appreciate the thoughts, to be sure."

"How's Archie been since he moved back?"

"Oh, he's been great to have around. But he's getting restless here. I could see it in him when he was just a boy. That's why we sent him off to McAllister."

"Just like his Mom."

"Yup. Hell the kid even looks like her." Frank's attention wandered to the fire, "He's working tonight. I'm not sure on what. No, he's going to have to move on sooner or later, that's why he didn't get an apartment or buy a house. He thinks it's to take care of me, and to a degree that's true. But he's also leaving himself room to move. He doesn't know it, but that's why."

"Has he said where he'll go?"

"Naw, I don't think he knows himself. Probably Europe again. He says it's good for wandering."

"Frank aren't you coming with us?" It was Midge's voice. "The food is supposed to be divine, I heard Mira Semmes, Caterer was doing it."

"Sorry Midge. If you'd gotten me before I settled in front of the fire, I might have rallied. Right now we've only got another fifteen minutes until my pants come off."

"Oh Lawd!" Midge said and turned on her heels.

Derrick laughed and hoisted himself out of the chair. "Coming Love." He said and tossed the letter into the fireplace where it blackened and burned.

Fourteen

The Panda Party

HER LIVING ROOM HAD NOT BECOME VERSAILLES, or New Orleans, or Peking, for that matter. It remained the living room of a woman with a taste for French style and lot of family money. Robert Chu noticed the DVD loop playing on the two 40" flat screen plasma screens had started again. He reckoned this to about twenty-five minutes of cuddly shots of Panda's frolicking amid the bamboo shoots and not copulating. Chu and his tuxedo stood before a grumpy trio, Mr. Lee, and Mr. Qaun, and another Mr. Qaun (no relation). They looked strangely alike in their not-quite-out-of-fashion tuxedos. Six eyes stared at Chu; tired, edgy, and puffed like cereal from air travel. Beyond them, throughout the enormous house, a few more small groups of Chinese diplomats moved about the room with a more congenial air. Mrs. Oaks held court in the living room, just under the plasma screen hung over the fireplace mantel like an oil painting come to life. She was convinced that the television-as-art flat screens were her idea and was very proud of them.

Then there was the long gone Lord of the Manor. Walt had arrived late last night and spent the morning in bed until the party people had driven him to the office all afternoon. He planned to spend tomorrow in his beloved study. Walt loved the fact that no one but himself ever went in there. He stood on the other side of the living room with another group, made up of both Chinese and Westerners. Chu thought he looked pale and tired from flying across the world.

Walt Oaks was a small man; not very tall and skinny. He was that sort of skinny that had and would endure a lifetime despite little to no athletic ability and an undying love of bacon. On the top of his pate, the hair was thin and wispy, but he would never be bald. He had a full smile and was generally liked for the easy-going manner his wife found so frustrating. The group he attended was standing near the door that led to the side porch where Mrs. Oaks and Mira Semmes had stashed cigars, enormous glass ashtrays, and a small bar stocked with beer, port and whisky.

Chu's heart skipped when he thought he saw Tara glide into the room. While the resemblance was striking, the lady coming into the room and heading towards Walt Oaks was a little heavier, a touch more matronly, and her brunette hair was kept with more sophistication than Tara's blonde locks. Vivie O'Neil joined her father and was gaily introduced to the group of men.

Chu scanned the room again for Tara. Then he turned to Mr. Lee, "I'm going to check the perimeter."

"I appreciate your vigilance, Mr. Chu, but there is no one here yet. Do not arouse suspicion buy snooping around."

Chu glided away through the marble of the entrance hall as a single thunderous knock came from the other side of the front door. Taking hold of the enormous pull, Chu swung the huge door open without waiting on Mrs. Oaks. Two dignified couples, smiling in the fumes of pre-party cocktails, were taken aback. Undaunted, Chu bowed deeply with a fluid grace and smiled. "Welcome," he said, "I'm Robert Chu, with SinoTel Americas, please come in. Your hostess will be along shortly." The two women were immediately disarmed and smiled, letting him take their hands as they came through the doorway. Their husbands followed, smiling and nodding to Chu politely.

Coming up the driveway was another pair of elegantly dressed couples. Chu heard Mrs. Oaks coming from behind into the grand entrance hall, calling, "Suzy, Amanda, So glad you could come. John, Richard, oh you boys have cleaned up nice."

They guffawed nicely. Chu slapped John on the shoulder, "Mr. Oaks and the cigars are through that door, Gentlemen." Then he kept moving through the entrance hall.

He found Tara in the sunroom wearing a red and gold Mandrin dress with a slit so far up the side that Chu knew she was wearing a thong. Her hair was in a traditional oriental bun, but one of her loose forelocks had come free and dangled over her eyes. It took Chu a moment to realize that she was not alone. A man was explaining something to her-and not one of the beautiful people, either. He was wearing a pair of pressed khaki trousers and burgundy sport coat of unnatural origin, and tie that was most likely fifteen years old. It was, in fact, his school tie from McAllister, and this was as close to black tie as Kelso Truitt was capable. "Your mother wants this DVD of the pandas to loop all night. I disabled the stereo, I'll hook it back up in the morning."

"No music?"

"I put some background music to the Panda, your mother gave me the CD's. Listen, that's Miss Saigon I think."

"You can't dance to that."

"Do panda's dance?" Truitt asked and sipped his Mountain Dew from a champagne flute.

Chu cleared his throat, "Miss Oaks."

Tara cut a glance his way and lifted her finger, she was about to continue her argument with Truitt when something clicked. Instantly a smile painted itself across her face, "Bobby Chu…you made it!" She took his hand. Chu's heart skipped again as her face neared his. Then, just before the moment of impact, the trajectory changed and they touched cheeks. "Don't tell me you dragged yourself out of the Jamaican sun to this cloudy little pig-path for a pair of pandas?"

"I'm afraid so." He said smoothly, recovering his calm.

"So," Tara said, throwing out one hip and planting a fist on it, "Who'd you come with?"

"A crew on business."

"Yer on a date with three grumpy blue suits, aren't you?"

"I've got them in black tie tonight – they aren't happy about it." Chu winked and gave Tara a winning smile, "Frees up to entertain you."

"You are entertaining, aren't ya little buddy." She said, which wasn't the reply for which he'd been fishing.

FROM THE STREET, THE HOUSE OF OAKS looked like an enormous French Chateau in dark weathered blue and crème. The house and topiary were dramatically lit with the expert placement of white lights. The wide front lawn was gracefully bisected by the arch of the illuminated circular driveway. One expected the pile to be set among the sloping hills of a vineyard, but this was more than the walled confines of the subdivision could bear. As a point of fact, the nearest neighbor wasn't more than ten yards away from the far wall of the Chateau. It was an enormous Spanish Mission style house. The Oaks' other neighbors were installed in a graceful adaptation of Tudor England except that the garage really didn't look like a carriage house. On the far side of the Spanish Mission stood a Greek Revival mansion that would have made Scarlet and Rhett proud.

All of this made Archie want to sing "It's a Small World After All." He refrained.

Ugly Sue was busy telling him he'd made a mistake. "We shouldn't be here this early. There aren't enough people here yet. This is dangerous."

"Apparently we aren't the only ones interested in this safe. We need to beat the rush."

"Archie, this is dangerous business-you need to be serious."

"Alright then, I'm not leaving Bunty in there alone one second longer than I have to. How's that for a serious answer?"

"Just look out for Tara. I just hope that silly twit is near the door. The sooner she splits us up, the better."

"I've been meaning to ask you-" Archie lowered his voice. They were still only half way up the driveway but both politeness and caution were creeping over Archie's manner. "Why are you so sure she's gonna split us up?"

"She just will."

"Why? How do you know? I hope you aren't basing this whole caper on *that* sack of hormones."

Ugly Sue stopped short and looked Archie in the eye, "Bunty was right, you really do have a black hole when it comes to women."

"She said that?" Then he started on towards the house again, "I think she's told me that before...when did she tell you? Y'all went to the bathroom together, didn't you?"

At precisely 7:34, Archie stepped into the entrance hall behind Ugly Sue. It took about a minute and a half for Mrs. Oaks to stop fawning over him and what a fine young man he'd become. She was so proud, the whole family had all kept up with his exploits over in Ireland and were very glad to have him back in Memphis. Vivie is here, and y'all will have to catch up. So sorry about your mother, how's Frank holding up?

Mrs. Oaks was saying pretty much anything to keep talking and not think about the alarming color of Archie's date.

"She's like a tidal wave." Ugly Sue said as they stepped into the living room.

"Terrifying." He said. Bunty was coming out of the kitchen with a tray of somethings. She came through the room without really stopping for anyone to inspect the tidbits. Tara was in a corner with Robert Chu, looking around the room while he talked. Mr. Qaun made an attempt at the hor's dourves tray as Bunty came rolling past. He wasn't quick enough. Bunty crossed the room and positioned herself in front of Archie, blocking Tara's line of sight. "Egg roll?" Bunty sang in a bouncy voice, "That's sweet and sour on the side." The tray wobbled and both she and Archie sent a spare hand to steady it. There, underneath all that fried goodness, Bunty passed the customized Rolex into Archie's palm. Without wiping the idiotic smile from her face, Bunty said to Ugly Sue, "Your kit is in my car. There's another one under the Walt's desk. Looks like we've got competition."

Then Bunty moved away from them, heading towards the sunroom on the far side of the entrance hall. "Archie Gilmur." Tara sang from across the room. Archie smiled and slipped the Breitling off and into his pocket as he clasped the Rolex around his wrist.

Archie was watching Bunty walk away; she moved slower now, easier. The next fellow that attempted a egg roll actually got one. Then he said something sly or clever to Bunty as he snacked on a second roll and Archie recognized her "aw-you" smile.

"Don't act like you didn't hear me." Tara said, standing close and placing a long leg between he and Ugly Sue.

"I'd recognize that voice anywhere, Tara. You remember Norah?"

"Of course I do. So glad y'all could make it. Norah, love the dress. I didn't think I'd make it myself after Sunday Brunch. You've got to watch this one, he broke out a bottle of absinthe and then got away from me after lunch. Or maybe it was the green fairy, who knows. Listen, we do have some unfinished business. We won't be a second but I have to borrow Archie here." Back to Archie, "Vivie is just dying to see you, Dear. You don't mind, do you Norah? I'll have your man back to you before you can say Moo Shu Pork."

"Not at all, Tara. Listen, Archie, don't fall into any black holes while you're gone."

"Oh he's in good hands."

Ugly Sue smiled, "I don't doubt it."

Tara took Archie by the hand and guiding them into the sunroom. "That waitress, she looks familiar." Tara nodded to Bunty, who was ignoring them.

"Which one?"

"The one that doesn't look like a waitress."

Archie shrugged his shoulders and fumbled with a pack of Dunhills. "Black pants, tux shirt. What's the big deal?"

"Those clothes aren't rented, Dear." She said. Archie shrugged again as he lit a cigarette and handed it over to Tara. "You're such a boy. Still, she looks very familiar."

"Small city. Probably works all the parties."

"I'd remember those pants, she looks great in them."

When Bunty left the room with her tray, she had a decided swish in her hips. Archie lit another cigarette. "Careful, Tara, you'll give her a swollen head."

"She can't possibly hear us."

Archie checked his watch, "It looks like no one's late for your mom's grand soiree."

"It's Dad's people."

"But it's your mom's party."

"Won't argue there. Hey Archie, why'd you run off so quick the other day? And that absinthe was sooo good. You even left the bottle."

"Is the bottle still with us?"

Tara bit her lower lip, "The *bottle* is."

"Ha! Well at least I know it went to a pretty cause. Listen, you said Vivie was around?"

"Oh she is, I just don't want to share you just yet."

Across the house, in the kitchen, Bunty tapped on the barely visible piece in her ear. "Mind the black hole, Arch."

Ugly Sue watched Tara drag Archie off into the sunroom. God only knew what she'd try to get him into in there but she hoped it would take at least a few minutes. Robert Chu was in another room, tending to his masters. If he recognized her, he hadn't let on. The far-off words of her American trainer in the South Pacific all those years came back to her, *Your shield is your face, beautiful enough to go anywhere, and not striking enough to be remembered.* Damn Americans over-think everything.

Ugly Sue lit the staircase without looking down to see if she was being watched or followed. She wasn't. At the top of the stairs, she turned and peered down the hallway. It was exactly how Archie had described it, right down to the molding that didn't quite match the color of the ceiling.

Then there was Dickey O'Shea, standing in the hallway, looking directly into Walt Oaks' office. He stood like Michelangelo's David. Ugly Sue had to admit, as she came down the hall, that he looked good. It was a well-cut and snug fitting tuxedo, then she saw the lace at his cuffs. Before she could duck into Vivie's former room, Dickey turned and looked at her with his one good eye. "Can I help you? The bathroom's downstairs."

"Oh thank you."

Dickey continued to stare at her and took a step forward, "Don't I know you?"

Ugly Sue laughed and closed the gap between them, "Oh I don't think so, I'd have remembered you."

"The eye patch, huh? Well it's new. Have I seen you in the jewelry store?"

"Do I look like a woman who buys her own jewelry? Now the bathroom downstairs is taken, could you be a dear and point me the way up here?"

Dickey didn't moved, "You look so familiar."

"Oh you aren't going to use that tired old line on a gal in search of the loo?"

"Are you from here?"

"I'm from South Carolina."

"What brings you here?"

"Searching for the bathroom." Ugly Sue pointed over his shoulder —"the master bedroom I take it? There'll be one in there. Listen, Jolly Roger, stand guard for me." She brushed past Dickey quickly, turning her head, pretending to take in the pattern of the wallpaper. She was aware, as she stepped into the gilded master suite, that Dickey had still not moved.

Being resourceful, Ugly Sue used the facilities while she was hiding there. A quick check of her make-up and she stepped back into the master suite to hear the shrill cackle of Mrs. Oaks saying to Dickey O'Shea, "Why are you still up here? If you're looking to make a grand entrance, remember just whose party this is."

Ugly Sue stopped. This was a problem. A darker-than-vanilla woman coming out of her bedroom and Mrs. Oaks would be trailing her all night. It didn't matter how proud of Archie they were.

"Now Dickey, do come downstairs."

"I'm no ornament, Mrs. Oaks."

"Aren't you?"

"Mrs. Oaks, I'm just… got a gut ache."

"My God, Dickey, you're a bundle of nerves."

"Nerves? I got a hold of some bad sushi."

"Dickey, I don't pay you to be quite so graphic. Walt tells me all about his bowel problems and look where it's gotten us."

"I'll just wash my hands and meet you downstairs."

Ugly Sue crossed the master suite in silence over the thickly padded carpet, keeping close to the hand painted walls. There was a tiny dressing room on the far side of the room, she needed to get there before Dickey trapped her in the bathroom. He was thinking about her too hard to not eventually come up with where he'd seen her face.

She slipped into the dressing room and pulled the door almost closed. Mrs. Oaks and Dickey were now just outside the master suite. "Look, Dickey darling, I can't have you orbiting around the bedroom like you've got the run of the place. My husband is in town you know. God, he's in the house." She laughed loudly. "C'mon honey, I want to show off your talents. Well at least some of them. Don't make me put a gun to your head."

A light went on in Dickey's head. "Yes!" He barked.

"Well, Dickey, I'm glad we see eye to eye."

"Yes, of course Mrs. Oaks, I would never leave my favorite client to those vultures downstairs." He winked and gave her a slap on the behind. "Yes, I'll see you downstairs in just a bit."

"You seem to be feeling better. Hurry now." Mrs. Oaks scurried back down the hallway. Dickey turned into the master suite, and stepped into the bathroom.

Ugly Sue had moved further back into the dressing room and backed into a small regency chair, pushing it into a low shelf serving a vanity table. Assorted diamond jewelry was scattered over the table. "Clever." Ugly Sue muttered and picked up a large cocktail ring. It had recently been reset.

"Hello." Came Dickey's voice from the bathroom.

"Damn fool, can't even knock. But clever."

"Hello." He came again. Now he was in the suite, trying to reckon exactly where she'd gone off. If Mr. O'Shea was as familiar with the boudoir as he appeared then he'd be looking her in the face in about twenty seconds. Ugly Sue backed into the silky folds of the dresses along both walls on the theory that men are scared of women's clothing if not actually hung on a woman.

Dickey stepped into the dressing room. "Where are you?" he said quietly. "Oh God you old cow, why don't you lock up your jewelry. Not that it's worth anything now." Then he stopped and sniffed the air. "Chanel." He whispered and the barrel of the silenced Beretta came out of the fold of a silk kimono and pressed itself into the side of his head.

"Well Captain Ahab, your nose works better than your eyes, ahem, eye."

"You're the twat from Vanderhorn's, the one with the suitcase full of diamonds." Dickey said, his hands slowly, gently, rising above his head.

"And you're the one taking Mrs. Oaks' jewelry and replacing it with, from the looks of it, moisonitte."

"Are you FBI? I want to talk to my lawyer."

"No."

"No? I've got my rights, lady. This is America damnit."

"That's cute, but I'm not FBI."

"Then who're you with?"

"Someone who doesn't give a fuck about your rights or lawyers."

Then it all went black for Dickey.

Ugly Sue stood over the crumpled body, turning the cocktail ring under the bright even lighting. It glinted and formed a prism but it wasn't brilliant. The old cow would never know the difference. Ugly Sue tossed the cocktail ring onto the dressing table and peered into the master suite. Then she looked down at Dickey. "You little prick." She took hold of his lapels.

THE BLACK LINCOLN PULLED UP TO THE CURB in front of the Oaks' house, but didn't take the approach. "Thank you driver." Vik said absently and handed over a five and ten dollar bill, "You'll stay on call."

Mr. Carl ran a private taxi service consisting on his gleaming black Lincoln Town Car and himself. "The name is Mr. Carl, if you'll like. And I'll stay on call till mornin' if you wanna pay me for that long. That alright?"

"No."

"Then Mr. Carl ain't on call, Mr. Makarin." Mr. Carl eased back in his seat and eased the black cap on his head, "You see, I've got other customers, Mr. Makarin. Lotsa people depend on Mr. Carl to get them here and there in a little bit of style. Jest like you. Yeah, you jest give old Mr. Carl a call bout, say, twenty minutes before you gots to go and I'll be around shortly."

Vik was considering exactly how incensed he should be at this. "What if I have to leave quickly?"

Mr. Carl breathed hard and propped his elbow over the back of the front seat. "Well now, if its that urgent, maybe you ought to consider havin' Mr. Carl on call."

The alligator wallet came out of the dinner jacket and Vik handed over three crisp twenty-dollar bills. "I don't want to wait any twenty minutes. I want you outside!"

"Very good, Mr. Makarin, very good." Mr. Carl put the money in his coat pocket. "Listen, I'm gunta get something to eat, cupa coffee. That alright with you, Boss?"

"Didn't I just pay you to stay put?"

"You ain't plannin' on leaving in the next fifteen minutes are you? I'm sure there lots of good food…a high rent party like this. You can't get through the food line in fifteen minutes. Unless you on a diet. You ain't on a diet is ya Mr. Makarin?"

Vik rolled his eyes, "Fifteen minutes – or you're fired."

Mr. Carl was comforted by the fact that $60 cash for fifteen minutes of work really wasn't a bad scale. "One quarter of an hour, Boss. Not a second longer." Mr. Carl came around the car and opened the door. Vik hoisted himself out of the Lincoln and straightened his dinner jacket without making eye contact.

That gave Mr. Carl a chuckle.

Vik Makarin made his way up the long drive and the knot tightened in his stomach. Why hadn't he had a pre-engagement bracer? Because Mickey Boy had called him and specifically brought it up. *No drinking, Viktor Borisivich.*

Mickey Boy, it's a cocktail party.

Champagne, if they're passing it around. BUT NO VODKA!

It was like telling a fish not to swim. Vodka was pure, like water. Vodka fortified their people against harsh winters and long darkness. It fortified Vik against these insane, pushy western women who overran America. One of those strangely analytical women he'd met in New Orleans a few years ago had once made the absurd comment that Vik was shy, or worse, afraid of women. Crazy bitch. Just a crazy American bitch.

Now he was on the front steps and the knot tightened again. Maybe Dickey would be at the door. Hell he was throwing the damn thing wasn't he? Dickey would be at the door. They'd have a drink or two and Vik would go upstairs to the safe. Then everyone would be off his back. He'd have another drink and talk to some women.

The door swung open after a single violent rap of the knocker. Vik recognized the ring on Mrs. Oaks' finger and instinctively made a short, quick bow. "Mrs. Oaks, I presume." He took her hand. "I am Viktor Borisivich Makarin."

Mrs. Oaks ate the old world style up with a soup ladle. She snatched a champagne flute off the Beidermeir table in the entrance hall handed it to Vik. "Mr. Makarin, I hear that your little shop is the place to go to find the most wonderful pieces."

"You flatter me. I try." He said and drained his champagne.

At first Mrs. Oaks was taken aback, but then figured maybe it was a Russian thing. She didn't offer him another glass on the suspicion that breaking stuff was another Russian thing. She excused herself and the nerves gripped Vik again. Where the hell was Dickey O'Shea? Damned Irish pikey was probably passed out drunk somewhere.

ARCHIE WAS MENTIONING TO TARA that he hadn't seen Vivie all night. "That's okay, Archie. Old boyfriends aren't really the best thing for marital bliss. I think boredom is."

"I thought you said she was dying to see me."

Tara lit a cigarette, "That doesn't mean anything good will come of it. Now where in the hell did you get that absinthe? That was fabulous."

Over her head, Archie saw Vik Makarin come into the entrance hall and knock back an entire glass of champagne in front of a stunned Mrs. Oaks. He checked his watch-closely-"Hey that's Vik Makarin who just came in. I'll bet he's thirsty."

Tara turned, gave the old man a look and shrugged, "Who's he?"

"Someone who needs to keep drinking." Archie said.

"Is something wrong with your watch?"

Then Bunty came out of the kitchen with a tray of champagne flutes, stopping only once to let a couple swap glasses. The swish went into her hips and a smile cut across Vik's dry face. "Champagne, Sir." She said. "You're empty handed."

"Yes." He said and took a flute.

"Does your wife need one?" Bunty offered with a smile.

Pathetic relief washed over Vik's face. "Of course she does. How awful of me to forget her." He took another glass and Bunty moved away quickly. Vik took the glass in two gulps and set on a table, wandering into the den with the second glass dangling from his fingertips.

On the porch beyond the den some men were smoking cigars. Vik was feeling better now and had just finished his 'wife's' glass of champagne when Bunty appeared at his side to clean up the evidence. "Listen, if you're tired of the girlie champagne, there's a proper bar right over there. Whiskey and port." Bunty looked him over and winked, "I might be able to sneak out a bottle of vodka, if that's your poison."

Vik took another flute of champagne, "You are an angel, my dear."

"It'll be our secret, okay. You tell Mira Semmes, caterer or Mrs. Oaks I broke with theme and it'll get ugly."

"You are beautiful. It will be our secret."

His angel flew away with a half empty tray. Vik, feeling a little fuzzy, and more confident, checked his watch and cursed Dickey O'Shea.

He stepped onto the screened-in porch and took a cigar, lit it and poured himself a glass of port. He drifted towards the far door unnoticed by the Memphis insiders. Then he was stepping into the side yard, puffing on the cigar and sipping what he had to admit was excellent port.

IN THE SUNROOM, Archie tore his attention from Tara's mostly exposed thigh and watched Vik move toward the outside door of the porch. "What the hell is Viktor doing out in the side yard?" He said into his Rolex.

Tara rolled her eyes, "He's taking a piss, Archie. You boys will have a squirt anywhere."

"God bless us, Tara, everyone."

He took her hand and dragged her into the entrance hall. "I don't wanna go public, Archie. Please, not just yet. Gotta let mom loosen up."

From the entrance hall Archie could see into the kitchen. "Stay inside!" He barked into his watch.

Bunty's head twitched as she stepped out the kitchen door.

"I'm not going outside, Archie." Said Tara calmly, "I'm not wearing a bra. Christ, I'd put somebody's eye out."

"Listen Love, can you and your blinding nipples excuse me for just one second. I've got business crap I've got to attend."

"All you people work. It's not for me." Tara gave the room a quick scan for Robert Chu. Before she could give Archie formal permission to leave her, he was gone. He was in the kitchen, popping an egg roll in his mouth and disappearing up the back stairway off the garage.

Tara turned to find her sister looking off in the same direction. "Hey Vivie, how're Mom and Dad holdin' up?"

"Mom, she's like a tank. Dad's doing alright. Was that Archie?"

"Where?"

"Going up the back stairs. How long has Archie been here?"

Tara smiled, "For a while. I've had him in the sunroom all night."

Archie emerged into the empty upper hallway and went straight to Vivie's old room. The room was dark save for the moon from above the windows and the floodlights below them. Crossing the room, Archie found the cord under the window treatment and pressed his face against the pane of glass and peered downward.

Below him, by the tree Archie had used to climb into Vivie's room, (and subsequently Vivie) were Bunty and Vik. They looked to be shooting vodka. Vik did, at least. While the old Russian dramatically threw his head back to take the snort, Bunty would do the same but tossed the hooch over her shoulder.

"Get inside, Bunty. He's dangerous." Archie snarled into the Rolex. "I'm in Vivie's room. Just get back to work and he'll forget about you-"Bunty laughed dramatically by the tree and poured out another round for them. "Just get inside."

"Who are you talking to?"

Archie froze. He hadn't heard her come in. How long had she been standing there? He couldn't really bark about privacy, it was her room, or at least used to be. Archie turned to see her like a very real ghost. If she'd gained weight, gotten a layer of thick skin with marriage and motherhood, Archie couldn't see it now. Vivie stood in the moonlight of her childhood room, hips set out and holding an unlit cigarette.

"Sorry about that. It was a phone call. A bit noisy downstairs."

"Won't argue that."

Digging in his pants pocket, Archie fished out a lighter, "Let me get that for you." The small blue flame danced up from his fingertips. Bunty and Vik were still out by the tree.

"I'm not going to chase that fire around." Vivie said.

"Of course you won't." He crossed over to her and lit her cigarette. She never broke eye contact, Vivie was like that.

"I heard you took Tara to lunch yesterday."

"Long story, it's not what it seems. I don't know what impression she's got but I'm sure it's wrong."

"Probably a good thing. There is no way in hell that you can live up to a crush she's had since she was ten."

Archie smiled, "How're things Vivie? Wouldn't have guessed that you still smoke."

"I don't really. I've got a hall-pass, Roger's got the kids while I'm being a good daughter, do the cheerleading thing for the family firm."

He could see it now, a little older, heavier but not much so, strangely even more beautiful. "I always knew you'd get it picture perfect, Vivie. You were smart to get short of me and all my foolishness."

"You were the one who ran off to Europe, Archie. Besides, like I said, Roger is home with the kids." She let that one linger and took a drag off the cigarette. "Would you like a puff? It's awful, I bummed it off Tara. I *think* it's tobacco."

"No thank you. I don't guess that y'all aren't so hard up you can't get a babysitter."

A long drag. "I don't guess that we are." Then she smiled, "So how are you boy-o? I've been thinking about you since Isobel died. God I loved that woman. How's Frank holding up?"

"Pop's fine. He's better. Listen, I stepped into your father's office earlier…"

"Ha! So did I."

Another long, awkward drag.

Vivie smiled, "If I thought it would do any good, I'd meet you in there again."

"It wouldn't."

"Nope." Vivie turned and walked to the doorway, "Take care of yourself Archie. Kiss Frank for me."

"I will. On the forehead."

DICKEY O'SHEA WAS AWARE OF THE PERFUMED folds of delicate fabric tickling his nose. The reverb between the walls of his skull was low and squeaking and painful. His eyes swam in and out of focus in the dim light. *Where in the hell am I?* It smelled like Mrs. Oaks when she was dressed – he was starting to like her better that way.

He tried to roll to his side but he couldn't. His hands were bound, and his feet. It was cold. He felt naked. Dickey tried to thrash the delicate fabric loosely laid over his face away. The skull boomed with pain as he did. It was cold, he could hear the sounds of a party far off. Or was it just muffled. The party! Why was he so cold? The thud along the side of his face boomed and Dickey was aware of some genital shrinkage. The word *heavy* drifted around while he racked his brain as to what he was supposed to remember. There was a reason he was there-but where? He had a job, needed to do something. Something heavy.

UGLY SUE BENT DOWN TO STUDY THE SAFE. Archie, whatever else she might think of the charming buffoon, had a good eye for detail. Under the massive desk in front of the safe, was a small metal kit. She checked the door and set the case atop the desk and opened it. The equipment was basic, but of a better quality than she was used to working with. This stuff wasn't Russian made despite the

Cyrillic letters. She placed the electric stethoscope at her ears and squatted before the safe, placing the pad against the wall, next to the dial. She spun the dial a time or two, slowly, then quickly, then slowly again. There was nothing. She'd need to go hi-tech. Pretty in its foam inset was an electric meter about the size cell phones used to be. Another check of the door and Ugly Sue set the meter against the safe. Three yellow lights lit up along the face of the meter. When the locks turned and the pins opened inside the safe wall, they would turn to green. Slowly she began to turn the dial and watched the meter. The yellow lights, lined neatly up on the bottom of the display, never flickered.

A deep breath. *Calm down Daisy, you're going too fast.* She lifted her fingers off the dial and dried them on her leg. Softly she blew lightly on her finger pads. Even in this world of lasers in Polynesian jungles, touch still did, and always would, play a crucial role. *Slow down, Daisy. Touch.*

Archie's voice came from the hall, "Ugly – open up." In an instant the door opened, without speaking Ugly Sue was back at the safe and Archie checked the window. Vik and Bunty were no longer by the tree.

Ugly Sue was again trying the meter on the safe, still the three yellow lights remained unmoved. "This thing has been customized." She said. "I'm going to need the drill."

Archie set the bag on the desk, crossed the room and opening the door in the paneling. "Why is this unlocked?" he muttered and turned on the light. A dim red glow washed from the small room and faded as the panel swung very nearly closed again.

On one of the monitors he caught site of Uncle Derrick and Aunt Midge. Midge was holding court before a trio of enthralled Chinese diplomats and Derrick, who appeared to be disappointed in the caviar, was talking to Bunty. "That's not good." Archie muttered and kicked the drill at his feet. "That's odd."

GROWING UP, MRS. OAKS ALWAYS IDOLIZED the older local beauty who'd managed to marry herself to an older Scottish aristocrat. At an engagement party for Midge and Derrick, the young Vivian Wallace (now Oaks) had gushed drunkenly over Midge's catch. Enough so that Derrick felt compelled to tell her that Scottish

Baronettes were not really aristocrats. It didn't matter – he and by proximity Midge, would always be higher life forms to Mrs. Oaks.

Now they were standing in her entrance hall. Mrs. Oaks didn't remember inviting them, thought they lived in Virginia, but she wasn't about to say anything. Perhaps Archie had brought them. Where was Archie? She could see Tara, who was busy hiding from that oily Chinaman named Chu.

Uncle Derrick's eyes crept over the grand sweep of the staircase. About mid-way up was a pretty girl who he thought was an old girlfriend of Archie's. She looked more like the Vivian Wallace of all those years ago than the woman now gushing at Midge. Midge was telling Mrs. Oaks how surprised they were to get an invitation and of course they wouldn't have missed it for the world. Then a voice from another room caught the old soldier's ear; he wasn't nearly as deaf as he lead his wife to believe. Stepping around the other two, Derrick continued his study of the staircase but glanced into the kitchen. Bunty was picking up a tray and being shadowed by Viktor Makarin. She moved quickly away, focusing on the caviar she was carrying and then disappeared from sight.

Midge was still chatting with Mrs. Oaks. "Well, Vivian, why don't you introduce us to your diplomats. Derrick and I lived in Hong Kong for a few years. Oh God, it was forever ago. You know I think he was a stockholder in the old Colonial Telegraph & Wire."

Bunty reappeared in the living room, carrying the tray of caviar awkwardly. Waving a paw to get her attention, "Excuse me ladies." Derrick coughed and moved towards the living room.

Midge gave Mrs. Oaks one of those you-know-men eye rolls. "Well there you are. She is a pretty thing." Then a bright smile, "At least he's got good taste."

Mrs. Oaks apparently felt that Bunty's looks didn't actually salve the situation and gave a deliberate "tsk, tsk, tsk." Then she lightened up, "Midge, you will have to met Mr. Lee, he's awful. He has two attendants, both named Mr. Qaun. They look like executioners."

At first glance, Bunty stared back at Derrick with panic. She could see him peer back into another room. There was nothing for it but to take the man some caviar. Crossing the room with a smile on her face, Bunty moved the tray before Derrick.

"How goes it, Ms. Carrick?" said Derrick.

"Pretty good Mr. Gordon. I didn't know you were coming?"

"Ha, neither did Mrs. Oaks." He looked at the caviar, and a wicked but charming smile floated across his face. Like he knew exactly where a dirty joke was going.

"Would you like some caviar?"

"Of course." The caviar was set atop a dollop of cream cheese on a small triangle of toast. Derrick snatched the toast with a cocktail napkin. He never ate the morsel and kept looking intently at Bunty. He cleared his throat, "Now what's all this? I'm delighted to see you m'girl. You look spanking. Is that nephew of mine not paying you enough? He's got plenty of money. Don't believe him when he says he hasn't." The half grin spread fully across his face, he seemed to be looking for a reaction.

"Try the caviar."

He popped the toast into his mouth and cut a sideways glance in Mrs. Oaks' direction. She was leading Midge to a trio of Chinese men in bad tuxedos. "This is Russian, and illegal. Where did you get this?"

"You've got a very sophisticated tongue. How can you tell?"

"It tastes like it was tinned in an oil refinery. Now why do you need a second job…and why one flogging black market caviar?"

Bunty tucked a strawberry blonde forelock behind her ear. "Ski vacation with the girls. I'm trying to earn a little spending money. Go shopping."

"Oh how about that. Jolly good. Bunty Love, why didn't you just ask for an advance?"

What was annoying Bunty was the certainty that Derrick was enjoying this little game. "Look, Uncle Derrick…uh…Mr. Gordon…Archie doesn't know about this."

"Not that I'm not happy to see you. I just thought you'd be in a cocktail dress."

"So did I. Listen Mr. Gordon, can we keep this quiet?"

Rocking back on his heels, Derrick never lost eye contact with Bunty. "Really. Keeping him in the dark, eh? I could have sworn I saw his car – that God-awful Scout – outside the approach."

"Is it?" Bunty stammered, "He'll be so disappointed."

"What a remarkably bad liar you are. What have you two got brewing?"

"What? Oh God, I've got to run."

Vic came stumbling out of the side porch grumbling at the cell phone in Russian. He swept through the room and took Bunty by the arm. "My assistant is a worthless gypsy, he's no good. He's here but I can't find him. But you, you are an angel."

"I'm starting to dry out Vik." Bunty cooed and moved back to the side porch the stairs. She was aware that Derrick was watching her performance. Actually everyone was.

Mrs. Oaks didn't know what to make of the scene. Midge grabbed her arm, "Don't you absolutely hate these diplomatic affairs!" she said by way of all encompassing explanation.

Vic moved her out of the way, "Not now, little girl."

Bunty bit her lip and pouted. "Just a taste, Mr. Makarin."

"My apologies…but something of mine was stolen and I really must get it back." He turned ascended the stairs.

In an instant, Bunty had crossed to the kitchen and swiped the now half-empty bottle of vodka. Bounding up the stairs, she closed the distance between them.

At the top, Vik turned to Bunty. He smiled but it was far off and sinister. "Little girl…you are beautiful. But I have business here. You don't want to be involved."

Bunty took a belt of vodka and kissed Vik deeply.

"Here." she said, her face still close to his, "You're thirsty."

Vik put a hand to the small of her back and led her to the first door from the top of the landing. They moved into the room, cold from the air coming in the open window.

There was a blast to the head, things went white and then purple and splotchy. Vik opened his eyes and steadied himself against the door jamb. The pretty waitress was stand beside him, holding the vodka bottle like a sheleghly."

"Why did you do that?" Vik asked.

"Why are you still standing?" Bunty brained him a second time with the bottle. Then a large hand came around Vic's chin and Bunty was confronted with a large swathe of Gordon plaid. "If you could let me have that bottle, Miss Carrick, I'll show you how this is done." Derrick clubbed Vic who slumped into a heap. "You see, Love, it isn't a matter of strength, you've just got to hit them just so." He dragged Vic into the closet. Bunty was dumbfounded. "I feel like I'm in the regiment again. Is there anyone else you want to kiss?"

"It was like a catcher's mitt soaked in vodka. I'd kiss you right now but I don't want to get on Midge's bad side."

"Best give it to Archie. Now where is the lad?"

"I dunno, I did see the nympho's big sister come this way."

THE LOCK IN THE HANDLE POPPED OUT and the door swung open. He stood in the doorway and said, after blithely checking his watch, "As of three hours ago, Mikhail Boyorov was still sunning himself on what passes for a beach in Cuba. Not at all at the bottom of the Archipelago like I asked."

Ugly Sue, caught in the very act of lining the drill bit with the door of the safe, stood dumbfounded. "Could you at least close the door?" she asked hoarsely, and fingered the power switch at her thumb pad. "Look, Rowan, there is more to this than you know."

"I sincerely doubt it."

"American companies are involved, multi-nationals."

Rowan shut the door and stepped into the room, his fingers resting gingerly on the high shine of the desk. "American multi-nationals are always involved. You really ought to know this by now. You see, Ugly Sue, I don't need another detective, I've got them and analysts running out my ears. What I need is a heartless drone to remove one ex-KGB arms dealer in Cuba from the equation. Need I remind you that one of you is going to be dead by the end of the week."

"You may not make it either, Rowan. Don't forget what you hired me for."

This brought a smile to Rowan's lips – now it seemed faintly familiar. "Quite frankly I'm a bit hazy on what it is you do."

The panel on the other side of the room opened and out stepped Archie, Ugly Sue was still poised at the safe, drill in hand. Archie looked at the other, "Hey Uncle Derrick, how do you two know each other?"

Fifteen

'Round Midnight

THE INTERNATIONAL DEPARTURES GATE at the New Orleans Airport the night before the Mardi Gras is a lonely place. It's an odd time to leave the city. The tall Chinaman in the cheap suit felt very conspicuous. The sensitivity to racial profiling being what it is, he normally was not stopped while traveling, but tonight the travelers leaving the city for destinations abroad were few and he could feel the custom officer's eyes baring into him. "Could you step aside, sir?"

The man coolly did as asked. He took off his shoes and opened his coat wide. The search was professional and efficient. "Open your bag sir?"

"Pardon?"

"Your carry-on, Sir." The tone of the officer's voice changed. Another officer drifted closer.

The man snatched the bag and ran. He heard the voices calling after him and he turned quickly into a gate, shoving through the door and down the ramp that opened into the air ten feet above the tarmac. He took the jump and came down as best he could. His heel came over a patch of oil-slick concrete and turned. That was all it took. His ankle snapped under him as he heard commands to stop screamed from behind.

Inertia had him, he kept falling forward. Then they were shooting and the searing pain ripped through his muscles. The broken ankle went forward but didn't stop him. He turned and fell on his back. The life was bleeding out of him as he stared up into a cloudy night.

Footsteps were running towards him.

DERRICK STARED AT UGLY SUE. "Put down that drill, I've got the combination!"

Ugly Sue put down the drill, "How?"

"The same way I found you, darling."

"How do you two know each other?" Archie repeated.

"Archie Gilmur is your nephew!" Ugly barked.

Derrick was looking at Archie, "Ugly Sue here worked for me."

"I'm still-"

"She tried to kill me." Archie explained.

"She pissed in her whisky there. She was not supposed to be there, in Jamaica. Not then anyway. She failed her assignment...then overstepped it to keep from being liquidated." Without passion he looked back at Ugly Sue. "And she's going to have to pay the price for it."

"Don't worry about the shooting, we made up."

"Archie, I'm sorry you're involved in this."

"Well it isn't your fault, Uncle Derrick. Strange coincidence, really."

"You were telling the truth!" said Ugly Sue, "You honestly thought you were in Jamaica for a corporate job?"

"I was. The fella from DeltaComm hired me to check out the security systems."

Ugly Sue leaned in over the desk, "In all the information you stole, all that data on corporate officers and personnel, did you ever find the fella's name who hired you?"

"No."

"Have you spoken to him since?"

"I haven't made my report." Archie said and then he was looking at Uncle Derrick, not his face but the .9mm Sig Sauer that had come out of his jacket. It was vaguely pointed at Ugly Sue.

"She's right, Archie. The man from DeltaComm was a plant. CIA."

"Your own uncle used you as a pawn."

"That's quite enough!" Derrick said quietly and stepped to the desk, placing the gun in the small of her back. "Archie, we needed you to do what you do best. The safest way to do it was to keep you in the dark. When Ugly Sue broke orders and showed up at the

SinoTel facility that night, your ignorance saved your life. The smallest details were planned out, except for this one breaking rank."

Archie had never seen Uncle Derrick's aristocratic calm fail him, but now, beneath it, he could see a fury rage. It dawned on him that Derrick was most likely going to kill Ugly Sue right in front of him.

The same thought occurred to Ugly Sue. "It's called the US-UK agreement." She said, "The laws of the US and Great Britain forbid either from spying on their own citizens. It used to not be a problem, the world was a cloudier place and media leaks were easy to stop up. Now it's a little different." Ugly Sue continued and Derrick, while still furious, did nothing to stop her. "Now, the United States out sources spying on its own citizens to the Brits and vice versa. Makes the world much more convoluted. Really clouds up those 60 Minutes exposes. Isn't that right Rowan?"

"To a degree. Archie, we hired you to do what you do best. You were looked after, I hope you believe that."

"Why me? Don't you have people for this sort of thing? I've taught myself some tricks, but I'd thought your own people would be better at this cloak and dagger business."

"Your line of work, plus your history with the Oaks made you perfect. Again, ignorance to the bigger picture was your best shield."

"Don't connect the dots, Archie," Ugly Sue snorted, "that'll get you killed."

Derrick nudged her with the Sig Sauer but said nothing to her, "I had hoped that you'd come work for me."

"Does Aunt Midge know any of this?"

"Some. She was totally opposed to the idea of you working for me-if that helps."

"What about Pop?"

Derrick laughed.

"It was Pop's idea wasn't it?"

"This place is killing you, M'lad. You need a bigger stage. You can't spend the rest of your days chasing after desperate housewives and philandering husbands."

Archie shrugged his shoulders, "It was getting a bit old." He saw a sadness in Ugly Sue's eyes. Not fear, just sadness. "What's her real name?"

"Archie this really isn't-"

"You threw me into this."

"Daisy," Derrick said, "Daisy Adreas."

"Nice to meet you Daisy." He turned back to Derrick, "Who exactly do you work for? The Brits or us?"

"You're half a Brit yourself, m'lad. It's hard to explain. I work for an agreement, really."

"This US/UK agreement."

"Precisely."

"It's called U-suck?"

"Amazing." Derrick smiled, "All our cryptographers and code breakers and you are the first one to notice that."

"Really?"

"Good God no!"

Ugly Sue chimed in, "Yeah, you two are definitely related."

"That's been a joke since day one. We'd have gone with something else but the Americans always demand top billing."

"National character flaw."

"I'm well aware of that...I've been married to your Aunt for forty years." The he nudged Ugly Sue, "Go get Robert Chu!"

"I think I just need to get the hell out of here."

"And how far do you think you'll get?"

"Alright. Bring him back up here?"

"Please."

She got up, looked at both of them and said, "It's a hell of a family business." She walked out of the office.

"You weren't really going to kill her?" Archie asked.

"Let's not talk about that right now." Derrick crouched in front of the safe and worked the dial. Then the door swung open and he set the contents on the desk. "Have you got a briefcase with you?" Derrick asked, still looking at the neat pile of bound papers and envelopes before him.

"Hold on." Archie went to the closet and returned with a slim black briefcase that looked perfectly normal.

"Hey now," said Derrick, "that's sharp."

"Knowing Mr. Oaks, this thing has got a pair of throwing knives and strand of Krugarands in the lining."

Derrick breathed hard. "That halfwit. Listen to me, when we're done up here I want you to tell Miss Bunty here to scat. I didn't think you were going to drag her into this." He looked back over his shoulder, "Where'd the lass go?"

Archie smiled, "I haven't seen her in an hour. I notice you haven't dismissed me."

Bunty was down the hall. The situation had relaxed when Derrick brained the old Russian, so had her bladder. When Derrick stepped into the office, Bunty headed down the hallway to the master bedroom in search of a bathroom. Her head was swimming and she stepped in the bathroom quickly without turning on the lights. It was strangely cold in the room but she relaxed. She emerged from the master bath thinking that Archie had mentioned Uncle Derrick having been in the SAS, and she thought he was hot in a Sean Connery sort of way. Then she heard the voice and saw the naked man tied, spread eagle with silk scarves on Mrs. Oaks' bed. The man was suffering from shrinkage. "Whose there?" the man hissed, "untie me." Bunty moved closer to the bed and pulled the sheet from his face. He wasn't entirely nude, he still had the eye patch. "Ahoy Matey! You've got a naughty bag of tricks."

"Untie me."

"Oh, what's the fun in that?"

"Then cover me."

Bunty decided right then to go downstairs and really push the caviar. She turned on her heels and stopped as the image of Mrs. Oaks' violent red lipstick flashed across her mind's eye. Dickey thought her laugh was evil.

UGLY SUE CAME DOWN THE SWEEP of the front staircase certain that she looked smashing. Then it was into the reception room. On the first causal scan of the room, she didn't find Robert Chu. Then, appearing at her side was Bunty with a tray of caviar. "How goes everything? Haven't heard from upstairs."

"Things have gotten complicated." Ugly Sue took a toasted round of caviar.

"Hold it. Don't eat it. Mr. Gordon thinks it was tinned in a oil refinery."

"Who?"

"Archie's Uncle Derrick."

Ugly folded the napkin over the caviar. "Bunty, you need to get the hell out of here."

"Where's Archie?"

"Upstairs."

"I'm not leaving him here."

Ugly Sue set the squished napkin on a butler's tray and said, "Suit yourself." Ugly Sue made her way across the room. The party was lively but mellow. The continual loop of the frolicking pandas on either side of the room cast a dim light over the partygoers. Across the room, she spotted Mr. Lee.

The Manchurian did not recognize her, but Chu was nowhere to be found. Mr. Lee, on the other hand, was enthralled by the presence of a small, smartly dressed woman with a drawling Southern accent. Two other Chinese men seemed to be standing in attendance. Without knowing why, Ugly Sue knew this was the one Archie called Aunt Midge.

She held a glass of champagne with one hand and the other flitted around in an animated twitter. "Well," she was saying, "I thought Hong Kong was grand. But Derrick tells me that you can't play polo on the side of a mountain, so it was never really his cup of tea." Then she turned to Ugly Sue, "The champagne is delightful, dear. Do go get some."

"Yes ma'am, I think I will." She said and drifted off towards the side porch and clouds of cigar smoke.

There she found Robert Chu.

Tara couldn't tell if Robert Chu was drunk or desperate or some fatal combination of the two. He'd been hanging around her all night and while Tara wasn't sure exactly what it was Chu did, he wasn't here for his social connections. Robert had taken to puffing arrogantly on a cigar. Then she looked over his shoulder (every time Chu approached her, she allowed him to back her to the wall so she could get a view as to who was coming and going – it freed her periodically when Chu grew tiresome and also drove the boy wild with jealousy. A win/win in Tara's rather thin book).

The girl who'd come in with Archie drifted onto the side porch and looked as if she were searching for someone. Tara assumed it was Archie and this brought a smile to her lips. She waved Ugly Sue over.

Ugly Sue crossed the room and zeroed in on Tara without so much as a glance at Chu. "Have you seen Archie?"

"Oh no, I set him free an hour ago. He hasn't found you yet? That's strange," she leaned in, "I mean the party isn't *that* big, is it?"

Ugly Sue winked at Chu. "No party is that big." Just lightly, the pads of her fingers brushed the back of Chu's hand. "Don't I know you?"

"You do look very familiar. What was your name again?"

"Sue." Ugly Sue said slowly.

Tara watched them. "So Robert, you were telling me about Jamaica."

After an embarrassing pause, Chu's attention drifted back to Tara, "Was I?"

"Ah, Jamaica." Ugly Sue cooed, patted his arm, and drifted out of the room. Chu turned to watch what Tara could already see: hips swaying that certain way.

Chu turned back to Tara. Her jaw was set. He let out a plume of smoke and said, "I've really got to go check on Mr. Lee."

Tara gently plucked the cigar from his mouth, "Want me to hold this?" She placed it between her pouting lips in another certain way.

Chu was enjoying the sudden dynamic shift. "Suit yourself. I'll be back." He turned and left the room. In the reception room, he found Ugly Sue picking a glass of champagne from a tray. She looked over her shoulder and smiled. Then she left, passing him on the far side of the room. He followed her up the staircase.

The office door opened and Ugly Sue entered, floating across the floor and drifting into one of the armchairs, facing the doorway with a wicked smirk. Then Chu came into the doorway and stopped, "Why so formal? There's a much more comfortable room down the hall."

"That's for married people – where's the fun in that?"

Chu came into the room and closed the door. Pain exploded behind his eyes and a blood-fueled heat gathered beneath his left cheek. He was being pushed backwards by a man and recognized the feeling of an H&K P7 pressed into the flesh of his neck. Then he was shoved into the other armchair and a number of hands where on him. Duct tape was being torn. Just as his eyes were swimming back into focus a strap of tape went over them. Then his ankles and wrists were bound to the chair.

Then a needle went into the fleshy side of his neck. "This very well may kill you, Mr. Chu-" It was an older man's voice. Hard to place the accent, like a Brit who'd lived abroad most of his life. "But it won't leave a mark. I hate messes."

"I don't think you know-"

"I think I know very well who's downstairs, Mr. Chu. And who isn't. I need something from you, that's why I've invited up here to this lovely office. What I want to know is where Mickey Boy is sending that yellowcake you boys at SinoTel bought from him."

"What yellowcake?"

"Not the moist delicious kind - uranium." Said Archie

"What would SinoTel want with nuclear yellowcake?"

"Precisely the question I was going to ask you. We picked up a report from our man in Panama—something about a plan to 'defile the most vile holy day in Christendom.' Why would a Chinese Telecom parts manufacturer want to do that? Are you planning to blow up an Easter Egg hunt? A little out of your knitting, I think."

Ugly Sue watched all this, Rowan standing behind Chu, one hand with a firm clump of Chu's short oily hair and the other holding the syringe steady. She knew what he was doing, what wasn't entirely clear was why Archie was crouched silently at Chu's side, and crawling his fingers slowly over Chu's shoe and up his pant leg.

"What's that?" Chu's voice wavered and his ankle strained against the duct tape.

Ugly Sue smiled, she almost laughed. Then she spoke slowly because she had always spoken slowly in Jamaica. "It's you friend, Bobby Chu, Anansi Coupé."

The crawling hand passed his knee. "Ugly Sue?"

"Tat's right. Ole Miz Cassat told me you biz-ness."

"No – she didn't trust you. You are a half-breed."

"Jess like you. Maybe that's why she tell me. Tat Anansi Coupé, he might powerful mojo. Then you is dealing in powerful tings. Tings that sparkle and go boom."

Archie was creeping along the thigh and in no mood to handle genitalia. He crept up to the torso and stopped. Ugly Sue really needed to speed up the show up or Chu was going to figure out the scam. Still there was Uncle Derrick and that freakishly large syringe he'd pulled out of the pocket of his dinner jacket. Ugly Sue nodded and Archie continued his crawl up Chu's torso.

"Mr. Chu-" Derrick started, "I don't know what religion you've got here, or just where the bloody hell that great hairy spider came from, but what I've got is going to burn through your bloodstream for a few hours while you think about the Almighty and your insides liquefy. If you've got any hexes on your soul, you'd best clear them out now."

"Oh Bobby Chu got him a hex of a foul sort."

"IT'S NOT AN EASTER EGG HUNT!" He blurted out.

DERRICK WENT DOWNSTAIRS TO GET BUNTY. Ugly Sue stood guard at Vivie's door and Archie was shoving Chu out the window. "Quit struggling. It isn't much of a jump – I used to do it when I was sixteen."

"You and Tara?" Chu asked and Archie pushed him through the casing.

"No, her older sister."

Chu seemed relieved.

"I didn't get nekkid with Tara till last week. Hot little body. Very clean. Now jump."

He jumped. It wasn't until Chu hit the grass, cracking all the ribs on his right side, that Archie noticed the limb was gone. "Bunty, you could've told me about the branch."

"On my things to do." Bunty called back.

Looking up from the cold ground, Chu was unsure what he saw. He thought it was a small Celtic caterer with an industrial pizza cutter.

Archie leapt to a lower branch and came down the tree with enough dexterity to keep hold of the P7 as he hit the ground.

"You know," Bunty said, "I feel a little exposed here." She brandished the pizza cutter.

"Here take the gun."

"Will that thing go off?"

"On occasion."

"I'll stick with the pizza cutter."

"Well wipe it off, Chu here could get an infection."

Bunty looked at Chu, "You hear that? Stay in line."

Chu tried twice to stand on his own, but the pain from his crushed ribcage burned through his muscles and his lungs couldn't take in the air. Then Archie pulled him to his feet and they walked around the side of the house, staying in the shadows.

On the street Archie dropped the tailgate of the Scout and ordered Chu inside. He and Bunty climbed into the back after him. They duct taped his ankles and wrists behind his narrow back. The tape wasn't torn roughly as before, but in neat strips by Bunty's new weapon. Covering Chu with a tarp, they climbed into the front seat and started the car. "Really Archie, the boy might die back there. It smelled like someone delivered a calf back there."

"I think Pop did once."

"The funk better come out of these pants."

"What about the shirt?"

"The shirt is your problem."

The Scout rolled down the street and stopped in front of the Oaks' house.

"Bunty, go inside and get Ugly Sue-Norah- you know who I mean. Then get in your car and get out of here."

"I'll meet you at the office."

"No Bunty, go home. In fact don't go home, pack a bag and take a vacation. Any place but here, New Orleans or Jamaica."

"Not hardly."

"Don't go to Panama either. How about South Carolina?"

"No way Archie. I don't know what you've gotten yourself into – but I'm in it too." Bunty hopped out of the car and ran inside.

MR. QUAN APPROACHED MR. LEE FOR THE SECOND TIME. The smiling woman with him nodded her head at Mr. Quan. Mr. Lee turned to him, annoyed. "This gentleman appears to need your attention, Mr. Lee." Midge said. In their chat, Midge had failed to mention to Mr. Lee that while she and Derrick were in China, she'd taught Chinese to American and British children. She smiled blankly while Mr. Quan spoke to his boss in unremarkable grammar and a Cantonese inflection. Mr. Quan told Mr. Lee that Robert Chu was nowhere to be found and didn't answer his latest page. And while Midge's grasp of Chinese came from 50-year-old textbooks she was sure that Mr. Lee mused that, Miss Oaks-number two daughter- the nymphomaniac-was to blame. Nymphomaniac being the word she was unsure of.

In the entrance hall, Mrs. Oaks was showing a departing couple to the door and turned to see Midge Gilmur's Aristocratic Scottish husband coming down the stairs with Archie's (his nephew's!) noticeably tawny date. At the sight, Mrs. Oaks was awash in comforting waves of *Schandefreude*, that a late-in-the-game marriage scandal of her childhood hero had taken place at her grand event.

That was simply too rich. She smiled widely at the pair as they came down the steps.

Derrick saw her face and thought Mrs. Oaks was having a moment of wind. Then he turned into the reception hall and Ugly Sue turned to the porch. For Mrs. Oaks, this was a dream come true. She couldn't wait to tell Dickey. And just where the hell was the boy? Sadly, all dreams must end. At that very moment not only was a desperately nude Dickey O'Shea tied to her bed wearing more lipstick than a baroque whore, but Walt Oaks was going upstairs to the Master bedroom to use the bathroom in piece and quiet.

Midge spotted Derrick, "Mr. Lee," she said, "It was marvelous to meet you, I see my husband, would you like to meet him?"

"Regrettably," Mr. Lee started formally, "this trip is business for me. But you have made it a pleasure as well."

"The pleasure is mine." Midge said and drifted across the room to where Derrick stood smiling.

"How did it go Love?"

"Oh he was charmed until his little goon came along. Archie…how bad is he involved?"

"Very deep. I'm sorry. It's the French Operative's fault. I'll take care of her as soon as I get him out of this."

"You're the one who got him into this. You and Frank. Don't blame the girl, you know the affect the boy has on women."

"I know the affect they have on him."

"That seems to be part of the problem doesn't it? We all know he's clueless." Midge took the lapels of her husband's dinner jacket. "Derrick, this has gotten out of hand."

"No, Midge, he's doing fine. You should be proud."

"It's dangerous."

"Who dares-"

"-wins." Midge finished. "I know."

In the back of the truck, Chu rolled over and kicked away the tarp. "Settle down back there." He leaned over and took a can of Dr. Pepper from the floorboard and hurled it into the back. Chu groaned. Archie looked at his watch – it had stopped. The Rolex came off and the Brietling went back on. It was twelve fifteen.

Then, finally, Ugly Sue emerged from the front door, coming quickly down the drive. Archie thought she moved like a cat. She climbed into the car.

"Where's Bunty?"

"Leaving, we put the drill in the back of her car. She said we were going to rendezvous at the office. Where's Chu?"

A defiant groan drifted in from the back. Archie thumbed over his shoulder.

"Nice tape job. How'd you do that?"

"Bunty helped. Have you got the briefcase?"

"What briefcase?"

"The one with all the crap from the safe. The reason we're here!"

"I thought you had it! "Uncle Derrick!"

"Rowan!"

"Who?"

"I could tell... have to kill you though."

"Right."

They looked at each other until Ugly Sue said, "This ought to make Christmas dinner at your house interesting." Bunty's Volvo came down the driveway. "Let's go Archie."

Archie pulled away from the curb and turned into traffic. Ugly Sue looked back at Chu for a long time. "Let me check those bindings." She climbed into the back and slid her hand into the inside of Chu's jacket. She drew out a thin wallet and slid it into the small pocket sewn into the underside of the wide ribbon around the waist. She climbed back into the front. "Your girl Bunty did a bang up job."

"Yeah, she's good like that."

Downtown, they parked the Scout below the window of the Tantallion Group office. Archie and Ugly Sue stood behind the Scout and looked at the motionless figure in the back. Bunty had caught up with them but, Bunty being Bunty, decided to park the Volvo in her reserved space in the parking garage across the street.

"Christ, He's not dead is he?" asked Archie.

"Hard to tell, Archie. The smell back there might have killed him."

"It's like you people don't have farms in France." Archie shook his head and climbed into the back of the Scout. He took Chu's pulse at the carotid artery. "He's alive." Archie came out of the back. "Passed out from the pain, I'd imagine. I thought you spy game sorts were tougher than that."

"I am."

"I'm sure you are. Not tough enough to smell dog-in-a-truck, though. Look, I don't feel like hauling his dead weight up to the office." Archie covered him with the tarp. "Bunty taped him up pretty good...see the nice edges?"

A great many things passed through Ugly Sue's head but she said nothing while Archie locked the Scout.

Bunty emerged from the steel door of the concrete parking bunker across the street. She'd lost the tie and short apron and came across the dark street in the tuxedo pants and shirt now open at the neck. She looked stunning. The smile on her face, visceral and breathy, lit her entire body. Ugly Sue waited for a moment at the door to the office building, turning to find Archie still at the Scout waiting for her.

Roughly two minutes after the trio disappeared behind the building security door, signed in, and disappeared up the elevator, a black Lincoln came around the corner. It pulled up next to the Scout and sat idling as Mr. Quan got out into the cold night wearing a pair of coveralls over his suit. Around the front of the truck he came with a wide skateboard in his hand. Setting the skateboard down, Mr. Quan sat, then laid back on it, and guided himself smoothly under the Scout.

Another three minutes more and Mr. Quan rolled himself out from under the Scout, took up the skateboard, and got back into the Lincoln. He started the engine, gunning it against the cold at the same time he put the gear to drive. The car leapt forward, it's rear trunk panel connecting harshly with the front panel of the Scout, rocking both cars violently. Mr. Quan cursed himself loudly and stopped. Gently he extracted the car from the Scout with a grating scrape, and drove off.

Inside, Archie stepped into the elevator. Bunty and Ugly Sue had taken either wall, facing each other, they were scowling. The implications of this Archie failed to note although it did occur to him that Bunty was still carrying a pizza cutter that belonged to Mira Semmes, caterer.

The car moved up to the soft jazz of Chuck Mangeone's "Feel's So Good." The girls were still glaring at each other. They weren't staring at him, which he took as a good thing. Archie pulled on the lapels of his dinner jacket. The doors opened. He motioned for the ladies to exit. They were locked. "Suit yourself." He muttered, stepping between them and into the hallway. He was unlocking the office door when Ugly Sue came out followed by Bunty.

He opened the door and stepped aside as the two came barreling into the anteroom. Then in Archie went, heading straight for his office door. Bunty was already there – Archie stopped. "I'm changing clothes." She said flatly, stepping into the office and closing the door.

Archie looked at Ugly Sue, "You're the pro, why are we here again?"

"Her idea."

"Since when do you listen to Bunty?"

"She said it was your idea."

"Since when do you listen to me? Listen, what the hell is your problem?"

"Nothing. Your secretary is the one with the tiff."

"Well I know why she doesn't like you-there's the trying to kill me thing, and worse, writing her in as the help on this ridiculous adventure of yours. But what have you got against her?"

"You really are clueless, Archie."

"That, Daisy, is entirely beside the point."

"Get off it. You aren't the only guy who wants to stuff his secretary."

"Bunty? Don't be stupid."

Ugly Sue rolled her eyes.

"Now why did I drag your ass to that party again?"

"To break into the safe-before the Chinese did."

"And did we?"

"Yes."

"And what have we got to show for it, Daisy?"

"Don't get clever," Ugly Sue snarled, "Clever will get you killed."

"By you? You couldn't kill a cat. I don't know why Uncle Derrick hired you. Fuckin' frogs can't finish anything without our help."

"I heard that!" Bunty called from behind the office door.

Then Ugly Sue's Beretta was in Archie's face and he wasn't moving.

The door opened and Bunty said, "I'm glad to see y'all are getting along."

Archie moved away from the gun and Ugly Sue lowered it. He stepped into the office, around Bunty, who was now in a black sweater, jeans, and tennis shoes. Archie moved into the cold pocket of air between the open window and his desk, taking a cigarette from the pack on the desk and lighting it. Bunty turned on the air purifier.

After a long drag, Archie looked down at the Scout. It seemed to rock on its wheels. "Fuck."

"Language! That's twice. Archie, go to the jar."

"Chu's moving again."

CHU WAS AWARE OF A KNOCK TO HIS SURROUNDINGS, then an awful dog smell, then a horrible scraping noise. He opened his eyes, it was black, a complete absence of light, he tried to move his arms, but they were numb, no it was more than that, they were bound. So were his ankles. How had he gotten here? He remembered Tara Oaks. He always remembered Tara Oaks. Then he'd followed that girl from Jamaica upstairs. It would drive Tara mad. But what had happened upstairs?

A stabbing in the neck, a spider-Anansi-crawling up his belly and the girl, Ugly Sue, laughing at him. No, it wasn't Ugly Sue laughing at him but Miz Cassat. Laughing at him from the grave.

Instinctively, without any thought at all, Chu's bound feet came up to where he could touch them with his hands. In the shank of his black Chelsea boot was a razor blade. He fingered it through the fabric of his pants, inching it out of the boot shank.

What was that girl, Ugly... (Ugly Sue couldn't be her real name)... doing at party in Memphis? That's just strange. A little too strange. Chu had trained himself not to believe coincidences.

With a little pressure, the blade came through the fabric it sliced. That was a shame because Chu really liked the way those pants fit. With the blade in hand he began to work on the duct tape around his wrists. Slow and steady, with a little outward pressure from the wrists was the way – too much sawing and the blade would get stuck.

Miz Cassat had been working for Mickey Boy. Mickey Boy liked pretty girls. While Chu was aware that Miz Cassat liked pretty girls as well, Ugly Sue wasn't one of them. Where the hell was he? Chu vaguely remembered falling out of a tree. What was he doing in a tree?

His wrists came apart and Chu sat up, flinging the tarp away. He tore the tape from his lips with a yelp and took in draughts of air into his lungs. Sweat oiled his face, he was in the back of an old truck, but where? The blade went between his ankles and a moment later he was free.

Ugly Sue was working for Mickey Boy! Of course! Chu thought. He flipped over the seat and slid behind the wheel of the Scout. He opened the center console, certain he'd find a screwdriver or a hammer and wasn't disappointed. With the flathead screwdriver, he removed the casing of the ignition switch and leaned in to hot wire the car.

Ugly Sue was working for the Russian…but she worked with Miz Cassat…she would know how to remove the mojo the old witch had hung on his head.

These and other misguided theories were interrupted by the explosion that incinerated Robert Chu and his favorite tuxedo.

THE GIRLS HIT THE FLOOR as the explosion rocked the building and rattled the glass panes. Archie, who was still pondering his uncle's involvement in the current ya-ya, watched with a certain detachment as the Scouts twisted hood came upward, hung momentarily at eye level, and fell back into the burning heap below. He sighed heavily, "Why am I not surprised?"

Sixteen

Airplanes and Ticking Clocks

TUESDAY

The phone rang and David Meeks felt his hand come down on the leather tray that contained his watch, wallet and spare change, sending it to the floor. Valerie had moved the phone to her side of the bed. Now he was fully awake and the phone rang again. He rolled across the empty bed and groped in the dark for the receiver. That his wife was so desperate to have the phone close on her side of the bed, just in case, was made even more frustrating by the fact that Valerie now slept in little Amy's room and had for two months.

On the third ring, Meeks got the phone to his ear, "David Meeks...." The voice on the other end of the line said something, a fairly average something that didn't quite register. "Um…" David was supposed to know what to respond. The caller spoke again, slowly, the hints of that Scottish brogue fading in his ear. "No thank you, I don't have a cat." The brogue was satisfied and began to speak again. "Okay…New Orleans? A situation? Care to speak up? Alright, I'll be at the airfield in…give me an hour….Look, if that plane takes off in thirty minutes it won't have me on it. Forty-five minutes. Who's flying? Alright." He hung up the phone and rolled out of bed, snatching a pair of khakis off the floor and staggered into them. He took a denim shirt and tweed coat off the chair in the corner and grabbed a tie from the closet door that, had he been wake for longer than three minutes, would have noticed didn't match. Then he was down the hall, in Jack's room, gently shaking the boy's shoulder.

"What's up Dad?" Jack asked sleepily.

"C'mon, we're going to Aunt Kim's."

The boy roused himself, pulled jeans off the floor and a sweater over his head. He was pulling on a pair of tennis shoes when his eyes caught the clock. "Is it Amy?"

"No, she's fine. Well, she hasn't changed." Meeks said from the doorway, putting a heavy palm on Jack's shoulder as they stepped out into the hall.

"Why can't I stay here with Mom?"

Now they were standing outside Amy's room, looking in. Amy was asleep, the humidifier quietly running at the foot of her narrow bed. The bottles and monitors lined up on her bedside table with the precision and quantity of a chemist's shelf. Then, sitting vigil over Amy was Valerie; alert in the rocking chair, eyelids fluttering lightly but closed. She looked as if she were about to pounce at an instant sign from Amy. The rocking chair tipped forward, just slightly. She was, in fact, asleep. Meeks himself wouldn't have believed it had he not seen it so many times since Amy went ill.

Jack watched the scene by his father's side. "I'll get my toothbrush." He whispered.

Downstairs, in the kitchen, Meeks wrote a note to his wife. Jack was at her sister's house. He would call her from New Orleans. Jack appeared in the kitchen with his gym bag and got an apple out of a bowl on the counter. "Alright Pop, I'm ready."

THE PILOT HAD BEEN TERRIFIED TO BREAK CUBAN AIRSPACE and to actually land there was even more preposterous. But the one they called Mickey Boy had been very persuasive. The way the pragmatic young pilot saw it, there were two options: the Russian would pay the price they'd agreed upon and all would be well, or the Russian would kill him. As the helicopter touched the concrete slab of the helipad in the darkness, either option was out of his control.

Mickey Boy looked at the young pilot, who was fully focused on taking his machine down safely. The agreed upon fare for flying from Panama to Cuba-and keeping quiet about it-was roughly equal to a years salary for the pilot. Of course, there were cheaper methods of keeping folks mouths shut, but there was something about this young man that Mickey Boy liked. Taped to the control panel, the pilot had a creased photo of a pretty but tired looking woman surrounded by three little girls; his triplets. Mickey Boy knew this because the pilot talked incessantly about his girls. Poor things, they had to look like their awkward father.

Mickey Boy had used the chopper's radio to make a call that made no sense at all to the pilot. But there, waiting for them outside a shuttered hangar, was a man in olive fatigues. He carried a slim black suitcase with him. Hoping out of the chopper, Mickey Boy signaled the man and he approached quickly in the duck walk people do when approaching a helicopter. Mickey Boy took the suitcase and turned to the pilot. "I like you. There's a tip in the case for you, and here's another one...don't be stupid about spending it. Do you understand?"

The pilot nodded that he did. He stowed the case under the seat and took off with a salute.

The two waited until the chopper was out of site before moving to the hangar. "How is the move?" Mickey Boy asked.

"Just waiting for you. Ha, there's nothing left. I half expected you to come back in the *Kaa*, boss."

Mickey Boy shook his head, "No, everything goes. I sold the boats to those drug lords and chinks over at the canal for nearly what I paid for them. Need to be very liquid for the move."

"What about the-"

A friendly slap on the shoulder and the mechanic clammed up, Mickey Boy smiled, "Best not to ask so many questions."

"Yes, best not."

Inside the hangar, under the long high florescent lights stood Concepión in her flight suit. Her fists planted on her flung out hips. She stood before a Bombardier Challenger 870, a 106-foot jet that had originally been designed to hold up to seventy passengers before Mickey Boy and the crew got a hold of it. Mickey Boy left the mechanic and stepped up to Concepión. "Where are the lead lockers?"

"We got what we could on the plane, boss."

"I don't like this."

"We've been over this before. What don't you like?"

"This shipping my retirement all over the world unattended."

She laughed. It was the best way to keep her boss calm. "The Challenger has got enough yellowcake on it to live in the islands in luxury for longer than you're gonna live."

"I want to buy the island."

"We're also carrying enough, that if anything goes wrong, we are going to glow longer than the Northern Lights.

"Which is how long?"

"Pretty much forever. Listen Boss, we either had to smuggle it out or leave it here. We don't want the locals getting a hold of this stuff."

Mickey Boy knew that she was right but because he was nervous he liked to complain. "Telecommunications equipment, huh?"

"Yes sir. Bound for India. The Goain coast."

Mickey Boy looked around, "Fine."

"The mechanic appeared in front of them. "It's done Boss, the clock is ticking. Literally."

"Fine."

Concepión smiled at this, "How long until this little lair is a dusty memory?"

"Four hours. Concepión, how long till we're in India?"

"Twenty hours."

"That's enough time to become a Count, isn't it?

"As long as I'm not your Countess."

"Just a mistress, then. That's even better."

"Yes." Now Concepión was smiling broadly, "Just a mistress. On her own little island."

Mickey Boy shrugged his shoulders, "Sure, I'll buy you an island. A small one."

THE OVERLOADED JAGUAR E-TYPE came up the approach to the private airfield. Not far off, the Memphis International Airport, which looks as much like a set of Martini glasses as anything else, broke the horizon. Archie was driving, fast. A delighted Derrick was in the passenger seat with Bunty scrunched up on his lap. They came through the gate and Derrick pointed to the small jet that had already taxied up to the runway. Archie slowed as a man emerged from the plane.

All three climbed out of the car and the man approached, extending his hand for Derrick. He turned, "Archie, Bunty, this is Captain Perry. You're in good hands."

They all shook hands and Perry said in a professional clip, "Mr. Gilmur, Ms. Carrick, why don't y'all climb aboard and make yourself comfortable."

Derrick laughed, "Don't worry about the car, Archie-after the ride up here I need to get back home and chase Midge around the house."

"Well, sir, I do what I can." Bunty took Archie's arm and led him to the waiting jet.

"Bunty," Archie pleaded under his breath, "Let Uncle Derrick take you home."

She laughed as she lit the stairs, "I feel safer with the terrorists."

The interior of the jet hummed lightly with the vibration and noise of efficient engines. The plane had comfortable captain's chairs and fold away desks; a place where work was done. If there was a bar, Archie couldn't see it. He crossed the cabin to an urn of coffee. "It's fresh."

"Yes please." Said Bunty. She wasn't in the mood to work and lowered herself into the two-seat sofa facing the urn.

Archie poured out two cups of coffee and joined her there. "Seriously Bunty-"

"Archie stop."

"-I need someone to check in on Pop, should I get...detained."

"That's why I'm coming, so you won't get detained. Besides, I've got to fend off that Ugly Sue."

"I think we've seen the last of her."

"Good. I never really cared for her."

"You know I picked up that vibe."

"Well there may be a ray of light in that black cloud of yours."

Archie settled back into the sofa. Ugly Sue *was* gone, he thought. After the Scout had gone to the assembly plant in the sky, Ugly Sue grew nervous-the first time Archie had ever seen that. She demanded that Archie and Bunty stay in the office while she "investigate the accident."

"Well," Archie had looked at Ugly Sue, "Not entirely sure I'd call *that* an accident. And as for the investigation, it's pretty clear what happened out there." She just stared at him. Archie continued, "My theory is that the Scout blew up."

"That'd be my guess." Bunty offered.

Ugly Sue fumed, "Well this is dangerous business – why don't you two stay up here and leave it to the professional?"

Archie dug into his plaid pockets, "Alright, do you need the key?"

"Very funny." She said, "I'll be back." And with that she disappeared from the office.

Archie returned to the window as if on further inspection he would find the Scout less blown up.

Then the building alarm sounded.

Bunty had a theory: "The bitch snuck out the back didn't she?"

Archie made a call to the security company while Bunty mixed two whiskey and sodas-strong ones. Then, on the street below, a Jaguar E-type pulled up right behind what was left of the Scout. He realized it was his E-type and Archie was annoyed with Uncle Derrick, who was coming around the car and dialing his mobile phone. The phone on Archie's desk rang as he opened the window. "Hey!" Archie called to the street.

Derrick looked up-Archie dropped his keys. The old man caught the ring without a flinch. Behind Archie his phone continued to ring and Bunty answered it. "Oh hey Mr. Gordon. He's right here."

Archie took the phone, "Silver key – square head." He quit the line and smiled at Bunty, "Drink your drink, Love, we've got a visitor."

"You'd think with all this activity I'd be making more money."

"Life is strange that way."

Then Uncle Derrick was in the doorway, coughing and throwing his keys to Archie. "Where's the other one?" Derrick asked.

"Snuck out the back way. Just before you got her. Don't think she's coming back."

"She said she was checking out the Scout. She lied." Bunty offered.

"No, no my dear." Derrick said, "don't you blame yourself, she's doing what she's trained to do. She's skipped more experienced teams than the two of you."

Archie was watching his Uncle's brow pinch. He cleared his throat "So where is she, Uncle Derrick?"

"She ought to be on her way to Cuba. But if I had to guess she's on her way to New Orleans to cock it up entirely."

"Well, I guess I'll head down there too. Has the Jag got gas?"

"Archie." Derrick started.

"They blew up the Scout. Pop'll be pissed."

"Archie! You've done well. Much better than you know. But I've got a team briefed and they're already in place, or will be…" Derrick looked at his watch, "in about three hours."

"Do they know what the bomber looks like?"

Derrick frowned deeply. "You can ID the bomber?"

"I've met him, and the girl. There'll be two of them."

"Good God Man! Tell me what you know! I'll debrief our men in New Orleans."

"I think this'll need more than a police sketch and some fliers.

"Blast." Derrick's large paw fell on his nephew's shoulder, "I can't make you do it m'lad."

"I know it."

Bunty cleared her throat, "Why don't we just issue a red alert, like they do on the news over Labor Day."

"Too late. Cause a panic and the bomb would surely go off. Right now we've got to hope they stick with the time table."

Archie and Bunty were silent. She pulled the corduroy collar up around her face. "It's cold."

Archie closed the window. Bunty never unbundled the coat.

"Midge'll have my head if I let you go."

"I've met the fella. Reckon I'll just go point him out to your people in New Orleans. Then it's up to the professionals."

Derrick cleared his throat, "I'll arrange a plane to fly you down."

"Uncle Derrick, I've got a question: What was in the safe?"

At this Derrick laughed, "Nothing. Stock certificates, a will, trust documents, soft porn. I've got a man close to Oaks, he's not a problem."

"Van Clair?" Asked Archie. "The man who said he was from DeltaComm?"

"Yeah, that's the chap." Derrick smiled, he looked at Bunty, "He rather fancied you."

"So I felt."

"I didn't know what Ugly Sue was doing up here. That half-wit is chasing ghosts. She's put you and a great many people in danger. She's going to get people killed." Derrick looked over his nephew, mulling something over. "What are you carrying these days?"

"H&K P7."

"Good, listen, find your man-neutralize the threat. This Ugly Sue, she's a bit of a loose cannon. If you see her, and this isn't a priority, but if you see her you could tie up a loose end for me-"

"UNCLE DERRICK!" it was the loudest explosion anyone had ever heard come from Bunty. "Archie here isn't killing anyone on purpose!"

"Just thought I'd ask." Derrick looked intently at Archie. "You'll outlive this day, and come home safe."

"You aren't giving the Saint Crispin's Day Speech are you?"

"I guess not now."

And that's how it ended. Derrick made a quick call neither Archie nor Bunty understood, and they all went down a climbed into the Jag.

Now he and Bunty sat alone on the sofa in the center of the empty cabin. The quiet vibration and hum interrupted from time to time by a comment from Captain Perry, but the occasional squawk wasn't enough to wake Bunty. She had drained the scalding coffee and settled into Archie's side and instantly fallen asleep. But Archie's brain was humming, trying to fold in the wall of information that had been coming in all night. He had barely touched his coffee because if sleep came, Archie wanted to be ready for it. It didn't.

As a point of fact, his brain was still churning out scenarios and probabilities. It was pointless though, he just didn't know what was going to happen and didn't like it. He was certain, however, that he hadn't seen the last of Ugly Sue.

THE GREAT DRUNKEN MASS SWELLED AND CHURNED around them and Yavi felt like a dinghy in the ocean. Alice, being taller, was taking the choppy crowd better than he. She laughed, clapped her hands over her head and swayed her hips. If she hadn't told Yavi that they were drinking non-alcoholic daiquiris, he'd have thought she was drunk. She sure as hell looked like she was having a good time. To Yavi, though, the world in this vile little Quarter seemed to be an impenetrable wall of shoulder and sweating necks.

Yavi ducked away from Alice and stepped away from the crowd. Beyond them, two mounted police officers trotted by on horseback, blowing on their brass whistles for the crowd to part. That caught what was left of the crowd's attention span like a mini-parade. He stepped into a trinket shop.

The shopkeeper was a plump little lady, tired but cheery and more than a little drunk. She took in Yavi as he ducked into the store and pretended to shop. Their eyes then met and her round face was awash in compassion. Yavi needed to work on his poker face. "Oh sugar," the woman said, "Just wait till tomorrow, that's when the party gets started."

"Tomorrow?"

The lady looked at her watch, "Well, tonight, I reckon. The crowd'll thin out at daybreak, they'll all stumble off and go to bed. So will I. But the whole quarter will be rollin' again 'bout noon. That's the Mardi Gras of course, I've got to stay open the whole week, all the damn time 'cause there is money out there in that crowd. Might put a daiquiri machine in here. You need a tee-shirt?"

Go to sleep at daybreak, hide during the day. It's the way they moved in the army and this was no different. The mission would be safe. The little fat lady was speaking to him, "Pardon?"

"Where are you from?"

"Paris."

"Paris, France. Well isn't that something, I guess the whole city is from France, really."

"How do you mean?"

"New Orleans, Louisiana – started out as a French colony."

"Yes, a French Colony." Yavi said.

"Is this your first time in America?"

Yavi checked his watch and then the disposable cell phone in his pocket. *He should have called by now.*

"First time, honey? In the states?"

Alice came into the shop, beamed and smiling with the crowd from which she stepped. Before they'd left the hotel, Yavi watched her take a straw from a hurricane and drip a few sloppy red dots on her linen blouse. Now it looked slightly worse; her shoulder looked like it had been shot. Still she beamed, "There you are! Have you heard from your cousin?"

"No." Yavi said.

"Really, I thought that was why you ducked in here."

"I thought my phone was ringing but it wasn't." He said absently and they shuffled out of the shop together to stand on the sidewalk under the critical glare of the shopkeeper.

"Damn foreigners." She muttered.

"Why hasn't he called?" Yavi asked. "This is irregular."

"You know Bobby Chu, he's probably got some girl pinned to a mattress."

"He should have called by now."

Alice took his hand, "It isn't his war, Yavi. We know what to do."

They stepped back in the gross flow of the mob. It was less than a block later when Alice saw it. At first she thought nothing of it but then some vague revulsion lurched in her stomach. She was looking at a very accurate sketch of Yavi's face and a passable one of hers on a flier posted on a wall. "Wanted for Violation of Patriot Act." It said over the faces. "Believed to be in New Orleans." It said below. Then there was a phone number. Both scanned the parameter for police.

"They are looking for a couple. We'll split up. Go straight to the hotel. I will be there shortly. We will take different routes. Once we get there, we will be quiet until nightfall. If they come to the door before I get back-"

"-set it off on the balcony." Yavi didn't wait for an answer and headed off down the street. He told himself not to move to quickly, to smile, but not too broadly. The streets were crowded, and from where he was they would be until he reached the hotel. *Stay in the crowd.*

A quartet of college students were inhaling nitrous cartridges, laughing hysterically, and falling over into cars and each other. Yavi sidestepped to avoid them and saw, across the bobbing heads, another flier with his face on it. He ducked back into the crowd. Two girls stopped to take in the flier across the street and his heart leapt. *How many of these posters were there? If there was one, there could be a thousand.* He was moving faster now, weaving his lean frame between the bulk of drunken Westerners. Another side step. Then there was the annoyed scream of an American girl. Yavi turned to see the girl-hands out, inspecting the bright red stain on her top and the huge plastic cup between her feet. "Asshole!" she screamed.

"Excuse me." He muttered. Yavi wasn't looking at her anymore, but beyond her shoulders to still another flier. Somewhere down the street the brass whistles of the mounted police sounded. They were getting closer.

"Hey Asshole!" it was a male voice, "What the fuck?"

"Sorry!" Yavi turned back down the street. Some sailors were inspecting a flier. A heavy hand fell on his shoulder, then Yavi was spinning back around.

"Fuckin' foreigner!" The man screamed as his fist connected squarely with the bridge of Yavi's nose. He fell into some other bodies, male ones that simply pushed him out of the way. Then he was on his knees.

The police whistles were louder now, beyond the din of the crowd Yavi could hear the cadence of hooves on cobblestones, they were coming closer, fast.

He scrambled to his feet again, ducking the glistening and sparkling bodies. The horses moved past him. Yavi stepped onto the sidewalk and kept moving, *Don't look back!* he commanded himself as he turned to take in the scene he'd left behind. The sailors were still studying the flier. One of the mounted police was wheeling his horse around, blowing hard on his whistle.

The darkness of the alley was too much and Yavi side-stepped the throng and disappeared into its fold. Between the tall brick walls, both the light and the noise from the Quarter became distant. Moving along the wall, Yavi ducked under a flight of steel fire stairs, pressing himself into the recess of a locked door. Across the narrow alley, staring at him, Yavi saw a hand painted sign.

On the street the mounted patrolman passed in and out of sight slowly. Then Yavi moved under the single bulb that hung cockeyed over the door across the alley. The sign had a word that Yavi had first seen in Jamaica but still didn't understand, TAROT, and beneath it was a word he did know, WICCA. Yavi knocked on the door and it opened almost immediately. There before him stood and tall black man made even more so by his desperate thinness. His shirt was open and dirty and the smooth skin beneath clung to his ribs and abdominal muscles as if it had been sprayed on. "You want to see?" The man asked in an accent Yavi couldn't place.

Again he looked down the alley, then at his watch. The man said nothing and didn't move. His wide mouth was littered with gold teeth when he smiled broadly. Then Yavi's thoughts jumped to Robert Chu's bizarre fear of spiders. Alice had told him that Chu thought the old witch had cast a spell over him. Yavi looked down the alley again, "Can you cast a spell?"

"Come in and tell Gustav what you want."

"You are Gustav?"

"I am."

"Your shop is hard to find." Yavi said as he looked around the room, "It's strange that anyone finds it." The room felt, even in the darkness, obscenely dirty.

"Dis ain't no trinket shop. Those who know, dey can always find me. Now, what do you want from Gustav?"

Yavi smiled and tried to look reverent. "I want a curse placed on someone." He looked at his watch, he'd wait inside for a few minutes.

"Dat's bad mojo, man. Who do you want to hex? A lady perhaps?"

"Yes, an old girlfriend – Alice."

"Ah, love warps the soul, don't it? Did she leave you for another?"

"Can you do the hex?"

"I am Gustav – I can hex this, I can hex that. I am Gustav. Let me ask you somethin' though."

"Alright." Yavi looked at his watch.

"Why you wanna hex some poor girl when you cursed yourself?"

"What?"

Gustav smiled and shut the door behind them. "You consumed by the things dat you hate most."

The room was very dark.

ALICE STEPPED AWAY FROM YAVI before he'd finished echoing her order back to him. She turned away and painted a wide, toothy smile across her face. As she moved into the throng, her hands clapped over her head and her hips swayed to whatever music poured from the nearest bar. Alice never looked back and danced her way across the nearest intersection, lightly, the way she used to before she was declared unclean by the good people of Allah.

On a lamppost a flier-*the flier*-hung and was being read by a small gang of partiers. Looking straight ahead, Alice stood face to face with the yawning doorway of the KITTY KAT BAR. In she danced.

Inside the music thumped loudly as girls danced on the wide serpentine bar blowing police whistles to snatch what attention they could. Not that they needed much help: there were four of them that Alice could see and they were dressed alike in black short shorts that showed the bottom swell of the rear end, blue bikini tops and police hats. Their thick belts "holstered" a bottle of tequila on either hip. They smiled and pranced and passed out shots to the boys who stuffed dollars into their pants and never got change.

Alice moved deeper inside, looking for a place at the bar far away from the girls on drink patrol. But America is a country of great competitiveness. Girls who'd come in groups together or with the boys who clamored for the drink patrol climbed onto the bar as well. They danced alone or with each other. Alice sat on a far corner, next to a sloppy waitress station. A girl-on-girl kiss, more of a snog really, drew thunderous applause. That was funny. How long had it been since she'd been in the West?

Other than the point she'd been making to Yavi the day before, it had been years since Alice had tasted alcohol. It was as if she dried herself out enough, the uncleanness that her family and neighbors were so good to point out would turn to dust and blow away. But it wouldn't. Here she was, just hours from martyrdom and Yavi, the staunchest of the good people, still thought her unclean. She thought about the wicked, handsome smile on the Russian arms dealer's face. What would she do with 72 virgins? She ordered a daiquiri and drank in the cool frappe. Suddenly, as if on cue, the drinks patrol laid heavy on the whistles.

Alice couldn't help but move to the music as she watched the girls play their games on the bar. To get that drunk, to parade yourself like a prostitute, these girls couldn't possibly be happy. But then, neither was she, the prospect of seeing paradise tomorrow wasn't as peaceful as she'd hoped. But still these girls were free to dance however they wished, so they had something on her.

He was tall and well built and clean-shaven although at this hour the shadow of a course beard visible on his brown face. He approached her lightly and smiled. Alice smiled back. Standing near her stool he never took a seat. "New Orleans takes a little getting used to." He said.

Alice noted an Indian accent. "You aren't from here."

"Neither are you. My family is from Kashmir." He laughed, "Nowadays that makes people take long looks at you, but I'm over here studying banking and finance. My name is Sanjeev."

"Alice." She said, "I'm from Saudi Arabia."

"Alice can't be your real name."

"It is. My mother had a pen pal in England, ever since she was a little girl and I was named after her."

Sanjeev smiled, "That's a good story. Are you a student?"

"University of Georgia," she said, "Just here for the party. So Sanjeev from Kashmir, how do you like the US? Are you going back home?"

"It's fun." Sanjeev said and tipped his beer to the dancing girls, "Not much too it though. In the end, I'll get homesick. Are you going back?"

Alice smiled broadly again, "No."

"If I were a woman, I wouldn't either." Again he used his beer bottle as a pointer to call out the girls, "They may act like trash, but it's their choice. I couldn't put up with the bullshit heaped on you women back home. My older sister lives in Birmingham, in England. She writes to tell me she wears blue jeans everyday."

YAVI WAS NO LONGER TRYING TO FIT IN, but trying to get back to the hotel as fast as possible. Strange visions of spiders filled his head and he was not entirely sure what had happened with the old witch doctor but now was not the time to sort it out. His hotel was just on the other side of the intersection and Yavi pressed on. Hanging about eye level near the main door was another flier. Then something caught his eye. He wasn't thirty feet from a Lucky Dog stand. A monstrosity like that would surely hide his face. He approached the vendor as he saw a couple stop and read the flier. "Gimme a Lucky Dog." The Vendor seemed slightly drunk himself. "One foot long Pok dawg fo da gentamen."

"Pork?" Yavi asked.

"Where you from? Of course poke! Goody, nuthun' but goody."

Yavi turned toward the hotel with the Lucky Dog in hand. The couple were still standing in front of the flier. Yavi was hungry, and he needed to hide. The West was unclean, the pigs were unclean. Alice was unclean. He approached the door and buried the dog unto his turned head. It tasted good, he was hungry. Upstairs his bed waited for him, he was tired. He was something else as well. Yavi was unclean.

ARCHIE COULDN'T BE SURE WHETHER TO ATTRIBUTE IT to Bunty's exhaustion or Captain Perry's flawlessly smooth landing but she was still asleep when the plane came to a stop. Archie looked out the window to see a ten-man contingent waiting on the tarmac. "Aw Shit." he muttered and reached over to wake Bunty. She was sitting up now, looking out the same window and taking in the meaning of the welcoming committee before them. "Don't worry, Bunty, it's just the Metairie Louisiana JayCees."

"I don't care who they are, we're negotiating my contract when we get back to Memphis, Asswholio."

"What contract? You have a contract? How the hell did you talk me into that?"

"I'm not scared of you, Archie! You fold like a cheap lawn chair."

"What does it say?"

"Oh, just the standard employment contract. Archie, what's up with the welcome wagon?"

Captain Perry emerged from the cockpit and said "Well folks, here we are!" as he opened the door.

"I haven't got a standard employment contract!" Archie continued, "I've only got one employee – you."

They moved up the cabin and stopped as the steps were rolled up to the plane.

"Archie, not now. Who are these folks?"

"Well," Archie explained. "If they're from Uncle Derrick, we're fine. Safe as milk. Or they could be from the good folks at SinoTel."

"And if that?"

"I guess we can use their network to call God and tell them we're on the way."

"You've got no faith Archie. God is probably preparing our rooms right now already. Or at least my room. Who knows where you're staying."

On the tarmac, David Meeks rubbed his eyes and stepped away from the group, and crushed out his cigarette underfoot. Since leaving Virginia, he'd heard from Jack, but not from Valerie. She might not even know he was gone yet. Then the two emerged from the plane behind the pilot. He hadn't expected the fella to be in a black dinner jacket. Nice touch. He had a private laugh and came across the tarmac with his hand extended.

Archie came onto the tarmac without being told who was in charge.

Meeks smiled, "You're Rowan's boy."

"I reckon so. Didn't meet Rowan until tonight though."

"Oh that's great. I don't like this, told Rowan that too. This is really sloppy."

Archie scratched his hip. "What's your name before I do something rash?"

"What are you gonna do, rich boy? You're pretty well surrounded." Meeks nodded to the contingent behind them and felt the P7 press into his temple. The kid was quick, and clever. He might work. Meeks smiled again and started to say something.

Archie spoke over him. "I may save your life...name please...and I don't give a fuck about your passwords. We haven't got time for that foolishness."

Meeks laughed, "Yeah, you're Rowan's boy. We've got a chopper, got a pretty big crowd to fly over tonight. Let's take a ride."

"Name please." He pulled back the hammer on the P7. A man in a NOPD patrolman's uniform took a step forward and then stopped, his hand on the service revolver at his hip.

Meeks put a hand up. "Commander David Meeks."

"That's not the name I was given."

"Rowan called me-"

Archie laughed, "Just kidding." He uncocked the gun and put it back in the small of his back, "Let's be friends now." The cop moved closer, hand still on the revolver.

"Jesus, little boy, we aren't playing games-"

"Oh yes we are. I've been up to my neck in you people and your games for a week now. It is a game...I don't want to play but I'm sure as hell not gonna lose."

"Get in the chopper." Meeks looked Archie over as they crossed over to the helicopter. "You're a little over dressed, Mr. Gilmur. James Bond isn't a real spy."

Archie turned back to the contingent, still huddled on the tarmac, "Officer, you can help us out. I don't know where Commander Meeks is taking me, but when I get there we're gonna need a couple of red fezzes."

"Now why in the hell do you need a couple of red fezzes?"

"These carnivals are all the same."

"What the hell are you talking about?"

"Just get them. We've got three choices, nuclear disaster, a frantic riot and nuclear disaster, or you get me a couple of queer red fezzes. You know, those goofy red things with the tassel on top."

The cop desperately looked at Meeks, who looked at Bunty who shrugged and said, "The man needs a fez to stop a nuclear disaster, get the man a fez."

"You heard the lady." Meeks said. "Look, it's 1:45 a.m. right now, on the Mardi Gras. There's bound to be a paddy wagon full of drunken Shriners somewhere in the city."

The cop shrugged, "I'll make a call. See what I can do."

They climbed into the helicopter with Bunty, Archie and Meeks in the back, the pilot and another in the front. The machine had barely come off the ground when the other in the front seat turned and as said, "Mr. Gilmur, first things first." The laptop on his lap was already up and running. "This is Edgar Holmes, he's a sketch artist. He's gonna draw our guy on that magic pad of his and that face will be all over the city, hell the world, before we land."

"Alright Edgar, where do we start?" Said Archie. Then he was shocked at the speed and accuracy in which Edgar worked. The image on the screen looked remarkably like the man Archie met in Jamaica.

"You said there were two?"

The sketch of the woman wasn't as well done, but Archie had only seen her from a distance and couldn't provide the details Edgar needed. "Alright." Edgar said, alternately reviewing the two images on the computer. "This is very good. I'll get these out."

"Are you done with Mr. Gilmur?" Asked Meeks.

"All yours."

"Again, I don't like this making spies out of businessmen and CEO's. But Rowan came up through SAS and he's told me to brief you. Here's what we know: A report surfaced from Panama. It was very threatening, dangerous stuff. When our man in Panama disappeared a few days later the alarms really went off. A Chinese corporation, SinoTel, had been donating a good bit of money to a terrorist cell in Morocco. In this report, there is a mention of acquiring fissionable material in South America. Well, if anyone was making nukes in South America, we'd know about it."

"But then Mikhail Boyorov popped up on the radar and you realized he was sitting on a mountain the obsolete Soviet era yellowcake."

"Obsolete? Hell, it'll still kill ya."

"Yeah but instead of a violent jerk, it's a prolonged pull." Archie said as the chopper banked right. From the window, he could see the crowd in the quarter, moved flowing the open doors along the street like inlets into a drunken river. The crowd didn't seem to register that they were above. The flow gathered around an enormous hurricane, the rim in the huge Plexiglas "cup" level with the roof of the three-story building in front of it. The banner across it read *WORLDS LARGEST HURRICANE!* And inside the cup the bright red frappe churned as busty girls poured the concoction out into smaller 12 once cups from spigots at the base of the thing. "Will you look at that?" Archie said and tapped Bunty on the shoulder.

Meeks glared at the gimmick, "You can take the boy out of the frat house-"

"Shut the fuck up, Commander. That's where they're gonna loose those bombs."

"Where?"

"At the three story hurricane."

"How do you know?"

"I saw them training. I thought it was an antenna SinoTel was developing for cell phone or WiFi..." Archie trailed off and looked out the window again, "It was just a big hurricane glass."

Now Meeks looked out the window. "God Almighty. It's tall enough, the exhaust from the pump motor would blow the cloud over the crowd."

"Oh Good Lord!" said Bunty, "It's even got a DeltaComm logo on the banner."

"We need snipers! Clear the quarter!" barked Archie.

"It's not that simple, Mr. Gilmur."

"Not that simple!?!" Screamed Bunty.

Meeks ground his teeth, "It's not that simple, little girl."

Bunty pressed her back into the seat and kicked a heel into Meeks crotch.

"Godammit!" He growled, "What is it with you two? We can't go starting a panic down there!"

"Commander Meeks, we are very close to having a nuclear disaster in a defenseless crowd!"

Meeks leaned in, close to Archie so that he could smell the stale coffee and cigarette on his breath, "We are always very close, on the verge, of a nuclear disaster, kids. Everyday that you go to work, go out at night, step foot in public, we are on the verge of a nuclear – fucking - disaster. Do you appreciate that? That is the world we live in. You think that 9/11 changed everything? Well it didn't, that was just the first one that slipped through the net. But we keep going. People like me work to keep people like you in the dark, so you'll go to work and the only superpower still standing will keep running. And the world will go on. In the dark. It's the only way."

YAVI WOKE UP AGAIN, and again, now it was 6:10. Each time it was visions and dreams of the witch doctor that woke him. Then, awake, he looked at the other twin bed and saw that it was empty, that Alice had not come back. He'd been asleep for roughly three hours. He was groggy and his head felt thick and his stomach extended. He needed to vomit and he thought again about the appalling sausage he'd eaten on the way through the lobby.

The flier was downstairs in the lobby.

Yavi snapped out of the bed and pulled on his shoes. After a scan of the room, he was sure that Alice had never come back. He picked up his russack, slung it on his shoulders, and moved to the door. No, the other way. He made a volte-face and headed to the balcony.

Then he was outside, moving along in the brightening day. There were still revelers on the street, but they were scarce. He jumped the barrier, and was moving along the balcony of the next hotel. At the street corner, he saw a smallish man was wandering alone in an olive poplin suit and a fez on his head. Yavi reckoned the fellow was a local because tourists didn't dress like that.

Pulling the straps of the russack tight, Yavi swung a leg over the balcony railing and climbed down to the street. He followed the fez for five blocks until the man began to fish around in his pocket for his keys.

From one of the outside pockets on the russack, Yavi retrieved a pre-paid disposable cell phone and dialed Alice's number. He let the other end ring fifteen times before hanging up and stuffing the phone in his pants pocket.

Ahead, the fez opened a gate. The two wide panels spanned the entire alley, with a smaller door cut into one of the gates. The man in the fez, swayed this way and that and tried twice to jam his key in the lock. Yavi was quickly closing the space between them. Finally, as the man turned the key in the lock, Yavi passed him. He stepped through the small door as Yavi spun around and slipped a finger between the lock and the door. He waited, five to ten seconds, for the man to return. He didn't.

Yavi pulled the door open and peered inside the alley. Three cars were parked along on side. The fez was climbing the wooden steps to one of the apartments along the back of the alley. Yavi moved quickly down the alley and up the steps. Now the man stopped at a light blue door and looked at Yavi coming onto the third floor gallery. "What da fuck you want?" the man spat. He had olive skin and dark, oiled hair coming out from under the maroon fez.

"I'm staying with a friend on mine, in one of these apartments, but I can't remember which one. His name is Botto."

The man looked at Yavi for a long time with intense, searching eyes. Then he smiled, opened his door, and stepped inside. "Yeah, lemme see which one he is."

Yavi stepped through the doorway after him, and the man turned around and put a knee into Yavi's crotch and two quick rabbit punches to the face before slinging him around and onto the floor. "You ain't lost! I seen your face all over. You dat fuckin' terrorist. Well welcome to America Abdullah!"

Yavi pulled the snub-nosed .38 from the waist of his pants and sprung to his feet. The man kicked out, high and hard, but Yavi spun on his heels. The kick went to the left. Then Yavi had the barrel in the man's mouth as he pushed forward and closed the door. Yavi swatted the fez off his head.

The shot was loud. The door, above and behind the exit wound was sprayed a deep maroon. The man slumped to the floor. Yavi locked the door and moved into the kitchen. The revolver had a leather cord tied through the trigger guard, from which dangled two small feathers. It was a nuisance, but Yavi didn't take it off because it was the old witch doctor's gun and he wanted it to stay that way. He wiped the gun down and washed his hands.

Then he got into the shower. The water pressure in the apartment was better than the spittle that came out of the hotel. Yavi stayed under the scalding, violent pressure for as long as he could. Washing away the stink that clung to him; the body laying in the entrance hall and the old witch doctor across the vile quarter, lifeless since Yavi had driven his nose up into his brain. The witch doctor had begun on a hex, playing up the wild and deranged voodoo from which he made his living. While the witch doctor spat and hissed his incantations, the look of horror on Robert Chu's face had crept into his mind. What had happened to the man? Yavi wasn't about to let it happen to him. So he took the heel of his hand and thrust it once, without warning or even passion, and driven the tall man's nose backward into his skull. Yavi didn't want to touch anything in the nasty place but the handgun would be useful.

Then the steaming water began to run lukewarm and Yavi got out and toweled off. The sleep was tugging at him. Why the hell had Chu not called? He lay down on the bed and closed his eyes.

ARCHIE AND BUNTY LAY LIKE SPOONS IN THE HOTEL BED. In the adjoining suite Meeks was running a small crew from the makeshift HQ on the twelfth floor of the Jaubert Bros. Hotel. Meeks came in and grabbed Archie by the foot, "Alright you two, proms over, wake up."

Archie opened an eye, "What's the time?"

"11:30."

"Fuck."

"Arch-" Bunty mumbled.

"Don't worry about it, Mr. Gilmur. I've got men watching the Hurricane. If he tried to do it now there'd be no one to nuke. Besides, with no one on the street that would make things too easy for the snipers."

Now Archie was craning himself upright, trying not to disturb Bunty-who, although awake, had not seen fit to acknowledge it. "You never know, Commander Dave, you might get lucky."

"That's not something I'm gonna bet the house on."

"When's this party gonna get crankin'?"

"Few hours. We've got a long day ahead of us. Listen, we've got your description of the two all over the quarter. We blanketed the damn place, but I have a question-"

"No, I won't describe them again, and don't show me the picture. I barely remember what I told the sketch artist...it was a long night... but I know enough about the brain to know that the more you describe something the worse your memory gets."

"You've got some strange theories."

"I suppose. But y'all are depending on my brain, not the other way around." Archie shoved Meeks back into the adjoining suite. "We need another computer."

"Why?"

"Because I installed a trap door in the SinoTel Global network last week-about the same time you were losing track of your man in Panama-and SinoTel monitors all usage of company credit cards. They even monitor usage of DeltaComm cards. Not sure if the good people at DeltaComm are actually aware of that, though."

"Doubtful."

"Anyway. If I were sending these clods here, I'd give the smart one an unactivated credit card, that they could use in a bind but would not really exist until the day of the job."

"You have the brain of a real shithook."

"Thanks. That'll get me through the hard times." He pulled the PDA and Truitt's key fob out of his pocket. There is a list of unactivated cards, on this thing somewhere."

"Do you know where?"

"Not really, we'll have to ask Bunty. She's really the bookkeeper of the company. But all we have to do is find one that's just been activated here in town and we'll find our bombers."

"Well about that."

Archie rolled his eyes, "You cocked it up, didn't you?"

"We found what we think was the hotel room. The clerk said he had a man and a woman who fit the description staying there. We came in, but the room was deserted. We've got a crew stationed there."

"I doubt they're coming back now."

"Mr. Gilmur, shut up and let us do our job."

"Your job, as I understand it, is to shoot the fella I point at."

"Basically."

"What if they've got this bomb hooked up to a cardiac monitor?"

"Oh you are a bastard. The snipers have darts. A hit will knock the bomber out, but won't stop the heart. We also get to interrogate the hell out of him later on."

"That's sounds fun."

Meeks ground his teeth, "Oh, it will be. And where we're holding him won't be all over the news either."

"Probably for the best, really." Archie looked at the computers and surveillance equipment that littered the once elegant room. "God, that's a mess. Listen, get Bunty to search for the credit cards. She knows how to do it. Where's my fez, I need to hit the street?"

Meeks thumped over his shoulder, "The mini-bar."

"Wow, y'all brought a plastic pirate sword. You government fellas think of everything."

IT WAS LATE AFTERNOON WHEN YAVI WOKE. Padded into the entrance hall to look again at his handywork. He'd never taken a life before and now there were two dead by his hand in less than a day. The .38 still lay on the kitchen counter. Yavi went back into the bedroom and turned on the television as he fingered his way through the closet. He chose a khaki poplin suit, white shirt and red tie. He dressed deliberately sloppy, the way he thought American businessmen carried themselves.

The local news was on. Something about a daring smash and grab job at a jewelry broker in the Quarter call "Vanderhorn's". The reporter called the place a New Orleans institution. Explosives had been used, taking the security grate off the structure completely. There were no suspects. Then Yavi found himself looking at the hotel room he'd abandoned earlier. The talking head next to the footage was reporting that the police were not commenting on a possible connection between the hotel raid and the fliers that were now posted up and down the streets of quarter. Homeland Security had upgraded the Terror Alert from Yellow to Orange, but also failed to give any detail as to why.

He got a fresh cell phone and called Alice. There was no answer. Footage of the parade routes in the quarter showed that the crowd for the most part either hadn't seen the news or didn't care.

Yavi couldn't believe that this was a religious ceremony.

ARCHIE CAME OUT OF THE HOTEL ALONE still in a very wrinkled dinner jacket and Gordon plaid trews. The fez, planted catawampus on his skull was slightly used. The plastic pirate's cutlass was in his right hand. Archie pulled away the plastic blade away from the hilt, partially revealing the thin, serum coated blade beneath. A quick head check and one of the two field officers who were shadowing him gave a sober shake of the head. Archie slipped the ridiculous blade back into place. *These guys really do think of everything.* The two trailed Archie as he made his way down the street to the next intersection and turned, continuing down the street, moving towards the three-story hurricane.

In the dimming afternoon sun, the hurricane churned and swirled in the glass. The next street further still, the first in a long line of floats began to roll past, flinging beads, panties and moon pies to the bleating crowd. He made his way to the parade route, checked down both side of the street, and made his way back to the hurricane.

Another man in a fez caught his eye, then another. Archie lifted his cutlass into the air and hollered into the crowd, his call being matched by yet another man in a tall fez. This one didn't seem to fit, though, it seemed too big for him. The sleeves of the man's poplin coat were too long, and his shoulders were swimming in the coat. Over his shoulder was a canvas russack.

"*Laissez Le Bons Temps Rouler!*" Archie called.

This Yavi understood but didn't know why the apparently Scottish man in the plaid pants was yelling at him. *Laissez Le Bons Temps Rouler!*" Yavi called back with a smile.

Now Archie was very close and slapped him on the back. A uneasy fear gripped Yavi as Archie lingered too long on his face.

On the roof, the sniper posing as a maintenance man got the signal through his earpiece. "Negative." The sniper said into the microphone in his collar, "They're moving too fast. The crowd is too wild."

Yavi was walking fast now, toward the Hurricane. He turned to look at Archie, who had dropped back slightly. Archie waved his plastic cutlass and smiled.

Yavi bolted.

ALICE WAS WATCHING A VINCE VAUGHN MOVIE on pay-per-view when the day shift manager pressed the *BATCH SEND* button on the credit card machine. The phone was ringing on the dresser, but Alice ignored it. Then, after a good giggle fit Alice rolled off the bed and went into the bathroom. Crumpled on the tile floor was the dirty pair of blue jeans and her stained linen top. She was washing her hands and scrutinizing her face. She was wearing a pair of black stretch pants and a French blue fitted shirt. Her hair was shorter now, thanks to an afternoon in the hotel saloon. Alice thought she looked good.

One block away, a certain number and name went red on a computer screen and Ugly Sue's eyes went wide. She'd been searching the SinoTel network through Archie's doggie door for twelve hours now. The wallet she'd lifted from Robert Chu lay beside the laptop. Along with it the lay a list of names and credit card numbers. Now there was the movement for which she'd been looking. One Alice Shannarah was staying at the Le Meridian Hotel – had checked in this morning using her DeltaComm company card and apparently had treated herself to a spa day. Strange behavior for a suicide bomber.

Ugly Sue jumped out of her chair and looked out the window. She could actually see the hotel. Almost checked in last night herself. She counted 15 floors up as she slipped her pistol into the small purse. She looked at herself in the full-length mirror before going public: jeans, artist smock, and K-Swiss running shoes. Nothing remarkable, something that would slip through a crowd.

BUNTY HAD JUST HUNG UP, for the seventh time, with Truitt. She scrolled through the accounts on screen again. The third line down blinked red.

"Hey Bunty…" Meeks was saying.

"Hold on… An Alice Shannarah checked into the Le Meridian hotel here in town using an DeltaComm credit card that's never been used before. Room 1524."

Meeks spun around to the nearest field officer. "How far away is that?"

"Five blocks."

"Call it in, let's go!" He turned back to Bunty, "Good work Ms. Carrick. Keep watching, stay in touch. I don't want this turning into a wild goose chase. Stay on the money trail." With that Meeks and the field officer were out the door.

UGLY SUE KNOCKED TENATIVELY ON THE DOOR marked 1524 and called out, "Housekeeping." There was no answer and Ugly Sue did a head check and used the pass key she'd lifted off the maid who was now in a drug induced sleep in the linen closet.

The door swung open and she stepped inside, drew her gun and checked behind the door. Then she swept the room: shower, armoire, closet. The room was empty. The television was still on and the towel by the sink was still damp. She kicked the discarded clothes on the floor. Then she was back into the room. In the seat of the armchair on the far side of the unmade bed was a canvas russack. She crossed the room. Then she heard, almost felt, the lock turn and the door fly open. Ugly Sue spun around, dropping to one knee as Meeks shouted, "Drop the gun! Drop it!"

"Drop your weapon!" Ugly Sue screamed back.

The blast and thump of fired shots filled the room. "Drop it!" someone yelled.

THE SNIPER ON THE ROOF heard the field officer bark, "Godammit they've gone inside. The target knows he's been spotted." The number two sniper, on the roof across the street from the huge hurricane, crossed the roof. "Get back to your position." Said the sniper. "They've gone into the bar. We'll wait. Get back to your position. He's got to come up on the roof!"

Downstairs, Yavi pushed into the bar, weaving and shoving drinkers out of his way. The crowd parted for the small frantic man, shouting him down but staying open for the one in pursuit, screaming into his dinner jacket that a positive ID had been made. That's when the fliers, the terror alerts and early morning police raids clicked in the collective consciousness of the bar.

The two field officers shadowing Archie reached the doorway as a wall of screaming people began to empty into the street. They shouted for calm, but the wall pushed them further back on the cobblestones.

Yavi made it to the back of the place against the opposing push of patrons. A young waitress appeared in a hallway from behind the bar, Yavi shoved her aside and barreled down the length of the narrow hall. Archie hurdled the girl and pressed after Yavi, moving fast under the weight of the russack. "Positive ID!" Archie screamed into his dinner jacket. *Where the hell were his field officers?*

Two sets of steel doors were on either side of the narrow hall. Yavi stopped short and dove to the right, stumbling into the small kitchen of the restaurant next door. Archie pressed through the doors just as they slammed shut – "Positive ID!"

The line cooks and waitresses went for cover. Then Yavi was in the back of the dining room watching the rucas from next door pour onto the street outside. He was heading for the wide circular staircase in the back of the old building. Yavi lit the staircase taking steps two at a time. Archie came through the room, hitting the stairs, pumping upward in three step leaps.

Archie closed the gap between them and adjusted his grip on the plastic cutlass. His legs burned and pressed himself into one more leap. Yavi spun around and delivered a roundhouse kick to the side of Archie's skull, sending his head against the bare brick of the wall. His hand went limp, and Archie heard the blade clatter against the steps. Bouncing off the wall, Archie ducked low and sprung forward again. Yavi pulled the gun from his belt as Archie came into his torso. He fired wide.

The first of the two field officers leapt onto the staircase as the slug ripped into his stomach and dropped him instantly.

Yavi hit Archie with the grip of the revolver and twisted free. Both scrambled up the steps, Archie pulling the P7 free of his back. Yavi leapt up the sweep of the staircase as Archie fired, sending up a cloud of brick dust from just over Yavi's head.

On the ground floor, the field officer called in for help. "Man down- positive ID –heading to the roof – snipers at the ready!"

On the roof, the sniper turned and trained his rifle onto roof access door. "He's coming this way number two."

The third story of the restaurant was a dusty storeroom. Yavi kept hold of the russack and pumped his legs up the final set of steps to the roof. The access door burst open – Yavi spun to the right and dropped to one knee and fired once as the sniper turned to the noise and realized the target was on the roof of the adjoining building. The shot was lethal and the sniper fell to the gravel roof.

Archie was flat on his belly over the threshold of the access door and fired once. *Don't hit the russack!* The shot was wide across Yavi's face and he fell forward, holding the burning streak across the bridge of his nose. Across the street, number two waited for Yavi to appear over the wall for a clean shot. Yavi sprang forward, turning his back to Archie, and fired across the street. Archie took aim, the russack, and all that yellowcake, covered his target.

Number two leveled his rifle but Yavi dove over the firewall separating the rooftops.

"Stop!" Archie screamed, scrambling to his feet. Yavi popped to his feet and leveled his pistol. It dry fired. Archie trained the P7. "Stop!"

Yavi threw the pistol wide over the street and laughed. "Shoot me and see what happens! Stop my heart! Laissez le bon temps rouler!"

Number two across the street fired a shot into Yavi's knee. The target buckled as Archie leapt the firewall and bolted across the roof.

On all fours, Yavi scrambled to the motor pumping the Hurricane around in its huge glass. Yavi lurched forward on two feet and reached into his coat pocket.

Then Archie was on him, hooking his arms under Yavi's shoulders and pressing the russack between them. Yavi planted his leg to stop Archie but the blown leg folded over. Now the two were moving forward and Archie twisted forward to plant a foot on the low wall over the street. Legs snapped straight, Archie ducked forward and they were moving through the air. Archie let loose of Yavi and felt his face press into the Plexiglas the same time fluid rushed into his mouth. He gripped the rim of the glass, pulling himself up and hiking a drenched leg over the rim. An enormous bubble erupted from the bottom of the hurricane. He kept sliding over the rim until his feet were dangling over the empty street.

The girl who'd been serving drinks before she took cover under the bar grabbed an empty cup and poured herself a drink. "I wouldn't drink that Love!" Archie called from the top of the glass, "It's gonna have more of a kick than you want."

"They aren't connected, Sir." She said sensibly. "It's just sugar water in that glass."

"Not anymore."

Then Archie lost his grip on the rim on the slick Plexiglas. What was left of the crowd gasped as the girls scrambled away from the bar. On the way down, Archie grabbed the banner spanning the glass. It slowed him down only momentarily.

THE DOCTOR WHO SET ARCHIE'S BROKEN ANKLE had been nice enough, but with the pain medicine, it was hard to tell. Bunty had run to the Gap during the procedure and bought some clothes that looked much hipper than Archie felt. She showed up with the clothes and closed the room curtains to the gathering night.

"There's another bomb!" Archie said. "Forget about the clothes and call Meeks, where the hell is he? The doctors don't know anything, they think I'm outta my fuckin' head – where's the female bomber? She's out there Bunty, out there with another bomb!"

"Archie, lift your leg." Bunty said and pulled the boxers over his thighs. "We got her."

"How?"

"Tracked a just activated DeltaComm charge card to a hotel here in town. Your doggie door worked."

Archie let out a deep breath. "I don't pay you enough."

"Fine words, but will you remember them when the drugs wear off?"

"Not likely."

The doctor came in as Bunty was tying Archie's shoe and he was tucking his white shirt into a pair of crisp khaki's. The doctor drumming his fingers on the stainless clipboard and announced, "I don't like it, but a fella from the Navy wants you released immediately."

"Where am I going?"

"To the morgue." Said Bunty.

"I don't like that either."

The escort of police outriders cut a clear path for them from the VA hospital to the city morgue. David Meeks met them there, standing in the green tiled room next to a body on a stainless steel table. Archie drew up along side the table, leaning on the hospital issue crutch. "So you got her?"

"Need a positive ID." Meeks said and snapped away the crisp white sheet."

Bunty gasped, burying her head into Archie's shoulder. The smell of formaldehyde was overwhelming as Archie's eyes scanned Ugly Sue's lifeless body. "That's not her. Not the bomber."

Meeks ground his teeth hard, "What do you mean it's not the bomber. We found her in the hotel with a sack full of-"

"It's not her."

"You're mistaken."

"Her name is Daisy Adreis."

"You mean to tell me that this woman isn't the bomber, but you do know her?"

"Yeah, she's French national. Worked for Rowan. You'd have known her as Ugly Sue."

"Aw shit!" Meeks dropped his head into his hands. "She was working for us? Are you certain?"

"Commander – this woman is not Arab – and she tried to kill me last week."

"I thought you said she worked for Rowan?"

"We had some trouble connecting the dots."

Meeks looked up, beyond the table and beyond Archie. "Aw shit." He repeated. "It looks like we've got some collateral damage."

Archie turned to see Uncle Derrick come into the morgue. "Archie, I am glad to see you bipedal. Well sort of." Then to Meeks, "What's the damage? Oh...I see." He stared at the body on the table.

"If the military had been in charge-"

"We would be waiting for a bomb in our Easter basket." Now Derrick was close enough to grip Archie by the shoulder.

"The bomber is still out there." Archie said.

Meeks shook his head and cleared his throat. "But she ain't got a bomb. We recovered it from the hotel. Enough yellowcake to make a nasty dirty bomb. No detonator though. Wonder what happened to that?"

"You lost her! This is an enormous fuck all!"

"She can't do a thing without her bomb." Meeks said.

Bunty squeezed his hand and said the only thing that popped into her numb mind, "That's twelve fifty."

"What?"

"The cuss jar."

"You kept count?"

"No. It's a guestimate."

"Go to hell you silly bitch."

"I'll see you there, Asswholio."

Meek shook his head, "Don't worry kids, we've got the money trail."

THE RENTED FORD TAURUS was moving east on Highway 10, passing a sign pointing the way to Biloxi, Mississippi. That wasn't the final stop for Alice, though. She was repeating the name on her credit card, still unused, to herself. It sounded foreign to her, so she kept repeating it until it simply was her name. Ms Shannarha's short life began and ended in the billing department of the Le Meridian hotel. She would keep repeating her new name until she reached Athens, Georgia – whenever that was.

Alice had no idea how much money she was sitting on, literally, under her seat. She'd left the Kitty Kat last night to find Mickey Boy's man in New Orleans. Didn't entirely know why until she saw it locked up and decided right there to use the detonator to blow the security door out of its frame. She'd count it in Athens. She headed east.

Further east still, somewhere over central Africa, a Bombardier jet carried a man calling himself Count János Kossuth, toward a resort on the India Goian coast. He looked at the photo of his new Hungarian passport and smiled. His mistress leaned in, "Not bad, Count. Looks like an old lover of mine."

"What happened to him?"

"He used to work for the KGB in Cuba."

Mickey Boy laughed, "What happened to him?"

"Who knows, he had a fierce career."

THE END

Printed in the United States
88065LV00002B/118/A